CAGES

and

CROWNS

CELAENA CUICO

Hardcover ISBN: 9798988716945

Paperback ISBN: 9798988716952

eBook ISBN: 9798988716938

Edited by: Veerie Edits & Vilandra Cuico

Cover by: Gigi Covers

This book is dedicated to the ones who were by my side during the terrifying leap from dreamer to author; to the ones who supported me and made sure I didn't lose myself in this journey or in my past; to the ones who read Elaenor's story and resonated with her hope and her desire to be loved.

The Diadem series wouldn't be happening without any of you.

The Diadem

Glass and Bone
Cages and Crowns

The Diadem Journals

Elaenor

The Soulless

Persephone

Pronunciation Guide

Characters

Elaenor: EL-luh-nor

Evreux: EV-row

Sybil: si-BILL

Amaya: UH-my-uh

Thelonious: THUH-lone-ee-us

Kassius: CASS-ee-us

Nithe: NEE-th

Ni: NI

Bijoy: Bee-joi

Davel: DUH-velle

Demos: day-MOS

Delarus: dill-AR-us

Icana: ick-CAN-uh

Selkath: SELL-kath

Wyclif: WHY-cliff

Ela: EL-luh

Cynfael: SIN-fell

Welan: way-LEN

Danieas: DANE-e-us

Malathea: MAL-uh-THAY-uh

Places

Chatis: shuh-TEEZ

Noterra: NO-tare-ruh

Rakushia: RUH-koo-juh

Labisa: luh-BEES-uh

Khailes: KHAL-us

Delaquar Lake: DELLA-car

Brauntie Lake: BRON-tee

Colveil: coal-VEEL

Vaneau: VAN-oh

Tatus: tate-US

Ovobia: OH-vo-BEE-uh

Zivell: ZIV-elle

Aeqerian: ack KEER-ee-un

Dorin: DOOR-in

Port Tobeo: toe-BAY-o

Senaya Sea: sin-NY-uh

Roally: ROW-uh-LEE

Viridiana: ver-RID-ee-on-uh

Playlist

Losing Myself – Mia Baron
Carry You – Ruelle (ft. Fleurie)
Atlantis – Seafret
Sand – Dove Cameron
So Cold – Ben Cocks
No Good – UNSECRET (ft. Ruelle)
I Found – Amber Run
Fortunately – Bellabeth
History of Man – Maisie Peters
You're Losing Me – Taylor Swift
Burn – David Kushner

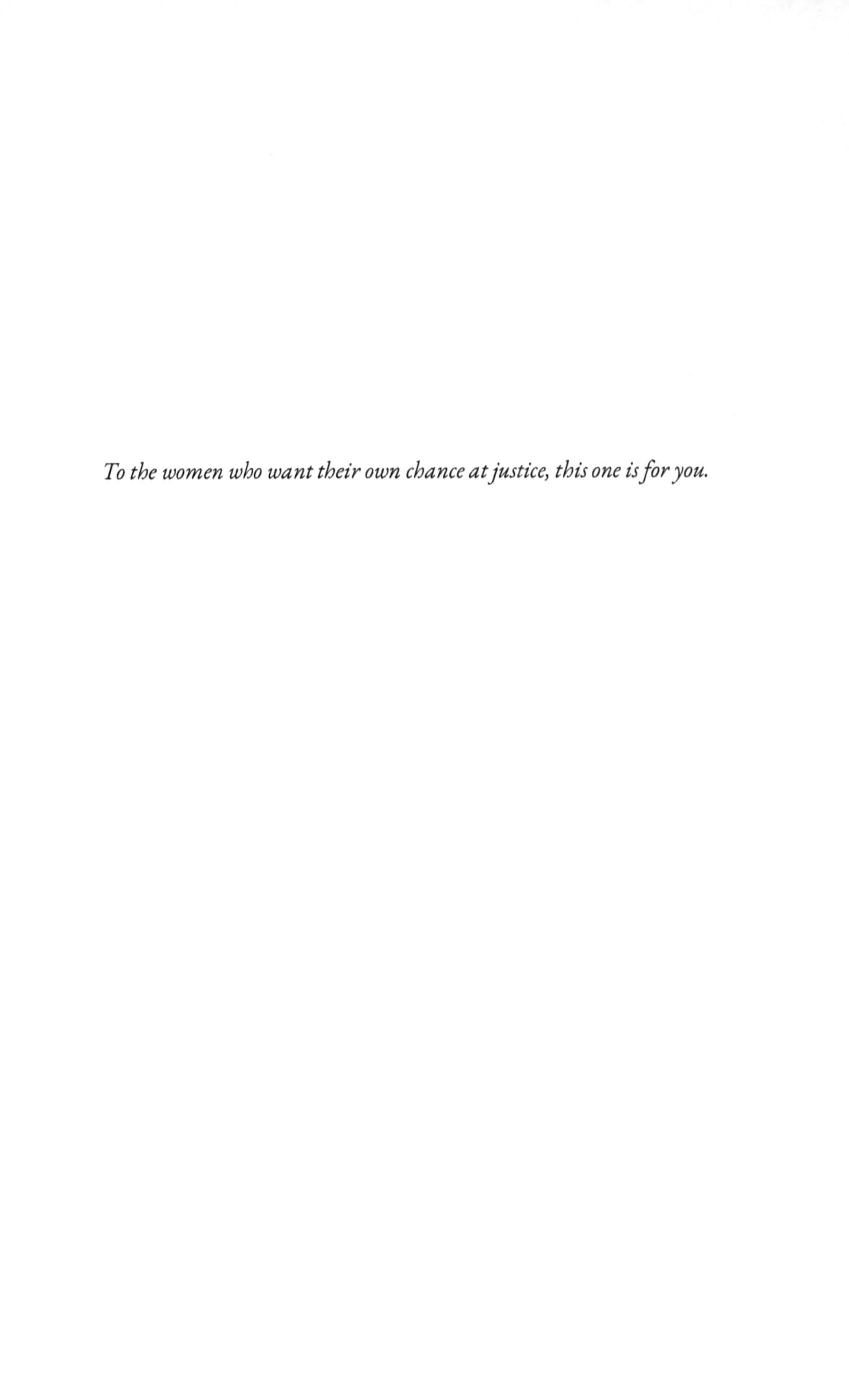

To the women who want their own chance at justice, this one is for you.

RAKUSHIA
CHATIS
DELAQUAR LAKE
ROALLY
VANEAU
RAUNTIE LAKE
NOTERRA
RAUNTFORD
CRA
PORT TOBEO
TELLAVID

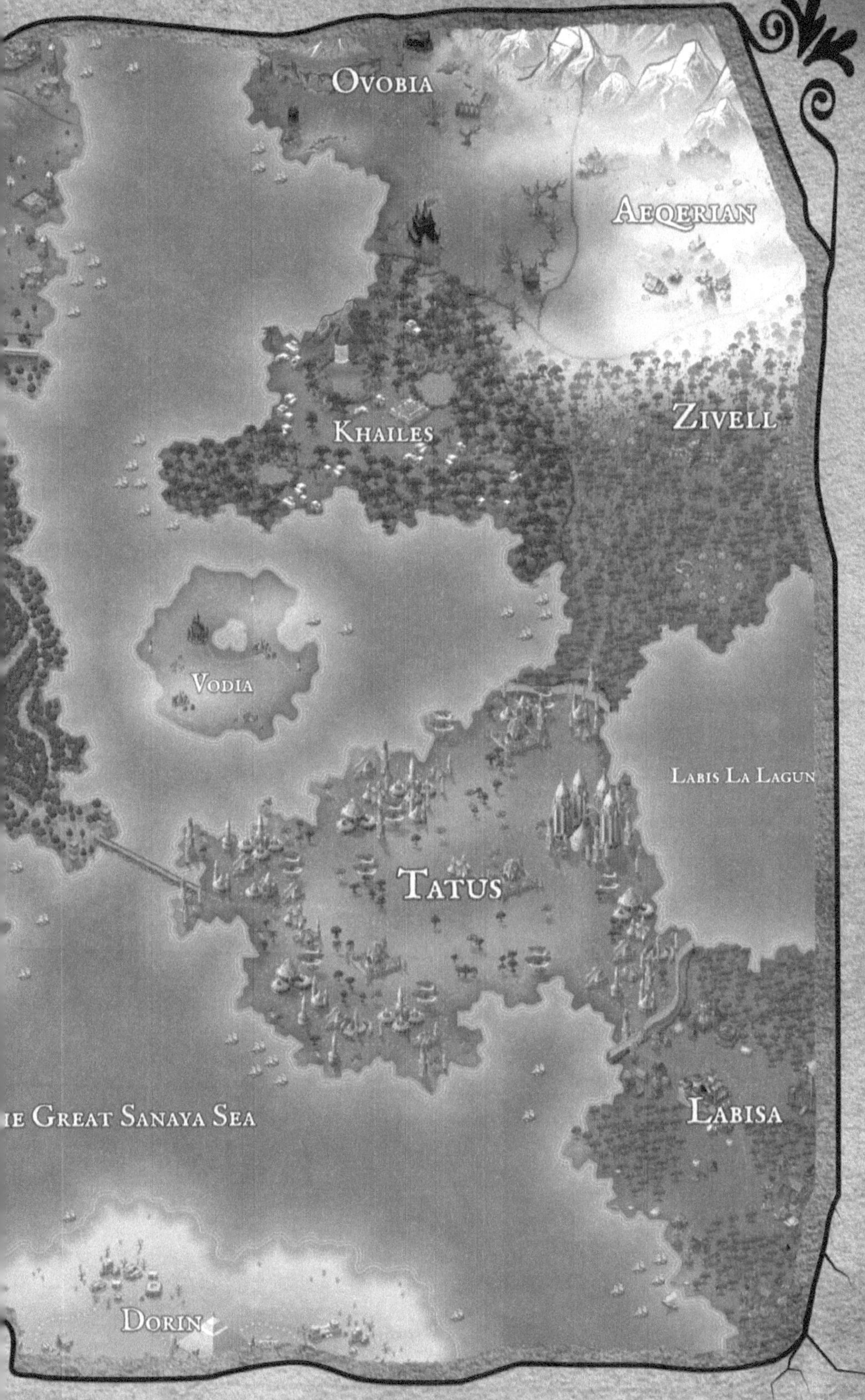

OVOBIA
AEQERIAN
ZIVELL
KHAILES
VODIA
LABIS LA LAGUN
TATUS
THE GREAT SANAYA SEA
LABISA
DORIN

Trigger Warnings

This book is a compilation of my thoughts and experiences. While princesses and magic are something from fairytales, the troubles of women in the modern world are very much real. Suicidal ideation, abusive relationships, sexual assault; those are all things I have experienced in my short life. In a way to prevent myself from succumbing to the ideations of death, I turned the horrors I have faced into a story of perseverance, strength, and the power of finding someone who makes you want to live. But I also threw in magic and fantasy because, why not? I only hope that as you immerse yourself into the world I have created, you find the strength to fight for yourself.

***Cages and Crowns** includes triggering situations such as graphic violence, miscarriage, gore, murder, graphic language, disordered eating, suicidal ideation, depression, PTSD, anxiety, rape, psychological and physical abuse in relationships, kidnapping, torture, branding, decapitation, confinement, and the use of drugs for compliance.*

Prologue

"Nora!" She screamed into the vast emptiness. Darkness had fallen, yet she still wasn't able to find the little princess with the raven-colored hair. Her eyes struggled to adjust to the lack of light as she peered through the endless tree trunks and foliage. "Elaenor!" She called out again, her voice hoarse. Her slippered feet slid over the rocks as she trekked through the dense trees.

Elaenor loved the forest, *loved* to explore, but she never disappeared without letting anyone know where she was going, especially *here*, so far from home. The trees shook in the wind, raining leaves down around her in slow, billowy movements as if time itself slowed down. Goosebumps spread along her bare arms, but it wasn't the cold causing her senses to tingle.

This forest was *alive*, she felt it every time she entered, but could never understand why. Could never understand *what* it was that was watching her. She could see the shadows. See them creeping around the trunks, moving as if they were living beings ready to devour her whole.

She took a slow, deep breath as an orb of silver light formed in her palms before breaking off into five equal pieces and shooting out in all directions. The orbs illuminate the trees as they fly by, temporarily causing the shadows to scatter. She could feel it in her bones, in her *mind*, as the aether searched for the girl. She sensed as it reached something, or someone.

Someone not as pure as the child she was looking for.

As if on command, silence blanketed the woods. The trees stopped moving, leaves stopped raining down. No sounds could be heard besides that of her thundering heart. She stood still, listening, waiting, but she knew who was approaching. She spun around and faced the woman standing behind her. Silver light dripped off her hand like liquid before absorbing into the forest floor as she took in the threat.

"Amaya! What are you doing out here?" She bellowed as she rushed over to her friend, light dissipating. Amaya's golden hair was coiled tightly around her head in a coronet, her gray eyes deep and lifeless. A large, swollen belly strained against the silk of her dress. She was too far along to be wandering in the woods, especially without the guards who usually swarmed her like locusts.

"Sybil, I can't find the boys." Amaya responded; her voice deeper than normal. Ancient power brewed underneath, waiting for its moment. Sybil swallowed down the fear pooling beneath her skin, the shadows that tried to find a home in her veins pressing in on her. "Have you found Nora yet?" She asked as she reached up to tuck a stray curl behind her ear. Something was different, her skin pale and her eyes dark as if she was losing an internal battle, a battle she'd been fighting for over a decade.

Sybil shook her head, a confirmation that the children had run off, probably together. "She said she was coming out here to play with the boys, but I didn't expect them to be out this long. We must be returning soon, Viktor will worry." She explained, confusion and concern crossing her features. But her concern was not for the children, instead it was for the darkness that bled out from her friend's skin as if it was a living being, as if it was swallowing her whole. Too many years have passed since the last time she was well – since the last time the darkness was controlled. "Amaya, how are you feeling?" She scoffed as she took in her friend's tone.

"I am fine, you mother hen, just ready to give birth already." She deflected, her hand coming up to rest on the bump straining against her gown.

"Kassius will be arriving in Chatis soon, maybe it is time for you to see him again." Amaya didn't respond, she just stared. The darkness and silence were near suffocating as they stood face to face, a challenge gleaming in Amaya's eyes. This wasn't her, this person in front of her just wore her face, but it wasn't her friend, her *sister*, staring back. Just as she opened her mouth to speak, a shrill scream echoed around them. Both women jumped and turned towards the noise as the little princess and the young princes ran through the trees.

Elaenor's curly hair was tangled and filled with leaves and twigs; her pale dress caked in mud. A small welt was growing on her rounded cheek as she threw her arms around her mother's waist. One of the princes, Tobias, had a look of mischief brewing in his stormy grey eyes, almost rivaling his mother's. Theo, the younger of the two, looked concerned, worried, as he stared at the small girl clutching her mother's skirts. He watched her as if he felt her pain and her fear.

"My little love, what happened?" Sybil asked, as she knelt down in front of her daughter.

"Toby pushed me down a hill." Elaenor whimpered, her fingers clutching the hem of her dirty dress as she looked up at her mother.

"Tobias!" Sybil scolded as she stood, grabbing Elaenor's hand. "How many times have we told you to be gentle? She isn't as strong as your little friends in the village." The young prince rolled his eyes and left without responding, heading back towards the palace. His attitude was always astonishing, always sounding alarms in Sybil's head. It was all too familiar, too much like someone else...

"Theo, how many times have I told you to watch out for Nora when you take her into the woods?" His mother snapped. Theo's blue eyes were lined in silver as he tried to plead his case, but Amaya brushed him off without remorse, ignoring him entirely. "Come here, miracle." Amaya crooned to Elaenor, reaching for her. The little princess grasped her hand, the latter swallowing her tiny palm whole. "What did I tell you last time this happened?" Tears welled up in Elaenor's eyes as she looked up at the queen. Sybil shifted nervously as she watched her daughter and friend interact. Something was definitely wrong with her; she could feel it. Feel the presence of something dangerous pressing in all around her, waiting to strike.

"That princesses shouldn't be–" Elaenor started to speak.

"That princesses shouldn't be running amok in the woods. Now why have you disobeyed me?" Amaya cut her off, her eyes glaring holes through the small child's face. Elaenor trembled and took a step back, but the queen held her hand tightly, preventing her from getting too far.

"Amaya, she is just a child. She is allowed to enjoy all the same things the village children do, all the same things your *sons* do." Sybil's hand wrapped around Elaenor's arm as she pulled her away from Amaya's grip, tucking her into her side.

"How do you expect her to be queen when she can't even keep a dress clean?" Amaya's snide response had followed a scoff, one of disinterest and irritation.

"I don't want to be a queen." Elaenor whispered, looking up at her mother.

"Little love, I know, but it is your destiny." Sybil responded as she wiped tears off her dirty cheeks. "You have no idea what life has in store for you. You are going to be so powerful, Nora. So powerful, and strong, and you will be so happy." Elaenor's blue eyes sparkled with unshed tears, mimicking the stars that she loved to fall asleep staring at.

"Not as powerful as my son." Amaya quipped as she looked at the small girl. "He will be your ruler and to whom you must answer to. You are–"

"Amaya!" Gray and blue eyes clashed as the silence dissipated. The trees once again came alive, the wind once more rustled the leaves.

"I am tired. You should return to your home." Amaya commanded, turning away from the Chatisian royals. Theo's eyes darted between his departing mother and the little princess before running after her.

"Mama, is she angry because the baby doesn't want to be in there anymore?" Sybil tore her eyes away from her friend, the shadows following the queen, and looked down at her daughter.

"Malathea isn't ready to come out yet, little love. But she will soon and then you'll have a new friend to play with." They started to walk, following after the others.

"How do you know it's a girl?" She asked as she held her mother's hand.

"There are some things I just know. One day when you are older, you will know things, too." Sybil gripped Elaenor's hand tightly before they disappeared into a cloud of silver mist.

Part One:
Cages Of Iron

Chapter One

I don't look up from my wine glass as the door to my bed chamber opens. My head is propped up against a stone post as I lounge on the balcony, the sun warming my tanning skin. We had another snow fall the other day, which isn't common for spring, but it is finally melting away, succumbing to the encroaching heat. As promised, the spring flowers truly do fill every inch of this godsforsaken place. The green hills are littered with various blooms, their colors creating a rainbow, but it's the wisteria trees that are filling the air with their suffocating floral scent and various shades of purple.

I don't know why I expected them to lie about something as trivial as flowers; I'm just having a hard time trusting anything that comes out of *his* mouth.

Speaking of the devil incarnate, he clears his throat behind me, his not-so-subtle way to command my attention. I sigh as loud as humanly possible, letting him know how much I detest his presence, not that he cares, before tipping my head back and draining the rest of my glass. I spin around in my seat and face him; his mask of the golden boy is blank and unreadable, irritating me to no end. I can never tell if he is in here to bother me or if he has somehow received word about Elaenor and her location. Though, I suppose if there was important news for me to learn, it wouldn't be coming from him.

"To what do I owe this pleasure?" I purr as sweetly as I can. He's not stupid enough to mistake it for excitement at his presence, but he still doesn't react.

He never does.

"I am being told you still refuse to leave your room?" He raises a single brow and I roll my eyes, I guess bothering me is his goal for today. His better-than-thou air of superiority is getting really fucking tiring and I want nothing more than to hit his perfectly groomed face. I can barely stand to look at him, much less join him and the others outside the walls of my chamber. What does he expect? Am I supposed to act like I am not stuck in this barren hole of a country?

"This is less a room and more of a prison." I sneer, reaching for the wine bottle on the small table next to me. The berry red liquid splashes into the glass, but only fills it up halfway. I pout before slamming the bottle back down on the table, the glass clinking loudly against the wood. Another bottle empty and yet my heart still isn't full, and my mind still isn't numb.

What will it take to be free of the demons taking residence in my head?

"You are not a prisoner here, Scarlett, you know that." I can tell he's irritated, but he never loses control. He always has the same stupid, straight smile. One that could almost be mistaken for contempt if I knew it wasn't hiding his pain and anger towards the current state of our lives. Why he never shows emotion, never gives in to his feelings, I don't know. One of these days his emotional well will overflow and he'll snap.

I just hope I am far away when he does.

"Well, not being able to go home, nor be rid of all of this ridiculous yellow decor," I wave my arms around the room, gesturing to the lemon hue plastered everywhere from curtains to bedding to rugs. "Kind of feels like torture. What sort of color even is yellow?" He sighs and runs his hands through his perfect inky hair, save for that single white streak that seems to be darkening to gray as the days pass. I know it's not a good sign, but I refuse to acknowledge it.

I refuse to acknowledge what it means, or what they *think* it means.

"It's gold, Scarlett, not yellow." He's trying to control his temper, but the ice in his tone peeks through. I don't even try to hide the smile of amusement that plays at the edges of my mouth as his stony resolve finally cracks.

"Have you ever seen the color gold? Because this isn't it." I smirk before draining my glass again. The wine is sweet and bitter at the same time, burning its way down my throat. It doesn't taste nearly as good as the pink wine Elaenor had in her room, but now I know why it was so sweet; it was drugged. I can't help but feel slightly jealous. I wish I had a wine that made the days pass without notice.

I guess that makes me a shitty person.

"It isn't a very easy color to capture unless it's constructed of metal." He shrugs. Are we really debating colors right now? Is this what I have to look forward to during my never-ending days in Rakushia? I'd rather drive a dagger through my eye than spend the rest of my life like this.

"I hardly think that's true considering most of Emery's closet is lined in gold." I stand and step off the raised balcony. He watches me as I make my way over to the bar cart that holds another five empty bottles of wine. I dig through them, hoping to find another I haven't already drained.

"Yes, a closet I have heard you pilfered half of." He responds, his uninterested tone trailing off into a sigh as he watches me.

"Might as well look good if I am stuck in this hell hole." I mutter under my breath. My hand drops in defeat at the collection of empty wine bottles.

None left.

"Need I remind you that you are here as a guest? You have nowhere to go. Your home was destroyed, your fiancé has been murdered, and you, my lady, are homeless. Would you rather I leave you to be taken by Noterran forces? Or would you prefer being dropped in the barren rubble that used to be Chatis?" I clench my teeth as I bite back the retort brewing in my mind.

I'd rather he be dropped *under* the rubble of the country he did nothing to save.

It's been three months. Three months since Theo, Elaenor, and Donovan were supposed to make it to the border. Donovan snuck me out of the castle during the location change from the infirmary, where I spent the better part of a month fighting for my life, to the dungeons. As soon as I could stand and there was a plan to have me transferred, I was snuck away, strapped to Bijoy, and brought here. That was four weeks after Rhea's death, meaning I have been in Rakushia now for *six months*. I guess I should be grateful I at least got to bring my horse, but all I can think of is Rhea. Her head cleaved in two while she was trying to save Theo, just for him to die too. Bile rises in my throat as I remember her eyes, open but unseeing.

The only reason we know Elaenor is alive is because of some bond or whatever Enzo seems to have with her. The white streak in his hair spreads the closer he is to her, it's a sign that she is connected to him or something. No one really knows for sure. Enzo's father knows a little about their connection, but even his knowledge is questionable. He says one thing, only to contradict it later, as if he is just in the dark as we are.

Enzo's lighter streak has been slowly darkening for days now, which we believe is a sign that Elaenor isn't doing very well. Either she has been moved and there is more and more distance between them, or her strength is failing. He can't even call out to her anymore, although he believes it has something to do with the drugs Tobias is pumping into her, and not that she is dead.

Enzo saw her memories the night it all happened. It was during dinner, and one of the first and only nights I left my room. He was fine throughout the first half of dinner, but suddenly started screaming. He was grabbing his head, pulling his hair out from the roots as if he was trying to get rid of some unseen force. His face was turning red from pain, his breathing ragged, and then it was gone just as fast as it came on.

He saw through her eyes. She was screaming, and somehow her mind connected to his, allowing him to see and feel what she was in that moment. He said he saw her kneeling on the ground in the throne room with Theo and Donovan's heads laying on the marble, blood pooling everywhere and soaking into her dress as she's forced to stay on the floor. He hasn't been able to connect to her since.

I am grateful that Elaenor is alive, that Tobias hasn't killed her...yet. It means we have a chance at saving her, but all I can think of is the cost. What is the cost of her survival? I love her, she is my best friend, but all I can think of is who's next to be sacrificed because of her? And for what? What is the purpose in all of this? Theo is gone. Rhea is gone. Donovan is gone.

Who's *next*?

I step away from the bar cart and drop onto the sofa, pinching the bridge of my nose. I can't think of any of this right now. I can't allow myself to succumb to the emotions that are just one second away from destroying me.

I need more wine, or something stronger.

"Scarlett," I can hear his footsteps seconds before the cushion next to me dips down. "I know this has been a really hard few months for you. I sympathize. I want nothing more than to rescue Elaenor and put an end to Tobias and his men. But we are at a standstill. We have no idea where she is, what is happening to her, or what to do." I drop my hand and meet his gaze. His eyes have lightened, their normal bright green is gray today, saddened. While his face is freshly shaved, I can tell he feels anything but fresh. Bruises bloom under his eyes, a sign he hasn't been sleeping. None of us have. But that doesn't change our current reality, it doesn't change anything. Nothing we do will *change* her life.

"I don't know what you expect me to do." I wanted venom to coat my tongue, but a broken, child-like voice comes out instead, revealing how I truly feel.

Weak and powerless.

"There is a lot you can do. You can join in on the council meetings and provide insight considering you are the only one who has lived in the palace. You could provide ideas. *Anything* that isn't just sitting in here and draining the wine cellar." I shake my head. I have no use, no purpose, to their crusade.

"I have nothing to offer." I whisper, eliciting a groan from him. He quickly stands and crosses the room.

"You have two choices, Scarlett. You can either help or you can leave. I have spent the last six months defending you, but the kings who currently run this palace have very thin patience and they will not allow you to stay and drain resources if you aren't of use."

"Enzo–" I turn in my seat to look at him standing by the door.

"Choose wisely." He doesn't even spare me another glance before slamming the pale wooden door behind him. I throw my head back on the cushion and close my eyes.

I don't know what he expects me to do. I can't see the future, I can't fight, I can barely even talk battle strategy. What does he think I am capable of doing?

A soft knock echoes across my room and I open my eyes as the door opens again. Laenie walks in, wearing a loose beige dress that flows around her like liquid. Her chestnut hair is braided into a long braid that hangs down her back, her brown eyes looking more amber today, more alive. Erik walks in behind her, shutting the door. His ginger hair is cropped close to his head, his skin looking tanner by the day. He's wearing a black tunic cut close to his body to show off his stature, seemingly copying Nithe and Enzo's wardrobe choices. He has his sword strapped to his belt like always, the hilt a beautiful forest green. The color of Chatis, of *home*. He offers me a smile as they both walk over to the couch.

"It isn't even noon yet Scarlett, please tell me you aren't already drinking?" Her voice is soft, she's always been the quieter and more reserved person out of the three of us. However, her time here in Rakushia has brought out a new side of her. She's happier, smiling more, and has even been learning how to ride a horse. I hate to admit she has been more attentive towards Bijoy than I have.

"Not enough to count." I murmur as she collapses next to me. Erik sits in the chair across from us, propping his feet up on the table.

"Is today going to be the day you get off your ass?" He smirks and a little bit of light enters his soft green eyes. He, too, has been flourishing in Rakushia.

It seems I'm the only one that hasn't.

"What would you have me do, Erik? Train with the guards like you and Emery, plant flowers like Laenie, discuss battle strategy with Enzo and Nithe?" I snap, narrowing my eyes. I know I shouldn't take out my frustration on them, but I have no other outlet.

"Anything besides getting drunk would be great." He grins, flashing his teeth, before winking at Laenie. They have grown close over the last few months. She used to have feelings for his brother, Lord Danieas, but he stayed in Chatis and was part of the casualties after the bombing. Her and Erik were able to escape with Enzo's help, the knight in shining armor for everyone. Elaenor and I thought Erik was dead, at least that's what Tobias had said. Turns out he was alive and thriving in Rakushia instead.

Erik was here before Laenie or I. Enzo intercepted him on his way back to Chatis and brought him here, after ensuring Elaenor's letter was delivered. King Viktor and Tobias knew he was taken by Rakushia, but they thought he was killed, so that is what they said happened. I hate admitting that Tobias thought he was protecting Elaenor by saying he succumbed to his injuries instead of being tortured and murdered. But he wasn't, he was brought here where he has been helping ever since.

Sometimes I wonder if Tobias truly believes he is the good guy in all of this. Does he genuinely believe Rakushia is full of psychopaths torturing families and beheading kings? Or does he know which side of history he is on?

Laenie was next. She arrived shortly after Rhea's death. She was walking the grounds of the palace checking on the flowers, like normal, when Erik and Enzo took her. She was terrified, of course, but as soon as she realized what was happening and that Rhea was dead, she came willingly. She's become quite attached to Emery and Erik since then, and I don't blame her. Her entire family was murdered, as was all of ours, but she was alone here. I have them, and in Noterra I had Elaenor.

Enzo truly is a white knight, and it pisses me off even more. How he knew they were important to Elaenor, I have no idea, but he seems to know a lot. He says he's a seer and can see the future. He can hone it to get a certain idea of a specific timeline, but everything has been fuzzy for him since Elaenor arrived at Noterra. He doesn't understand what it means, but his father, Kassius, has been helping him adjust quite a bit to the changes in his abilities.

Kassius is just another one of the surprises I found when I arrived here. I spent the last nearly ten years thinking he was dead, but he wasn't. He was helping to create a council, an army, for Elaenor to wield when she became ready. When she became *queen*. He always knew what would happen, but I don't think he expected the death toll to grow so quickly. He was blindsided like the rest of us, doing what he could without gaining attention. However, that didn't stop me from giving him a piece of my mind when I saw him.

Despite the predicament we are all in, everyone here in Rakushia could have done more. Could have done more to stop this, more to protect Elaenor, more to reduce the number of deaths. Even Theo could have done more. He expressed his concerns about Tobias to me when we first met. I should have listened, and he should have done more to convince me.

Maybe none of this would have happened if we *all* did more.

"I saw Enzo leave; does he have any news about Elaenor?" Laenie's soft voice is the only thing keeping me from throwing something at Erik.

"No, he had nothing to say about *Elaenor*." I scoff.

"Have you seen his hair?" Erik asks, his voice quieter. I meet his gaze and nod. I still hold hope that maybe we are wrong, that maybe Kassius truly doesn't know what the light hair means. "He said he can't feel her anymore, whatever that means."

"He's said that for three months, Erik. Nothing has changed other than his hair. How do we even know if he is telling the truth? What if they really are the enemy? How have you both come to trust them already?" I question as irritation and nausea bloom in my belly, fighting for dominance. I run my fingers through my long hair, but they get caught in the tangles and I abandon it, throwing it back over my shoulder. I really should bathe; I can't even remember the last time I changed clothes.

"They have been nothing but kind, Scarlett, how can you even say that?" It seems Laenie has taken that as a direct insult. I think out of all of us, she has fully become a subject of Rakushia in more than just name. She loves it here.

"We don't know if what they say is true. What about what Tobias said and did? What about what *Viktor* said and did?"

"We *always* knew they weren't good people, Scar." Erik interjects.

"Doesn't matter. We were still fooled. Tobias still killed Rhea, and Theo, *and* Donovan. He is still torturing Elaenor while we sit here and drink expensive wine and wear nice clothes."

"No, that is what *you* are doing, Scarlett." Laenie's voice raises in volume, iciness replacing the usual warmth. I turn to face her to see her brows are furrowed and her jaw is clenched. "*You* are the only one who is doing nothing to help. We are all trying to get Elaenor out of there. You are the one wasting away in here being nothing but an *almost*-royal pain in the ass." My eyes widen in shock as she stands and heads to the door. "Get your shit together and do something or do us all a favor, and leave." She steps around the table and Erik stands to follow her out.

"Laenie–" I start, but Erik raises his hand.

"She's right, Scarlett. You're going to lose her too if you don't change.

You're going to lose everyone, and there aren't many of us left." His lips press into a thin line before he steps into the hallway, closing the door behind him.

I scream and throw a pillow at the spot in the doorway they just vacated, but it barely makes it across the table.

That's twice now that someone has given me an ultimatum and I fucking hate it. There isn't anything I can do. I am powerless, both figuratively and literally. I have nothing to offer. I have no skills, no strength and no stupid magic that everyone else seems to have. I have nothing. I blink away the tears filling my eyes as I lean back into the sofa.

Birds are chirping outside, the wind lightly whistling through the trees. It sounds peaceful, like what a normal life would entail. But that is not what I feel. I don't feel peaceful and happy. I don't feel content.

I feel lost.

Chapter Two

The Caged
One Month Ago

    The cuffs dig into my wrists and ankles with every movement. The collar stabbing into my throat, cutting so deep it nearly hits my spine, but I don't give him the satisfaction. I don't let myself feel the burning, all-consuming pain encompassing my whole body. Even as I feel each flick of his wrist, each time the blade slices through skin and muscle. Each time he begs for me to scream, I don't.

    I haven't in weeks.

    I don't whimper. I don't beg. I don't plead. I take it. He wants to see me in pain, but he won't.

    Not anymore.

I feel nothing. I don't feel sorrow or anguish. I don't feel the empty pit in my heart where Theo and Donovan's corpses will always sit. I don't feel the longing I used to feel. The longing for acceptance, for love. I feel absolutely nothing. I am numb. I *have* to be numb. I won't survive otherwise.

"I have to say, my love, your behavior is...surprising. Are you not afraid?" He asks, his voice filled with dark amusement as he picks up another instrument from his table of torture devices. The table that keeps growing and growing as the bladesmiths continuously construct some new contraption to inflict as much pain as possible. I wonder if they know it isn't a criminal being subjected to their masterpieces, but instead their queen. The one they are sworn to protect with their life.

Tobias has kept me in the dungeon for a while, but I can't be exactly sure how long. There are no windows, so the passage of time is an illusion. It could be minutes or days, it could have been months, and I wouldn't know the difference. A year could have passed, and it would have felt just as long as a single day.

This is the same place he held Jeremiah all those months ago. The same place he holds all of the prisoners he wants something from.

But what does he want from me other than the satisfaction of seeing me bleed?

Of seeing me in pain?

Is this what he has always wanted? A body to destroy? My body is his for the taking, that I cannot control. But my mind? That still belongs to me. He doesn't get it. He doesn't get anything from me that he can't physically take.

My mind and my sanity. That's all I have left. All I have left of the girl I used to be, and he doesn't get to take that away from me.

Nobody gets to take that from me.

"No." I croak, my mouth dry and cracking. I can't remember the last sip of water I had, the last meal I ate. Blood; that's what fills my stomach. The blood I am forced to swallow when I cough it up from my lungs. There is nowhere else for it to go.

"I don't believe you." He murmurs, his voice soft and amused. If I didn't know any better, if I wasn't lying strapped to this slab of rock, I would almost take his tone as one of endearment. One of love and playfulness. But the entertainment he likes isn't something I also enjoy.

It's something I can't wait to inflict on him.

"That sounds like *your* fucking problem, not mine." He chuckles and walks over to me. He's holding a thin blade with some sort of spikes on it, but I don't look at it. I look at him. I always look right at him, into his eyes, as he slices into me day after day.

"I don't think you'll be feeling that way soon, my love." He says softly before running his fingers lightly down my cheek.

"Fuck off." He sighs, but I can see the hunger flicker in his eyes.

"That mouth of yours, it makes me want to do such *despicable* things." He's smiling, both dimples on full display. He waves the device in front of my face before moving to my stomach. I can feel the sharp edge slice through my skin before the short spikes catch on muscle and tendon, ripping through them. I grit my teeth but keep my eyes open, letting the tears escape of their own free will.

He's drawing something, *carving* something into my flesh, but I don't move. It burns, and I can feel the warm blood pooling on my abdomen before dripping off my sides and onto the stone table that is stained with the blood of his other victims. My limbs begin to shake, sweat beading along my hairline, and I bite down even harder, tasting the metallic liquid pooling in my mouth. He stops and I let out the silent breath that was trapped in my lungs, my limbs still vibrating from the pain. "Nothing?" He asks before he shuffles farther down the table.

The blade presses into my thigh, a long slice down to the knee. I can hear the snapping of my own tendons as he rips through them with ease. My breathing grows ragged, but I keep my mouth closed and teeth clenched. Tears pool in my eyes and drip down the sides of my face. My jaw cramps from the pressure and I feel as if my teeth are going to crack if I bite down any harder. My arms pull at the shackles as my back arches against my will. *Fuck*.

He's going to win. I can't do this.

I'm losing.

"Tell me, Ela, what would it take to hear you scream?" He pulls back and I fight through the sobs threatening to break through my blood-filled throat. I can't do this. I can't.

"You won't break me." My voice is hoarse, strained, as I relax against the cold stone.

"We'll see about that." The tip of the scalpel slams into my stomach, burrowing deep. I flinch and shut my eyes. *Breathe, Elaenor*. You can do this. "Hmm, I'm disappointed." He rips the spiked blade out and tosses it. I can hear it hit the stone wall of the dungeon before landing on the floor, echoing through the empty chamber.

"With what?" I stammer, blood and spit flicking off my lips, my heart pounding in my chest. Black edges around my vision and I know that unconsciousness is near. I never thought I would beg for the moments I wouldn't be conscious, the moments I was unaware of everything happening.

"I wanted to hear you scream, Ela. *Scream* for me." He's frustrated, his brows furrowed, and jaw clenched as he leans over me. His hair has grown, it now flops into his eyes as he bends down. His sharp jaw is lined with stubble, as if he hasn't had the time to properly clean up. Part of me wants to care for him, I think it's the part that used to love him. The other part of me wants to take a blade and slam it straight through his temple. I want to watch the light fade from his eyes before he gets the opportunity to end me.

"No." I whisper, any semblance of energy gone. He growls before grabbing something off the table. I can hear a click and then I feel the heat of the torch.

"Scream." He demands.

"No!" I say again, this time louder.

"Very well." I feel the torch grow close until it is pressed up against my bare stomach. The pain is all-consuming as it blisters my flesh. My back arches as I buck off the table. I'm biting my lip so hard it's drawing blood as I fight against the screams tearing at my throat. I will not give in. I can never give in.

"*Scream*, Elaenor!" I hold my tongue as my flesh burns away. As the pale skin marred with his torture is melted away. The heat is pulled off and I smile, a small chuckle escaping my delirious lips as I collapse on the table, numbness spreading through my veins.

"You won't win." I whisper between laughs. He's staring down at me, bewildered. "I. Will. Not. Break!" I spit at him, but it doesn't reach his perfectly smug face. I'm shaking. From pain, from disbelief, from anger. From everything. My body incapable of staying still. Tremors explode down my limbs; I feel as if I'm vibrating.

"I already have." He turns away, stomping out of the room as my laugh grows in volume. The slamming of the dungeon door echoes around me. I laugh so deeply I can feel the blood pooling underneath me from my many wounds. The wounds that will be gone when I wake.

I still haven't been able to figure out how he is able to heal me with no trace of the torture I've endured. Not a single scar left behind from his escapades besides the *T*he branded on me all those months ago.

He wants to know why I'm not scared?

It's because the wounds are always gone, leaving me wondering if any of this was even real.

Chapter Three

The Caged
Present Day

I'm cold, but that seems to be the norm these days. My wrists and ankles are protesting against the metal tightly clamped around them, I'd think they'd be used to it by now. He left the balcony doors open when he was done with me, leaving my naked body shackled to the bed, my limbs pulled in different directions leaving me fully exposed.

It's always the same.

The same ending. The same position. The same dread that fills my body and infiltrates my bones.

It's been three months *at least*. I only know that because I have been counting the days that I remember. There are 72 scratches on the back of the nightstand. 72 days I have remembered to count.

How many days have I forgotten?

I know that I was unable to mark the days I spent in the dungeon, which is why I am estimating three months, but something is telling me it's been longer. Nothing feels right, as if I am living someone else's life, but maybe this is what trauma feels like.

Maybe this is what it feels like to truly be helpless.

The icy spring air flows throughout the room, causing me to tense. That only makes the shackles dig deeper into my skin, burrowing into my flesh. I wince silently. I learned quickly how to hide my pain. Not because I had to appear strong, but because no one cared about the pain I was in. The only person interested in how I feel is Tobias, but that is only because he *enjoys* the sight of my pain. My screams for help, every flinch and wince as he slices me until I am nearly unrecognizable, only to pump me full of drugs and do whatever it is that makes me heal almost instantaneously as if nothing has even happened.

My brain doesn't heal as fast though, my mind slow to recover. The days blur together and I often find myself questioning what truly happened. Did any of it actually happen? Am I insane? Are these moments of pain and terror just dreams like the one I had about Chatis?

When will I wake up?

I can't fight the full body tremors wreaking havoc through my body as I shiver, the chains rattling from the movement. The shaking always comes, it's a sign that the hemlock is wearing off. A sign that my body is craving it, something I can't even fight. He's made me addicted to it, the numbing haze that overtakes my senses, making me forget.

Tobias has been using poppy root less and less lately with the hemlock. He wants me to remember. He wants me to remember how he touches me, how he uses me, what the pain feels like. He wants me to remember every single second of my miserable life. He wants to break me, but I won't let him. I *can't* let him.

But if I do, if I succumb to the depression eating away at my mind, who will I become? Will I become a husk he can control even more than he already is? Is living this life, like this, even worth it anymore?

Davel is standing by the door, his hand resting on the pommel of his golden sword. He's my least favorite of my rotating jailers. He stares at me, intently. He watches Tobias touch me, hurt me, *rape* me. And then, when Tobias leaves, he stands as close to the bed as he can while he touches himself, finding pleasure in my pain, in my blood. It doesn't help that Tobias keeps me tied up like a dead deer, for all who walks in to see. Naked, chained to the bed. Not a single part of my body is hidden.

I guess I *should* be grateful I'm not dead. That I am not lying in an unmarked grave like I am sure Theo and Donovan are. Like I know everyone in Chatis is.

Graves I'll never get to visit.

The day Tobias brought me home, I could barely even think. I could barely even breathe. The smoke was so thick, I was choking with each breath. My bare feet were getting sliced up from the rubble and shattered stained glass. The leftover bones were burned and reduced to ash. It smelled awful—like sulfur and charred meat.

He paraded me around, holding me close to him with a metal collar he has kept around my throat since. I had no words for what I saw, for what was left of my home. He read off the list of casualties as if he was reciting a task list. Chatis was small, but the death count totaled to 481 people. Nearly 500 people were murdered simple because I pissed off Tobias.

My father. My friends. My people.

All dead.

I'll never forget that it was my fault. I will never get their faces, their names out of my head. For ten years I dreamt of glass and bone, but it wasn't a dream, it was a premonition.

One I could have stopped.

I haven't had a single dream since that night. I don't know if it's the steady stream of drugs Tobias has been pumping into me, or if I just have no more visions to see. I have tried nearly every day to reach out to Enzo, but the connection is gone. I feel nothing. Part of me is convinced he never existed. That I imagined him to get away from the horrors I'm experiencing.

Another part of me believes that it was the glass dagger, the one I am convinced he left for me in the woods, that fueled our connection. When Tobias broke it, it shattered everything. That is what I keep telling myself, because if that is true, then I am not crazy. I am not growing mad. I am merely a person who can see the future, uncontrollably, and that I have someone out there who I can connect to.

Or maybe I *am* insane.

I take a slow deep breath as another breeze filters through the open doors, causing my nipples to harden and goosebumps to spread along my bare skin. Even back in the dead of winter he tried to freeze me, and he almost succeeded. Laris was on duty, and if he hadn't thrown a blanket over me, I would have died from frostbite.

I almost wish I had.

I haven't seen Tano in weeks and Laris will barely look at me. For three months he has been averting his eyes, only speaking when needed. He's the weak link. I plotted for days on how to exploit that, but I eventually gave up. Any hope I have of getting out of here is gone. No one is coming to save me. No one should.

I'm not worth the sacrifices everyone has made already.

The door opens and Lydia walks in with Malia trailing behind her. I asked where my other two ladies went, but it seems they were dismissed after everything. They glare at Davel before making their way over to me. They are coming to bathe me, like clockwork. I don't offer them a smile, nor do they offer me one. Davel follows behind Malia, producing the key to unlock me. She and Lydia stand off to the side while he walks over to me, his armor rustling. Their eyes harden as they wait, as they know what comes next. I brace myself.

Davel has a smirk plastered to his face as he reaches over the bed. His hand trails down from my breasts, his fingers brushing the hardened peaks of my nipples, before sliding down. His fingers slide against the apex of my thighs softly and he bites his lip and snorts.

Every day it's the same. He watches Tobias, he touches himself, and then he touches me. Sometimes it is more than this, more than a brush of a finger, but I don't let myself remember those days. I don't let myself remember the feeling of him pressed up against me as he has me bent over the side of the bed. The feel of his hands squeezing my sides as he slams himself inside of me. I can't let myself remember how he told me Tobias would never believe me as he empties himself on my back, wiping the evidence away before anyone can see it.

I can't, because he's right.

He never believed me about Jeremiah. Almost to the point of my death. If he hadn't seen first-hand what he had done, I don't think Tobias would have *ever* believed me.

I keep my glare fixed to him and he stops his caress before winking at me. Davel gets to work on the shackles holding me in this position. I nearly groan as they fall off my wrists and ankles, the pressure finally releasing. When he's done, he slowly lets his eyes trail over my naked body, licking his lips. I force myself to sit up and slide off the bed, pushing past him with shaky legs. His hand grabs my arm, pulling me into his side. He leans down, pressing his nose to my hair before inhaling loudly. I rip my arm from his grasp and stumble towards Lydia, who catches my shoulders before I fall into her.

My stiff limbs protest the movement, and if my ladies didn't stand on either side of me, I would probably fall. They lead me to the bathing chamber where a tub full of steaming liquid sits. They don't say anything as I step into the water. I hiss as the hot liquid burns the sores on my ankles and the shallow slices along my stomach from this morning that haven't yet healed. When I'm fully settled in the bath, Malia gets to work scrubbing the blood from my skin as Lydia detangles my hair.

I close my eyes and relax, it's the only time I can. The only time I feel safe. I used to fight.

Fight Tobias. Fight Davel. But all the fight I have in me is gone. All that's left is a full-body numbness. I don't protest, I don't speak. I don't do anything but exist. It's the only way to keep my sanity.

I don't even remember falling asleep, but Lydia's soft hand on my cheek wakes me up. She smiles at me before helping me up and into a warm towel. They are silent as they help me dress in a deep crimson gown. Lydia brushes oils in my hair and places my crown atop my head. A routine, a ritual. That's what this has become. Every day is the same. And every day I refuse to look in the mirror because I always see the same thing.

Graying skin, bones peeking through as if I didn't have an ounce of fat on my body. Dark and puffy under eyes. Burns, cuts, brands, and bruises covering nearly every inch of my skin on the days I haven't yet healed. The deep welts on my ankles and wrists that seem to blister more and more every day, despite what Tobias does to force my skin to regenerate.

And lastly, the mark on my neck from the collar.

The iron collar is composed of short and sharp spikes that push into my skin. Every time I move, they dig deeper, sometimes piercing through. It's how he gets me to stay still, stay *pleasant* in front of court and guests. It's thin enough to be hidden by a gown or be mistaken for a simple necklace, but still sharp enough to cause continuous pain, continuous sores.

I slip into my heels and follow my ladies out of the bathing chamber. Tobias is already back, speaking to Davel. He smiles upon my entrance, his tan skin and golden hair looking healthier than ever. He's wearing his kingly cloak of crimson fur and his usual silk tunic and trousers that are in a black so deep that it seems to swallow all light, pulling the shadows around him like a magnet.

"My love!" He smiles as he reaches for me. I stand my ground and he pulls me into his arms, planting a rough, wet kiss to my lips. I don't reciprocate,

I never do. He pushes me away slightly and I nearly stumble. Cold fingers brush my neck and I hear the clanking of metal before I feel it being snapped into place. I bite my lip as the sharpened points settle against the deep wounds already in my skin. Tobias is smiling, excited by my pain.

He always is.

"We have much to do today, Ela. We have court shortly, where we have to, yet *again*, speak to the citizens about their inability to manage themselves. Then we have a special guest coming to speak with us. You might know him as Thelonious?" My eyes snap to his, shock evident in my face. The King of Rakushia is here? That's impossible.

He's dead.

"I know, I know. You are probably thinking, '*I thought Labisa beheaded him*'. Well, my queen, so did we. I guess we were wrong." He shrugs before grabbing my arm and pulling me with him out of the room. His fingers slide down to my hand, threading through mine. I let him.

I much prefer holding his hand than the chain he used to strap to the collar to walk me like one of his hunting hounds. Anytime I would speak, or honestly do anything he deemed disrespectful, he would yank the chain. The only person who got him to stop was Apollo, and only because he damaged my esophagus and I almost suffocated on my own blood. He stopped using the chain after that, but the collar stayed.

"Imagine our surprise when he was found stumbling through the woods wounded and starving. He's been healing with Pakin the last couple of days, and now he is ready to talk with us." I turn to look at him and wince against the metal spikes.

"Will we offer him safe harbor?" I ask, my voice hoarse. His eyes widen at the sound of it. It's been weeks since I last spoke, and I don't know why I chose today to break that streak of silence. Maybe it's the prospect of seeing someone who may actually care for me, a family member.

Someone who may be able to help.

I have to hope that Tobias enjoys it when I speak, especially now as his eyes soften. His hand reaches out and he strokes my cheek with his thumb. I can see it in his eyes, adoration and *love*. Part of me wants to get lost in his eyes, in the way he's looking at me, but I know that isn't the only side of him. Tobias carries masks around as if they are costumes to don when appropriate, and the mask I most often see if not the one he's wearing now.

"Of course we will, my love. We are going to help him get his country back." He says matter-of-factly as he drops his hand from my face and threads his fingers through mine again. We stroll down the hallway, servants and guards bowing as they pass. They don't look at me. They used to. They would stare and gawk, but Tobias stabbed the last person who looked a little too long, right in the middle of the hallway, so now I am just invisible.

"Is it wise to enter a war at this time?" I speak again, my voice rough and weak from disuse. We knew war with Labisa was coming, but it's too soon. What would happen if we agitated them? If we allowed them to cross the border? What about the innocent lives that would be lost?

"We have no choice, Ela. They will come for us. They will come for you. You were nearly taken once before," He pauses and turns to face me. His brows are furrowed, and his eyes are filled with sorrow. I know Tobias cares for me, but this act of the scared husband is just that, *an act*. He himself has hurt me more times than I am even aware of, yet he is acting saddened by the thought of my trauma. I don't believe it. "I won't let them take you again." He slides his hand up from mine to the back of my neck, before dropping his forehead down to rest against mine.

"It is not my safety that I am worried about. I am worried about those who reside near the border, those who do not have hundreds of kingsguard to ensure their survival." I retort, genuine fear fueling my words. We have too many citizens who are unarmed, who are vulnerable. Would he protect them?

"Your empathy is one of the things I love most about you." His lips press softly to mine, and I fight the urge to flinch. "Do not worry about our people,

Ela. I will ensure their safety." I nod shallowly as he steps back and continues down the hallway. I believe him. Regardless of our relationship and our situation, he *does* care for them. He cares for Noterra, and I think at the end of the day, he would keep them safe. I have to believe that.

"Is Thelonious going to be alright?"

"Yes, he was quite dehydrated, but he has been healing quickly. I don't know how he managed to stay alive all of these months, but I am sure we will find out when we speak with him." I nod as he pulls me into the throne room and up the dais.

Chapter Four

"Just blow the fucking palace to the ground." Nithe mutters from my left, nursing his cup of whiskey. He's always quick to jump to the extremes, not caring for the deaths that will follow. He has always been dramatic, even as a child. He would either be the one crying and over exaggerating some ailment, or being a bully to the other lords' sons. I guess I should be grateful he was always kind to me, but then again, I think my father scared him enough to keep in line. Kassius may look non-threatening, but he has the uncanny ability to freak people out, *especially* children.

"Nithe, for once in your life, shut the fuck up." I whisper back to him, and he sends me a scathing look before rolling his eyes and downing his glass.

"They have been debating how they are going to kill Tobias for months but haven't come up with a legitimate plan. Are you saying blowing the damn thing to the ground wouldn't be the easiest thing to do, Enzo?" He has a point, but I can't let him know I agree with him. That's the last thing his ego needs. "It's made mostly of glass anyway, it'll be easy." He shrugs and sets his empty glass down, reaching for the decanter in the middle of the large, oak table.

"We aren't going to blow Noterra up. The goal is to eventually place Elaenor there, isn't it?" I press, constantly having to remind him why she's important. He's been calling her an inconvenience since we all came to Rakushia, even though he knows what she means to the rest of us. That she herself is a miracle and will help reunite all of the kingdoms.

Thelonious was more than gracious enough to host not only the King of Labisa and their crown prince, but also my father and I. My father spent quite a lot of time here while I was young. He was close to Elaenor's mother, Sybil, and left me either here in Rakushia or in Labisa with Nithe, where I grew up, when he would visit her. I always begged to go, but he wouldn't take me. He would tell me about his time there. How Sybil's daughter was stubborn, but sweet and caring. He spoke about her often.

When I turned seven, I started to shock nearly everyone I touched. I was terrified and hid in my closet for two days after nearly giving my nursemaid a heart attack. My father was gone and returned to find me missing. When he eventually found me and I shocked him, he sat me down and told me what was going on.

He called us seers, and said that Sybil and Elaenor were seers too, but that they were also witches. That electricity was being caused by a bond that I had with Elaenor. She was distraught, her mother had just died. She was unintentionally channeling all of her energy into the bond, but it was keeping her alive. He told me the king tried to blame him for Sybil's death, but he wasn't the one who did it. He was the one who found her and the Elaenor sized pool of blood days after the attack happened. No one even noticed the queen and princess were missing.

It took weeks of my father teaching me how to channel energy for me to find her, and we believed that when we did, it would be a body that was found instead of a living, breathing little girl. All I kept seeing were trees and water. I was seeing the bottom of a lake for days and days, and I was convinced she had drowned, but she hadn't. She was sleeping down there, at the bottom of The Delaquar. I still to this day don't understand how she survived, but somehow, I found her.

She was rescued the day after.

The buzz under my skin stayed pretty constant throughout the years after that, and whenever I wanted to, I could push until I could feel her. I felt her worst moments. I felt when her father beat her and whipped her. I felt her sorrow as she thought about suicide. I was angry, wanted to get her out of my head as much as possible, and so I left. I was headed to Chatis, leaving Labisa where we currently lived, when my father stopped me.

He said it wasn't time, but it would be soon. A year later we came to Rakushia with Nithe and the King of Labisa. We've been here ever since, but nearly 8 months ago I was told to go. My father gave me a shard of sirenstone and sent me into the woods outside Chatis. We knew she was leaving; she was headed to Noterra. I had to find a way to get to her, make her take the stone.

I was shocked when I laid eyes on her for the first time. I wasn't supposed to let her see me. She was absolutely beautiful, but saddened—broken. Her hair was just a mass of unruly, black curls that almost sparkled under the little sunlight that broke through the clouds. Her skin was pale, but I could still make out a small spattering of light freckles along her nose.

She wasn't scared when she looked into my eyes, nor when she chased me through the woods. She was quick, but I was faster. I dropped the sirenstone and, like I'd hoped, she stepped on it. The stone needed blood to activate it, and I got it. It strengthened our connection and I no longer had to strain my own power reserves to reach her. With that connection, I felt everything. I could get into her head; I could even shadow walk so she could see me as if I was really there. She could touch me, and I her.

But that came with its own problems. I saw when he hit her. I saw when he drugged and raped her. I saw everything he did to her and every time she forgave him. I saw it all, but I took it for granted. Every second I can't feel her—can't *see* her—I regret ever hating that ability. I regret not taking her with me in the woods that day, but I couldn't intervene.

That's the one thing I've had to promise: not to intervene until it was time.

And now, I can't feel her. I can't see her or speak to her. It ended one day, and it took my father explaining it to me to understand what it meant. He said we still had a connection, but the stone had to have been destroyed. It was the only way the connection could weaken. We couldn't exactly fact check that assumption, so we have just been riding on the belief. The belief that the stone was destroyed and not her, because if it isn't true and she is dead, I don't know what that would mean for us.

Ever since we came to Rakushia, Nithe has been an annoyance, even if he is my best friend. He says it's because he hates being here and wants to go home, but I think he just doesn't believe the truth. He doesn't understand who Elaenor is, and honestly, I didn't either at first.

I'm convinced Nithe will be forced to marry her, which he believes also. He doesn't want it. He doesn't want *her*. He complains and says she's a child, even though she is just shy of a year younger than him. I just think he prefers his women wild and willing, and he calls Elaenor broken.

I call him an asshole.

I also don't think he ever believed he would ever have to marry. He's used to getting his own way, sleeping with every available, and *unavailable* woman he can find. He's wild and untamed. His father hates it, but before now, he didn't have a need for his son to bear an heir or have a wife. While Nithe is the heir to Labisa, his father is convinced that he will remain king forever.

"What if she doesn't even want it?" Nithe whispers. He's hoping she abdicates, because that would be the only way he wouldn't be forced to marry her. But if she abdicates, who will take over?

"Then that will be her choice." I shrug.

"Are you two done?" Thelonious, the King of Rakushia, is a kind man, but his patience is fading. He has been a gracious host, but I don't think he thought we would be here for over a year. He believes in us and our mission, and he was a friend to Sybil prior to her death. He wants Elaenor on the throne just as much as we do, but it is not without a cost. It seems we are losing people left and right.

"Yes, Your Grace." I bow my head softly and sit up in the chair I currently occupy. Nithe snorts next to me before downing his glass again and sighing.

"We need someone who can get in. Someone who would be let through the palace gates. I had thought that would be Theo, but it seems his affection for the princess got him killed before we could get to him." Davenport, Nithe's father and the King of Labisa, *isn't* a kind man. He strictly refers to Elaenor as the princess instead of the queen, which is what she is. I'm almost convinced he's going to force Elaenor to marry *him*, putting him on the throne. Nithe's mother, Arya, died when he was young, as did mine. Leaving us to be raised by our fathers. While I had someone who cared about the greater good, Nithe's father cares more about power and how to get it. Maybe Elaenor and Nithe have a lot in common in that regard. I don't know how either of them grew up to be good people.

"We have no one else we can risk sending." My father speaks up from my right. He's been quiet during this meeting. He says he feels something. Something in the air. He hasn't had a single vision since Sybil's death. He said she was his other half and when a seer's other half passes, their power often goes with it, if it's not absorbed by the other. Instead of absorbing Sybil's power, her death wrecked him and left him without his abilities. While he can no longer see what is to come, it didn't affect his intuition. He always knows when something is going to happen.

Shifting is an ability I am told only I have. I don't remember my father ever being able to do so, but he said he used to. I, however, have only learned to shift this last year. It started as something random, like a cat or deer, but then I was able to channel it. Control it. My shift of choice is a raven. They are quick, small, and intelligent. Nobody questions a bird flying about, but they would question a cat or deer.

"I could go." Thelonious's voice doesn't waver. He stands at the head of his council table, hands planted firmly on the pale wooden table.

"They think you're dead, Thel. That will do nothing but cause problems if you show up at their door unharmed and healthy." Davenport sneers.

"What if we make sure I am *not* unharmed and healthy? Make it seem like I have spent the better part of six months wandering the woods. I'll stay out there for a few days, get dirty, hungry, maybe even ill. They'll believe I escaped. It will be the same lie they spun about Erik being murdered when he was here all along." Everyone is quiet for a second. I glance at Nithe whose eyes are focused on his father's.

"What about Lyla?" My father speaks up again. "Her and Emery are due back any day now with Mal, are you going to leave before saying goodbye?" The queen and the princess went to Labisa for a few weeks, for safety, taking my little sister with them. We were worried about Tobias infiltrating Rakushia, so we had to take precautions. Labisa is on the other side of The Divide, and Tobias wouldn't risk sending an army that far when we are stationed on his northern border already.

"If I stay, I won't be able to go. I won't be able to leave them. This is our only shot, Kass. This will get me close to her." My father reluctantly nods, understanding. I hate it, but he's right. He can get in.

"So it's settled, then? You'll live in the woods for a few days and then get into the palace, make the boy king think he's harboring you, and you'll get close to the princess. Then what?" Davenport's voice is filled with amusement and disdain. As if he can't even decide whether he should laugh or yell.

"Make sure the king doesn't kill her, or she doesn't kill herself." My eyes flash to his, and I can almost feel it. Feel her life draining away. She would kill herself. She'd be weak if she didn't even consider it. If the choice was to stay and be abused and tortured, or end your life and experience peace in the world beyond, why wouldn't she choose the latter? I wouldn't blame her, but I hope she doesn't attempt it.

She just has to hold on a little bit longer.

Nithe and I are dismissed, but we linger in the hallway, waiting for them to be done and hoping they have some sort of information or plan that they can share with us. They don't keep much from us, but sometimes they do prefer to speak just the three of them, which does nothing but irritate me to no end.

"I don't think this will work." I admit. Nithe is leaning against the dark wood of the wall, his head back and eyes closed.

"Do you have any better ideas?" He mutters.

"No." I pace, my hands on my hips. "I still can't feel her. Not after the stone was destroyed." My leather shoes smack the stone floor as I walk back and forth, filling the silence.

"Maybe you aren't trying hard enough." He says, disinterested.

"Or she's dead." Nithe groans and pushes off the wall.

"Enzo, I get that this girl is important, but is she truly worth all of us dying? All of us risking our lives to get her to safety?"

"You don't know her." I snap, my face heating.

"Neither do you!"

"I watched her grow up from afar, I watched her get beaten by her father and get up again. I watched Tobias rape her, torture her, and then drug her to make her forget. I have seen first-hand her struggles and I have been able to do *nothing.* I know her better than most." My hands clench into fists, anger brewing beneath the surface of my skin.

"Sounds a little like you are in love with a girl who doesn't even know you exist." I don't hesitate, my clenched fist meeting his cheek before he has a chance to deflect, sending him sprawling on the floor.

"*Fuck you*, Nithe." I spit, but he just laughs as I walk away.

Chapter Five

The Caged
Present Day

"Come forward and state your complaint." Welan bellows out into the crowd, his voice echoing in the silence. The throne room is packed to the brim, with the crowd spilling out into the hallway like one giant wave of people. This isn't the first time I've attended court with Tobias, but it never gets easier. Hearing their woes and fears is one thing, but sitting in the same room I watched Theo get beheaded in is worse. A small, elderly woman limps up to the bottom of the dais before dropping to her knees.

My gaze fixates on the shiny marble below her, my pulse quickening. I can still see the blood pooling next to me, the heads rolling on the floor. My pulse pounds in my ears and I can feel a tremble run down my spine. I force myself to look away, sending shooting pain into my neck as I jostle the collar. I swallow loudly, forcing the bile creeping up my throat back down.

"What have you come to request from His Grace?" Welan speaks again. The woman's head is bowed, her gray hair tangled and knotted. She's wearing a beige gown made of linen, with speckles of dried blood and dirt towards the hem. I slightly lean forward as I take in her appearance, the exhaustion evident on her face.

"Your Grace, I ask that you send aid to the town of Tellavid. It has been raided and all of our homes have been ransacked. We have no food and no shelter that isn't destroyed. We ask that the crown supply emergency assistance." Her voice cracks as she stays on her knees, her eyes cast downward. Her hands are knotted together nervously, and I fight the urge to go to her, to help ease her worries.

"Who is it that has attacked Tellavid?" Tobias speaks. His voice is loud, bellowing out into the crowd. People shift, uneasy, and I can see a lot of them are dirty and tired. How many of those attending court were there during the raid?

"We believe it was a group of savages hailin' from Ovobia, Your Grace. They carried spears and dressed in nothin' but cloths hangin' from their hips." I am not familiar with the country of Ovobia, and I have my father to blame for that, but I vaguely remember seeing it on a map north of Tatus. Maybe now would be a good time to get geography lessons.

"How can you be certain it isn't Labisa?" Tobias pushes. He wants nothing more than to pin any threats on Labisa, and I don't blame him. They already killed the Rakushian Queen, and the princess is still missing. What is going to stop them from killing innocents? Tellavid is part of Port Tobeo, which means they had to come by ship if they were to arrive unannounced. But why wouldn't the guards stop a ship filled with Ovobian men? How would they have even gotten far enough to infiltrate Tellavid?

"Did they come by ship?" I quickly clamp my mouth shut as soon as the words leave my lips without thought. I'm not supposed to speak during court, but I couldn't help it. I look to my right, where Tobias is sitting on the matching throne to mine. He isn't glaring at me though, his eyes are focused on the woman, awaiting her response. I swear I see a hint of fear pass through his eyes, but it's gone in less than a second.

"No, Your Grace." She lifts her head and looks at me. "They came from behind. The land side, not the port side." They came *from* Noterra, not the ocean. It couldn't have been another country, unless they funneled out of Rakushia, but even then, they would have been spotted well before they made it all the way to the bay. I open my mouth to say just that, but Tobias cuts me off.

"Very well. The crown will supply medical equipment and food to assist in healing the people of Tellavid. We will also arrange our emergency funding to be distributed equally amongst the affected families, to ensure they can rebuild without strain." She nods, relieved, and stands, limping towards the back of the room as people part to let her through.

Tobias rises without saying anything, signaling that he is done for the day, his jaw clenched. We have been here for hours, and there are still so many people seeking the attention of their king, but they will have to wait. I follow suit, standing from my own throne and walking over to offer my hand to Tobias, which he takes.

It has become an act; one I was quick to learn. I play the dutiful wife, the queen that speaks only when spoken to. In turn, I live. Although, I feel the alternative would be a better option. I wouldn't call this living.

I am *surviving*.

Tobias turns and pulls us out of the room without another word. The door to the council chamber opens and he guides me through with his hand on my lower back. I focus on keeping my head up and steady, as any slight movement causes the spikes to shift. Once the door back to the throne room closes, his hands leave my back, and he walks around the table to the bar cart. I can tell he's angry, but I force myself to remain steady. My pulse skips as my eyes snag on the door on the far side of the room.

The door that leads down.

"Remind me, Ela, when have I ever given you permission to speak during court?" He asks, his back to me. I tear my eyes away from the door and take a slow deep breath before answering.

"Never." I whisper, wiping my sweaty palms on the skirts of my gown.

"Exactly." He walks over to me, carrying his glass of whiskey. He sets it down on the council table before stepping closer. He lifts his hand and I flinch, but he just brushes hair from my face, tucking it behind my ear. "You don't need to be scared of me, my love." He whispers, his thumb brushing my bottom lip before he bends down and kisses me.

His lips are soft against mine, gentle. I fight against the trembling that seems to always be present. His tongue forces my lips to part, and I resist the gag forming in my throat. His free hand snakes around my waist pulling me against him. I can feel his growing erection pressing into my lower belly and my hands dampen. Sweat beads along my hairline as the pounding in my ears quickens. *Breathe, Elaenor.* Thankfully, someone knocks on the door and Tobias pulls away from me.

"Your Grace, King Thelonious of Rakushia is here." Welan says and I force myself to straighten and swallow the bile sitting in my throat.

"Send him in." Tobias calls back, returning to the table where his whiskey is after brushing his hand along my cheek again.

Thelonious walks in and I nearly gasp, my hand flying to my mouth. His normally golden skin is a deep red, sunburnt and dry. He's thin, as if he hadn't eaten in weeks. He is freshly dressed but looks as if he has been on the run for months, which I suppose he has.

"Elaenor." He smiles as he walks in, coming right to me. Relief pools in his eyes as he sees me. "It's so good to see you." He throws his arms around me, and I return the hug, tears springing in my eyes. "My, how you've grown." He pulls back and looks me up and down, his eyes catching on my neck and the iron collar.

"It is so good to see you, uncle." I whisper, fighting the sob working through my throat. He's my father's cousin, but as children he told me to call him uncle. He is the last living family member I have. His thumb gently wipes under my eyes, taking the tears with it. He turns away from me and smiles, looking at Tobias. I bite my bottom lip and clasp my hands in front of me, begging the trembling to subside.

"Your Grace." He bows quickly before offering his hand to Tobias.

"It is good to see you have healed well, Thelonious." Tobias responds, shaking his hand. It isn't common for kings to not bestow formalities when greeting one another, but Tobias forgoes tradition, no doubt seeing himself as better than the Rakushian King.

"Yes, well you have been more than instrumental in my recovery." They take their seats at the table and I hover behind Tobias, my place when in the council room. Thelonious's eyes glance at me nervously every few seconds. I cock my head in question and hiss as the collar moves. I bite my lip to keep from wincing and straighten my neck.

"Are you alright, Elaenor?" He asks as he rises and steps over to me. "Are you ill?" Tobias stands quickly, grabbing Thelonious's hand before he can touch me again.

"She has been unwell as of late, but she is recovering quickly." He gestures towards his chair again. "Please, sit." His voice is anything but regal, and if I was scared of Tobias, I would take it as a threat.

"Of course, Your Grace. Pardon my intrusion. I will always see her as the small girl I once knew." He explains as he glances at me knowingly. He knows. He *has* to know. Anyone who saw me, saw how I looked, would know I was not a willing participant to whatever Tobias does to me.

"I am no longer that girl, uncle." I say, causing Tobias to look over his shoulder at me.

"Sit, Elaenor." Tobias snaps and I take the seat next to him. He holds out his hand and I take it. His thumb caresses my palm and I try to ignore the nervous jitters spreading throughout my body. The jitters responsible for the brief feeling of relief knowing that I am no longer alone. I have family with me. "Please Thelonious, tell us of your troubles."

"Please, call me Thel." He responds before furrowing his brow and sighing. "It started one evening; we heard the shouting. It wasn't long before we were pulled from bed and thrown on the ground. Men wearing indistinct armor and black cloaks were yelling, and I had to watch as they beheaded my dear Lyla." He takes a deep breath and looks over at me.

"They were screaming, asking where Emery was, but I pretended to not know. I only hope she got out in time." He swallows against the lump in his throat, and I almost want to reach out and grab his hand, but something in his facial expression looks off. It looks *forced*. I glance at Tobias who is staring at him with wide, calculated eyes and pinched brows, buying every word.

"How did you escape?" Tobias questions.

"I was in the dungeons when I heard a bomb go off, no doubt ruining a part of my home." He shakes his head. "The blast knocked the doors loose and I was able to simply walk out. I stayed in the hills, hoping to find Emery, but then I saw them publicly declare my death, saying that they beheaded me. I was shocked, because I was very much alive, so I took that as my chance, and I ran. I have been wandering for weeks, ill and hurt, until one of your men found me." He looks up at me, his eyes narrowing for just a second.

Something is off, something is wrong. I almost want to warn Tobias, but I don't. If he came to cause Tobias harm, I don't know that I would stop him. I don't think he would hurt me, plot against me, but he might be helpful in my situation.

I need to get him alone.

"I am forever grateful for your rescue, Your Grace." Thel continues.

"We are happy to have found you." He pauses. "But I have a stipulation for assisting you in recovering your home and your country." Tobias leans forward, his hands clasped together, releasing mine. He takes a slow breath before looking up at Thelonious.

"Name it."

"I want your support in my ascension to High King, ruling over the entirety of the continent." I nearly gasp and Thel's mouth parts slightly. My eyes widen as I stare at my husband, the man who is about to start a war pitting every kingdom on the continent of Viridiana against each other.

"Forgive me, Tobias, but I am only one king. There are nine," he glances over at me again and his face softens. "Forgive me, *eight* other countries you must appeal to." I fight the lump in my throat at his mention of Chatis. The country that once was, but is no longer. My home. His eyes narrow slightly as he turns back to Tobias. "Countries who have never bowed to anyone but themselves since the death of King Jahara nearly twenty years ago. How do you wish to achieve this? How will you convince kingdoms to give up their birthright?" Thel is firm but careful. He knows how to talk around the subject in a way that doesn't raise suspicion, but still questions Tobias's sanity.

The sanity I have been questioning for months.

"It's simple." Tobias says, leaning back in his chair and sliding his glass of whiskey off the table. He takes a slow sip, sighing after he swallows. "Follow me, or die."

Chapter Six

The Bound

My nose is still bleeding, even after two hours. I throw another rag down and take a swig of my whiskey, savoring the taste as it burns its way down my throat.

Fucker.

He was supposed to go easy on me, we were sparring, not *actually* fighting to the *death*. Enzo never knows how to hold back. He's been too angry, too unstable since he felt Elaenor last. He's slowly becoming unhinged, and a lack of control is dangerous, especially right now when everything is so tense. Right now is when we should be in control. Should be methodical. *Should* have a plan. But we aren't and we don't. We are going into everything blind. Doing everything without a plan. Because we don't know what to do. It's been months and we *still* don't know what to do.

The windows in my room are open, letting the spring air filter in. The flowers here have been blossoming like crazy, setting off my allergies. Who knew I would have an allergy to wisteria?

Wisteria is the nation's flower, and all who need or want it, have to buy it from here. It's a simple flower that can either fill a room with a thick floral aroma or be used to kill or decapacitate. Much like hemlock and poppy, it has many uses, and every godsforsaken inch of this country is covered in wisteria trees and pollen. It's a wonder Rakushia's citizens haven't all accidentally killed themselves, although Emery always tells me the flower has to be prepared a certain way to make it toxic. I can't imagine a country would allow their entire nation to be filled with plants that could kill anyone who it came into contact with.

Unless that person is Tobias. He probably would and he'd call it population control.

To combat my allergies, Master Lenus has been giving me a tonic made of honey and elderflower every morning, which has been helping, but now with my nose busted it just makes it worse. I can't even take a deep breath without choking on my own blood and snot. My irritation peaks as another wave of pain shoots up my nose. I reach for the rag again as a blur of gold and white barrels into my room.

"What happened to you?" The intruder taunts as she throws herself on the bed. My chambers here in Rakushia are small compared to my room back home in Labisa. A small writing desk sits in the far corner, a single sofa in front of the fireplace, and a four-poster bed in the center of the back wall. A door by the bed leads to the small bathing chamber and dressing room. I don't have a balcony here, which I despise. Even Scarlett got a balcony and she's nothing but a pain in the ass. Not to mention the large room they set aside for Elaenor when she eventually arrives. A room fit for a queen, as Enzo said.

It's bullshit.

"Good morning to you, princess." I plaster a smile on my face and turn in my chair to face her. Her golden blonde hair is shining in the sunlight, pooling around her like molten metal. Her hazel eyes are glowing in the bright light filtering through the open windows.

"Let me guess, you were an asshole to Enzo again and he finally let you have it?" She's smiling as she takes in my bloody nose, her rosy lips splitting to show her straight teeth. Emery is one of those people who is effortlessly beautiful. Whether she is wearing a dress worth more than someone's house, or in her fighting leathers. She is the type of woman men go to war for.

"Emery, have you nothing to do but bother me?" I feign annoyance, my free hand on my chest as I wipe at my nose.

"Oh don't act like you don't enjoy my company, Nithie." She winks as she stretches out on the bed, her dress spreading around her like liquid. She knows how to tease me, make me want nothing more than her skin on mine to ease the ache settling in my limbs, but after a single night when I first moved here a year ago, she hasn't been willing to cross that line again, regardless of how much I try.

"Oh *I* enjoy your company, it's you who doesn't enjoy mine." She giggles and sits up, propping a pillow behind her head.

"I enjoy your company just fine, Nithie, it's your dick I'm not fond of." I snort and throw the bloody rag back on the desk where it lands with a wet slapping sound. I glare at the cloth before turning towards Em.

"That's a first." I mutter.

"Well, I prefer something…more feminine." She says slowly, cocking her head to the side.

"You can say you prefer girls; I don't care. In fact, I would be *more* than willing to be a spectator during your enjoyment of women." I walk over to the bed and climb up next to her. She hits me in the face with the pillow, my eyes instantly watering as she hits my already bloody nose. "*Ow.*"

"Pig." She spits and I gasp before rolling on top of her, holding her down with my thighs. Her small frame is lean, comprised of honed muscles that make her lethal. I'm not afraid to admit that she would win in the ring. She's trained her entire life to be a weapon, and a weapon she is. A *wraith* as her father calls her. The greatest weapon in his arsenal.

"That's quite rude and unladylike."

"You are very heavy, my prince. Maybe consider a diet?" My eyes widen and she freezes. "Don't." She warns. I don't hesitate, my fingers find her armpits and she squeals so loud she could rival a hog. "Nithe, stop!" She half-screams half-laughs as I tickle her. Her body bucks underneath mine as she tries to get free, but I keep her pinned.

"Take it back!" I can barely hear myself over her screaming as my fingers tickle any part of her I can touch.

"Can you guys maybe shut the fuck up?" I jump as a snarky, feminine voice erupts from behind. Whipping my head around, I see Scarlett standing in the doorway with her hands on her hips. Her jaw is clenched, brows furrowed, and eyes narrowed so much she could rival a cat. Her brown hair is in a messy braid, the blue dress she's wearing hanging off her awkwardly. She's lost a lot of weight since she was first brought here, but I suppose an all-liquid diet tends to do that. I roll off of Emery and prop myself up against my headboard.

"Better?" I snap. She has a habit of being annoying at the most inconvenient times. Well, it's *never* convenient for her to be annoying.

"You two are disgusting. If you insist on being in a room next to mine, the least you can do is keep it down when you are doing whatever it is you are doing." She crosses her arms in front of her chest and squints her eyes in my direction.

"Don't be such a prude, Scar. We weren't doing anything." Emery is breathless, and I can almost hear her heart pounding in the awkward silence. She sits up, propping her elbows up behind her as she brushes her golden tendrils from her eyes.

"I am the farthest thing from a prude, as *you* know." Scarlett scoffs, but a glimmer of amusement flashes through her brown eyes. I glance between the two of them. Emery is sucking on her teeth and Scarlett is staring her down. I can almost feel the tension radiating off of them.

Oh. *Oh.*

I can barely contain my laugh as I slide off the bed with widened eyes.

"I'll leave you two alone, just stay off my bed." I chuckle as I push past Scarlett, exiting *my* room.

"I don't know what you are thinking, but you're wrong!" She yells after me, which only makes me chuckle louder, the sound echoing off the bare walls.

Good for them. I think Em could do better, but honestly Scarlett needs to blow off some steam if she's ever going to become a productive member of this group. Which she needs to become soon, or my father will push her out of the palace. Scarlett is stubborn, strong, but she couldn't survive out there. Not when we are on the brink of a war.

My footsteps echo off the wooden stairs as I descend to the bottom floor. I head towards the council chamber, hoping to get my father alone. He doesn't withhold much, but he tends to be more secretive when there are others around. And ever since Thel left, he's been holing up in there with Kass, not allowing any of us to join them. I know the three of them are old friends, but I wouldn't be surprised if my father was trying to find a way to absorb Rakushia as his own country. Although that shouldn't be his priority, Elaenor should.

I have questions, complaints, concerns, all of the above, in regard to Elaenor and his plans, and I'm hoping he'll answer at least one of them. The one that will also affect me.

Like I expected, the Labisian King is in the council room, pouring over the map like usual. The council chamber is a small rectangular room that holds a table big enough for ten. Golden banners line the walls, showing off the Rakushian flag. A yellow background with a bundle of purple wisteria in the center tied together with a rope. Why they chose yellow to compliment the purple flowers, I'll never know.

It's not the most attractive color combination.

However, the rope is an ode to how this country started. These lands were once slave territory, and the continent's ancestors forced those who were magicless to do hard labor. They worked in mines, chopped trees, and more. All for a few bites of bread a day. Each slave was tethered to the next with rope so tight it sliced through their skin. Hundreds of years passed with that being the norm, but King Jahara was a savior and Rakushia became a beautiful country again. I think everyone expected it to stay that way until King Jahara III and his nephew were murdered, and King Evreux took the crown. With how Tobias is, I'm not too sure that the continent's weak will be safe.

"Father." I announce my presence as I make my way around the table to peer over his shoulder.

"He's moved more of his men to the border, I wouldn't be surprised if he pushes through within the next week." My father mutters. He's moved a few rose shaped pieces on the map closer to Rakushia.

"How many men does that make?" I ask. Each rose signals 100 people and I can currently see seven pieces on the map, with two rolling in his hand.

"Nearly seven hundred and eighty, if our intel is correct." His voice is quiet, disinterested as he thinks.

"Do you know if Thel got to the palace?"

"Yes, he did. I received a raven from Ren. He said he met with Tobias and Elaenor this morning."

"So she's alive?" We haven't had eyes on her in weeks. Ren tries his best to send correspondence when possible, but it's hard. If he got caught, he'd be executed. Last we heard, he hadn't seen her in days, unsure of where Tobias kept her. She hadn't been to any of the court holdings, any of the royal meals or events. She was gone. For all we knew, she was dead. But I knew he wouldn't kill her. He wants something from her, and he wouldn't risk losing it. He has to have somewhere in the palace that others don't know about. A place he could keep her close without being seen.

The plus side to Ren's collaboration with us is that we have Elaenor and

Tobias's wedding certificate. It never even made it to the vault in Noterra after their wedding. After it was signed, it was sent off that same day by Donovan. They are still legally wed, but all we have to do is burn it in the presence of a reverend and it'll be annulled.

Why we haven't done so yet, I am not sure. Maybe they want to do it once Elaenor is here, so she can be a witness? Or so Tobias doesn't have a chance to force her to sign another before she's rescued.

If she's rescued.

I'm hoping they opted to wait to give her a choice in the matter. Let her make the decision to end her marriage and enter a new one. I know Thel would be on board with that, he loves his niece, but I know it isn't something my father would agree to. But this isn't our decision, it's hers. Maybe she loves him? I can't imagine that she does, but how would any of us know what she's feeling right now?

"As far as this morning, yes. I don't know where she's been these last few weeks, but she is in the palace now. She was at court today." He's quiet as he ponders. We have 4,000 men stationed in Labisa, ready to move when we say. I don't doubt we could win against Tobias in an all-out war, but many lives would be lost. More than necessary. We were supposed to petition other countries for their armies, but they all wanted to wait and use Elaenor. Use her as the reason for their cooperation. Honestly, even if Elaenor died, she would still be useful. She could be a martyr, igniting the other countries into a rebellion to remove Tobias from the throne. Not that I am hoping for her demise, but she's useful either way.

"Father, what are your plans where Elaenor is involved? What happens after we rescue her?" I sit down in the chair adjacent to him, watching as his furrowed brows relax.

"She is the heir. As much as I hate it, her future son would be the rightful ruler of the entire continent of Viridiana. We need to control her, garner her trust. I expect nothing of her but a puppet to play with." I nearly scoff at his indifference. I may not be a fan of Elaenor and what she means, but she deserves more than this.

"So you just want to use her? Do you think she'll be so trusting after her time with Tobias, that she will listen to anything you have to say?" I counter.

"She won't have a choice. She will wed upon her arrival, and you will put a child in her before she has the chance to say no." He doesn't look at me, his eyes still pouring over the maps as he suggests I impregnant a young woman who has spent the last few months being tortured.

"Father, I will not force myself on an unwilling woman." There is no way he can force me to do this, to *marry* her. To force her to carry my child.

"Then make sure she's willing." He retorts without looking at me, his tone indifferent and tired. He sighs as he sets the wooden roses back on the table.

"I don't remember agreeing to wed her." I snap. It's not often I verbally disagree with my father, but I won't stand by and be another one of his puppets.

"I don't remember asking your opinion, son." I stand, the chair nearly toppling over as I plant my hands on the table, leaning forward.

"Father, *please*. Enzo would be a much better husband than I would." Not to mention he already loves her. My eyes plead for him to listen, but his just harden in return.

"*Enzo* isn't the crown prince. *Enzo* isn't my son. If you will not marry her, *I* will." He snaps, his voice rising. I cross my arms in front of my chest and lean back. He *would* marry her. He's that sick and twisted that he would force a girl who is younger than his own child to be his wife. He wouldn't be a kind husband; he would do more harm than good. She truly would just be a shell for him to control after that. She would be better off with Tobias than him.

"There is no discussion to be had, is there? It is either you or me sitting on the throne beside her one day? I don't want to marry her, but I will not subject her to a life chained to you. I know more than anyone how horrible that life would be." He doesn't respond. He knows how I feel about him, about his use of women as toys to play with until they are broken. He almost coerced Scarlett to be his newest pet, but he couldn't deal with her attitude. I just don't think he liked that she had boundaries. Ones he couldn't cross without seeming like he was forcing himself on her—which he was.

I don't want this life for myself, but I do have a chance to keep Elaenor from entering another marriage like the one she's in. I'm bound to her, one way or another.

I don't even know why I care about any of this; why I care about her. At this point in time she doesn't even know I exist.

"You will wed Elaenor, and you will become the king, that is final." The door opens and I glance over at Enzo as he barrels in.

"Anything?" He's breathless as if he ran all the way here, his hands gripping the back of a chair with an iron fist.

"Thel put eyes on her this morning. She's alive." I inform him as I take my place in the chair behind me. His shoulders drop back to a normal height as the tension leaves his body.

"What is the plan? Did he say anything else?" He asks as he pulls the chair out and drops into it.

"Yes." My father's voice drops, a little more than a whisper. My head whips back in his direction. He's hiding something.

"Father, what else did Ren say?" He clears his throat and slowly sits into the chair behind him, swirling his whiskey in his hand.

"He said she's ill. He doesn't know with what, but her skin is pale, she has wounds and bruises covering every inch of visible skin, and he said there was a silver collar fitted with prongs around her neck." I choke, my mouth falling open.

"*What*?" Enzo's voice is so loud I jump.

"Enzo," I raise my hand to get him to relax. The last thing we need is him losing his mind and shifting into something obscenely large, like a whale.

"What is going to be done?" He snaps, his fingers digging into the wood of the table.

"As of right now, nothing. Thel will ensure she stays safe." My father states, disinterest coating his voice like ash. He doesn't care if she's safe, he just cares if she's alive and able to create heirs.

"How?" I pipe in, he has to have a plan.

"I am not sure."

"We have to go. *Now.*" Enzo snaps, shooting back out of his chair.

"Child, you do not command me or any of our armies. We will move when *I* say we move." The Labisian King's voice raises in volume, sending goosebumps down my arms. He only snaps when he's angry, and I can tell he's getting to that point. As much as I hate it, he's in charge here. His word is law until Thel returns.

"You can't expect us to sit around while she's chained up like a dog."

"You will do as you're told." His voice is even as he holds Enzo's glare. I flick my gaze back and forth between them, my palms growing sweaty.

"*You* are not my king." Enzo snaps before rushing out of the room. I roll my eyes and sigh. One thing Enzo tends to do is throw tantrums like a child when he's stressed. Most of the time he's even, stoic, but when it comes to Elaenor he's unhinged and rash.

It's going to get him killed.

"Talk to him, Nithe. If he attempts to cross the border right now, he will cost us everything." My father orders as he goes back to peering at the map. I nod and sigh, before standing and following behind.

Chapter Seven

The Protector

My heart is racing, my breathing ragged as I lean my forehead against the cool glass. *Breathe.* Every time I get upset, I can almost feel the feathers brushing up against my skin, begging to be released. Shifting is new for me. Something that has been brewing beneath the surface, *literally*, for months now. I can control it, for the most part. At least what I shift into, which I am grateful for. I accidentally shifted into a horse one day when I was sparring with Ni, and he pissed me off. That was a shock.

My father said the ability to shift came from my grandfather. I guess it's a trait that can only be passed onto male children. I asked him about my grandmother, and he said she was a witch, like Sybil and Elaenor. I wonder if that's how he met her.

I can sense his presence before he speaks, and I sigh. He can always tell when I'm stressed and on the brink of losing control. He may not have his seeing abilities, but his intuition when it comes to my sister and I, has never failed him.

"What happened?" His voice is soft. Not that he is without emotions, but he never lets them show. The only time I saw him genuinely break down is when Sybil died. It was the first and only time I had seen him cry.

"He's using a collar. A collar fitted with *spikes* to control her." I spit out, clenching my eyes shut and pressing my forehead harder into the glass.

"Has Dav received word?" I can hear him collapse in one of the green settees placed around the small sitting area. The library in the Rakushian palace isn't large by any means, but it's comforting, warm. It's also rarely used so it's my favorite place to escape, to hide.

"Ren sent a raven. I guess Thel met with Elaenor and Tobias today. She's alive, but she doesn't look good. She looks sick." I told him what exactly Ren said, watching for his reaction. I don't miss the fury that flashes in his eyes, even if it only lasts a second. He loves Elaenor, probably as much as he loves his children.

"I don't know how much I trust Ren to be honest with you, son. He's been working for Tobias's father for years, and now Tobias himself. He may claim to be on our side, but he has stood by and watched as Elaenor is tortured. He may be a man of the church, but he is watching as a young girl is in need of help. He could be doing something to assist her."

"He has never lied." I turn and face my father. His dark hair is cropped close to his head, his yellow eyes are soft, tired. He's wearing a long sleeve tunic and breeches, light but still warm enough to stave off the last of the spring chill.

"That we know of. Regardless of his honesty, he hasn't stepped in. He hasn't helped us, or her. He's provided information. That's it."

"Information we wouldn't have otherwise." I counter.

"I'm just saying, don't get hung up on anything until we receive a raven from Thelonious himself." He says softly, as if he's being cautious how he speaks to me.

"I doubt they'll let him be alone in any capacity for quite some time, father. Tobias doesn't sound like a trusting man." He snorts and runs his hand through his short strands. I step away from the windowsill and drop into the settee across from him. His eyes are fixed on the window, wonder and calm settling in.

"Have I ever told you what Sybil called Elaenor when she was younger?" I shake my head. It isn't often he speaks about his time with either of them, but I long to hear all of the stories he has to tell.

"Starlight." He smiles and looks down at the floor, thinking. "She used to say her hair was as deep as the night sky, but was so shiny that it glittered like a thousand stars. She was so beautiful, so at peace when in her mother's arms. You two would have gotten along. She was stubborn, but she was free and adventurous. You would've influenced each other to do risky things, I presume." He chuckles softly, his eyes softening as he looks up at me.

"Tell me about her." I say quietly, hoping he'll keep talking.

"Elaenor?" I nod and he relaxes a little more into the plush cushion.

"She loved the trees, to be outside. I think she got that from her mother. Whenever I was around, she was either reading some book far too adult for her age or begging to go exploring deep in the woods and mountains. I went often, accompanying Sybil and Elaenor as they traipsed around, explored. Chatis is mostly trees, much like Noterra, but it's cloudy and humid. You had to run to keep up with her as she played, she would disappear in the fog, only to sneak up and scare you moments later." He laughs and I allow myself to smile.

"She sounds mischievous."

"That she was."

"Do you think she's still the same?" I think I know the answer, but I don't truly know. He ponders for a moment before looking at me.

"After Sybil died, and I escaped Viktor's claims of my involvement in her death, I went back a few times to check in on her. I never saw her leave the palace grounds. Not even once. I was able to get into the palace one day when Viktor was elsewhere. It was when she was fourteen years of age. Still young, but it was seven years after her mother passed. Seven years since I saw her last." Unshed tears in his eyes catch the light, and he blinks them away quickly.

"How was she?" I whisper.

"She was broken. I don't mean that to sound as horrible as it does, but she was no longer the little girl I knew and loved. She wasn't in her room when I searched for her, but in the infirmary. She had deep wounds across her back, so much so that stitches were barely enough to keep the skin closed." My eyes widen and my lips part.

"My gods." I whisper. I can feel my throat close as a lump forms.

"It was Viktor, he whipped her. Scarlett was asleep beside her bed, watching over her and holding her hand. I didn't mean to scare her, but I did. She remembered me though, she remembered who I was. I asked her what happened, and she told me. I guess Elaenor begged to leave, begged to go to the lake for a few moments just to feel the water on her toes. The Delaquar was one of her favorite places to go with Sybil." He sighs and rolls his lips. "Viktor whipped her for even asking to leave the walls. I sat with her for a few moments, ran my fingers through her frizzy curls. She was medicated, so she never woke while I was there. Scarlett told me she'd take care of her. Even at such a young age, she was strong enough to defend her, to protect her as best she can. Scarlett may not be okay right now, but she's strong. She'll get there." I ignore his comments about Scarlett and focus on Elaenor. How could a father whip his child into pieces?

"I don't understand how someone could do that to their child."

"She isn't his child, Enzo. Despite the fact that he raised her. She has been in captivity for almost nineteen years. She has never known freedom." He explains.

"She still won't, not here. Not with Davenport in control." I scoff and lean back. I hate the king, almost as much as I hate Tobias.

"Enzo," he warns.

"You know it's true. He is either going to force her to marry Nithe or he'll marry her himself."

"We don't know what's going to happen. All we need to worry about is bringing her to safety."

"This isn't safety, father. This is just another cage decorated with crowns and expensive clothing." I spit, venom coating my voice.

"She will be safe here. I'm not going to let anything happen to her, not again. I never should have let her get on that carriage to begin with." He tries to reason, but anger seeps through my skin like sweat. Everything that has to do with her—it just makes me angry. Feral even.

"You always said we couldn't intervene."

"We can't, it upsets the balance of life, but I can still be regretful of my lack of involvement–" His voice cuts out as the ground rumbles, and a deafening boom breaks up the otherwise silent palace. Rubble and dust fall from the ceiling as everything shakes. My fingers dig into the arms of the settee I am occupying as my widened eyes meet my fathers.

Nithe stumbles in, his face red, and his breathing labored.

"The palace, it's been bombed."

Chapter Eight

The Caged

Tobias's grip is firm as he drags me back to our rooms. The meeting with Thelonious didn't go as well as he'd expected. While he pledged his loyalty, he isn't entirely convinced the other eight kingdoms would bow to him, and I'm not either. He's going to have to kill them all. There is no way any of them will willingly name Tobias High King when the last High King died 20 years ago.

My heels are clicking against the marble loudly as I half run to keep up with his pace. If I slow down even a little, the collar around my neck pokes into my skin. Laris is standing with the door open to our chambers and shuts it as soon as we cross the threshold.

"Tobias." I whisper as he drags me to the couch. His fingers flex once before loosening. He releases my upper arm and I release the breath I had been holding.

"This will work, Ela. It will work." He's pacing and I take the chance to sit down on the couch, careful not to jostle the steel pressed to my throat. My back cramps as I relax into the cushions, finally releasing the stiff posture I was forced to carry.

"I know." I whisper softly. He's muttering to himself while he paces. "Can you take the collar off now?" I ask. His eyes soften as he looks at me and nods. He pulls the key out of his pocket and quickly unlocks the metal clasp. I groan as the spikes pull free from my skin; the pressure being replaced with a burn. I reach up and grasp my crown, pulling it free from my black hair and set it on the table in front of me.

"Think of what this could mean, Ela."

"What?"

"If I am High King, that would make you a High Queen. We could rule the entire continent together. Viridiana would be ours. All of it." His eyes are wide, filled with excitement. He collapses on the couch next to me, his hands harshly grabbing my face. His lips are merely a breath from mine. "This will work." I nod, unsure of what to say, and he releases me.

"What happens next?" I ask. He sighs and props his feet up on the table. As he opens his mouth to speak, the door to our chambers opens and Davel walks in. My eyes narrow and he smirks at me quickly before Tobias can see.

"It's done." He says. Tobias nods without looking at him.

"I am not entirely convinced Thel is on our side. I need to control him." I tear my eyes from Davel to look back at Tobias.

"How so?"

"He cares for you, get close to him." My lips part in shock.

"How?" I repeat.

"I want you to have lunch with him tomorrow. It'll be here in our chambers, and Davel will keep watch. I just want you to feel him out." He looks over at me. "You can do that, right? You aren't going to cause any issues?" I shake my head, excitement bubbling inside. He's going to actually leave me alone with someone other than his guards or my ladies. He leans over and cups my cheek again. "You are different today, more behaved." I don't respond, I just keep my gaze fixed on his. "I like it." He leans forward and presses his lips softly to mine. He forces them to part with his tongue, and I allow it.

I glance nervously behind him; Laris has turned and thankfully Davel is gone. Tobias pushes me onto my back, and I fight the wince as my unhealed wounds stretch. I open for him, knowing that if I allow him access without hesitation, there would be no need to punish me.

One of his hands reaches up to cradle my head while the other settles in between my legs. I can feel my dress being pulled up and hear the rustle of his pants they are pulled down. I don't move. His hand finds my bare waist, ripping through the lacy undergarments. I don't have a second to prepare myself before he thrusts into me with one push of his hips. I clench my eyes shut, trying to force myself to enjoy the feeling. He's quick, panting in my ear and pressing kisses down the side of my throat. His teeth graze my neck before he bites down, and I gasp. My body jerks and he groans at the movement.

"I want you to come for me, my love." I fake a moan and wrap my arms around his neck as he brings his mouth back to mine. I lift my hips in tune to his, begging for any form of pleasure, but it doesn't come. Not even a little bit. He shudders above me and I feign a release at the same time as him. He's breathing heavy, his body pressed up against mine. *"My Ela."* He whispers as his nose nuzzles into my neck. I force my eyes open, a single tear finding a way to escape my iron resolve.

I don't cry. I don't beg. I let it happen. I let every moment happen without any emotions attached. That's the way it has to be. He pulls out of me with another moan and sits back, pulling my dress back down.

"Laris, you are free to leave." His eyes are sharp, narrowed, as he meets my gaze. *No.* My eyes widen, and I sit up. I didn't do anything wrong. He can't punish me. My pulse skips and my breathing grows ragged as the shadows seem to pull from the walls and surround us.

I didn't do anything wrong.

"Tobias?" I squeak, my voice strained.

"Yes, Your Grace." The door softly shuts behind him and Tobias rises with a sigh.

"Do you think I am stupid?" I shake my head, my mouth opening and closing in confusion.

"I don't understand." I whisper.

"Get up." I rise, shakily and his hand whips out, slapping me. He grabs my shoulders before I can fall over, keeping me upright. "I am not an idiot. I know what it sounds like when you come, Ela." My hand flies to my cheek as I shake my head.

"Tobias–" He slides his hands down to my arms before dragging me to the bed.

"Shut up!" He throws me onto the mattress, and I quickly stand back up. His hand whips out again and I taste the blood in my mouth this time. I fall onto my stomach, my heart pounding. My breath is nothing more than short rasps. I hear my corset rip and then the feel of the icy spring air on my bare back. I bite my lip as he drags me back to the edge of the bed, my legs hanging off.

His stomach presses into my back, his mouth next to my ear.

"I want to *hear* you, Elaenor. I want to feel you. I *know* you love me. I know you love when I touch you." His hand slides down my back before settling in between my thighs. His pointer finger gently brushes my clit and my tortuous body jerks. I bury my face in the bed, willing my body to not respond. To not enjoy his touch. He presses down harder, and a small whimper escapes my lips. I bite my lower lip, fighting against the growing heat pooling low in my core.

"That's it, Ela." He whispers, his lips pressing into my shoulder blade. His finger slides down before slowly entering me. He pulls back out and adds a second finger, causing my body to shake with anticipation. I know he can feel it, the gathering heat, the wetness. He pumps inside of me and my back arches against him.

Tears spring from my eyes and I fist the bedsheets. I hate this. I hate him. I hate myself. I hate that I find even an ounce of pleasure in his touch, in this. My legs are shaking, my core pulsing with each thrust of his fingers. Delicious heat curls low in my abdomen and I shudder again.

"Gods." My moan is muffled as I press my face harder into the bed. Tobias sits up, his fingers slipping out of me before his cock replaces them. His hand snakes around, torturously pushing on my clit as his hips slam into my backside.

I cry out at the feeling, at the pressure brewing deep inside me. His hand finds my back, his fingers splayed out as he fucks me. As I let him.

As I *like* it.

I don't fake it this time. My toes curl and I start to shake before a loud cry escapes my lips and I erupt around him. He comes right after me, his shout echoing throughout the room. Our matched breathing is ragged, gasping as we come down. He doesn't slide out as he lays down on top of me.

"That's what I wanted, my love. Was that so hard?" I shake my head, the bed soaking up the tears I shed before he can see them. He pulls out of me, and I sit up, my legs unsteady. My ripped dress falls down around me, leaving me bare. I can feel a combination of my arousal, and his seed dripping down my thighs. I step out of the heels I was still wearing and walk towards the dressing room.

I keep my bottom lip firmly planted in between my teeth as I clean myself up and dress in leggings and a tunic.

If you don't let yourself feel, if you don't let yourself care, none of this will matter. You will survive. A voice, one that seems so similar to a person I know I'll never see again, echoes through my head. I almost want to agree, say that I understand. But I don't.

I don't know if I want to survive.

When I exit the dressing room, Tobias is lounging on the bed, his ankles crossed and a lazy smile on his face.

"Come here." He holds his arm out for me, and I hesitantly join him, nestling into the crook of his arm. I inhale the scent of cedar and smoke, a scent I will never forget. A scent I hate and crave at the same time. A scent that terrifies and calms me simultaneously. His arm tightens around me and I blink back the tears in my eyes.

I hate what happened. I was scared he was going to hurt me. I thought that was why he sent Laris away, but he didn't. He wanted me to find release. He slapped me. He was rough, but he was doing it for *me*. At least I think he was.

What is wrong with me?

Why am I searching for any ounce of redemption? I sniff once, cursing the snot gathering in my sinuses.

"One day, things will be different. Things can be how they used to be. Back when we were happy. That's what I want." I don't say anything for a moment. I know it's what he wants, but I don't think we could ever go back to that. Not unless he drugs me to forget, and I am so close to asking for it. Asking for the numbing haze that makes being alive a little more bearable.

"I don't know if that is possible, Tobias." I whisper. He cups my cheek, tilting my head up so that I'm looking at up him.

"I love you, Elaenor Rosenthal. With every fiber of my being, I am yours." He leans down, pressing a sweet and soft kiss to my lips. I don't know what to think, what to feel.

What I feel in this moment is broken, confused. Could things actually be different? Could he truly love me, and I him? Could we make this marriage work?

No.

He killed Theo. He killed Rhea and Donovan. He massacred an entire country. There isn't a single part of him that is good. But there doesn't need to be. He just has to believe that what I feel is happiness—peace. Because if he saw the storm brewing inside me, he would kill me before I had the chance to erupt.

"Can I ask you something?" I say when his lips leave mine. He nods, his hand still cupping my face. "One night. Can I have one night without the chains?" I soften my eyes and stare into his icy blues. He smiles softly and brushes his thumb across my bottom lip.

"Yes." Tension releases from my body and I almost cry in relief. One night. I get *one* night without the shackles tying me to the bed. He kisses my forehead and I lay back against his chest.

The steady beat of his pulse thrums in my ears and I fall asleep in his arms for the first time in months.

He stirs before I do, waking me up. Night has fallen, casting darkness around the room. I sit up and look around. Laris never returned, leaving us without a guard for once. I can't remember the last time I slept without an audience. My hair falls over my shoulder, messy and tangled. Warm lips press to my arm, and I glance over at Tobias.

"It seems we slept the day away, my queen." He murmurs before sliding off the bed. I cross my legs under me, unsure of what to do. He goes to the bar cart, pouring himself a glass of whiskey, as a knock sounds on the door. "Enter." Tobias calls out as he comes back to the bed. His fingers gently brush a lock of hair away from my face, tucking it behind my ear, and I find myself giving him a genuine smile. His eyes lighten in surprise and my smile drops.

You don't feel this way, Elaenor. This is for his benefit, so he can drop his guard.

Don't make this *real*.

"Your Grace." Davel is the one who speaks as he walks over to the bed. "Reports have returned that Tano has been captured, as suspected."

"And?" Tobias asks without looking away from me. His soft fingers running along my jaw, sending a shiver down my spine.

"It was successful. Minimal damage to the palace. Very few guards exited the premises, and instead, the prince along with three other companions, were the ones who apprehended him." Tobias tears his eyes away from mine and looks over his shoulder briefly.

"Good. That is all." He says, dismissing the guard. Davel bows and winks at me before leaving. I fight the urge to scowl, knowing Tobias would question it. Davel convinced me Tobias wouldn't believe me if I told him the things he does to me. He didn't believe me about Jeremiah. He wouldn't believe me if I told him one of his most trusted guards touches his possession. And if by some miracle he did, he would punish *me* for it.

"What was that about?" I ask, hoping he'll share some part of his plan with me.

"Reassurance that there is nothing for us to fear from Labisa. Their war efforts are being run by children." I nod as he leans down and kisses my forehead, my eyes focusing on the sky outside the balcony. The deep purple and blacks, the sprinkle of stars.

Some part of me feels something.

An inkling that something is to come.

Something neither of us are prepared for and I have no desire to warn him.

Chapter Nine

The entire palace shakes, dust falling in clouds from the ceiling. I stumble down from the balcony, catching myself on the settee before I fall to the ground. I hold on to the cushion, waiting for the shaking to stop. My ears are pounding in tandem to my pulse, and I clench my jaw. The shaking stops after a few seconds and I slowly rise from where I was crouched, adrenaline pulsing through my veins. I glance around and see nothing but dust outside the windows.

What the hell?

I run to the door, throwing it open. The hallway is dark, most of the torches were knocked out of their holders. Laenie's door opens, and she steps out with Erik close behind. I don't even comment on the fact that they were together, and instead, I grab her hand and frantically search her for injuries.

"Are you alright?" I ask her, and she nods. Erik places his hand on her lower back protectively, and we look around. "What the hell happened?"

"I don't know." Erik responds, his voice clipped.

"Come on." I spit out, tightening my grip on Laenie's hand as I pull them to the staircase. We hit a crowd of people as we make it to the bottom floor, all trying to get to the bunkers. I steer us past the door that leads us down to the basement and pull us into the throne room.

Davenport is already there, his hands on his hips as he stands in front of one of the thrones. Enzo and Kassius are standing off to the side, looking confused. Mal is standing behind Kassius, holding onto his arm. Her strawberry hair in its usual messy ringlets. Her yellow eyes are wide, terrified, and I feel for her. No ten-year-old should be in the middle of a war.

"Where is my son?" The King of Labisa asks, staring right at me, and I glance around. Why is he looking at me?

"I am not sure, Your Grace." I respond softly.

"He was the one who alerted us of the bombing, but he didn't follow us to the throne room." Kassius interjects.

"It was a bomb?" Laenie speaks up softly, and I turn to look back at her. Erik has his arm wrapped around her, holding her tightly against his chest. My throat constricts at the love in his eyes, the possession he has over her. I want nothing more than for someone to look at me like that.

"*Someone* find my son." He says slowly and sternly, his teeth clenched as he looks around.

"I'll go." Enzo speaks up.

"No, please don't go." Mal whimpers, fisting his tunic. He bends down and wipes her tears before kissing her nose.

"I'll be right back, Malie." He whispers. He's good with her, with his little sister. She idolizes him. I didn't have siblings growing up, just Elaenor, Laenie, and Rhea. But the way he treats her makes me realize I wish my little brother never died. I could have been that for him.

"I'll go with you." I interject. Enzo rolls his eyes in my direction as he stands but doesn't stop me as I follow him out. His hands are shoved in his pockets as he walks through the halls, I can see the tension radiating off of him in waves.

People are still pushing to get to the bunkers, and I almost feel like I should send Laenie with them, but Erik will keep her safe. "Where is Emery?" I ask as he steers me towards the back of the palace.

"Probably wherever Ni is." He mutters and I sigh. I know we aren't the best of friends, but I'll never get over his attitude. Why is it that he insists on treating me like I am less than him? As if I am not worthy of respect?

We step out into the courtyard, debris and crumbled stone scattered about. I cough as I inhale dust and Enzo sends me a scathing look. What is his problem? I look around and see that the back wall to the training room and another storage room is gone, wood and stone rubble in its place.

"What is that?" He asks as he tilts his head to listen. I can't hear anything, but he must have. He quickly unsheathes the dagger on his thigh and takes off. I stumble after him, barely catching myself from falling. I lift the skirts of my gown as I pick up the pace, trying not to lose him. He weaves in and out of the rubble and the people running before he reaches the front gate.

Nithe is there, a sword to someone's throat. Emery has an arrow knocked and aimed at the man's head. He's alone, wearing a dark cloak, his hands held out as a sign he isn't a threat.

"*Why?*" Nithe yells, his sword pressing farther into the man's neck. I can see a small trickle of blood sliding down his throat from where the blade slices into his skin.

"A distraction." The stranger spits, and I instantly know who it is just from those words. I can still hear his voice, see his face, as it was *his* arrow that hit me that day. In all the confusion, all the blood and chaos, he was the one who aimed for Elaenor and hit me instead.

He was the one who almost killed me.

"Tano?" I question, and he whips his head around. It's *him*. "Oh gods." I run at him, screaming, and if it weren't for Enzo's arm snaking around my waist, I would have tackled him. "Where is she? What did you do to her?" I scream, trying to break free from Enzo's clutches. I dig my nails into his arm, trying to get loose, drawing blood.

"Who is he to you, Scar?" Emery asks, her voice loud and commanding. I am seething, wanting nothing more than to rip his eyes out of his skull and shove them down his throat.

"His name is Tano. He's one of Elaenor's guards and the person who shot me. He was aiming for her and hit *me* instead." I spit between ragged inhales as my feet dangle. Enzo is holding me up in the air as if I was nothing more than a bag of flour.

"I *was* one of her guards." Tano retorts with a sneer.

"What has he done to her?" Nithe asks, dragging his attention back to him.

"She is nothing more than a husk at this point. One we have all been eager to play with." Enzo gasps behind me, his grip loosening a fraction as my feet touch the ground. I kick out at his leg, hoping to break free from his grasp, but he moves me at the last second, lifting me back up.

"Let me go!" I yell, squirming in his arms.

"No, you're just going to hurt yourself." He snaps, his arms tightening.

"I'm going to *kill* him." I spit, my eyes glaring holes into Tano's smug face.

"Scarlett, please." Enzo whispers. I can feel his forehead press into the back of my neck and only then do I realize he's shaking. He's *actually* shaking. I stop fighting and listen to his slow deep breaths as they fan across my bare skin.

"Guards!" Nithe yells, and men file out of the dust clouds. "Take him to the dungeons and make sure he doesn't escape." He drops his sword at the same time Enzo releases me, but he keeps his hand loosely on my arm. Tano is pulled to his feet and dragged back towards the palace. I watch as he disappears into the half-crumbled walls of the courtyard.

"What did he mean by a distraction?" Emery's arms fall as she drops the bow, sticking the arrow back into the sheath on her thigh.

"He had to know he wasn't going to get out of here alive." She replies as she looks over at me. I watch her eyes quickly scan my body, searching for injuries. I can see the brief look of relief cross her face before she looks away. My pulse skips in surprise. Surprise that she cares enough to look at me like that.

"But what was he trying to distract us from?" I reply. He was here for more than just causing minor damage to the palace. He was looking for something. "Tobias wouldn't send one of his favorite guards to die unless it was for a purpose."

"Do you think there could be others?" Enzo asks, tearing his eyes away from the area Tano disappeared in and looking at Nithe.

"The guards are searching every inch of the palace. If there are, they'll be found." He replies, disinterested. His focus is elsewhere. His hands clench into fists as he stares off in the distance.

"Your father is asking for you, Nithe." I say, remembering the reason we came out here in the first place. He rolls his eyes in my direction and pushes past me. I stumble to the side before whipping around to smack him. Enzo's warm fingers slip from my arm and grab my wrist before I can make contact. I glare at him while he shakes his head in warning. He doesn't release me as I watch Nithe's back.

"I don't have time to speak to my father, I have someone to deal with."

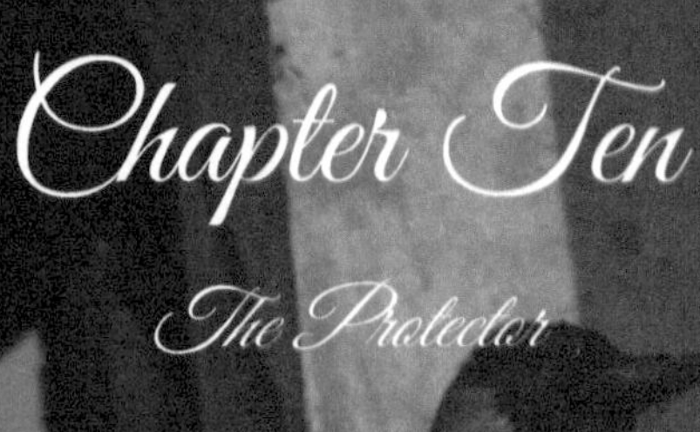

Chapter Ten

The Protector

I follow Ni back into the palace, leaving Scarlett and Emery to head back to the throne room. They don't need to witness this. Although I am half convinced Scar would want to contribute to his torturing in some way. He almost killed her, and he almost killed Elaenor. He deserves what's coming to him.

Nithe leads me straight down to the dungeon, past the bunkers, to where Tano is being shackled to the wall. His hood has fallen back, his entire face exposed, but all I see is weakness. This man—this *fragment* of a protector—was supposed to be Elaenor's guard. He was supposed to protect her, but he didn't. And now he's here, causing damage to our home.

Nithe and I are both silent as we wait for the guards to finish with the tethers. When they do, they hastily bow to the prince before exiting, leaving us alone.

"Tano, is it?" Nithe asks, crouching down in front of the guard.

"And who are you?" He sneers, sweat beading along his brow.

"I'm the last person you are going to see for a while." Nithe's hand snakes into his boot, pulling out a short dagger. He slices it through the air, splitting Tano's cheek open in a millisecond.

"*Ni*," I warn, stepping forward. Usually his father, the king, is the one who tortures people. This isn't like him. Nithe has always been against torture, against hurting without reason, but right now, right now Nithe isn't himself and I have a sneaking suspicion it has something to do with Elaenor, and that thought causes confusing emotions to flick through my mind.

"Here is what's going to happen, Tano. I am going to ask you questions and you are going to answer them. Every time you don't, I cut something off. I'll be generous and start with your fingers and not something you'll really miss." He lifts his hand and presses the blade against Tano's thumb, where it is hanging from the wall behind him. He tries to wrench his hand away, but the tight shackles don't allow it.

"*Fuck you.*" My heart skips a beat and I take a step closer to them, my hands clenching together.

"While I appreciate the offer, Tano, no thank you." Nithe clears his throat. "Where is Elaenor?"

"At the palace." He spits, his eyes narrowed.

"Good job. You *do* listen!" He moves the dagger to Tano's pointer finger. "Is she alive?"

"Yes. For now." His voice shakes as he looks down at the blade pressed to his knuckle.

"Where is she being held?" It's there, and I almost miss it, but the edges of Tano's lips twitch as if he is trying to hold back a smile.

"In the royal chambers where she is shackled and naked, ready for any and all to—" Nithe barely flinches, and the pointer finger is gone. Tano's screams echo off the stone walls, and I step back, watching the blood steadily drip down his arm. Bile fills my mouth and I swallow it down. *Gods.*

"That was for being disgusting." He mutters.

"Why do you want the queen so badly? What is she to you?" Tano asks, *begs.*

"She is our *salvation.*" Nithe whispers and my eyes widen. That was the first time he has ever acknowledged Elaenor for what she is. What she could mean. This *is* about Elaenor. This whole side of him, his change in demeanor. What did I miss? Why *now*? "Why are you here Tano?"

"A distraction." He spits again.

"I got that the first time. *What* are you distracting us from?" He keeps his mouth shut, and another finger is cleaved off. I flinch as it falls to the floor with a fleshy smack. Tano yells out, his face going red from the pain. I can see sweat beading along his hairline, dropping past his temple. He's a weak excuse of a man. I can almost guarantee that Elaenor takes the pain and the torture better than this. "Answer me!"

"He wanted to see how many you had at the palace."

"Who?"

"The king." Tano spits out.

"Why?"

"He was trying to find a weakness." Nithe leans back, the dagger spinning in his fingers.

"Did he find it?" I'm the one who speaks this time. I step closer to Tano, blood steadily dripping off his hand. "Was there another with you?" He hesitantly nods. "What is he going to tell Tobias?" Nithe glances back at me before leaning forward and pressing the blade to another finger.

"Answer him."

"He's going to tell him that the palace is weak, unguarded, and that the only ones who even made a move to protect the palace were the prince and princess.”

“Is he going to cross the border?” Nithe presses. Tano doesn’t answer and another finger is gone. “Is he going to cross into Rakushia?” He asks again. Tano nods, and another finger is gone. I flinch as the guard screams, the shrill sound bouncing off the walls. His hand is left fingerless and pouring blood.

“Just kill me.” He whimpers and Nithe smiles, his amethyst eyes sparkling in the dim light.

“I can’t do that. I have too many questions left to ask you.” Tano’s eyes widen as Nithe’s turn black. A small puff of smoke escapes his nose as he exhales, and I don’t have to look down to know that Tano’s trousers are no longer dry.

“This isn’t you, man.” I shake my head as I take in the blood splattered over every inch of his body.

“Someone has to be in control. Someone has to figure this shit out, and it sure as hell isn’t going to be our fathers.” He pushes past me, and I grab his arm, cringing at the wetness I feel. At the blood soaked into his clothes.

“Do not turn into your father, Nithe. You just murdered a man. Murdered him as if he was nothing.”

“He *was* nothing!” He growls, leaning in so close I can smell the smoke on his breath.

“No, he was a chance to get into the palace. A chance to learn more, and you took that away from us.”

“Away from you, you mean. Away from *you*. You don’t actually care who Elaenor is, all you want her for is to be your mate. You are the one who isn’t thinking of the bigger picture. She is more than just a body to potentially warm your bed—”

“Fuck you, Nithe. That is not why I want her safe, and you know it!” He pushes past me, shaking off my grip, and I spin around. "Where are you going?"

"I have to inform the king of what *I* learned from our prisoner."

"What you *tortured* out of him, Nithe. Tortured. Do not go down this path of darkness. Don't. Because if you become anything like your father, I will make sure Elaenor never even gets close to you." I threaten. He spins around to face me again.

"I don't want to marry her! Don't you get it? She will be tethered to me, forever. She doesn't deserve that. She doesn't deserve someone like me." His voice cracks, the edges of his pupils darkening from the emotion, from the lack of control.

"Do you think Tobias is any better?"

"No! Gods, no. I don't think she should be married at *all*. She's a child. She deserves to be free." He sputters, his hands coming up to run through his shaggy hair.

"She is the same age as us, Nithe." I retort.

"That isn't the point. The point is that I don't deserve her. She doesn't deserve me. She should just be left alone."

"Because you believe that, is *why* you do deserve her. You care whether or not you want to admit it. You have come to care for her and that terrifies you."

"It should have always been you who marries her, Enzo. Not me." He shakes his head, stepping back.

"It was never going to be me. I'm not a royal, I'm nobody." I snap, my voice growing louder. I don't even hide the anger and jealousy coating my voice. It was never me and it never will be. She doesn't belong to me and that is the hardest truth I'll ever have to swallow.

"Enzo. I can't do what they are asking of me. I will ruin her. I will be a weakness that she cannot afford." His eyes grow frantic, searching mine. He's scared. I have never seen him this way.

"You think she'll fall for you. That's what scares you. You're scared that she will fall in love with you, and you will have to care for someone other than yourself—"

"No!" He takes a slow, deep breath before meeting my gaze. "What scares me is that she *won't*."

Chapter Eleven

The Caged

I awake in the morning, unshackled. My arms feel better than they have in weeks. The welts less red and my muscles finally loose. I stretch out, sighing as I take in the massive bed. I curl back up in a ball, pulling the blankets up around me, relishing in the warmth.

Tobias was soft last night, caring even. We ate together, talking about nothing in particular, and then he held me again as we fell asleep. He was gentle and reminded me so much of the man he once was. I frown slightly thinking of the old Tobias. He was kind, but he was also doing the same things to me at night when I wouldn't remember. He's always been this way; I just didn't know. But I know now.

Could things actually be different? Can I pretend to love him in a way that doesn't end up with me actually feeling that way?

The blankets are ripped off of me and I gasp. Davel is standing next to the bed, a smile plastered to his pockmarked face. His crooked teeth are biting into his lower lip, and I want to gag.

"What do you want?" I snap, sitting up.

"Do you know where your husband is?" I look around the room, seeing that it's empty. I shake my head. "He left to visit Tellavid. Meaning he will not be back until this evening." I almost say something sarcastic, but the look in his eyes tells me that I am not about to like what he has to say.

"If you touch me again, I will tell him." I warn, a lump already forming in my throat. He chuckles loudly, and I flinch.

"Do you think he'd believe you, *whore*? Who hasn't been in between your legs?" He reaches forward, snatching my ankle. I kick out, but he grabs my other foot with his free hand. I kick as much as I can, but his grip is strong. He yanks me down, settling me against the edge of the bed.

"Get off of me!" I scream. I reach around, clawing his face. I leave deep gouges along his cheek, narrowly missing his eye. Blood pools in the wounds instantly and his eyes widen.

"You bitch!" His fist flies out, hitting my temple. My neck makes a weird cracking sound and I cry out as pain radiates down my spine. I can hear his pants dropping and I shake my head to clear the fogginess. He has my legs trapped in between his thighs and I kick out. I get a leg free and plant my foot against his hip, shoving him back. Panic barrels through me as I try and get free.

He trips on his pants and falls off the raised platform, landing on his backside. He shoots back up, righting his pants, as I scramble across the bed. My heart is in my throat as I throw myself over the other side of the mattress, landing hard on the marble floor. I get back to my feet, ignoring the pain snaking down my back and the bruises no doubt forming on my knees.

He jumps over the bed, reaching for me, but I dart out of the way at the right time, sending him sprawling across the ground. I run as fast as I can, and get to the door. His hand tangles in my hair, yanking me back against him. I feel strands rip from my scalp, and I scream before sending an elbow back, hitting his nose. He falls back to the floor, taking me down with him. His arm around me loosens just enough, and I slide out of his grasp. I get the door open and fall face first into the hallway.

I scramble to my feet and run as fast as I possibly can. I don't pass a single guard, a single servant in the hallway. I reach the stairs and fly down them, my bare feet sliding on the slippery floor. My nightgown is short, and I know I am probably going to give anyone I pass an eyeful of my body, but I don't stop.

I can hear him running after me, and I fully let the tears fall as he gains ground. Where the hell is everyone? I cross through the side exit and see the stables. Not only do I see the stables, but I see Tobias is still sitting on Wyclif talking to a man in a red cloak.

His head shoots up in my direction and he quickly dismounts, fury pooling in his eyes. He meets me halfway and I throw my arms around him.

"He–he tried to rape me." I spit out, breathlessly. He holds me close to him and I can feel as his head snaps up. His hand holds my head against his chest, his arm wrapping around my back.

"She's lying." Davel retorts, just as breathless. "She tried to run."

"I didn't, Tobias. Please believe me. He said you were gone, headed to Tellavid and that you wouldn't believe me." The words tumble out of me in a single breath along with a steady stream of tears.

"That's not true!" I lean back and grasp the sides of Tobias's face, begging for him to believe me.

"If you love me at all, look at me. Look at what he did." I can feel the blood dripping from my hairline, feel the muscles in my neck spasming from whatever he did to it. His eyes search my face, taking in every scrape and bruise.

"Put him in the dungeon." I nearly melt into him as a sob escapes my throat. He bends slightly and I wrap my legs around his waist as he lifts me. He's walking, and I think he's going to take me to the palace, but we step into the stables. Silence blankets us and it almost feels as if the shadows are pushing in around us, giving us privacy. He sets me down on a workbench and pulls back. He brushes hair away from my face and I wince when he touches my temple.

"What happened?" He asks as he searches my skin for every wound.

"Tobias, he said that he wasn't the only one who's touched me." I whimper and his eyes snap back to mine.

"What?"

"He said that he wouldn't be the first." My voice cracks and I suck in a shaky breath. I'm not pretending this time. The pain and desperation I feel is real. And I hate to admit that the comfort of being here with him is real too.

"Are you saying that others have touched you?" His voice is deep, edged in anger.

"Not to my knowledge, but have you ever left me *alone* when I am too drugged to remember? Have you left me alone during any time I could be vulnerable?" He ponders this for a moment and then his face hardens before shock settles into his features.

"Gods, Ela, I'm sorry." He pulls me to his chest, and I relax into it, into him. Cedar and smoke wafting around us, mixing with the scent of hay and horse, and for once I feel safe in his arms. *Elaenor, what are you doing?*

He carries me back to our room after that, watching as Apollo checks my neck and my head. I pulled a muscle in my neck, but thankfully it's nothing serious. I change with the help of Lydia, and when I exit the dressing room, Tobias is still there.

"Are you still going to Tellavid?" He nods and tucks a stray curl that escaped my braid behind my ear.

"Yes, but Laris will be with you. Just him." I nod and he kisses my forehead. "Are you still up to having lunch with Thelonious?" I nod again and he rests his forehead against mine. "If things stay like this, my Ela, how they are right now, I think we'll be okay." I close my eyes and keep them closed until I hear the door softly close. I'm not going to be okay.

Thel is already in the banquet room when I leave my chambers to join him for lunch, the guards keeping a careful eye on him. I had thought we'd be having lunch in my room, but it seems I am trusted enough to be in public without Tobias keeping an eye on me.

Laris escorts me to his table, and I take a seat. Thel's eyes widen as he looks at me, seeing the new bruise on my face. One of the servants comes by, setting a plate in front of me. The smell of potatoes and roasted chicken hits my nose and my stomach growls. I never ate breakfast as I opted to stay in my room and away from people.

"My Gods, what happened?" He whispers.

"One of the guards." I respond, looking down.

"They hurt you. Does the king know?" I nod and take a sip of the water in front of me. He glances around, seeing that the guards have given us room to talk. "I want the truth, how are you?" I roll my lips, contemplating how much to share.

"I am alright." I say slowly.

"Elaenor, I know that is a lie. Look at you."

"I will be okay, uncle." He leans forward.

"They will come for you." He whispers and I nervously glance around.

"What?" I whisper back.

"They will come for you, just hold on." His hand reaches out and takes mine, squeezing it. I search his eyes, my chest fluttering.

"Who?" I say softly.

"Who do you think?" He questions, tilting his head. A quiet gasp leaves my lips. He can't mean...

"Enzo?" He nods and my mouth falls open.

"How? I don't understand. What really happened in Rakushia?" He shakes his head and leans back, taking a bite of roasted potatoes.

"I can't tell you everything right now, but I am here to ensure you are okay. They will get you out, you just have to wait."

"I can't really do much but wait, uncle." I reply and take a small bite of chicken.

"What has been happening?" I chew slowly and glance around.

"I don't remember much. He uses drugs to keep me compliant. Some moments are fine, but then other moments I think he's gone mad." He tilts his head softly. "I think maybe I've gone–" I feel the brush of air as someone steps up behind me.

"Your Grace, I am to escort you back to your room."

"I haven't finished my meal, Laris. I *just* got here." I reply, taking another small bite.

"It is the king's orders."

"It was the king's orders for me to have lunch with my uncle, was it not? The king isn't even here." I snap back.

"The king has already returned." I whip my head around.

"He left just a few hours ago, Laris." He grips my arm and yanks me out of the chair.

"Ser, that is the queen you are manhandling!" Thel rises from his chair, his hand reaching out to grab Laris.

"It's fine, uncle. I will see you later." I say quickly. The last thing I need is him ending up in the dungeons. I shake Laris's grip off and follow him out of the room. "I was in there for five minutes, I don't understand–" A hand snakes through my hair, yanking me back.

"You forgot something." A deep voice growls in my ear and I freeze.

"What are you talking about?" I stammer as I feel Tobias's hot breath on my neck.

"You forgot your crown." My mouth opens in disbelief and then I am being pushed forward.

"Tobias, this is ridiculous." His hand tightens against my scalp as he drags me up the stairs. Servants hurriedly pass us, refusing to look. *"Tobias."*

When we get to the room, he throws me against the couch.

"Why did you take it off?" He yells, slamming my crown on the table. I push myself up into a sitting position and look at him.

"I forgot it, I'm sorry." I reply. He snatches the crown from the table and slams it down onto my head, the teeth digging into my scalp. I flinch, but don't let the pain show.

"Never take this off! Do you understand me? You are my *queen*." I nod, tears pooling in my eyes.

"I'm sorry." I whimper. His fingers squeeze my cheeks, his eyes filled with rage.

"Laris!" He snaps.

"Yes, Your Grace?"

"Apollo, needle, thread. *Now*." He demands, and the door closes quickly after him.

"Tobias?" My eyes widen and I can feel the shaking coming on. The fear as adrenaline pumps throughout my body.

"You don't fucking take it off. Ever. You are a goddamn queen not some whore. You don't *ever* take it off!" He yells, his face inches from mine. His eyes are red, frantic.

"I said I wouldn't." I stutter as he rips me off the couch. He drags me over to the chair by the vanity, tossing me into it. It nearly topples over, but he catches it just in time. He grabs two of the cuffs he uses to attach me to the bed and straps them around my wrists. "Tobias." He connects the other end to the arms of the chair, holding me down. "Tobias, what is happening?" My heart is pounding in my ears, my breath forced as I try to swallow the lump in my throat.

The door opens and Master Pakin enters with a small basket.

"Your Grace?" He asks as he makes his way over to us.

"Make sure she can never take her crown off again." He snaps. My eyes widen in panic as I look at my husband. My king. My torturer.

"Tobias, please!" I cry out, pulling at the shackles holding me down.

Laris joins Tobias as he orders him to help hold me down. Master Pakin doesn't say anything as he comes around behind me. I can hear him rustling around in the basket before his fingers are in my hair.

"No, no. Please." The tears are flowing freely as I stare up at Tobias. The first poke of the needle elicits a scream from my throat. I can feel the thread pulling through the skin and then another poke. I'm squirming as much as I can, but Laris and Tobias are too strong.

No, no, no, no. It's been weeks.

Weeks since he tortured me beyond shallow wounds.

Weeks since he has kept me in the dungeon, bloody and destroyed.

Again and again the needle goes in and out of my scalp. I can feel the blood dripping down my neck and tickling my forehead.

In and out.

In and out.

The needle and thread weave through my skin.

The pain is indescribable. It feels as if he's ripping my scalp off of my head, peeling it away one layer of skin at a time.

I'm screaming, my throat going raw as I cry out. I shut my eyes, squeezing them as tight as I can. Willing for anything to make the pain go away. Begging for some sort of reprieve.

A room flashes behind my eyes as electricity shoots through my veins like lightning. Yellow banners, a man with black hair and amethyst eyes staring at me, as if he's worried I'm going to snap. As if he's concerned for my safety.

Who are you?

My eyes open again and I'm back in my room, Tobias's face close to mine. He's straining as I struggle against him. As I try to get away from Apollo and his needle. His face is red, sweat beading on his forehead, his icy blues almost black.

I squeeze my eyes shut again and I can see the room. An older man with white hair is sitting in a large chair, a glass of whiskey in his hands. My eyes glance down, and I can see a set of olive tinted hands gripping the back of the chair, veins pulsing under the skin.

I open my mouth and scream.

The purple eyes flinch, his mouth opening in shock revealing perfectly straight teeth and pointed canines, before everything goes dark.

Chapter Twelve

The Bound

"I don't think I have ever said this before, but I am proud of you son." Enzo scoffs next to me, his hands loosely holding the back of the chair.

"I did what I had to, and now we know what he's planning." I respond, tearing my eyes away from Enzo's irritated face. He'll get over it. I never thought of Enzo as weak, but I don't think he has the stomach to do what needs to be done. What *had* to be done.

"I just wish I had the chance to interrogate him myself." My father says with a sigh, and I know a lecture is coming.

"What other questions would you have asked, Father? I found out as much as I could. I found out where she is. I found out how many men are stationed at the border. I found out what the purpose of the bomb was and what truly happened to Chatis. What else would you have asked?" I fail at hiding the frustration in my voice. I clench my hands into fists under the table.

"For starters, we could have asked *exactly* where the princess is so we wouldn't have to guess which room is the royal chambers."

"*Queen*. And it doesn't matter anymore." I correct him and run my hands through my hair. "Tano is dead. I promise to leave the next prisoner for you."

"Yes, because *that* is all that truly matters. That I have a prisoner to torture." He snorts and collects the papers in front of him into a neat pile. "Nithe, there is more to being a king than torturing prisoners and gathering information. You need to learn when to be ruthless and when to think of the bigger picture."

"Father, I do not *wish* to be king. I have no desire to rule a country, or an entire continent." His eyes widen and he slams his hands on the table, his fury unrestrained.

"Do you think you have a choice? That I care whether or not you want the position? This is your birthright. This is your duty, and as my son you will become the king and you will do the role justice. You don't get wants and desires. You don't get happy endings and dreams. You get a wife, you get a crown, and you make heirs. Do I care if you love her? No, of course not. Find yourself a whore or a mistress and stick your cock in them if your wife is unwilling. But *after* you make heirs. *After* you force her into a coronation and take the power from her."

"Father—"

"I swear to the Gods, Nithe. I will not allow you to ruin this. Your recklessness, your *selfishness*, will not cost me the continent. It will not cost me Viridiana. If it does, if you do anything to sway that girl to abdication, I will end you. I will kill you in your sleep before you have the chance to fight back. I will marry that girl myself and make sure she never breathes another free breath. You think her life is hard now? I will make her wish Tobias was still her husband." His eyes are narrowed, his hands clenched in fists as he leans on the table, getting as close to me as possible. I can feel the adrenaline, the disgust, coursing through my veins.

My father has always been a monster. He has always valued power more than love and family. It was something I was quick to realize and quick to get over as a child, but now I don't know if I can. He is cursing Elaenor, cursing me, to a horrible life. A life where neither of us can even breathe without his approval. That isn't a life she should be forced into. That isn't a life at all.

But what am I to do? Fight him? Argue? None of that would come out in favor of me and my wishes. He would win. He always does.

There is only one option. I have to—

Enzo gasps and I whip my head around to face him. His eyes go bloodshot, and his hands grip his scalp as he drops to his knees.

"Enzo!" I yell as I scramble to the ground next to him. His eyes are squeezed shut; his mouth open as he screams as loud as he possibly can. He's scratching at his hair, pulling strands out. I grip his wrists, forcing him to stop. "Enzo!" I yell again, restraining him as best as I can.

As fast as it comes on, it fades and he drops to the floor, his body relaxing.

"No." He whispers. I slowly release my hold on him, my eyes catching on his hair as I watch it darken from root to tip, fully saturating the once white strands.

"Enzo?" I whisper.

"I could feel her. She was in my head. She was seeing through my eyes. I could feel it." Tears line his emerald eyes, panic filling every crevice, every feature of his face as he holds my stare.

"What are you saying?" My voice is little more than a whisper.

"She was connected to me. And then all I felt was pain, as if someone was sewing something into my scalp. She was screaming. She was screaming so loud, and I couldn't help her." He raises his head, tears freely pouring down his cheeks. "Please, we have to go." He grips my arms, shaking me. Pleading for me to understand.

"Father. She's in danger." I angle my body to face my father, where he is pouring over the map as if he didn't just threaten me. As if Enzo screaming was just as consequential as a fly buzzing in his ear.

"She's been in danger this entire time." He mutters, uninterested. Enzo's skin is rippling, black feathers sprouting when I turn back to him. He hasn't gotten a hang of his shifting yet, and it can still come on under extreme emotional changes. And right now, right now is extreme enough to force the change.

"Breathe, Enzo." I remind him. His eyes hold mine, and I can see it. I can see the stupidity—the recklessness—pass across his face. "Don't—" Before I can stop him, he pushes my arms away, his fingers turning into talons before a sharp burst of black light replaces his body. When it fades, a single raven is in his place. His bright green eyes look at mine once, before he flaps his wings and barrels into the hallway.

Chapter Thirteen

The Caged

My head is on fire, it's burning and throbbing as if it's been lit alongside firewood. I can taste the blood in my mouth, thick and metallic as it coats my tongue, making it hard to swallow. I try to open my eyes, but they feel swollen and unresponsive. My pulse skips and I fight the panic brewing in my chest. I try to move, begging my limbs to cooperate. I can feel my arm twitch, as if it's waking up, before I feel the prick of something in my leg. I flinch as ice spreads through my veins, and then the darkness comes again.

I can feel something wet on my face, a cloth, as someone wipes at my skin. Soft, and slow humming fills my ears as someone cleans me. I try to force my eyes to part, but they still fail to respond. I can hear rustling as the cloth pulls away. I fight to inhale as water is poured over my head, my scalp stinging in response.

I feel cold. So cold.

"You can't be in here, miss." Someone says. I think it's Lydia, but I can't tell. I hear rustling, heels smacking the marble floors, before a cold hand grabs mine. "Miss—"

"You need to help me, Elaenor. Please." A panicked, lyrical voice flits around me, one that sounds so familiar but so foreign, and then I am gone again.

"Nora," his voice is soft, a whisper. His fingers brush my cheek and I try to pry my eyes open to see him. "Stay strong, Nora." *Theo.* My mind screams as I fight as hard as I can to see him, to keep him here. "I love you."

"I think he's going to kill me. Please, wake up. *Please.*" Someone is shaking me. I feel so warm. I feel as if I am on fire. I groan as I beg my body to cooperate with my pleas to move. My eyes finally part just enough to see fiery red hair and eyes such a deep green that they remind me of home. Her brows are furrowed, there are bruises across her hairline, and I can see just a little spattering of dried blood on the edge of her mouth. My eyes close against my will and she shakes me again. "Elaenor." She whispers, and I can feel her hands trembling as they hold onto mine.

"Nylah?" I whisper, my throat protesting.

"Please, Elaenor. He's going to hurt the baby. He's going to hurt my son." She sounds so sad, so broken and desperate. I want to help her, but I can't. All I can do is sleep.

Croaking. I hear a deep, demonic sounding croak echoing around the room. My eyes open to a marble ceiling and I find I am in my bed. Bright sunlight filters through the windows, reflecting off the shiny walls, illuminating the empty room. A chill runs down my spine, causing an involuntary shiver. I'm freezing and glance down to see I'm naked, not a stitch of clothing on my body, but there's also no chains.

There are fresh bruises and cuts along my stomach and thighs. The *T* brand on my stomach is as bright as ever. Bones poke through my skin, alluding to my obvious malnourishment. I look around the empty room and see that the balcony doors are open. The sky is a bright blue, not a single cloud to be seen, but that's not what pulls my attention. A single raven is sitting on the railing, staring at me. Watching me as if it has more than a bird's intelligence.

I sit up and wince as my unhealed cuts stretch. My head is pounding and heavy, as if it is filled with stones. My hand reaches up and I feel something cold and sharp. Something familiar. My other hand joins as I feel around my head, the pain is almost all-consuming. It feels as if something was sewn to it. I pull at the metal and cry out as my scalp feels like it's ripping.

Because it is.

Oh Gods.

I slide out of the bed, the icy marble nearly causing me to slip as I collapse into the vanity. My crown is sewed to my head, the diamonds stained slightly crimson. My hair is wrapped around the metal of the diadem, frizzy and untamable waves knotted around it.

"No." I whimper, disbelief coating my tongue like ash. I grab the brush off the vanity, trying to smooth out my inky tresses, but all it does is yank on the stitches. Tears form in my eyes, and I throw the brush down, knocking cosmetics onto the floor. "This can't be happening." A broken sob escapes my mouth and I bury my head in my hands.

He is mad. *Insane.*

He *sewed* my crown onto my head because I forgot to wear it. We had a great night, a perfect and normal night. He made me feel safe, and happy. And then in the morning he defended me without hesitation. He ensured my safety and cared for me. He acted as if he truly loved me, but this—this isn't love. This is control, this is power.

This is madness.

The croaking behind me makes me flinch as I remember the strange bird. I hear flapping and whirl around as the raven comes directly towards me, its wings beating furiously. I duck out of the way as it almost hits me, nearly scratching my face. The tiny black bird slams into the vanity mirror and lands in a lump on top of the dark wood. I stare at its lifeless body for a moment before it stirs. The raven pulls itself up and shakes out its wings before it turns and looks at me.

"What do you want, bird?" I cry out. Its intelligent eyes are green, a super bright, almost bioluminescent green that seems familiar. It's staring at me as if it knows me, as if its human. It's eyes drift from my scalp to my stomach before its pupils widen in what could almost be mistaken for shock. I glance down at my naked body, the brand and unhealed wounds on full display, before quickly grabbing the dressing robe on the back of the chair with shaky hands.

It's just a bird, why do I feel so indecent?

Once the robe is fastened, I stare at the raven again. There is a green sheen to its inky feathers, glowing in the sunlight streaming in from the windows. I hesitantly reach out and it stays still as my fingers brush one of its wings. They are soft, silky. It closes its eyes briefly, as if it is enjoying my touch, before reopening them.

"Hello." I say softly. Its wings open and shake, and I jump back before it has the chance to come near my face again. It hops up in the air before landing on my hand. The little beak pecks at my palm, tickling the sensitive skin. "Who are you?" I ask as it jumps off my hand, and back onto the vanity. It uses its beak to pull at the drawers, digging through them and throwing things around.

"What are you doing?" I almost yell out, but my voice comes out as a confusion-soaked rasp. The raven digs through until it finds a pot of lip stain. It yanks it out of the drawer and points at it expectantly with its beak. I raise my eyebrows in confusion, a bewildered giggle building in my throat, before hesitantly bending down and pulling the cork out of the tiny pot. It sticks its beak in the crimson lacquer immediately before hopping back onto my arm. I stand frozen as this tiny bird wipes its beak along my arm. The red paint leaves streaks on my skin and I stare at it in both shock and awe. It jumps off my arm and I glance at the marks left behind.

Four tiny lines across my wrist.

E.

My eyes fly open, as wide as they can go, as I stare at this bird. This tiny black raven sitting before me, whose body could be no larger than the size of my hand.

It can't be.

"Enzo?" I whisper. He nods and I nearly collapse, my free hand shaking as it grips onto the back of the chair. "No. No, that's impossible. How can that be?" His eyes soften and he jumps back on my arm. I watch as he writes out the letters: *W, A, I, T.* "Wait?" I whisper. He nods again and I feel tears pricking behind my eyes. He jumps in the air and flies in a circle around the room before returning to me. His wing lightly brushes my cheek before he soars through the open balcony doors and disappears.

This isn't real. This is a dream. It has to be. My gaze is fixed to the open sky, my heart pounding furiously in my throat. *He's coming. He's going to come for me.* Thel said he would, but this isn't real. He can't be a bird. There is no possible way—the bedroom door opens and Tobias walks in, a wide grin plastered to his face.

"My queen, I am so proud of you." I whirl around to face him, quickly rubbing my arm on the side of my robe, hoping I smudged the lip stain enough to make it illegible, if he even notices in the first place.

"What?" I croak, my palms growing sweaty. He saunters over to me, mischief and excitement clouding his eyes as he clasps my cheeks between his hands.

"He is so beautiful." His eyes flit back and forth between mine as he waits for a response. His hot breath fanning across my face. He looks like he is going to cry.

"What are you talking about?" I whisper.

"Our son, Cynfael." My pulse skips and a soft, terrified voice fills my head. *Help me, Elaenor.*

"I don't understand." I turn towards the door as I see movement, his hands releasing my face so I can look. An older woman walks in with an infant, no more than a couple of months old, a dusting of copper hair along his head. He's wrapped in a deep gray blanket, his eyes wide and curious. "Tobias. Whose child is that?" I ask, afraid that he'll speak what I already know aloud.

"That is our son, Ela." His voice is full of irritation, irritation that I don't recognize this child that *isn't* mine. This child that belongs to another. Tiny blue eyes meet mine. Oh Gods. *Nylah.*

"Tobias, where is Nylah?" I whisper as the baby is pushed into my arms. I take the small bundle, and the tiny child *coos* in response. She asked me for help. It wasn't a dream. She asked me for help, and I could do nothing.

"She's gone." He says matter-of-factly before grabbing the whiskey off the bar cart.

"Tobias, did you kill Nylah?" My voice cracks and I look up at him. He pours himself some of the amber liquid and downs it before answering me.

"She was trying to take our son, it's treasonous. I had to protect our family, Elaenor." He drops the glass back onto the bar cart and I fight the overwhelming urge to scream, to panic.

"This isn't my child!" I snap, a choked sob escaping my throat.

He killed her. He killed Nylah. I can't believe it. I don't believe it. This. Isn't. Real. Cynfael *coos*, and I close my eyes, fighting the tears.

"Tobias, where is she?" I ask, keeping my eyes closed, but he doesn't answer my question.

"Take care of him, my love, that's a future king in your arms." He turns without another word, leaving me with a child that isn't mine, and fear brewing deep in my abdomen.

Chapter Fourteen

"How long are we supposed to wait?" I snap, restlessness pulling at my bones.

"Hmm?" A tired voice pipes up from my right. I glance over at Scarlett who is half asleep on the settee. Her pale blue dress is wrinkled and wrapped around her like a tourniquet. Her chestnut hair is free, spread out along the pillow beside her head. Her skin is deepening, less pale and more golden as she spends less and less time in her room. She looks beautiful, peaceful, as she lays there.

She has been joining us outside the walls lately. She comes when Nithe and I check the lake, ensuring that none of the Noterran forces are laying claim to it. That alone has vastly improved her health, and she is no longer malnourished and weak. She's strong. She's exactly as my father described.

Scarlett and I have grown close these last couple of weeks, despite all odds. Despite our earlier hatred for each other. I don't necessarily believe it was ever hatred, just discomfort. Discomfort that we both were hurting and in pain as we wait for Elaenor, but instead of fighting each other, we realized we worked better together. Not in any official way besides our need for comfort, for release.

She has started to spend some evenings in Emery's room and the days in mine while we wait. While we wait for either progress or news that Elaenor is gone. It's a weird situation, one that mostly benefits Scarlett, but not a single one out of the three of us are complaining, at least not to her.

It's been a month since I saw Elaenor. One month since my hair returned to completely back to black. I was tired of everyone staring at it, so I cut it all off. Scarlett actually helped me, she found me losing my mind and going at it with a blade. I had small cuts all over the top of my head as I kept nicking my skin. She sat me down, told me to relax, and took the blade to my scalp. She was quiet as she worked, but I watched her in the mirror. I watched her eyes glisten with unshed tears. I watched her hands shake and her shoulders pitch inwards as she stared at the black strands. She was hurting, but she helped anyway. My hair has grown a bit since then, but so has our affection towards one another. So has our desire to bring each other comfort.

"How long should we wait until I go back?" I ask, my eyes still searching her soft face for any hint of regret. I keep thinking she'll change her mind and decide it isn't me she wants to spend her time with. I know feelings weren't supposed to get involved, but I find I am calmer in her presence. She brings a feeling of peace I never expected. I look away, forcing myself to take a deep breath. Distance. I need distance.

But I don't want it.

"You aren't going back to Noterra, Enzo. You'll get yourself killed." She murmurs with a sigh. I hear something drop to the floor and I glance back over to see the book she was reading laying haphazardly on the rug.

"We can't just wait around forever, Scar. I need to do something." She sighs and stretches, her feet ending up on my lap. I rest my hand on her ankle, squeezing it slightly.

An unlikely alliance, that's what Nithe called us. I'm not going to pretend I don't get more out of this arrangement than sex. She talks about Elaenor, tells me about her personality and how they grew up. How she was wild and stubborn, but loyal to her friends. How she would sneak away with Scarlett and explore areas where her father couldn't find them. It's almost like having Elaenor here.

Gods, that sounds terrible. Scarlett isn't a replacement for her.

"If you go into the palace without thought, you aren't going to be alive long enough to help anyone. Do you really think this will be easy? If you fly in there as a tiny little raven, how do you expect to leave with a full-grown woman?" She sits up and tries to pull her ankles from my lap, but I don't let her. She scoots closer, her hand coming to cup my face. I look at her, her chestnut eyes ringed in gold. Her thumb slides across my lower lip and I lean forward. Her lips are soft as they press against mine and I sigh. Berries and sugar, that's what she smells like. I inhale as her breath wraps around me.

"Promise me." She whispers before kissing me again. "Promise me you won't just fly in there." She pulls back and I reach forward to brush a loose tendril of hair from her face.

"I promise." She leans forward again to kiss me, and I reach over, gripping her hips and pulling her on top of me. Her thighs settle on either side of mine, my hands sliding up her back. She kisses me back with fervor, her tongue clashing with mine. Her hips grind against me, and I moan into her mouth. "What do you want?" I whisper before pulling her closer, my lips trailing along her jaw and down her neck. She moans as she shifts above me.

"You." She responds, her voice deep and husky. It doesn't take long for my breeches to be undone and her skirt to be pulled up. She slides down slowly, her mouth open and eyes shut. "Gods." She moans as she settles into my lap.

I grab her lip with my teeth, pulling her back to me. I taste the tiniest hint of blood as her tongue finds mine. My fingers squeeze her hips roughly, forcing her to move against me. I relish the feel of her wrapped around me, warm and wet. I groan as she rises up on her knees, almost freeing me completely, before slamming back down. She does it again and I nearly come undone at the feel of it. Her breasts brush against my face as she rises and I yank her corset down, pulling her hardened nipple into my mouth. I bite down gently before sucking on it to ease the sting. She cries out and moves faster, her hands pulling my mouth back to hers.

"Fuck, Scarlett." I moan into her lips before throwing my head back. She presses her lips to my throat as she rides me. Her teeth graze my skin and then she bites down. A yelp escapes my lips, but the sting shoots straight to my cock. I shake under her, and she cries out. I feel her core clench around me as she finds her release. I move her hips back and forth, letting her ride the wave of her orgasm, milking as much of her as I can. She pushes my hands away and greedily moves on her own, slamming into me over and over. I feel her legs beginning to shake again, her second release coming, and I press my thumb down on her clit.

"Enzo." She cries, and I yell out as I come. My body shudders under her and she finds her second release a moment later.

We are left panting and sweaty, but she doesn't move. Her hands are resting on my chest, her forehead pressed to my shoulder. I turn my head slightly, pressing my lips to her cheek. The sun is fading, with the only light coming from the roaring fireplace. It's still cold out, which is strange for early summer, but it's nice for moments like these. My arms wrap around her, holding her against me as she shakes with the aftershock. Her forehead presses against mine and I brush my lips against hers softly.

Scarlett has been on the herb that prevents pregnancy for a few weeks now, ever since that one day that changed our relationship, which I am grateful for. It means we can enjoy moments like this without fear of a child. Although part of me wouldn't be opposed to a child. Just not right now. War isn't an ideal time. She sighs and I tighten my arms around her as she nuzzles into my neck.

"Can I stay here tonight?" She whispers, her breath tickling my throat. My pulse skips and I find myself questioning my reaction, questioning the excitement I feel at her request.

"What about Emery?" I respond, trying to play it off.

"I just want to stay here, like this." She responds softly. I nod and she sighs again.

"Is she going to be mad?" Scarlett groans and I smile. I pull her head back and brush the messy tendrils away from her face. The movement sends a shudder through me again and I can feel her clench in response.

"I don't care." She whispers before her lips find mine again.

Chapter Fifteen

I can hear him slamming things, throwing stuff around as he yells at something. I throw open his door, expecting to see him doing something other than losing his mind. The anger fades from my face as I see the tears streaming down his cheeks. He has a blade to his scalp, shaving his all-black hair. Blood is dripping from his hairline as he nicks his skin.

"Fuck!" He screams and throws the blade. He plants his hands on the vanity and looks down at the wood. His back is shaking from his rapid inhales, his fingers tensing as they dig into the table. "Fuck." He whispers this time. I don't know why I watch him in silence, why I intrude on his tantrum, but I can't look away. He sighs and lifts his head, his eyes meeting mine. We both freeze, our eyes locked onto one another's.

My chest rises in tune with my rapid pulse and my mouth dries. I can still see the tears dripping off his jaw as he stays unmoving. As he watches me watch him. I move first, walking towards him. I don't know why I do it, but I grab the blade from the vanity and gesture for him to sit. His lips part as if he is going to speak before he reluctantly sits down.

I run my hand through his hair, relishing in the silky feel of it. My thumb wipes away a drop of blood heading for his eyebrows before I lift the blade. I hold it up against his scalp, waiting for his approval. I meet his eyes in the mirror, and he nods. It's silent as I take the first swipe of the blade, cutting his inky strands down to the root. I don't know if it's silence he's after, but I have to talk.

I need to talk.

"When I was six, my little brother and I were playing in the trees by the palace." I start speaking, his eyes locked on mine as I work. "I had just finished at the palace, as I wasn't permitted to stay on the grounds during the evening due to my age, and I was in my reckless stage. I liked to cause trouble." I smile, but the knot in my throat cuts it short. I blink back the tears and slide the blade again. Strands of hair fall down his face, piling in his lap. "We were running around, getting lost. He was only four, so he really had no choice but to follow me." I take a deep breath and adjust my hands for a better angle.

"He fell, smacking his head into the trunk of a tree. He didn't cut his head open, thank god, but what he did do is get sap all over his hair." I smile as I remember his chubby cheeks. "My mother was so angry. She tried for hours, long into the night, to get the sap out, but it wouldn't budge. At the end of those few hours, she handed me a blade and told me it was my job to cut his hair since I was the one who ruined it." I meet his eyes in the mirror, those green irises wide and round as he listens.

"She walked me through how to cut his hair properly. In the end, my brother was left with hair cropped close to his head. But instead of being upset like a normal four-year-old, he got excited that he had the same hair as our father. We laughed until the early hours of the morning before we finally fell asleep." A single tear falls down my cheek and I wipe it away with the back of my hand.

"What happened to your brother?" He asks, his voice thick and hoarse.

"A few years later, there was an attack on the city. A group of men who belonged to no crown. They burnt half of the town to the ground. The school was the first to be destroyed. I was safe, in the palace acting as Elaenor's lady, but my brother was in class. Nearly all of the town's children died that day." He doesn't speak, doesn't apologize, which I am grateful for.

It is silent for the next few minutes, tears pooling in my eyes as I cut strand after strand. I bite my bottom lip, willing myself to get through this task. When the last strand is cut, and his hair is gone, I step back. His eyes track me through the mirror. He watches as I set the blade down and turn to go.

His hand snakes out and grabs my wrist, spinning me around.

"I apologize for my part in your parents' death. I didn't know what Tobias was going to do, but we all had our suspicions. We all could have done something." His emerald eyes are swimming in pools of tears as he holds my gaze. I reach out, and he flinches, but I continue. My fingers brush the spattering of short hair along his jaw before my thumb brushes his bottom lip. His hand is still tightly wrapped around my wrist, holding it up in the air.

"Enzo," I whisper. His face, it's so sad. So broken.

"Scarlett." He responds, his voice clipped, strained. I don't know which one of us moves first, but his lips are on mine. They are warm, soft and full as they overtake me. As they worship mine. His tongue clashes with mine and then his arms wrap around me.

His hands are pulling at my corset strings while I pull at his tunic. My corset goes first, before he pulls his tunic over his head. His hands push the waistband of my skirt down and I step out of it while undoing his belt. Our breathing is erratic, labored as we fight to consume as much of each other as possible. He pushes me back and the backs of my knees hit the mattress. He falls with me and refuses to let our lips part as I scoot farther back on the bed.

"Are you taking—" He mumbles against my skin. His lips break from mine before trailing down my jaw and my neck.

"Yes." I moan, knowing that he is asking about the herb. His lips slide between my breasts, and I arch my back. He moves to the right, his tongue flicking out, teasing my nipple. I gasp as he takes it in his mouth, sucking hard. "Enzo." I moan as his hands slide down to my legs. I try to pull his head up to mine but he pulls out of my grasp.

"Let me taste you." He whispers against my flesh. I shudder underneath him as my fingers grip onto his shoulders. His lips move down from my breast, his tongue flicking out as he slides his mouth down my stomach. I shudder again, my legs wrapping around his shoulders. His hand slides up and up until his fingers pinch the nipple he just had in his mouth. I gasp again as I feel the pain head straight to my core, pooling in the growing heat. His fingers brush my thighs before lightly touching me through the thin underwear.

"Please." I moan as his fingers brush me again and he teases my nipple.

"Patience." He whispers as his teeth pull at the thin cotton waistband of my undergarments. His free hand grips the cotton and pulls, tearing it from my body.

I can feel his breath as it brushes against my clit, and my own breath catches. His lips press to my inner thigh, and I groan in frustration. He moves his head over and just when I think he's about to touch me, finally touch me, he kisses my other thigh.

"En—" I start to snap but stop as his lips close around my clit. His teeth graze the sensitive bundle of nerves and I cry out. His tongue dips down in between my slit and then inside of me. I groan as I pull my knees up, pressing them against his head, trapping him there. My hips move of their own accord, riding his face as if I have never been fucked before.

He moans against me, as he sucks on every inch of my skin. The warmth pools in my stomach, spreading down my limbs. My legs shake and I struggle to hold them against his head. He slides his tongue up just as he shoves two fingers inside of me. I yell out, my hands fisting the sheets. He pumps inside of me as his teeth and tongue continue their assault. I can't think. I can't breathe, and just when I think I'm about to come, he pulls back.

I gasp and lift myself up onto my elbows just has his lips slam into mine. Sweet and salty is his tongue as it wraps around mine. I don't have time to think before he shoves himself inside of me with a single thrust of his hips. I fall onto my back, bringing him with me as he grinds his hips against me. His lips leave mine as he presses his forehead to my shoulder. I wrap my arms around his neck, relishing in the feel of him.

"Don't stop." I whisper as my ankles cross behind his back, tightening the hold my thighs have around him.

"Never." He whispers against my skin. I can feel the heat pooling and the orgasm coming to a head. I can't hold it and I don't want to.

"Enzo!" I scream as I come undone around him. He shudders above me before finding his own release and collapsing on top of me.

Chapter Sixteen

The Bound
Present Day

"What's the deal with Enzo and Scar?" I ask from my place on the couch, a thin blanket thrown over me to stave off the nightly chill. Emery groans and sits up in her bed, her golden hair a mass of tangles. I smirk at the glare plastered to her face that she thinks is menacing. She is a formidable opponent in the ring and has knocked me on my ass multiple times, but she will always look like a harmless little kitten. "What?"

"We have an...*arrangement*." She responds, curling a pale lock around her finger as she pouts.

"Okay, and didn't that arrangement require her to spend nights with you?" She looks away from me and drops her hand. Her eyes glass over as she stares out the open windows at the star-filled sky. "Em, talk to me." I press, and she sighs.

"I told her I liked her, alright! I told her I cared for her, and she said she cared for us both." Her lip quivers as she finally looks over at me.

"You wanted her to choose?" I ask, trying to understand. She nods and I offer her a sympathetic smile. "You can't get mad at Scarlett for sticking to an agreement you both decided on. You both agreed that this would just be purely physical. In fact, all three of you agreed to that. Maybe she's not ready to be in a relationship." I offer. Who knows what could be going through Scarlett's head.

"Or just not with me." She mutters.

"You're jealous?" She nods again. "You know she likes men and women, Em. You can't change her."

"I know, but I sometimes feel like she likes him better than me." She whines and I sigh. We both know why Scar is closer to him, what holds them together, but she doesn't want to admit it.

"Don't compare yourself. That'll only cause issues later on. They are hurting, both of them. They have Elaenor in common and it's bringing them comfort. Let them figure out their shit and don't let your heart get involved."

"Well you and her have Elaenor in common, why aren't you out fucking her too?" She snaps and I roll my eyes. She deflects. Whenever there is a tough situation ahead of her, or something she finds uncomfortable, she snaps. She's done it since we were children because she doesn't like to confront her feelings, but she'll have to learn. Especially in this situation.

"Because, unlike Enzo, I am more or less engaged to Elaenor." I answer and she rolls her eyes.

"So? She's probably in her *husband's* bed right now." I glare at her, trying to ignore the anger brewing inside.

"So, I intend to *not* be a shitty person and sleep with her best friend."

"Fine, sleep with me." She quips.

"No."

"Why?"

"I'm not going to be a pity fuck, Emery." I snap. She groans and collapses back on her bed. I get off the couch and walk over to her, reaching for the hand she has laying across her eyes. I pull her arm up forcing her to look at me. "Give her time. Once Elaenor is here and everyone is fine, she'll come back to you." I squeeze her fingers and drop her hand before exiting her room, shutting the door behind me.

I take a few steps down the hall before throwing Enzo's door open, without knocking. Scarlett is in his lap, her head thrown back, and her eyes closed.

"Gods, you two!" I yell and she jumps. Enzo snaps his head in my direction.

"What the fuck, man!" He snaps and glares at me. I close the door and laugh as I make my way back to my room, dreaming of the hot water I was about to climb into. But I don't make it to my room. I stop as I pass a closed door, one that could someday be mine. I look around the hallway before pushing it open and slipping inside.

The room is large, bigger than even Emery's. A large balcony sits off the back wall, accessible through floor to ceiling windows. A huge four-poster bed sits to the side along with a sitting room, writing desk, and a door that leads to a giant bathing room and dressing room. There is more than enough room in here for two people. Enough room for us to have distance from each other.

This is Elaenor's room. And the room we would share if we married.

I walk up to the bed, my hand brushing the furs. Laenie and Emery decorated this room a few months ago, when we were hopeful we'd be rescuing her. They kept the yellow out of the décor, instead opting for blacks and greens that would remind her of Chatis and would look nothing like the bright white of Noterra.

My heart clenches and I hate the sadness that plagues me. I have no feelings for the queen, but all I can think of is what she is going through and what she'll endure before we are able to rescue her. The torture and the pain. The fear and hopelessness. How could anyone survive it? How could she even be well enough once rescued to lead an entire army, to take over the whole of Viridiana?

If what Thel had said is true, she's not well. The last bit of contact we had from him was after he had lunch with her, which only lasted a few minutes before Tobias took her away. She was cut up and bruised. He said it was one of the guards, which almost makes me wonder if people other than Tobias have been hurting her, *touching* her as well.

Enzo saw her that same week. He said she was worse off than even Thel could describe in the short letter he managed to sneak away. He said that her head was swollen, dried blood covering her forehead and neck. It was the crown that her deranged husband had sewn to her head for only the gods know what reason.

My pulse races and I fight the urge to punch something. This anger is new. I've always been level-headed and contemplative, but these last few weeks I've grown restless, as if I can't control my own emotions. As if this need to do something, to help someone is pressing down on me.

I shake my head and crack my neck to release some tension. I give the room one last look before I leave, closing the door behind me.

Instead of heading to my room, I take the stairs down to the bottom floor and walk out to the courtyard. Repairs after the small bombing have already finished, and the palace looks exactly the same. Tano was right, it wasn't an attack, but a chance to see who would defend it. Tobias knows there aren't many of us here. Our armies aren't stationed at the palace and if he brought one here, we couldn't take them.

But it wouldn't just be humans fighting his army, and I think that is one advantage that we have. Something even *he* can't predict.

The night is cold, but I can feel the warmth starting to make its way north. It would already be blistering in Labisa, in my home. It's been two years since I have set foot in my home country.

The trees are just as present in Labisa as they are Noterra, but they are different. Less of a forest and more of tropical paradise. Most places past The Divide are tropical, as if the barrier between our lands have some effect on the climate and not just on the magic.

I wonder if I'll ever see it again, or even feel the pressure release from my tense shoulders as I cross the unseen barrier. As I head towards my home.

Something is telling me that I won't.

Chapter Seventeen

The Caged

It's quiet and I feel like I can finally take a deep breath as I rock the growing child in my arms. It's still mid-afternoon, but he is past due for his nap and the days he stays awake are the days I start to panic at the motherhood I was thrown into. Usually one of the nannies comes and takes him so I can rest, but they haven't been as present today, leaving me to care for him alone. I don't mind it, sometimes. It's nice to have someone present who doesn't force you to act or speak. Just be present. That's all he requires of me. But other times, times after Tobias has been rough, I can't bear to look at that small child and not think of his mother.

Tobias has been gone for over two days now, doing something at our borders he said. He didn't tell me which border, but he was supposed to return today and has yet to arrive. All his trip has done is leave me with a four-month-old child that isn't mine.

Cyn has been good, he's a pretty quiet child, but I'm not his mother and he knows that. He knows I don't carry milk in my breasts, so instead I have to force bottles in his mouth. He is confused, and I don't blame him. He's barely out of the womb and his entire life has been uprooted. I am still unsure whether or not Nylah is dead, or if she is in the dungeon. I thought about sneaking down there, but I am not alone very often, nor have I ever really been able to explore the palace.

Laris has been giving me privacy when Cyn is here, letting me do what I need to do, and instead of being in the room, he stands guard outside. I feel less like a caged animal this way, but it's still a cage. I just have a child stuck inside with me.

I sway back and forth, Cyn sucking on a little piece of wood Lydia brought for him, when the door opens. I glance up as Malia walks in, her dirty blonde hair tied up in a knot. She smiles at me as she approaches and reaches for Cyn. The door is cracked, and I can just make out the edge of Laris's silver armor as he keeps watch on the hall.

"Any news?" I ask quietly. She sets Cyn down in his tiny bassinet, wrapping his blanket around him, before coming back up to me. She looks nervously over her shoulder before leaning in so she can whisper, her fingers lightly brushing my arm.

"I asked around and found an older couple in Tatus who claim to be Nylah's aunt and uncle. Her parents have passed, so they are the last remaining kin she may have." My heart skips and I nearly topple over in relief. Relief that parents aren't waiting out there for their child to return home that never will, and relief that there is someone else related to Cyn out there that isn't Tobias. "They have agreed to take in the child." She finishes and I grip her hands tightly.

"Thank the Gods." I whisper.

"Your Grace, we can take him tonight, before the king returns, but—"

She stutters and looks around as if she's searching for something.

"What?" My eyes briefly glance around.

"I worry for your safety, Your Grace." I exhale and release my death grip on her hand before stepping away. I turn towards Cyn, his curious blue eyes staring up at me, his tiny hands gripping the edge of the blanket.

He is who we should worry about.

"I am, too, Malia. I am concerned for how Tobias will react. Concerned that my life may be forfeit if we do this, but my priority right now is him. Cynfael can't be here. He needs to be with family, with those who would protect him from his father. There is only so much I can do, and I worry that any aggression he has shown Nylah, shown myself, may redirect to him. To his child." She's quiet as she comes to stand next to me, her fingers gripping onto the side of the basinet. I have no doubt that the worry eating through my mind is the same worry that is plaguing her. That she, too, has thought about Tobias and Cyn. What kind of relationship they would have.

"So what do we do, just act as if nothing is amiss? There is no way any of us would make it out of the walls before being caught. I wouldn't make it past the nursery before being stopped, Your Grace." I turn toward her, taking in the lines appearing next to her eyes. Her brows are furrowed, her bottom lip planted firmly between her teeth.

"No, I can't risk your life. No one's life should be in peril. This was my decision. My choice." She looks over at me, confusion washing over her face. "We stage a kidnapping." Her eyes widen, her lips parting. I stay stoic, strong. It's what my mother would want from me. What she would expect from me if she were here. Cyn. Cyn is whose life I need to protect.

"Elaenor..." She forgoes my title, her hand reaching for mine as sorrow replaces the confusion marring her lovely face.

"Take him tonight, or whenever possible, but we have to make it look real." I urge while trying to keep my voice down. I glance at the door again, Laris unmoved.

"I don't understand." She squeezes my fingers, and my gaze returns to her.

"Malia, I need you to find someone who is willing to hurt me, make it look like I put up a fight. Someone who could come in here undetected and take him. Someone we could trust to ensure his safety."

"Your Grace, I—"

"This is for him, for Cyn, not for me. We need to protect him. He is just a child, a babe. He can't be here, near the king."

"I know someone, someone in the village by Tellavid. Someone who could do as you ask, but what will become of you?"

"We don't need to worry about me. I'll be okay. I always am." Her shoulders drop and she reaches up to cup my cheek.

"I will see to it."

Night falls and I brush a tiny copper lock from Cyn's face, his beautiful blue eyes sparkling in the dim light as he looks up at me. He looks just like him, Tobias. I could almost imagine that this is what our child would look like, aside from the copper hair. A child who would be free to run around the palace. A child who could be happy. But that isn't what my child's life would entail. They would have a father who prefers to lash out instead of talk. Someone who favors aggression and blood to tenderness and care.

I can't imagine the kind of monsters his children would grow up to be. Who they wouldn't have a choice but to become if they wanted to survive.

"When you are older, Cyn, I will find you. I will come to Tatus, and I will tell you about Noterra and your father. I'll tell you the good and the bad, every part of the man he is. I want you to have a choice, a choice in who you live with. If you want to come live with me, once all of this is over, I will welcome it with open arms. You will always have a home with me." He *coos* and I blink back the sudden wetness in my eyes. I take a slow, shaky breath around the lump in my throat. "I may not be your mother, but I love you. You deserve so much more in this life. I hope your aunt and uncle can give that to you." I lean down, pressing my lips to his tiny forehead.

Time moves slowly. Malia promised it would happen tonight, but the fear I feel right now isn't for my own safety. I don't care what happens to me, but of the child in my arms. I only hope that whoever she found to handle this task is someone we can trust.

I don't jump when footsteps on the balcony echo through the room. A gloved hand spins me around, but I keep my eyes on the child in my arms.

"Please make sure he's safe." I whisper. "I will ensure you receive whatever you want as long as Cyn is safely taken to his family." The man doesn't speak, but I can see his dark cloak in my peripherals. I can see his gloved hands reach for Cyn. Reach for what could possibly be the only chance I have at being a mother. He's taken from my arms, and I keep my gaze locked on his as the blow to my temple knocks me to the ground.

My head feels as if it is underwater. As if my ears are filled with liquid and are unable to ascertain what the noises I hear are. I can hear mumbling, maybe even shouting, but it's too far away.

"Your Grace!" Yelling echoes throughout my head as the fogginess clears. My jaw is pounding, my throat dry. I force my eyelids to part as I look around. I can taste the metallic tang of blood in my mouth as I try to work a swallow. "Elaenor!" A rough hand shakes my shoulder and I slowly turn my gaze to Laris. His brows are furrowed as he leans over me, fear etched into his face.

"Laris?" I croak, my throat protesting.

"Are you alright?" I place my hand on the marble floor, pushing myself up into a sitting position as I take in the guards combing the room.

"What happened?"

"The prince, he's gone." My eyes widen and I glance around the room. The bassinet is tipped over, the balcony doors wide open. I scramble to my knees, my hand coming up to touch my temple. I wince as my palm grazes the bruise I have no doubt is growing.

"What do you mean he's gone?" I whisper, tears pricking my eyes. I planned this, I *knew* this was going to happen, but I still feel an overwhelming sorrow weighing on my chest as if a horse stomped on my heart.

"He's been kidnapped, Your Grace." His voice is soft, and I know he is going to get in trouble with Tobias. I foresaw this, but I knew he would be alright. I had to believe he would be alright. I almost feel bad. Laris is the only one who hasn't hurt me, who hasn't forced himself upon me.

I am helped to my feet and walked over to the settee where I collapse with a wince. A cool glass is handed to me by one of the menders, apprentices to Master Pakin, and I know it's the tonic. I take a sip and relish in the feel of it sliding down my throat.

"A rider has been sent off to alert the king. He should be here any moment; he was already on his way." I nod and the mender scurries off. I relax into the chair as guards search the room. I don't hide the tears sliding down my cheeks as they look for evidence, a few of them lingering on the balcony. Lydia and Malia come in and wipe what I suspect is blood off my face with a warm cloth. They each offer me a sympathetic smile, but the relief in their eyes is there. A blanket is wrapped around my shoulders as we wait in silence.

"What happened?" Tobias's voice is loud, and I jump. He rushes over to me, his cold hands brushing hair back from my face as he searches my eyes.

"I don't know. I was rocking him to sleep and then I awoke on the floor with Laris yelling." My hands are trembling as I bring them up to fist his tunic. "He's gone, Tobias." My voice cracks as he slides his hand to the back of my neck, holding me to his chest. He looks around the room, anger brewing in his eyes as he sees that his men have nothing. No evidence, no leads. They are just standing there, useless. The thought of his men being useless used to terrify me, because I knew they couldn't help me, but I have never been more grateful for their inadequacy as I am right now.

"Search the grounds and the woods. Alert every port town. He is not leaving this kingdom!" Tobias snaps, his voice deep and ancient as he orders his men. He sits beside me on the couch and pulls me onto his lap as everyone rushes out of the room. "It's okay, my love. We will get him back." I nod into his shoulder and relish the feel of his warm arms around me.

My tears soak into his tunic as he rocks me, his hand brushing hair out of my face. I close my eyes and let myself picture Cyn, a few years older. His copper hair shaggy and tied up, his blue eyes—

I gasp as I feel the pinprick in my arm. My eyes open, and all I see before the darkness takes over is anger.

Chapter Eighteen

The Caged

My head is throbbing, that's the first thing I notice when I awake. My mouth tastes like blood, my ears muffled. I try to open my eyes, but I am met with darkness, my eyelashes rubbing against something rough, like cloth.

"Tobias?" I whisper, my voice barely above a croak as my dry throat protests the act. I hear rustling around me, as if someone is moving things around, but I can't see. A sharp inhale of ragged breath leaves my mouth as I feel something slide down my arm, something sharp. "Tobias?" I call out again. My voice echoes and I know exactly where I am. He's brought me to the dungeon.

"You couldn't protect our son." I scream as the thin blade cuts through tendon and bone, the spikes catching on sinew and muscle. My back arches as I fight against the restraints. It's been so long since I've been down here. So long since he's tortured me like this.

"Tobias, please!" I beg, my voice cracking.

"What good are you if you can't protect our child? You failed!" I scream again as I feel the blade hit bone. My head is spinning, I feel like I am falling. I bite my lip, drawing blood. "You failed as a mother. You failed as a wife. You failed as a *queen*!" The blade disappears and then I feel his hand slide in my hair, fisting around the crown sewn in place. He pulls on it, ripping at my scalp. I can feel the strands breaking, feel the permanent stitches slicing through the delicate skin. I don't fight the scream as it feels like my head is being cleaved in two.

"I'm sorry! I am so sorry." I stammer out, sobs wreaking havoc on my body. I knew this would happen. I knew he would blame me.

"I don't believe you." His voice is close to my ear, I can feel his breath against my cheek, smell the whiskey he must have drunk.

"Things were better, they were better. I don't understand." I whimper as the pressure is released. His footsteps dissipate slightly, and I can hear him toss the blade he was using on the table, the metal clinking against the other instruments.

"They were, Ela, but you ruined that. You let our son, our *only* child, be taken by the gods only know who. Were you being reckless? Purposefully endangering our son?" Silence fills the room, the only noise my ragged breathing. "Answer me!" He snaps and I hear his hands slam down on the table, sending blades flying to the ground.

"No, I-I didn't stand a chance. Please, Tobias. I never saw it coming. I-I never saw it coming!"

"Now you won't see for a while." My pulse skips. I wait for pain, I wait for anything, but nothing happens. My hands tremble as I strain my ears, trying to listen.

"What do you mean?" It's quiet, my voice echoing around me. "Tobias?" He's gone.

My hands pull at the restraints, the metal digging into my wrists. I pull and push in every direction trying to slip free, but they don't budge. I slide my head down, attempting to catch the blindfold on something, anything, that might help me slide it off. I don't know how long I work, but it doesn't move an inch. My neck is cramping, my wrists and ankles burning. I can still feel the icy air brushing up against my open wounds. Every time I take a breath, it feels as if my arm is going to fall off. Tears soak into the material as I relax. There is nothing I can do. I'm stuck.

I hear shuffling around me, someone walking towards me slowly. "Who's there?" I whisper. Rough fingers graze my cheek, then I feel hot breath in my ear.

"Guess who?" His voice is deep, and I know it is Davel who is standing next to me. His rancid breath makes me gag and I turn away from him.

"Don't." I warn. His hand fists in my hair and yanks, exposing my neck and keeping me still. His lips are warm as they press onto my skin, his tongue flicking out to gather one of the tears dripping down my jaw.

"You always smell so good after he's done with you." I try to pull my head out of his hands, but he holds tight. His lips leave my neck, and I can hear his belt being undone. I can't go through this again. His hand slips from my hair and he's silent for a second. My pulse skips, my breath coming in short pants. I can hear my blood dripping off the table and onto the stone floor. My head is spinning, from pain and from blood loss. I *won't* survive this.

"Please, don't do this." I beg. It's pointless. There is nothing I can do to stop him. Nothing I can do to save myself.

"You almost got me killed, whore. I have been in these dungeons for weeks because you couldn't keep your mouth shut. You *owe* me." My ears strain, trying to ascertain where he is. His fingers brush my leg and then I can feel him climb onto the stone slab, on top of me.

My arms pull at the chains holding me down. I can feel my muscles straining, not wanting to cooperate. His fingers slide down my bare abdomen before thrusting into me. I scream out, bucking off the table as much as possible.

He rips his fingers out before settling over me.

"Stop!" I scream as his hand finds my neck, squeezing until no oxygen can make its way through. I gasp against the feel, searching for any tiny stream of air to inhale. His other hand finds my hip and lifts me up before thrusting himself inside of me. I scream out at the burning, blinding intensity. I keep screaming as he pounds into me over and over again.

"Don't stop screaming, whore. I *like it* when you fight." His voice is rough, breathy as he picks up his pace. My screams grow hoarse before turning into sobs. I can feel his legs shaking, his sweat dripping onto my naked skin. I can feel as he empties inside of me, pouring himself into me while simultaneously draining me of every ounce of sanity I have left.

I won't survive this.

The days and nights are long. I don't know how many days I have been in here, strapped to this table. There seems to be a rotation of who uses my body any way they wish. Davel, random guards whose names I can't remember, even silent men who make no noise that I can use to identify them. I used to scream, used to cry, but after the third guard emptied himself inside of me, I stopped.

I hear his voice sometimes. Theo's. I hear him telling me to hold on, hear him telling me he loves me. I know it's not real, but it's the only thing keeping me sane. Keeping me from descending into madness.

Tobias visits often. He slices into me, rapes me, and then knocks me out. I always wake up without wounds, without pain. All for it to start again. It happens too fast. Too fast to be poppy root. I can't figure out how it is he controls the speed in which I heal, only that it's consistent. I fall asleep, I wake up healed.

It's the same every time.

What if he can't heal me one day? What if whatever magical medicine he is using stops working?

I'm going to die down here.

I *hope* I die down here.

Something slams into my stomach, knocking the wind out of me. Hands come around my neck, cutting off my oxygen. I try to claw at arms and the person's face, but the chains don't allow it. I still can't see, the blindfold a permanent fixture.

"*Whore.*" He sneers as he suffocates me. Blood pools in my mouth and I fight to inhale as much as I can, but nothing breaks through. My body is on fire, as if lightning is shooting through my limbs, burning through every vessel and artery.

Burning through every remaining piece of my sanity.

Suddenly I can see it, amethyst and emerald. An odd combination. The lightest purple and the brightest green, calling me home.

Chapter Nineteen

The Bound

My eyes flash open, the bright sunshine streaming through the open windows. My breathing is ragged, sweat beading on my hairline. I take a second before I move, letting my racing pulse calm down.

I had the weirdest dream. I saw a star-filled sky and endless trees. It started raining, but it wasn't water dripping down from the cloudless sky.

It was blood.

I take a deep breath and sit up. My pulse skips as I look around and find that I am not in *my* room, but Elaenor's. Or what will be Elaenor's once she arrives. I don't remember coming in here last night. The last thing I remember is drinking in the library with Enzo and Erik, another evening filled with planning and preparing for the day we bring home the queen.

Nausea burns my stomach and I have the weird sense something is wrong. Something is pushing on my head, on my mind. Something telling me to run.

I slide off the bed quickly and step out into the hallway. Enzo is yawning, walking out of his room, his short hair disheveled and his clothing wrinkled. A slight glance behind him and I see Scarlett still asleep in his bed, blankets wrapped around her like a tourniquet.

"Something is wrong." My voice comes out hoarse, rushed.

"What?" He says between another yawn. He looks over at me sleepily, his eyes bloodshot.

"Something feels wrong." I repeat. He rubs his eyes and glances around as if he's expecting to see something.

"I don't feel anything besides hungover." He mutters.

"What is that?" I jump as Laenie speaks up behind me. I spin around, her dressing gown is tightly wrapped around her. Chestnut hair is messily pulled up into a knot.

"What do you feel?" Someone has to be feeling the same thing. This isn't just me.

"It feels like something is pounding on my head. Like pressure." Emery's door opens and she's rubbing her face.

"Gods, why do I feel hungover?" She grumbles, leaning into the doorjamb and glancing around at us.

"I feel fine." Enzo shrugs.

"It's her." Kassius is breathless as he crests the top of the stairs, with a tiny Mal right behind him, her strawberry hair in messy braids. "It's her. Something is wrong."

Chapter Twenty

The Caged

Everything hurts. Every part of me. My soul. My skin. My bones. I think I am dying, and if I am, I don't even mind.

I keep my eyes closed, absorbing the silence around me. My limbs are stiff, being held down by chains on the stone table. He was here all night, for hours, carving me up like a roast chicken. He was yelling, he was crying. He was hurt.

I don't know why I expected the few weeks of gentleness to continue. I knew what he was. I knew who he was. He'll never be capable of comfort.

I love him. I know I do. Even despite everything. I can feel that love, feel it as if it is a shard of glass piercing my heart, moving with every beat. *Gods*. What is wrong with me?

I flex my fingers, or attempt to. I can't really tell if they move.

I hope I'm dying.

What I do feel is a burning tingle in my fingertips. As if my hand strayed too close to a fire. As if it is burning through my skin, eating away at my flesh. As if it's spreading from my skin to the stone. Lightning bolts taking away everything I have left.

Chapter Twenty-One

The Bound

"I cannot allow you to go. It is not time." My father's tired voice is loud, and I am cursing the lack of coffee I have consumed this morning as I sit at the council table.

"We don't have a choice. She is *dying*." Kassius speaks up for once, disagreeing with my father. His voice is loud, desperate as he urges him to understand.

"You can't possibly know that." The King of Labisa is bored, irritated with our constant pressure to rescue Elaenor. Even now, as Kassius begs for him to listen, he doesn't.

"I can. *You* may not have felt it, but most of us did. The pressure, the pulse she sent. She is *dying*, Dav. That wave that we all felt, the one that woke most of us up, was her aether. It was searching, begging for help as a last attempt to save her. I could see it, pure, undiluted starlight. I could see her, or what is left of her." I whip my head in his direction, all of us stunned to hear he had a vision.

"What?" Disbelief coats my tongue like ash.

"My visions have gone, my ability to see, but something about her, something in her aether that she sent out, let me see her. She's in a dungeon, chained to a stone table. Her skin has been sliced open; salt poured in her wounds to keep her from healing. I fear she will not survive the day." His voice is soft, but I can hear the tremor. I can see the pain in his eyes. He once told us that she was like a daughter to him when she was younger. She was everything he hoped Mal would grow up to be—fearless and strong.

"You can't be serious." Enzo's voice is low. Scarlett is leaning against the wall, her hand in Emery's, her eyes lined with silver. Laenie and Erik are sitting to my left, watching Kassius as intently as the rest of us. Mal walks over and climbs into Enzo's lap, her arms wrapping around his neck as he rubs her back. She doesn't know Elaenor, or understand, but she's smart. She knows someone is hurt and that we need to help her.

"I've seen it. I've seen what I believe to be her death. If Tobias goes back to her, goes back to the dungeons, she will not survive. I saw the blade. I saw it slice through an artery. She bleeds out before he can stop it. It's an accident." My hands are shaking, and I stick them under the table, clenching them into fists.

"That isn't an accident, that's murder." Enzo growls.

"If you go, if you leave now without an army to back you, it will be a suicide mission. We do not have the manpower to send guards with you, nor will I risk anyone's life for something that may not even be true."

"We don't need guards. In and out." I speak up, turning back to face my father.

"Son," he warns.

"Just Enzo and I. No one else. We can cross the Delaquar by boat, it'll be quick. We would make it before the moon rose." I look over at Kassius.

"Would that give us enough time?" He shakes his head.

"The moon had not yet risen in this vision; it may be too late by then."

"We can leave now." Enzo replies as he guides his little sister off his lap.

"I can't allow it." My father snaps, his hands digging into the table.

"I have said it before, and I will say it again, you are *not* my king." My father's eyes harden as he stares at Enzo, preparing for another verbal battle.

"Dav. She will be gone, and all of this would be for nothing if they do not get her out." Kass cuts in, hoping to diffuse the situation. His eyes relax, his brows unfurrow.

"*Fine*, but you both go into this knowing you may not make it back. Knowing that you will not be rescued. You will *not* be saved." I nod and clamor out of my chair, following Enzo closely behind.

"Enzo?" Scarlett's voice is soft, and he spins on his heel to face her. "Bring her home." She whispers. She leans up, pressing her lips to his. He kisses her back, and I can almost see it, I can almost see love pooling in his eyes.

Emery is not going to be happy.

Chapter Twenty-Two

The Caged

His hands are tight around my neck as he thrusts into me. The whimpers are soft, barely audible, but I have no energy left. No energy left to fight. My physical wounds may be closed, but the mental damage is done.

There is no saving what is left of me.

It will be over soon.

Chapter Twenty-Three

He was rough, but he didn't touch me. Not in that way. He hasn't since she arrived. Since she arrived, things have been different. He's always been aggressive, but he's obsessed. Obsessed with her.

It's *her* fault.

Everything that has happened is her fault.

And now she gets to raise my son while I rot in a dungeon.

It's been two weeks since my son was taken. Two weeks I have sat in this dungeon, waiting to die. Will he kill me? Will he make it quick?

I've been well-fed. Enough bread and cheese to fill my belly until the next meal. No one has spoken to me, not directly, but I hear them whisper. I hear them whisper about the deranged king and the infant forced upon the queen.

My infant.

My son.

I can't stand the screaming.

It's too much.

The noises as he slices her open. As she sobs. As she cries.

She just keeps repeating that she's sorry.

He's mad, I think.

But I can't tell why.

It's my son. He's missing. I screamed when I heard. Pounded on the bars, pulled at the door. All it got me was a busted lip and raped by someone who was forced to wait their turn for Elaenor.

The stream of men defiling the queen has been constant. She stopped fighting. She just cries. Every time she cries as they call her whore and empty themselves inside her.

I'm going mad. I can't listen to it anymore. I can't.

They stopped feeding me. They are far too consumed with Elaenor to care about the other prisoners.

Davel started to visit me, though. I don't know when he was let out, but he is probably Elaenor's most frequent visitor, and mine. I think I'd prefer it if I were dead.

I think she would too.

It's dark. The dungeon only lit by a single torch. I don't know why I woke; I've been sleeping most of the time away.

It's quiet, which isn't normal. I'm used to her sobbing. Her pleas for a quick death. She won't get one. Not if she had anything to do with my son's disappearance.

My eyes linger on the cell door. The rusted metal bars and the lock that has been taunting me for over a month. My eyes stay affixed to the iron, and I can't tell why.

Until I see it.

It's almost as if it's alive, a snake or worm working its way over. My eyes widen and I stand, my back pressed against the wall.

It's beautiful. White and sparkling as if it's comprised of a million stars. The stream of light grows and climbs the metal bars, wrapping around them like lightning, or vines. The tip of it shoves into the lock and I hear the audible click, and then suddenly, it's gone.

Just like that.

I hesitantly step over, my knees weak from hunger. My hands grasp the metal rungs and I push.

An uncontrollable sob creeps up my throat as the door opens with a creak. I shuffle out, keeping a hand on the wall to steady myself. I pass another cell, a man half beaten crumpled in the corner. His hair a dirty brown, his skin pale. He watches me with brown eyes as I walk by. I could stop, try to help him, but I don't.

I reach the end of the cells, my ratty cloak dragging on the floor.

My mouth falls open as I turn the corner.

Elaenor is naked. Her body is clean, free of cuts and scars, but I know she's been tortured.

The table beneath her stained with old and new blood. The floor around the table looks the same. A cart with various metal instruments sits in the corner, blood and flesh hanging to each tool. My hand covers my mouth as I fight the urge to gag.

I need to get out of here.

My steps quicken as I shuffle to the door. The only one that leads up.

"Hello?" Her voice is little more than a croak, broken and weak. "Is someone there?" She asks. I pause, my hand inches from the door handle, before I turn and face the queen.

I take a long, deep breath as I walk up to the table. Her eyes are covered, a blindfold wrapped around. Her crown is on her head, blood staining the diamonds. Her lips are pale and cracked, her nails broken and bleeding as if they've been digging into the stone.

"I can feel you." She whispers.

"It's me." I whisper back. She flinches and her head turns in my direction.

"Nylah?" Her voice is filled with disbelief. "I thought you were dead." She shakes her head. "I begged him. I begged him to tell me where you were. I am so sorry—"

"What did you do with my son?" I cut her off. Anger brewing deep in my belly. If she had anything to do with him disappearing, if he's hurt, I think I might kill her.

"I'm sorry." She whispers.

"Did you hurt him?" She shakes her head, her hands fisting. "Where is he?" She's quiet for a second.

"Tatus." My pulse skips and I step away from the table. "He's with your aunt and uncle. I couldn't let him stay here. I was afraid of what *he* would do."

"You sent him away?"

"I was trying to keep him safe, Nylah. I promise. He is alive." I step farther away from the table. My footsteps silent.

Tatus.

He's alive.

Tears prick my eyes, and I can feel my pulse quickening. If I can somehow get out of the palace, out of the capital, I can get to Tatus. I can be with my son. I turn away from her, reaching for the door, but something prevents me from opening it again. Something at the back of mind telling me not to leave her.

"Tell him I love him." I hear her whisper, her voice barely audible. "I loved him so much." I glance over at the torture instruments, my eyes catching on a small blade. Without thinking, I snatch the thin metal into my hand and run back to the table.

"This is for him." I whisper as I shove the blade into the lock. The restraint around her wrists clicks open and I reach for the ones on her ankles. She's shaking, her body trembling, but she doesn't move when the last one falls away. "You are free, Elaenor. Go." I urge her, but she just shakes her head.

"I will never be free as long as he's alive, Nylah." She reaches up and pulls off her blindfold. Her blue irises are bloodshot, her pupils ten times their normal size. "Find your son. Be happy." Her lip quivers and she lays her head down, sliding the blindfold back on.

"Elaenor, you can leave. You can escape." I plead, my hand grabbing hers.

"I have no desire to live in a world where I will always be on the run. My place is here until he no longer breathes." I don't answer. I just stare.

This young girl, no more than eighteen, has been brutally raped and tortured. She has been abused for months, and I've spent almost all of them hating her. Hating that she has him.

But she saved me. I would be the one on that table if she didn't exist.

I almost was.

A tear escapes my eye, trailing down my cheek.

She's sacrificing herself. She's prepared to die, just to ensure he does.

She's doing it for me and for Cynfael. For herself.

"Every day I spend with my son, every breath I watch him take, I will think of you. I will not let the world forget your name, Elaenor, but you better fight like hell." I say, my voice wavering slightly.

This won't be the last time I see her. I can't let it be. Because if it is, that means he has won, and I can't live in a world where that is the truth.

I turn away from her, my hand finally closing around the handle of the only exit. I pause, only for a second, before I open it and run up the stairs.

Chapter Twenty-Four

The palace is silent as we near the wall. The trip across The Delaquar was quick and uneventful, mostly due to Enzo's ability to shift into a sturgeon and drag the boat across. I wanted to fly us, but it would only draw attention.

We crossed under the half demolished bridge to Chatis, docking on the other side. There wasn't a single guard manning the lake, watching for intruders. I silently thank Tobias for his stupidity and ego. We looked across the bridge once we were on land. We stared at the barren rubble that used to be Chatis. Used to be Elaenor's home.

All we could see was stone in large piles and trees knocked over, their leaves burned to a crisp. Smoke still lay heavy above the remains, as if it is forever burning. I don't allow myself to think about the bodies underneath the wreckage. All the people who will be forgotten by the world as time moves on.

By the time we reach the wall, the sun has set. We are both out of breath, exhausted, but we push on.

"Where did Scarlett say to enter?" I whisper as we lean against the stone wall.

"She said the stables have an entry point into the palace, we just need to get through without being seen." I nod and push off the wall. He's silent behind me as we follow the wall along.

I think we are both in disbelief. Disbelief that we are here, in Noterra, planning to rescue a queen that has always been a figment of my imagination. Not an actual woman. I knew she was here, all these months, but she wasn't real until today.

Until right now.

We find the stables and enter. It's dark, with only a small bit of moonlight to guide us. The moon has risen, and I silently plead for it not to be too late.

"What if we are too late?" I whisper as we slowly cross through the door leading to the horses. Each wall is lined with stalls, hay crunching under our feet. Only soft huffing and chewing fills our ears as we keep moving.

"We can't be. We didn't come all the way here for her to die. This can't be for nothing—" A sharp squeal causes me to gasp as I run straight into someone. My dagger is out and poised, ready to strike, but I freeze as I take in the pale face in front of me.

Hair that reminds me flames, of burning embers. Green eyes so bright they could rival Enzo's, shine in the moonlight. Her cloak is tattered, her skin sullen and dirty.

"Who are you?" She whispers, her voice hoarse.

"Who are *you*?" Enzo counters, stepping up beside me.

"Are you here for her?" She asks, tilting her head to the side as she glances back and forth between us. I hesitate, but nod once and her face relaxes. "You have to hurry. She's unlocked, but she refuses to leave. I unchained her, but she said she can't leave until he's dead. She's weak, she won't survive." Her voice comes out in a rushed panic, as if she's genuinely worried about her.

"Why are you telling us this?" I ask, skepticism coating my tongue.

"She saved my son, and in a way, she saved *me* from a life she is currently enduring. She needs help." She stares at me, her emerald eyes burning through mine. "Go through the double doors, there are no guards. The first room on your left is the council room. You can access the dungeon through there." She pushes between us, walking towards one of the horses. It's black, its coat glowing against the moonlight.

"Where are you going?" Enzo asks as she pats the horse's head.

"To live a better life." She unlatches the stall and pulls the giant mare out. "Tell her thank you. And tell her I took her horse, that I will give her a good life." She gives us a smile that doesn't reach her eyes as she leads the horse out through the back, leaving us.

Chapter Twenty-Five

The Caged

I can hear him coming. His leather boots slapping the stone of the stairs. He's not quiet. He never is.

"Did you miss me, my love?" He calls out from the stairs, his voice echoing around me. My fingertips dig into my palms, splitting the skin with my broken nails. I'm unlocked, untethered. All I need is for him to come closer.

The door creaks as he pushes it the rest of the way open. He inhales deep and slow as he walks up the table. He doesn't react, or he doesn't notice, that I am free. I am unconstrained.

His fingers brush my lips before they travel down my neck and in between my breasts.

"It's been a long day, my Ela. I missed you." He leans down, his lips pressing to mine. He tastes like whiskey. Cedar and ash mixing with the caramel notes of the alcohol, flooding my senses. My fingers tingle as he pulls away. They ache to reach out, ache to touch him.

Ache to drive this scalpel through his temple.

Nylah left it on the table after she escaped. Left it within reach. I have been holding it in my hand for what feels like an hour now.

Waiting.

He steps away, rattling to my right tells me he's digging for instruments. I wait.

I have all the time in the world. He steps back up to me, something cold running down my thigh. I don't feel it, really. I'm numb.

Numb to pain. Numb to emotion.

I am just ready. Ready for the end.

"Do you want to know what I was doing today, Ela?" Silence. "I was preparing our armies. They will be shipping out soon, they'll cross the sea to Labisa. Their country is defenseless without their king. So I'm going to give them a new one." The blade presses into my skin, slicing it open.

But I don't react. I don't feel it.

"Will you be going with them?" The blade lifts. "Will I?"

"You would enjoy being tethered to my bed for the days it takes to travel, wouldn't you?" I can hear him smiling, hear him picture it.

"I will go wherever you are. I will follow you." What he thinks is a sign of devotion, is a threat. A *promise*. We are both destined for it to be the end. Today is last day of our lives. But I won't give him time to grieve, time to beg.

His fingers trail back up my leg, smearing blood up to my stomach and then to my lips. He brushes them across, and I taste the metallic tang of my blood. He bends down, his lips touching mine again.

I open for him, let his tongue tangle with mine. Let him get comfortable. His hand holds my jaw, forcing my head to stay up, stay open. My pulse skips, my body tingles, and I know it's time.

My hand shoots out, digging the blade deep. Somewhere. He gasps, his mouth breaking from mine.

I rip the blindfold off, and nearly cry in relief as I see the blade jutting out of his neck. His eyes are wide, his mouth filling with blood.

I jump off the table, making a run for the instruments, but his hand catches my arm. He yanks me back, throwing me against the table. Pain lances down my spine as he leans over me.

"You are going to regret this." He says, blood gurgling out of his mouth, spraying across my face.

"You are going to burn in hell, and it will be me who lights the match." I spit. His hand grips my neck, cutting off my oxygen supply. I wrap my fingers around his wrist, trying to pull it off. His free hand grabs the blade and rips it out, black blood spurting all over my bare chest.

Black.

"Did you think a simple blade would be all that it takes to kill me, my love? You cannot kill what is already gone." My eyes widen, my lips part, and a choked gasp falls out. I watch as the wound knits itself together, blood soaking back into his skin as if it was never shed to begin with. "It wasn't herbs or injections that healed you every night. It was me. I was replacing every cell in your body, repairing every wound. I was remaking you each time so that you were made just for me. *By* me. I own your body and your soul. You cannot escape me, Elaenor." My vision darkens from a lack of oxygen, and I realize now that it won't be us dying today.

It will just be me.

He thrusts the blade deep in my thigh, so deep I can feel it slice through bone and nearly come out the other side. He rips it out, throwing it across the room, and I fall to the ground. I inhale sharply, my head pounding, as I look at the wound. Blood pours out of me like a fountain, and I know in that moment, he hit an artery. But it isn't pain I feel. It is a never-ending tingle, a never-ending feeling of something brewing deep inside. Something begging to come out. But I don't think I will survive if it does.

I don't know if I even want to.

"I want you to feel the pain I feel Elaenor. I want you to scream in agony. I want you to beg for your life as I strip you of everything." He turns his back to me, my vision darkening with each strained breath. I'm going to die here. My arm gives out, and I roll onto my back, unable to hold myself up. I force an inhale, but no oxygen reaches my lungs.

I'm dying.

It's as if time stands still, as if life is waiting to continue until I take a breath. A breath that doesn't come as my eyes close. As I succumb to the death that has been waiting for me.

Open your eyes. I can hear him, his voice, calling to me. *Nora, open your eyes.* Bright white light fills my vision as I force my eyelids to part. I expected to see Tobias, but it isn't him leaning over me. Shaggy blonde hair falls in front of his blue eyes, soft and pure. My hand lifts and I shakily touch his cheek, pleading for him to be real.

"I can feel you." I whisper, a sob working its way up my throat.

"And I you." A tear escapes his eye, trailing down his cheek to my fingers.

"Am I dead?" I ask. His hand reaches up to hold onto mine, his eyes closing briefly as if he's savoring every second of this moment.

"No, but you will be soon."

"I don't understand." I push myself up, my face inches from his. Sweetgrass flows around me, encompassing me in the scent of Theo.

"Things have been hard for you. More than I could have imagined. I'm sorry I didn't protect you. I didn't do anything to prevent this from happening and I am so sorry, Nora." My other hand reaches up, cupping his face as I stare into his silver-lined eyes.

"It's alright. I'm here now, with you." I smile and lean forward, aching for my lips to touch his.

"No, you can't stay here." He leans back right before our lips brush.

"I don't want to go, Theo." I shake my head, tears dripping down my cheeks.

"You have so much left to accomplish. So much left to do. There are people counting on you." He presses his forehead to mine and the tears flow freely. I shake my head and he grips the back of my neck. "I love you, Nora. I love you so godsdamn much, but you need to open your eyes."

"No." I shake my head, sniffing away the snot dripping from my nose. "No, I can't leave you. Please don't make me leave you. I have no one, and nothing. I'm alone. I can't do this anymore." He leans back, his ocean eyes holding mine. "Kiss me." I whisper. He pauses for a second, hesitating, and then his lips are slamming into mine. Tongue and teeth and tears. A moment I never want to end. His hands tangle in my hair, pulling me as close as he can before he pushes me away.

"I love you so much." He cries. "Open your eyes and fight. It's not your time."

"I don't want to leave you, Theo. I can't. I'm so alone."

"You are not alone. I have been here, this whole time, I have been with you. And there are people who love you, people who are waiting for you out there. Those who have been there, just waiting for the moment you are free." I shake my head. No. I can't leave him.

"I love you. Don't make me do this." My shoulders shake as sobs break through the lump in my throat. He leans forward and presses his lips to my forehead.

"Goodbye, Nora." His voice cracks and his hands disappear.

I open my eyes to darkness. A dark ceiling with only a single torch lighting the room.

I am no longer in pain, no longer struggling to breathe.

I glance over at Tobias, who is grabbing something from his tray of torture devices. Tears well up in my eyes as the scent of sweetgrass dissipates along with the feel of his lips. I take a single, pain-free breath before I open my mouth to speak.

"What else is there for you to take?" I say, my voice cracking. "You have taken everything from me already." My hands shake as I plant them on the floor and pull my knees underneath me. "I have nothing left. I have no home." I grunt as I force one of my feet to plant on the ground. "I have no family." My blood-slicked hands grip the table, and nearly slip as I pull myself up. "I have nothing to lose." I get out, my voice little more than a breathy whisper. I look up at him, his eyes going wide as he looks at me.

Blood is pouring down my leg. My body is on fire, but it's not painful, it's invigorating. Everything feels as if it is seconds away from failing, but I'm not.

I won't fail this time.

"You have everything to lose, Tobias." I take a shaky step forward. "You have a crown. You have a wife. You have a kingdom and a country full of slaves at your beck and call. You have riches and power. Armies and men. A son somewhere out there. You have everything to lose, and that makes you reckless. That makes you *vulnerable*. Do you know what having nothing makes me?" I ask as I take another strained step. My fingers start to burn, my limbs shaking as if they are being pumped full of adrenaline. And I know.

I know what it is that's calling to me. What it is that has been trying to break free this whole time.

My whole life.

"What?" He asks, his voice thick as he stares at me.

"Free." I whisper. The darkness edging my vision is replaced with light as I burst.

Lightning burns through every vessel in my body. Every cell being decimated as I let it consume me.

As I erupt.

Chapter Twenty-Six

A deep rumbling starts somewhere under where we stand in the stables. Men start yelling as rubble falls from the top spires of the palace. Glass shatters in succession, all of the windows blowing out. I grab the back of Enzo's tunic, shoving him against the wall as men race by, headed for the palace.

"It's her." I whisper.

"How do you know?" He whispers back.

"Who else would it be?"

Chapter Twenty-Seven

The Caged

Dust rains from the ceiling, coating us in a fine mist. Tobias's eyes are wide and red, his pupils dilated. His gaze travels from my feet to the top of my head where it lingers. A single trail of blood drips out of his nose.

"My gods, Ela." He croaks. A large cracking noise sounds above us, and I glance up to see a fissure forming in the ceiling. I catch sight of him in my peripherals before his body slams into mine.

My skull snaps off the stone floor and I am momentarily dazed.

"What are you?" He asks as he sits on my bare thighs. "What have you not been telling me?" His hands wrap around my throat, holding me down. I grip his wrists with my shaky fingers, a subtle buzzing sound filling my ears.

"Get off me." I croak, my voice weak.

"What are you?" He yells this time, his face inches from nine.

"Get off!" I scream. White flashes in between us and he flies off of me, his body hitting the wall before crumpling on the ground in a still lump. My heart races, my breathing labored as I force myself to sit up.

My hands are glowing white, and I stare at the veins streaking down my arms. *My gods.* I squeeze my hands into fists and tiny dots fling off of them, sparkling like stars.

Rushing footsteps pulls my attention away and I glance up just as the door opens, revealing a staircase.

"Your Grace!" One of the men yell, rushing to Tobias's side. The other two look at me with a combination of hesitance and duty fighting in their minds.

"Stay down, Your Grace." He orders. I grit my teeth and pull my feet under me. Primal rage pounds through my blood, filling every pore of my being.

"I will not be chained any longer." I say slowly. White once again fills my peripherals and I watch as their eyes widen. A shaky hand lifts a sword and I run at him, my scream echoing around the room.

He reaches for me, and the scent of charred meat fills my nostrils as he cradles his burning hand to his chest. I push past the other guard, my hand melting through the metal of his chest plate, before racing up the stairs.

My bare feet slip on the cold, stone steps. Rubble still rains down from the ceiling and I can feel my breath coming in short pants as exhaustion pulls at me. My legs feel numb, but I can feel the warmth trickling down my skin as the wound continues to bleed.

"Hold it together, Elaenor." I whisper to myself as I reach the top of the stairs.

I barrel through the door and gasp at the destruction around me. Glass and stone lay everywhere, coating the floor. I take a step further into the hallway, feeling it slice through my feet.

A feeling I know all too well.

I bite my lip and pick up the pace, racing down the hall. The stables. I have to get to the stables.

Rhythmic marching sounds in all directions and I skid to a stop. Two groups of men rush at me from either side, shields up and swords out. I glance at both of them, only a few feet away.

I can't take them on.

As I turn towards the other group, the wall of windows snags my attention. The glass is gone, leaving it open to the courtyard.

A courtyard that leads to the stables.

Panic wells in my chest and I swallow it down before I run.

Chapter Twenty-Six

The Bound

I hear men coming from all directions. Yelling about the queen. Yelling about the king being injured.

Enzo and I step out of the shadows as another group of men race by, paying us no attention. I glance out across the mist-shrouded courtyard. Flashes of silver armor and swords glint off the moonlight.

"We can't get through them all." I say softly, defeat barreling through my head. I grit my teeth and clench my hands into fists. "We aren't leaving—" I start to say, and then I see it.

Pale hair, the color of the moon, flows in the slight breeze. Skin the color of ash, covered in blood and not an ounce of clothing, jumps through an open window.

"My gods." Her eyes are frantic, her arms pumping as she races across the courtyard, but she isn't fast enough.

I can feel my heart break, feel it stop as time slows. She glances behind her, fear filling her features as she sees the crowd following. She pumps her arms harder, racing as fast as she can.

"She's not going to make it."

Chapter Twenty-Seven

The Caged

My arms can't move fast enough, the sounds of their armor racing behind me. My heart is pounding, ready to break through my chest.

I'm not going to make it. There is no way I can outrun them. Tears prick at my eyes as realization that my death truly is upon me, hits me like a horse.

And then I see it.

I see him.

Them.

Two figures step out of the darkened stables. Both with black hair, but their eyes glow different colors in the fading light. Amethyst and emerald. Calling for me.

The green eyes widen in panic. Enzo.

He's *real.*

They are both yelling, the other one ripping off his weapons. Enzo's hands are waving, his mouth moving but no words reach me. I push faster, I can feel the guards right behind me, ready to grab me. Ready to take me back to him. I won't go back alive. They'll have to ki—

"Get down!" The words break through the blood pumping in my ears. "Get down!" Enzo screams again and I throw myself to the grass.

Lilac light explodes, filling the courtyard before a roar deafens my ears. I squeeze my eyes shut, slamming my hands over my ears. A scream tears through my throat as I feel my heart stutter.

Heat lances my back as another roar shudders through my bones. A sound so deep, so *animalistic*, it infiltrates my very soul. Fire erupts around us, burning my skin. Screams echo around me. I part my eyelids slightly and look up. Another scream tears through my throat and I scramble to my knees.

Black scales of an underbelly tower over me, a light purple fire exploding out of the beast's mouth as he decimates the men who were behind me, turning them into nothing but ash.

My throat grows hoarse, and another stutter of my heart causes my breath to catch. I try to crawl away, my hands going numb as they grip at the grass before I lose feeling completely.

The wet ground caresses my bare skin as I collapse, a contrast to the heat around me. I vaguely see a tan arm reaching for me, but it doesn't matter.

Nothing matters anymore.

My eyes relax, staring at the fire catching as I take one last breath.

Part Two:
Crown Of Silver

Chapter Twenty-Eight

The Caged

My body feels like it's floating. As if I am nothing more than a speck in the sky, floating along with all of the other specks and stars. Floating with the other planets and universes. No desires or needs. No fears or sadness. Just existing to exist. But that isn't what is happening.

I wish I was just existing to exist.

It would be better than the alternative.

Better than the unknown.

Better than the pain that has followed me since the day I left Chatis. The pain that is a permanent reminder that happiness has never been in the cards for me. Fate has made sure of that.

My eyes flutter open, sunlight blinding me. I blink a few times, begging my eyes to adjust to the harsh light. Puffy white clouds and bright blue skies greet me. Birds fly overhead, trees rustle in the summer wind. It's quiet, calm. It almost feels surreal.

Am I dead?

Peace. This is what peace looks like. What I imagine the afterlife would be. What I imagine my mother is experiencing wherever she is.

What Theo is experiencing.

Something shifts below me, and I freeze, my eyes slowly panning over to the man sitting next to me.

His skin is tan, golden and slightly olive, as if he spends his time in the sun. His dark hair is tousled, as if he is constantly running his hands through it. His skin is flawless and smooth aside from a long scar that goes from his high cheekbone, through his eye, and up into his dark brow. It's a soft, flesh color, indicating it wasn't recent. His eyes are closed, his long lashes fluttering against his cheek. My eyes trail to his plush lips, perfectly framed and rosy. His jaw is hardened and sharp, with a spattering of dark facial hair; short and well-groomed. He is attractive, almost *too* perfect.

As if he is just as fake as the woods around me.

His chest is moving up and down, slowly and evenly as he sleeps. Every breath bathes me in the citrusy scent of bergamot, reminding me of summer. Reminding me of happier times. His tunic is a deep blue, cut close to his chest before disappearing under me, revealing the broad shoulders and defined muscles underneath. A black cloak is wrapped around me, fastened tight. My head is lying in his lap, one of his hands resting on my hair, his fingers locked into the strands around the crown as if he was holding me still. His other hand is resting on my stomach, almost protectively. His forearms are thick, corded muscles tensing as if he's dreaming of something unpleasant.

My breath catches as his warmth seeps into my skin, burning through the wool wrapped around me.

It's too much. Too much touching. Too intimate.

My pulse skips and I fight to keep my breath even as panic courses through my veins. My limbs burn as if they are igniting, as if they are reacting to my fear.

I shift slightly and he flinches. I sit up quickly, attempting to create some distance, and his arms pull away. All I see are trees as my head spins, pain encompassing my senses. I gasp as I clutch at my leg, digging my fingers into the flesh. I pull the cloak back and see a bright red burn across my thigh. The skin is mottled and blistered; dried blood caked around it. It's on fire, a clear liquid dripping out of it.

"What the—" I whisper, barely loud enough to hear as I grit my teeth to fight the scream tearing at my throat.

"Your wound—it was too deep. We had to stop the bleeding." His voice is deep and rich, but smooth as it infests my very bones. It's a sound I could get lost in if he wasn't a stranger. I take a deep breath, fighting the panic clogging my throat. *In and out, Elaenor. Breathe.* I look around and see that we are in a tiny clearing, tall trunks and falling leaves circling us as if to keep us from harm. My vision edges black as I take another deep breath. I visualize putting the pain into a little box, shutting the lid, and locking it. I take a slower breath this time, my tense shoulders relaxing a fraction.

"Where am I?" I ask. My voice is clear, bright, as if I haven't spent the last few days locked away; screaming and crying as a blade sliced into me, or as another guard entered me without consent. As if I wasn't just gritting my teeth in pain. My voice sounds as if it belongs to someone else.

"We are about an hour away from the Chatisian border." He responds, slowly and carefully, as if he's afraid I might do something. He hasn't moved, his body frozen, statuesque. Almost inhuman.

"What happened?" I don't remember much. I remember Tobias and this need to explode. This need to just scream and release all of the pain and fury I have been bottling up for nearly two decades. I remember his neck…it healed itself. His skin stitched itself back together as he admitted he'd been healing *me*. I remember amethyst and emerald. I remember thinking I was going to die. I remember the beast standing over me.

I remember feeling relief at the idea that it was the end. I remember a beast crouching over me—and then nothing.

"I am not entirely sure what happened before we got there, but you are out of the Noterran palace." He responds, almost diplomatically, without emotion. I don't know who he is, but he had to have grown up with some sort of status. He doesn't speak like a villager. He speaks like a Lord. My eyes fixate on the trees as I process. As I try to understand.

"This is real?" I whisper, afraid to raise my voice any higher. I feel as if the lump growing in my throat would prevent it. The lump building out of fear that this is just a dream and I'll wake back up underground, strapped to the table. There is no way this can be real. Just another false reality to fill my mind to protect me from the horrors I'm facing.

"This is real." He repeats. I look over my shoulder at him, his amethyst eyes making my eyes widen and my lips part. So light and so bright at the same time. So *familiar*.

"Your eyes...the color—"

"Elaenor." I quickly spin around, rocks digging into my backside, as another person breaks through the tree line, his deep voice echoing around the clearing. Tall, tan, with freckles across his nose. A sharp jaw and wide shoulders. Bushy eyebrows and thick eyelashes. But those aren't what surprise me. It's the bioluminescent green living in his irises.

The green I have seen before so many times.

A green that feels like home.

"Enzo." I whisper. His eyes are wary, gentle and careful as if he is afraid to scare me off. As if he's afraid I'm going to run.

He might be right.

Relief at knowing he is real, at seeing him in person, quickly fades away as rage fills my body. As anger and resentment boil to the surface.

They had months, *months*, to come for me. Months to offer some aid aside from disappearing completely and making me feel mad. Making me feel as if he never existed. But they never came. He disappeared and left me alone.

Alone and *suffering*.

"You left me. You disappeared without a trace. Why now? Why did you come for me *now*? Why did you wait until I was tortured and raped and—" My voice catches and I clear my throat before meeting his gaze. His brows twitch and lips purse as if he's confused by my question. As if he doesn't know how to respond. He cocks his head to the side slightly and takes a deep breath before responding.

"We were always going to come for you, Elaenor." The stranger says from behind. I force myself to my feet, swaying slightly and gasping in pain, before turning away from them. My wounded feet protest as they step on rocks and branches, the pain oddly familiar. My leg is cramping, and I feel this weird pressure in my chest, but I keep walking until I cross through the tree line, no plan in sight.

"Where are you going?" Enzo calls after me, his voice irritated, as if I am the one who's the issue here.

"I *didn't* need your help. I *didn't* need your rescue. I was *done*." I spit as I pick up my pace. I fight the nausea in my stomach, the burn slicing through my skin. I'm going to faint. Why am I so angry? None of this is their fault.

"Done?" The other man responds. Their footsteps trail after me, but they don't stop my walking. They don't attempt to restrain me, which I weirdly find nice and unexpected.

"I was done. With *everything*. I was ready for it to be over, and you took that away from me." My voice cracks again and I cough. I don't have time to break down. I don't have time for anything. A hand grips my arm and spins me around, making me dizzy. Green eyes bore into mine as he gets close. His breath fans across my face and I flinch at his proximity.

"You don't get to kill yourself. You don't get to be done. Too much is dependent on your survival. So stop throwing a tantrum like a child and come back to Rakushia with us." Anger brews in his eyes, his breath coming in quick, sharp pants. Surprise echoes around me.

"Excuse me?" I snap, attempting to rip my arm out of his grip, which proves unsuccessful. Terror builds in my chest as his grip tightens. "What do you mean too much is dependent on my survival?" Enzo's eyes widen slightly and his friend sighs behind him.

"Right now, we just need to get back to Rakushia." He says softer this time.

"No, *right now*, you are going to tell me what it is you mean." I retort. His nostrils flare and his grip tightens even more, pinching my skin. "Let go of me." I say quietly, but he doesn't react. The warmth from his hand is leaking through the cloak, soaking into my skin. The pressure just reminds me of him. Of *them*.

No.

It's too much.

My pulse skips and I force the adrenaline sparking through my veins back down. "Enzo, let go of me." His eyes flare open as he stares into mine, as if he sees something in my gaze. Slowly his fingers loosen, and he removes his hand and takes a step back.

"Your eyes." The other man says. I flick my gaze to him as he stares at me with a mixture of awe and bewilderment.

"What?" I snap.

"They are silver."

"Silver?" My voice squeaks as my hands move up to touch my brow. I blink a couple times, convinced it will clear away whatever anomaly they are looking at like a piece of dirt, but all that does is increase my heart rate. I can feel the panic setting in, the aftershock. The pain. It's all too much. I take a slow, deep breath as I try to relax, but it isn't working. My hands start to shake, to tingle, and I take a step away from them.

"Just breathe, Elaenor." Enzo whispers, his hands up with his palms out as if to show me he isn't a threat, but it doesn't matter. My hands fall to my side and clench into fists, nails piercing through the skin. "In and out, nice and slow." White edges my vision and I feel this pressing need to just scream.

"I can't." I close my eyes and shake my head. "I need...I don't know what I need." My breath comes in rapid pants, and I can feel the sweat beading along my hairline. Tears break through my shut eyes and a broken whimper comes out of my throat.

"Elaenor—" I hear one of them move and my eyes open.

"Don't come near me!" I snap, my hand flying out to stop him. I nearly gasp when I see the small sparks of lightning on my fingers, trailing up my arm. Sparks fly off of my skin, glittering as if they were comprised of stars. "What is this?" I stammer. The sparks travel to my shoulder and across my chest, tingling every part of my skin they come in contact with. They move down my body until I am glittering like the night sky. "Make it stop." I snap, my hands trying, and failing, to brush them away.

"Just relax, little witch." My eyes snap up to the stranger's and he flinches. Sparks fly off my hand and shoot towards him, singing his shirt. He yelps as his skin burns, his eyes narrowing. *What the hell?* I glance at my hand in confusion, and fear, before looking back at him. His amethyst irises dissolve as the entirety of each eye turns black, smoke puffing out of his nose.

"Oh my gods." I whisper. My feet scrape against the forest floor as I take a step back, my breath lodged in my throat. I take another step back and trip, sending me flying onto the ground. I catch myself with my arm as he crowds over me. Enzo just watches and waits. Patient and calm. I want to slap him.

"That wasn't nice." He *growls* and I can almost feel the blood drain from my face. He crouches down, his face inches from mine and I freeze. His hand grabs my face, his thick fingers squeezing my cheeks. The light edging my vision fades as I hold my breath, as my limbs shake with fear. His breath cascades over me. A scent that is all-consuming and suffocating. His skin is rippling as if it's moving on its own accord. A lavender glow spreads across his face and down his neck before disappearing under his tunic. The beast...

"*Oh gods.*" I whisper again.

"Alright, Nithe, she gets it." Enzo interjects with a sigh before putting his hand on Nithe's shoulder, but he doesn't move. *Nithe*. That's his name.

"She doesn't get to fuck around with magic and not understand the consequences. Do you know what you just did?" He snaps. I attempt to shake my head, but his grip keeps me still. My gaze locks onto his. "Your aether could have stopped my heart. You could have accidentally killed me without a second thought."

"I don't understand." My strained voice trembles as my gaze moves to his chest. To the heart I can almost see beating under its cage of muscle and skin. "I'm sorry." My eyes move back to his and I feel a single tear escape, trailing down my cheek. The black eyes staring at me fade back into white and amethyst, taking the glow under his skin with them. He releases my face, my skin almost burning where it had been touching his. "I'm sorry."

"It's alright, Elaenor." Enzo says, pushing Nithe away from me.

"I don't know how it happened. I don't know how to control it or even what *it* is." I admit, ignoring Enzo's outstretched hand and standing on my own.

"Aether is an extension of your will. It is something witches have, which is what you and your mother are. Yours happens to manifest as lightning or whatever *that* is." Enzo explains, his voice emotionless.

"Lightning." I mimic with a whisper. "I don't understand." Nithe sighs in annoyance and I spin to look at him. "Hey!" I yell, putting my hands on my hips.

"Yes, *Your Grace*?" He mocks with a bow.

"As of yesterday, I had no idea that I could do this. I don't even know what to think. I am confused. I am tired. I am in *pain*. And I am beyond exhausted with men thinking they can treat me like absolute trash and get away with it. If my husband can't—"

"Your husband *could*. And he did, *little witch*. You let him walk all over you and treat you as a common whore and not a queen. Don't expect others to not treat you the same, because they *will* until you prove to them you deserve otherwise." My mouth hangs open like a fish and my brain empties as I stare at this impossibly gorgeous man who called me a whore and said I deserved respect all in the same breath. "Close your mouth and move, I'd like to sleep in my own bed tonight." He finishes before turning away and stomping back to the clearing.

"Look, we all got off on the wrong foot. There is a lot you don't know and a lot we have to explain, but the longer we stand out here, the worse our chances of escaping are. We aren't safe until we cross into Rakushia, and we have to make it across The Delaquar first. So please," his fingers graze mine and I rip my hand away. "Please, just come with us." His brows furrow as he looks at me. I've seen him before but having him here in person is different. And I can't help but feel like he looks like someone else I know.

Someone who was close to me.

"Alright." I respond hesitantly, before pulling the cloak tighter around me and limping after Nithe.

Chapter Twenty-Nine

The Caged

We are all silent as we make the trek through the woods. They are dense, blocking most of the sunlight. While I spent a lot of time in the Chatisian woods, my time in Noterra didn't include a lot of exploring. But these woods, they feel...haunted. I feel this presence pushing down on me, making it hard to take a deep breath. Something is burrowing into my skin, begging to break through and take over. Neither of them acts as if anything is amiss, but I feel it. I feel *him*.

Nithe stays quite a bit ahead, saying that his magical ears can hear better than we can. Enzo started by walking behind me but has decided to stay directly next to me. I can feel his warmth and my sweaty hands ache to push him away, to keep distance. But I keep telling myself they are here to protect me.

But didn't Tobias say the same thing?

"Can I ask you something?" My voice is quiet, an underlying fear of talking too loud keeps me from raising it. Who knows who is out here, lurking behind the crowded tree trunks.

"Of course."

"Nithe, is he a witch too?"

"No, he's not." He snorts as if the idea is comical.

"His eyes...and that weird glow. I remember a beast—I don't know what I saw."

"Nithe is—he's not human. But neither are you and I." His avoidance at answering the question just piques my interest even more.

My eyes fix on Nithe's back, sweat soaking into his already dark tunic, making it nearly black. My bare feet constantly trip and slip on the forest floor, and I know I'll have a few more cuts marring my body after this walk. My legs aren't cold, though, which I appreciate, but every brush of the cloak and every strained step makes my leg cramp. I can feel the burnt flesh, feel the heat rippling off of it. I don't know what they used to cauterize the wound, but I only hope they didn't cause more damage. Though, that isn't what's making me nervous.

These woods just don't feel safe.

"What are *you*?" I ask, trying to distract myself.

"I am a seer, or a prophet as most say, but I am also a shifter." My eyes widen and stop, memories flicking through my head one by one. Silky black feathers with a green sheen.

The pot of lip stain.

"A raven. You came to me as a raven." He smiles, his eyes twinkling as he continues to walk.

"Yes, I did." Shock barrels through me. I remember the lip stain, the way he looked at me. But I didn't believe—I *couldn't* believe that was him.

"Can you only shift into a raven?" I start walking again, catching up to him quickly. "Or could you shift into something else?" I ask softly.

"I can shift into anything I can see. I have to know what something looks like in great detail prior, otherwise I can turn into something that lacks the ability to breathe, thus killing me." He explains.

"Could you shift into a horse and make this journey quicker?" I ask. Nithe snorts up ahead and I fight the urge to smile in satisfaction.

"I could, but Nithe would break my back if he tried to mount me." He replies, a laugh bubbling on his lips.

"There is no chance in hell I would try to mount you, brother." I snort this time and Enzo gives me a sheepish grin.

"How you can even smile is beyond me, Elaenor." The small twist of my lips melts away, and I look at the ground, fixating on my desire to not slice my feet up any more than they already are.

I don't comment.

I don't respond.

I stay silent the rest of the walk.

There are a lot of ways I can look at my life. I can feel sad about the childhood that was ruined. I can feel broken by the husband who thought torture was a good outlet for his rage. I can remember every moment he touched me, both with love and with anger. I can think about how I don't want to be alive, how my only goal and desire in life right now is to watch the light fade from Tobias's eyes.

All I want is vengeance. And I will stay alive until I get it. After that, I have no desire to breathe longer than needed. I'm too tired.

Whatever plans they have for me, they don't matter. I have spent the better part of a year acting, and I can do it for a few moments longer.

I have to.

My heart nearly stops when we crest the last remaining hill and break through the treeline, approaching a cliff. What lies in front of me is The Delaquar, shining brightly in the early morning sun, but that isn't what stops me in my tracks.

Just beyond the edge of the lake below us, the remnants of the bridge between Chatis and Noterra poke out of the surface. Burnt stone and rubble can be seen through the crystal-clear waters, marring what was probably a perfect lakebed. But even that isn't what makes me want to collapse into a pile on the dirty ground.

It's the sight of my home.

Rubble and smoke fill the open plain between the mountains. How there is still smoke, I have no idea, but it's there. White and billowy, more suffocating than the ever-present fog and mist.

The stone palace, nestled into the mountainside, is gone. Parts of it jut out into the open air, staircases leading nowhere. Glass from the windows sparkle in the sunlight. The town square that used to house merchants and festivals is buried under homes and shops.

Everything is just gone.

"I saw it right after it happened." I whisper, my voice hoarse. Nithe and Enzo both stop to look at me, and I don't miss the surprise crossing their faces. "He brought me here right after he cut Theo's head off in the throne room. Barefoot and half-naked, exactly how I am right now. He pulled me through the rubble with a collar around my neck." My hand raises and my cold fingertips brush the circular wounds on my neck. "He sat up high on his horse, holding a metal leash as if I was a hound. I could feel the glass and rubble slice through my feet to the bone. It hurt so bad I almost begged him, *begged* him to make it stop. But I didn't. I endured the pain. I let the blood drip from my wounds and soak into the grass, mixing with the blood of those who used to live there."

I take a breath, my pulse decreasing as I enter a deep numbness, a calm I only felt when Nylah left me.

"It was my fault. I angered him. He did this out of retaliation for what he believed was insubordination. Five hundred people lived here and every *single* one of them died. There isn't a single night I don't picture their faces. Faces I saw burnt beyond recognition. Faces that were just rotting skulls as the fire melted away their flesh. Glass and bone. I dreamt of it every night for ten years, and I never believed it was real. I believed I was going crazy, a child with an imagination. But I wasn't. I predicted their deaths and did nothing to stop it."

Enzo steps forward, but I don't acknowledge him. I push past the both of them and turn to start the small trek down the cliff edge to the lake, where a small, wooden boat sits.

I only make it a few steps before we hear it. I freeze as I listen, as do they. Pounding. Rhythmic pounding that sounds so familiar. I look at Nithe, his head cocking to the side as he listens with whatever magic flows in his veins.

"What is that?" I whisper. His eyes flash to mine and widen. Enzo grabs my arm and pushes me towards the cliff. Panic ensues as I nearly topple over the edge. "What are you doing?" I scream and try to pry his fingers off of me before I fall.

"Those are horses, Elaenor." *Horses.* He holds me steady near the edge, where I can feel the crumbling dirt falling.

"What do we do?" I step closer to Enzo, and away from the drop, his eyes staring at Nithe, who's staring back. "What do we do?" I repeat. Nithe nods and I look up at Enzo. "Enzo?" Nithe's hand grabs my wrist as he pulls me to him.

"You need to trust me." I pull against his hand.

"Tell me what is happening!" I demand. He grabs my face, his palms encompassing my cheeks as he forces me to look at him.

"You have to jump." My eyes widen and I try to shake my head, but his grip prevents it. "You have to trust me and jump." I glance to my left, right over the cliff edge to the rocks and lake below.

"No." I grab his wrists. "Please, I can't swim." He leans in, his forehead pressed against mine as he takes a long deep breath. The hoof beats grow in volume, and I start to hear the branches cracking beneath their feet.

They are close.

"*Trust me,* Elaenor." Tingles erupt from his touch, shooting through my veins and straight to my heart. His amethyst eyes bore into mine and I nod, inhaling the citrusy scent of him. I trust him. I don't know why, or what it is, but I trust him. He releases my face but keeps ahold of my hand, lacing his fingers through mine. I turn to Enzo, whose skin is rippling black. He nods once before a black cloud explodes from him, leaving behind a tiny raven. My heart pounds in my chest as Nithe drags me back from the edge of the cliff, towards the trees.

"Wait, no! What are you doing?" I stammer as my feet slip over the rocks. His eyes are focused on the cliff edge.

"We have to run to clear the rocks." He says softly. I can hear the beasts crashing through the underbrush. Just as I see the first snout, Nithe starts to run, dragging me along. Right as I am pulled over the edge, a scream lodged in my throat, I see Tobias's face. His eyes are wide, his lips parted in shock. He pulls the reins, stopping Wyclif before he can go over the edge with us.

My eyes stay locked on his as I fall through the air. Wind whips through my hair, snapping me in the face. I can't scream. I can't even breathe.

I just fall.

My back hits the surface, knocking the air out of my lungs. Nithe's hand slips from mine and I can barely see his purple eyes in the dark waters. Bubbles escape my mouth, my body going deeper and deeper. Sunlight barely reaching me in the depths.

I can see his hand reaching for mine, but he's not close enough. His feet are kicking, his body swimming deeper and deeper, trying to reach me.

I inhale.

Water surges into my lungs, suffocating me with its salty embrace. My body convulses and I can see a purple glow spreading from Nithe's fingers to his neck before my eyes close.

Something slams into my ribs, pulling me through the depths. I vaguely feel my body being dragged against rocks before someone's hands smack my chest and warm lips press to mine. Serenity is what I feel. Peace.

But something is pounding on me, something is blowing air into my lungs. Something—

Burning liquid explodes out of my lungs as I cough. I roll onto my stomach as I inhale desperately before vomiting what little there is in my stomach.

"*Gods.*" Someone whispers, and I glance over my shoulder. Enzo is soaked, his body rippling as if he is about to shift. I hear shuffling and coughing and see Nithe out of the corner of my eyes. "What the hell happened? You were supposed to shift!" Enzo yells as I pull myself up to my knees, my breathing coming in quick pants as I try to calm the burning in my chest.

"I tried, I couldn't. Something was pushing on me, dampening my magic. I *tried*." I cough again as I sit up fully, my lungs on fire. "Are you alright?" Nithe reaches towards me, something like fear filling his eyes, and I lift a hand, sparks flying off my fingertips.

"I'm fine." My throat is scratchy, and I don't ignore Enzo's hand, offering me aid to stand. I take it, his cold palm firm in mine. He pulls me closer, his hand resting on my back. I'm grateful for his warmth as icy water penetrates every part of me.

"We need to get on the boat, and across the lake before they come." I nod and let him lead me across the sand and rocks, to the boat that is tethered to what used to be the bridge. My chest aches, my body is weak. Shivers run deep in my bones, causing uncontrollable shaking. I need rest. I need food.

I climb into the boat without hesitation, collapsing onto the bench with a gasp in pain, Nithe and Enzo close behind. I note the small satchel under the seat and a stack of blankets. Nithe climbs in, immediately going for the oar, as Enzo pushes it off the beach. He hops in before the boat floats away, coming to sit across from me.

He reaches next to my leg, and I flinch. His eyes flick to mine, but he just grabs the satchel and opens it.

"Are you hungry? We have cheese and bread." He rummages through it. "Oh, and chocolate."

"If you touch my chocolate, I will push you out of this boat and you can swim to Rakushia." Nithe pipes up from behind me, where he is steering the boat towards the center of the lake. My eyes linger on the cliff's edge, where Tobias just was. He's gone, probably trying to get down to us before we can escape. His face though, it looked as if he was scared for me. As if he cared. "Elaenor?" I flinch.

"No, thank you." I answer, wrapping my arms around myself. "He looked scared." I whisper. Enzo sighs and reaches for my hand.

"Don't worry about him right now. Worry about you. Worry about getting to safety. If he was truly scared of anything happening to you, he wouldn't have been the way he is. He wouldn't have hurt you." I stare into his green eyes, knowing that what he says is the truth, but it's hard to accept. I still believe some part of him loves me.

"How long does it take to get across the lake? Will we be fast enough?" I ask, turning my attention back to the lake.

"Like this, hours, but I'll get us across fairly quickly." My brows furrow as he smiles and releases my hand. I wrap my arms around myself.

"How?"

"Have you ever heard of a sturgeon?"

"A giant fish that could probably eat a man, yes I have heard of it." I retort. His smile grows as he unlaces his boots.

"Want to see one?"

"Not really." I mutter, watching as he pulls his boots off, and then his socks, water dripping from them. "What are you doing?" He stands and winks before diving into the water. I glance back at Nithe, who is throwing a rope in the deep water, and pulling the oar out. I wait a few seconds before I peer over. "He isn't surfacing." Nithe ignores me and I can feel my pulse start to race. "Nithe, he isn't surfacing!" My voice raises and I stand, searching the dark waters for him. "Nithe—" The boat jerks and I fall forward. I suck in a breath right before I hit the water, but I never do.

A strong grip holds onto my arm, yanking me back into the boat. I fall against the seat, my spine instantly cramping. I clamor up, making sure the cloak is covering my legs. I glare at Nithe, who is pulling out a chunk of chocolate.

"You could have been more gentle." I snap.

"I also could have let you fall in the water, but I didn't." The boat starts to move quickly, water streaming behind us in waves. "Before you ask, yes. Enzo is down there as a fish pulling the boat, so I don't have to paddle for the next two days."

"Can he breathe under there?" I say, curiosity peaked.

"When he shifts, his lungs do too. He can breathe just as well as he would as a person on land." His eyes are focused on his chocolate, as he breaks the block into bite sized pieces with weird precision and concentration. I bite my lower lip and work up the courage to ask what I am really curious about.

"What can *you* shift into?" His chewing stops, as do his hands as he looks up at me.

"What?"

"Can you shift into a sturgeon too?" He swallows and tosses the chocolate back into the bag. He leans forward, his elbows on his knees, and I fight the urge to retreat. The distance between us shrinks as the boat suddenly feels too small.

"Who says I can shift into anything?" I suck on my bottom lip as I try to form a rational thought, but nothing comes to mind. His narrowed eyes don't look angry, they look curious.

"Your eyes, before, they turned black. And your skin had this purplish glow to it. And I remember this beast breathing fire. Enzo said you were supposed to shift—I just assumed."

"Well, assumptions are rarely correct." He leans back and props his feet up on the seat next to me.

"Then what are you?" I press.

"Tired, little witch." His voice trails off, disinterested as he stares at me. His eyes roam over me, assessing, before he smirks.

"Why are you calling me that?" I snap.

"You are a witch, and in case you weren't aware of your body size, you are very little. Little. Witch. It's really not that hard."

"I don't like it."

"How about Rosie?"

"Excuse me?"

"Your last name is Rosenthal, is it not?" He says as if I'm stupid, as if I don't know my own name.

"Well, yes—" I stammer.

"Do I need to explain this one too?" I clamp my mouth shut and wrap my arms around myself, shivers setting in from the wet clothes. I glare at him with the miniscule amount of energy I have left.

"No." I whisper after a second of silence. He grabs a blanket and wraps it around me, his fingers brushing my shoulders, before returning to his chocolate. I look at him, at the furrow in his brow. The concentration as he sorts through the food. Something about him feels different.

Feels familiar.

I pull the blanket tighter around me as I look away from him.

My eyes trail back to my left, where the Chatisian ruins sit. I can almost picture what it looked like before.

Before Tobias.

I don't even think I remember what before Tobias was like.

Chapter Thirty

The Caged
Ten Years Ago

"Your Grace! You were supposed to be up hours ago!" Blankets are ripped off of me and I groan. My eyes open to the bright light and stare at my ladies maid, or my *nanny* as my father calls her. Estelle is a plump, stout woman who has wrinkles permanently etched into her face from the frown that is always present.

"Leave me be, Estelle. There is nothing that demands my presence today." I snap as I pull the blankets back over my face.

"That is where you are wrong, princess! You have guests that will be arriving any moment." She rips the blankets back off of me and I sit up. My unruly curls falling in front of my face in a frizzy mane. I push it out of my eyes and glare at her.

Her gray dress is long, covering her from neck to feet. It's of a thin cotton with white lace detailing towards the hem. She dresses as if she's a woman of the church. Her gray hair is pulled back in a bonnet, not a single hair out of place. I scowl and she glares at me.

"Wipe that look off your face or it will get stuck like that." She snaps as she steps into my dressing room. I groan again and throw myself back onto the bed.

"Who is coming on such an awful day?" I yell after her. Today marks two years since my mother was murdered and Kassius was blamed. I hear the rumors that it wasn't him, but no one knows for sure. The only person who should is me, but I don't remember anything. I don't remember any of that day.

"The Noterran King will be here any moment." She yells back. I shoot up.

"Will the princes be joining him?" I call after her. I have known of my engagement to the crown prince of Noterra for years. Even at nine years of age, I know of my responsibility. I am terrified that I will be sent off to live in Noterra any day now. I swallow down my fear and slide off the bed, stepping into the dressing room.

"No, just the king." She replies as she pushes past me, a mound of blue in her arms. She throws the dress on the bed and motions for me to walk over. I hold my arms up like normal as she rips my nightgown off. The puffy dress is slipped over my head, and I turn to face the chair, gripping onto the back. This has become a routine, one I despise, but one that is required of me.

She pulls at the laces, and I gasp as the corset squeezes my ribs. I force myself to take short, slow breaths as she ties the corset as tight as it will possibly go. Another skirt is wrapped around my waist and tied into place. I can barely breathe and barely move, but that's the norm around here.

"Why is he coming today of all days, Estelle?" I ask as I collapse into the vanity chair, the skirts poofing up and nearly covering my face. I slam them back down into my lap with a sigh.

"He wants to pay his respects to your mother." I wince as she rips the brush from my hair. "Gods, child. You slept in too long, and I don't know what I am going to do with this hair!" She scowls at me in the mirror, and I smile back at her, my dimples coming through my round cheeks. Her face softens as she stares at me. "All will be well, princess." I nod and she squeezes my shoulders before gathering my hair up in a braided coronet.

Once I am readied, I am shoved out of my room, the giant dress feeling like a weight as I drag it across the stone floors.

"Where are the others?" I ask Estelle as she guides me down the hallway.

"They have been asked to stay out of the palace today."

"Why?" I press as we descend.

"I am unsure, it was a request of your father's." I frown at her as we reach the bottom floor. Flowers overflow from the vase at the entry table, the doors open to show a particularly nice summer day. Estelle's grip is firm as she pulls me into the throne room.

My father's gaze instantly hardens as he stares at me. His chestnut eyes seem black from this distance, his skin pale. He looks tired. I bow slightly before racing up the dais to take my place behind his throne.

"Once again you are late, Elaenor." He sneers at me over his shoulder. His green cloak with a silver collar is flowing over the armrests of the stone throne. Vines made of silver cord spread from his shoulders down, sparkling in the light filtering in from the windows. His crown is off-center, and I reach froward to straighten it. He looks over and his eyes soften just a hair before I clamp my hands back in front of me.

"I apologize, father." I reply. Silence ensues as we listen to the horses coming up the long drive. Gravel crunches under heavy-footed boots before turning into an echoing slap of leather on stone. My breath hitches as the king steps through the doors.

His hair is a beautiful golden color, his eyes so blue they glow across the vast room. His cloak is a deep blood red, his tunic underneath a silky black, matching his trousers and knee-high leather boots. He has a huge blade strapped to his hip, the tip nearly brushing the floor. He has a smirk plastered to his lips as he crosses the distance. He doesn't stop and bow like one should, instead he climbs the dais and stops directly in front of my father.

"Viktor, it has been too long." King Evreux says in a voice that sounds like nails on stone. My father stands and offers his hand to him. Their heights are parallel, standing over six feet tall. I can see anger in their eyes, mirroring each other. They could be twins if it weren't for the differences in hair and eyes. The king steps away from my father and looks at me.

"Princess. You grow even more beautiful as the years pass." He reaches for my hand, and I hesitantly place my fingers in his palm. He leans down and kisses the top of my hand, his eyes never leaving mine. Hot breath fans across my arm and I shiver.

"Your Grace, your compliment is appreciated." I reply before curtsying slightly. He smiles and releases me.

"I would like to visit her." He says, and I know he means my mother.

"I will escort you—"

"No. Elaenor will do it." He glances back at me. "Isn't that right?"

"It would be my honor." I reply, bowing my head slightly. I swallow the lump in my throat and take his outstretched arm. I guide him through the doors and down the hallway to the stairs that lead down. I pause, hesitant to descend, but his grip on my arm pulls me forward.

He's silent as we enter the underground tomb beneath the mountain palace. Torches line the walls, illuminating stone coffins and statues filling the space. All of the Pinewell's are buried here, however I won't be. I'll be buried in Noterra someday.

We walk over to the very back wall where a stone carving of my mother sits next to a large stone coffin. Tears prick my eyes and I glance away, focusing on the orange lights dancing along the gray stone.

"My son asks about you often. He wonders when you will be coming to stay?" The king asks as he releases my arm. I clamp my hands together in front of me.

"Whenever my father allows, I will be honored to live in your beautiful country." I reply softly, keeping my eyes downcast.

"You would, wouldn't you?" He snorts. "Tell me, child, are you happy here?"

"My father is a kind and gracious king. His kingdom brings me much happiness—"

"Do you say everything as if it's rehearsed?" He responds, turning away from me. His hand lifts before his fingers gently brush the stone version of my mother's cheek.

"I apologize, Your Grace."

"Your mother was a wonderful woman. Bright, untamed, erratic. She reminded me of freedom, of youth. Your father took that from her. He turned her into a scared and quiet queen who feared for her life. Sending her to him was my greatest regret." I stay quiet. Sending her to him? Is he the reason my parents married?

He sighs and steps up to the coffin, resting his hand atop it.

"You look just like her, Elaenor. I hope that you will be to Tobias what Sybil should have been to me."

"And what is that?" I ask, tilting my head in confusion.

"My salvation."

Chapter Thirty-One

The Caged

The memory barrels through me and I awake with a jolt. The sun is directly overhead and Nithe is leaning back, his eyes closed. I sit up, rubbing my eyes. Exhaustion pulls at me, beckoning to take over, but I force it down with a cough.

Evreux said I was to be his son's salvation. Did he know of the darkness inside of him? Did he know what he was going to become?

It feels as if no time has passed before we near the edge of Rakushia. I spent most of the journey looking over my shoulder, convinced that Tobias would be sailing across the waters with an army before I eventually fell asleep. But we met no resistance as we sailed, and I don't know why that bothers me. Shouldn't I be grateful?

A large splash to my right interrupting the silence makes me flinch as Enzo's head surfaces. His black hair is wet and plastered to his forehead, his smile wide and playful as he looks up at me.

"I'm going to need a very long nap after this." He says loudly as he pulls himself into the boat, soaking me again in the process. He grabs a blanket and wipes his face before wrapping it around himself. "You can row the rest of the way." He says as he kicks Nithe's foot off the bench. He groans and pulls himself up, snatching the oar into his hands.

"What do you eat?" I ask, mostly wondering if he eats in his animal form.

"Food, usually. A maiden preferably." My mouth falls open and Nithe barks out a laugh.

"I wouldn't think Sca—" Enzo's eyes widen and his arm whips out, hitting Nithe in the stomach and sending him tumbling over the side of the boat and into the water, the oar flying into the air.

"Enzo!" I gasp as I jump off the bench.

"Man, what the hell." I reach my hand out to assist Nithe, but he slaps it out of the way, pulling himself in. Far off laughing has me spinning around. Soft and feminine.

A sound I know.

I squint my eyes as I look at the shore. The span of white beach belonging to Rakushia. I can just make out a few figures, one of which has long chestnut hair blowing in the wind. My pulse skips.

"Is that..." I ask as I nearly fall to my knees. Tears well up in my eyes and I grip the side of the boat.

"They have probably been waiting for us all night." Enzo says softly.

"Oh my god." I clamp my hand over my mouth to suppress the sob making its way up my throat.

Scarlett. *Alive*. Unharmed and waiting for me.

Twin, golden buns atop a female head, standing next to Scarlett. *Emery*. Also alive.

Someone with dark hair cropped short, tall and standing a bit farther back. He seems stoic, careful. A smaller figure holding his hand, light hair in a braid over her shoulder. My body is shaking as we grow closer, as I start to see details.

It is then that I notice the man holding the little girl's hand is Kassius. The prophet who befriended my mother. The one who was beheaded for her murder.

The man who looks nearly *identical* to Enzo.

My lips part and my hand falls away as I stare at him, his yellow eyes getting clearer as Nithe rows us closer. My gaze stays fixed on his, and his on mine.

We hit the beach, but no one moves. No one says anything, except him.

"Hello, Nora." He says, a small smile crinkling the corners of his eyes, the eyes that look much older than they did when I saw him last. When I saw him for the last time over ten years ago.

"Kassius." I whisper. Enzo steps out, holding his hand out for me, but I don't move. I can barely breathe. "I don't understand."

"He's my father." Enzo says quietly, and my gaze snaps to his.

"What?" My mouth hangs open in disbelief. "Your father?" Nithe climbs out of the boat and treks up the wet sand to throw his dripping arms around Emery, hugging her tight.

"I told you I wouldn't get myself killed." He laughs and she hits his back as she pulls away.

"I'm glad." She smiles at him, affection brewing deep in her eyes. I glance down at Enzo's hand still in the air waiting to help me out, but I ignore it. Throwing a leg over the side of the boat, I climb out on my own.

The white sand is cool, soft, as I take a few slow steps. I can see Scarlett practically vibrating in the peripherals of my vision, but I can't look away from Kassius. The man who used to sit with me when I was a child, who would explore with my mother and I as we ran through the trees.

The man I never thought I'd see again.

"I was told you were murdered for the death of my mother. I cried every night knowing that my mother and the closest thing I have ever had to a real father, was dead." My voice is weak, strained, as I stare into his yellow eyes. Tears drip down my cheeks. "But here you are."

"I came back a few years ago. I came to see you, but you were asleep in the infirmary. Scarlett was there." My eyes flash to hers quickly before going back to him. "I wanted to make sure you were alright."

"I wasn't." I snap.

"I know." He says softly.

"You knew what he was doing to me, my father. You knew what Tobias was doing. All of you did. None of you did anything. None of you." My voice cracks and my hand flies to my mouth.

"Nora," he steps forward, his hand gripping onto the little girl who is staring at me with wide, yellow eyes.

"Don't. I don't want anything from you. I don't want anything from any of you. I wanted to be left alone, to be done. I was ready for it to be over. You never protected me, you never came for me, and when I *finally* accepted my fate, you took that away too." I take a step to my left, my hand reaching for Scarlett's. I hear her exhale in relief as she takes it and pulls me into her side. "I don't care what you want from me, you can't have it. There is only one thing I want in this world, and it's to rip Tobias's heart from his chest. I won't let you take that away from me too." I start walking, pulling Scarlett with me, as we trek up the beach to the path between the hills. I don't know where we are going, but I have to get away from all of them.

She doesn't speak, but I can tell she wants to. She keeps my hand in hers as we silently walk. My tears dry on my cheeks, the air warm and suffocatingly sweet. She guides us through the hills and within minutes they open up to a huge stone and wood palace.

It's not grand like Noterra, but it's still large. A half wall encircles the entire building. I can see guards with bright gold cloaks and silver armor lining the top of it. Horses are tied to stalls outside the palace. Small windows line the outside of the building, reflecting the bright sunlight. There are trees everywhere, but not as dense as home. Purple flowers hang from branches like vines, their scent almost too much. I hear someone sneeze behind me, and I flinch.

"*Damnit.*" Nithe mutters and I hear Emery laugh.

Anger is all I can feel right now. Anger and betrayal. It's not their fault, but I can't help but blame them, *hate* them, for not doing anything. For not stepping in.

But why would they?

They don't owe me anything.

"It's been over seven months since you were supposed to be here." Scar's voice is soft, hesitant.

"Seven months?" I whisper. "What day is it?" I ask, although I don't know if I really want to know. She doesn't respond for a second, so I turn to face her. Her skin is tan, tanner than I have ever seen it. Her hair is long and loose, silky and shiny like always. Her brown eyes are ringed in gold, sparkling in the sun. She's wearing a gray dress that hangs off her in billowy folds. She looks healthy, happy even. I smile slightly at her appearance.

"It's a few days past your birthday, Elaenor. It's the end of July." She says quietly. My smile falls as a choked sob escapes my lips and I clamp my hand over my mouth, my gaze holding hers in disbelief. The tears come and they don't stop. I start to shake, guttural sobs breaking up the silence. My legs give out and I land on my knees. Dirt and grass press into my skin, aggravating the cuts marring my knees.

It has been one year since I left home.

One *whole* year and yet nothing has gotten better.

Everything has gotten worse.

She drops down to the ground with me, her arms wrapping around my shoulders, pulling me into her chest. She squeezes me tight, and then I feel her shaking. She's crying too.

Another set of thin arms wrap around me as I cry harder than I ever have. As I cry for the person I never had the chance to become. The version of myself I will never know. I open my eyes to a set of light brown lined with silver and thick lashes.

Laenie.

We cry, together. All three of us. Cry for the year that has changed everything. Cry for the deaths that have occurred. Cry for the children we once were. I don't know how long we stay here, crumpled on the dirt hugging each other. I pull back first, my arms going around Laenie as I hold her close.

When I let go, I look around and see that everyone has left us. Everyone but one person.

Ginger hair sparkles in the sun, resembling flames. Pale skin and broad shoulders. A forest green hilt attached to a silver sword hanging off his belt. Another sob works its way out of my throat. A sob coated in disbelief.

In confusion.

Erik.

I push off the ground and run, barreling into his chest and nearly taking him out. His arms wrap around me, and his head buries in my hair. I can feel his body shaking as he holds on tight. He's warm, and whole, and *alive.*

"I am so sorry, Elaenor." He cries as he squeezes me tighter. I shake my head, emotions flooding through me like a tidal wave.

Everything has changed. Everything.

The walk to the palace is quick, as we stride hand in hand through the stone wall. Armed guards are running about, making sure everything is safe. I'm assuming Nithe or Enzo alerted them that Tobias might attack in order to retrieve me, but I don't think he actually will.

Why would he?

The grounds are filled with lush grass and wildflowers of every color. Nothing is dull, or drab. Everything is bright, welcoming. It reminds me of my mother somehow. Noterra wasn't drab by any means, but it was just green. Here, flowers of species I didn't know existed bloom freely. Wisteria trees press up against the palace walls, vines attaching themselves to the stone.

It's beautiful. A place I wouldn't be opposed to calling home if the circumstances were different.

Everyone stares as we near the open double doors, the pale wood bright in the sunlight. Scarlett's hand tightens in mine as Laenie lets go, stepping back to walk with Erik.

Confusion and surprise echo around the open halls as servants and guards catch sight of me, of the mess I am. They all bow and whisper as we step inside. I have no doubt my inky tendrils are caked with dirt and blood and a mess only a hairbrush and scissors can fix. Not to mention that I was naked aside from a cloak.

Scarlett leads me to a staircase, pulling me up it and down a thin hall. We move slowly as pain radiates down my leg and exhaustion pulls at me. Doors line either side, and an open archway shows a small library with plush couches and settees around a fireplace. We walk in silence as she guides me to a door that is slightly ajar. She squeezes my hand before pushing it open.

The room isn't grand by any means, the same size as my room in Chatis. Pale wooden walls are covered in torches and wildflower paintings. A plush bed sits on one side, gray and green blankets and wools draped over the thick mattress. A sitting room sits on one side, with a settee and sofa. The fireplace is lit, the flames warming the room almost too much for the season.

The back wall is covered in floor-to-ceiling windows, one of which is open, leading to a balcony. Another door sits off the room, leading to what I assume is the bathing chamber.

"This is your room. Emery and I have made sure it remained ready for you." Scarlett says softly. I take a step forward, my hand sliding from hers as I reach for the gray wool on the bed. My fingers slip through the fur, which is soft like silk.

"I don't understand any of this." I whisper.

"There is a lot you don't know." Enzo pipes up from behind me and I spin around. He's leaning against the doorway, his hands gripping the top of the frame. Laenie and Erik have slipped away, leaving me with Scarlett. Scarlett looks over at him, her eyes darkening as she rolls her lips. I've seen that look before.

"You two?" I ask, my voice cracking. Her eyes widen and she bites her bottom lip as she looks back at me.

"It's complicated." Enzo responds, sparing Scarlett the embarrassment. I take a slow deep breath, confused by the feelings whipping through my mind. I just nod.

"I would like to bathe and then I would like someone to explain what the hell is going on." I don't wait for a response as I walk over to the closed door, thankfully opening it up to reveal a large bathing room with a tub big enough to fit four, and closing it behind me.

Three separate women came in, assisting me in the bath. The water turned a cloudy shade of brown as all of the grime and blood was washed from my skin. My leg burned as the hot water washed over the mottled flesh. They kept sending glances to one another as they found cuts and bruises and scar after scar. They didn't speak, but I could tell they were concerned.

My hair was gently shampooed, and I nearly fell asleep at the feel of it, but my eyes stayed open, fixed on the wall across from me. I could tell they had to be careful to work around the crown. I almost asked them to remove it, but maybe it would be better done by a master or a mender.

I can feel exhaustion ravaging through my bones, but I can't sleep. Not yet. Not until I know it's safe. Adrenaline pumps steadily through my veins, keeping me awake, keeping me coherent. But it will soon run out and a dreamless sleep will be soon to follow.

The women dabbed a thick white cream onto my leg before wrapping it in a white cloth. They applied the same cream to my neck and feet, wrapping them as well. While they seemed to know what they were doing, I was still convinced I needed proper medical care. I had to ask for the master, they have to have one in the palace somewhere.

I was grateful when I was given a tunic and a pair of leggings, wanting nothing less than to be in a dress. I slipped the soft cotton on quickly before turning to the mirror to assess my appearance.

A strangled cry escapes my throat as I take an unsteady step back. The hair that I expected to be dark and coiled, was anything but. Icy locks that are soaked and dripping water down my back greet me instead. The color reminds me of the moon, of the white sand at the beach. Not a single black hair falls from my head, it is all just white. My eyes are bloodshot, the blue too bright for what I was used to. My skin is sallow and gaunt, my cheekbones looking too high and too sharp for the thin face that is staring back at me. The silver of the crown seems dull in comparison to the hair I didn't expect.

I don't understand.

I walk up to the mirror, my hand shakily reaching up to touch the strands that resembled my mother's the day she died. When did this happen? Why did this happen?

"It was white when we found you." I jump and whirl around to see Nithe standing in the doorway. His black hair is wet, flopping into his eyes. He changed into a gray tunic and a fresh pair of pants. His arms are crossed in front of his chest as he watches me. I can see dark ink wrapped around his forearms, disappearing into his sleeves. Swirls and scales of different sizes inked into his flesh. I tear my eyes away from them and meet his purple gaze.

"I don't know how." I respond, my voice weak, exhausted.

"I am under the assumption that it happened when your magic finally revealed itself."

"Well, assumptions are rarely correct." I respond softly, quoting him. His eyes widen in surprise before a ghost of a smile passes his lips. It falls quickly and he clears his throat.

"If you are ready, the king would like to speak to you." I turn back to the mirror. I look just as weak as I feel. I look broken. Used. And I was.

Time and time again.

But not anymore.

I force myself to look away as I nod.

Chapter Thirty-Two

The Caged

I'm quiet as I follow Nithe down the hallway and staircase I first went up. He doesn't say anything about the slower speed I force us to walk, or the limp that's present. He stays silent. He almost grabs my arm to guide me as we reach the bottom floor and go down another expansive hallway lined in pale wood, but he stops himself. We reach a room, a room that is familiar. I stop as I look at the wooden table and the graying man sitting at the head of it.

A sight I've seen before.

"I saw you. I saw all of this when Tobias was sewing the crown to my head." My hand slowly reaches up out of habit, my fingers brushing the cold metal. The man I am assuming is the Labisian King is just staring at me. His dark eyes are set in stone, set in cruelty. His aging face is wrinkled, his brows permanently furrowed. He's gripping a glass of amber liquid tightly in one hand, his yellow cloak almost covering every inch of his skin.

"Sit." Is all he says, his voice loud and commanding. I do as he asks and slowly sit down in the chair in front of me. I stare at the man from across the table just as intently as he stares at me. "You seem *better* than I thought you would be."

"What did you expect?" I respond just as sternly.

"I expected someone broken without a shred of sanity." He says with disdain as if the idea of me not being a mindless troll is disgusting to him. I squeeze my sweaty hands under the table, willing myself to be strong.

"Sorry to disappoint." Nithe clears his throat loudly, covering up a snort as he sits in the chair next to me.

"There is a lot we must discuss, but first," he holds out his hand and a man appears with a large piece of parchment. The page is bright, crisp as he looks it over, as if he is reading through it one more time. I glance to my right to see Nithe's hands tighten into fists. Where is everyone else? Enzo, or Kassius? Why is it just us three?

"Father, must we do this now? So soon? Shouldn't we talk first?" Nithe asks and I nearly jump. Father? Nithe is the Prince of Labisa? My eyes widen and he looks over at me, his face twisted up into a pained expression. As if what is coming next also affects him.

I was right. I guessed he had to be of noble birth, but this? This isn't what I expected. I was told that the true heir, the Labisian King, was the one who sent those men in the woods. Does Nithe know about that? Was he in on the plan to murder me? Panic courses through my veins as everything clicks into place. As every fear and every bit of anger starts to fall into place.

"What is that?" I ask, my nails digging into my palms as they fidget on my lap. I try to hide the fury in my voice, but they can hear it. I know they can.

"This, *princess*, is your marriage certificate." My eyes widen even further, and my mouth falls open as he looks up at me. I watch as he stands and makes his way over to my side of the table. The king places one of his hands on my shoulder as he leans in close, setting the certificate in front of me. I want to flinch away from his touch, but all I can do is stare.

My eyes are fixed on my signature at the bottom, Tobias's right next to mine. The Noterran crest pressed into red wax. This truly is our marriage certificate.

"I don't understand." His fingers flex, digging into my skin and I shift nervously. I glance up at Nithe, whose eyes are focused on his father's hand, his pupils darkening.

"Father Reynolds is a close personal friend of Rakushia, of *Thelonious*. After your marriage to Tobias, he brought this certificate to us." Tears well up in my eyes as I push the parchment away from me.

"What are you going to do with it?" My voice wavers as I speak.

"Elaenor," Nithe speaks up. "This is the only copy. If we burn this, your marriage is annulled. You will not be wed to Tobias anymore." I open and close my mouth, words failing me as I process what he's saying. I won't have to be his wife, his property anymore?

"But why? Why are you doing this?" I ask, my voice cracking. I clear my throat and take a deep breath before speaking again. "Why do you care who I am married to?"

"Because, *princess*, I want you to marry my son." His fingers flex on my skin and I close my eyes, trying to ignore the warmth soaking into my flesh.

"But, *why*? You tried to kill me." I ask again. His hand slides off my shoulder, almost hesitatingly, as he makes his way back around the table.

"I don't know what you are talking about." He says slowly as he smirks.

"The men in the woods, that was you." I saw slowly.

"What are you talking about?" Nithe asks.

"And when I crossed the border last year, men in cloaks ripped me from my horse. Drugged me—"

"These accusations—" He cuts me off.

"Are not accusations! They are facts. Those men told me who sent them. Who they were supporting. Why would you do that? I had done nothing to you."

"You were supposed to be brought here. Safely." He retorts. I can feel heat spreading through my veins. Heat ready to defend me.

"I don't believe you!" I yell.

"Father, what did you do?" Nithe stands, his voice loud and commanding.

"You belong to us, Elaenor! And it was only a matter of time before you arrived." *Belong*? I belong to no one.

"You are *deranged*!"

"You are not just the heir to Chatis, *child*! You are not just the once-queen of Noterra. You are the heir to it all, and if you want my support, *my* armies, you will ensure my bloodline is the one flowing through your children's veins." This conversation triggers a sense of deja-vu as I stare at the king. As I stare at yet another jailer. A jailer who never cared about my safety, just my presence.

"I don't know who you think I am—"

"Do you know who your father is?" He snaps. His hands digging into the wood of the table.

"Viktor, he is my fa—"

"No, he isn't, stupid girl, and you know that. You know who he is, you just haven't admitted it to yourself." My palms tingle and I can feel my pulse quicken.

"Don't speak to me—"

"Think!" He yells as he cuts me off again. My vision turns white in my peripherals and his eyes widen. I can't help the tingling spreading through my veins, igniting my limbs. I can feel the scream building in my throat, the scream that will ignite everything in this room.

"Little witch." Nithe warns and I look at him. He reaches for my hand, but his eyes snap up to the space above me. A warm, callused grip wraps around the back of my neck and the tingling fades, the light going with it. I gasp as everything dissipates, taking my anger with it.

"Why didn't you wait for me?" Enzo snaps as his hand releases my neck. I take a slow deep breath as he steps around the chair to my left. The veins in his right hand are white, glowing through his skin, and I watch as they dull until they are gone.

"What did you do to me?" I whisper, my voice barely audible.

"I don't owe you anything, boy." The king bellows, both of them ignoring me. Enzo says something before Nithe pipes up from my right. My eyes are flicking back and forth from Enzo's hand and the parchment as they all yell at one another, their voices drowning out into a dull buzz.

This is too much. I can't handle this. Too many people. Too many voices. My palms are slick against my leggings, and I can feel the sweat dripping down my neck. I close my eyes willing the paranoia, the *panic*, building in my chest to dissipate, but it doesn't.

I need to get out of here.

I shoot out of my chair, knocking it over, and run out of the room. The hallways are filled with too many people. They all stare at me, stuck between awe and fear. I want to scream.

I want to *explode*.

My breath comes in quick pants as I try to navigate my way outside. My shoes slap the stone floors as I turn and see an open door. I bolt towards it, relishing in the cool air as it flows across my skin. I keep running until I am near the palace walls.

I scream. The sound strained, and pathetic, but with the scream comes a release of power. Lightning shoots off my hands, hitting the stone. Sparks fly all around me, coating the dew-covered grass. I scream until I run out of breath and then it stops.

The light.

The power.

The pain.

Whatever it is, it just stops.

I place my hand on the stone in front of me, and then my forehead. It's silent, aside from the sound of birds chirping, wind rustling leaves, and the chatter of people walking about. But it's silent besides that. No loud noises. No fighting.

No sound of swords slamming into armor.

I don't know what I expected, but it wasn't this.

"You came here a few times when you were younger. Do you remember that?" Kassius speaks up from behind me and I take a deep breath. I step back from the stone wall and turn to face him. The little girl that was with him earlier is gone, leaving the two of us alone. His eyes are soft, expressionless. His hands clasped behind his back.

"I remember coming with my father once." I respond, out of breath.

"You came here with me and your mother quite a bit. You and Emery played when you were little. I think Nithe was here a few times too."

"Was Enzo?" I ask, wondering if I ever met him before.

"No, not when you were."

"I was told I spent a lot of time in Noterra as a child, that I grew up with Theo and Tobias, but I don't remember it."

"One of the gifts your mother had, as well as you I am assuming, is memory alteration. She took those memories from you. She was afraid Viktor would use them against you." My mother *took* my memories.

"That doesn't make sense."

"There is much you don't know."

"Everyone keeps saying that." He's silent for a second as he walks closer. His gaze snags on my hair and he reaches up slowly, fingering a lock in between his fingers.

"What would you like to know?" He says after a second.

"Why is my hair white?"

"Do you remember your mother's hair before she died?" I swallow the lump in my throat. *Oh gods.*

"Am I dying?" He smiles softly and drops his hand.

"Her hair wasn't white because she was dying, it was white because of her aether." His hands clasp behind his back again as he stares at me.

"She had the lightning too?" I ask.

"It's not lightning, Nora, it's *starlight*. What you are harnessing may look like lightning, but have you seen how it sparkles? It's starlight."

"Starlight." I mimic softly.

"Your mother had moonlight. It manifested like a mist or a wave of aether, not like yours." He shakes his head.

"How does that turn my hair white?"

"When you are at your strongest, your aether will manifest in different ways. For you, and your mother, your body slowly succumbs to that magic. It isn't a bad thing; it just means you're strong. Very strong." He smiles again.

"I don't feel strong." I mutter.

"I know Enzo appeared to you a few times, but do you remember his hair?" He tilts his head to the side, watching me.

"It was black, with a white streak. Was that his aether?"

"He doesn't have aether, but what you two have is a bond. That aether was being funneled into the bond instead of through you. It was turning his hair white instead of yours." He explains softly, but without prejudice. He doesn't sound irritated about my questions, he seems understanding.

"I don't understand. It's black now."

"Because you aren't connected anymore. Nora, when you are in danger, or when you are weak, you can channel Enzo, and he can channel you. When that bond breaks, or if you don't need to channel his strength, you can use your aether." He walks around me to lean against the wall.

"But how did our bond break?"

"Do you remember a piece of glass shaped like an arrowhead you found while in Chatis?" I nod.

"The one Theo made into a dagger." I recall quietly.

"Yes. It's sirenstone. It was made using his blood and a special crystal you can only get in Vodia. When you bled on it, it allowed your bond to become stronger. He could appear to you as if he were standing there in front of you. When the stone broke, it weakened your connection to one another."

"This is so confusing." I groan, defeat and resignation filling my mind.

"I know, it'll be a lot to absorb." We are both quiet for a second. "A few months ago, the white in Enzo's hair disappeared. We thought you were dead. We didn't know, or even think, that you were strong enough to not need him."

"How could I have possibly been strong? I was being drugged and tortured—" My voice cracks and my eyes widen as I turn to face him. "Tobias. He said that he was replacing my cells, healing me every single night with his own magic. He said he was constantly remaking me to be whole again." I admit. It can't be...

"He's young, and inexperienced. He probably was making you stronger every time he did it." Kassius says matter-of-factly. As if the idea of Tobias healing me isn't at all shocking.

"He didn't even flinch when I snapped." I say softly.

"Your starlight isn't enough to hurt him."

"What is he?" I ask, almost hesitantly. I don't know if I want to know.

"He's cursed." He offers, saying it as if I'd know what that means.

"What does that even mean?" My voice is little more than a whine, but he doesn't seem to mind. He steps away from the wall and holds his arm out, gesturing back towards the palace.

"Come, there are some things that I have to share with Enzo, too."

Chapter Thirty-Three

The Caged

I follow him back into the palace. Our footsteps silent as we walk. He doesn't take me back to the council room, but instead, takes me upstairs to the library. Enzo is already in there, Scarlett perched on his lap. Her eyes focused on him, as if she was afraid she'd never get the chance to see him again. I can't imagine that type of love, that type of devotion. I had it for Tobias, but receiving it? I ruined my only chance by not believing Theo, and now look where I am.

I look away from them and my gaze snags on Nithe. He's leaning against the window, his eyes filled with shadows. As if he's having a rough day. Or maybe he's just tired. I think we all are.

Kassius gestures for me to sit and I do, taking the remaining settee for myself. He stays standing and I pull my legs up to my chest, wrapping my arms around them. I wince as the burn on my leg rubs against the leggings. I need to find their master or whatever mender they have available. I need to be checked over. I feel ill, as if something is eating away at my insides. Maybe it's exhaustion or anxiety, but I feel like something is wrong.

"There are some things that I haven't shared with any of you. Things that only a few others know, Dav and Thel being two of them." He says, referencing the Rakushian and Labisian kings. Which reminds me—what happened to Thelonious? I open my mouth to speak, but Kassius continues. "I have my reasons for why I didn't share this with any of you, but it's time you know." He looks at me and then to Enzo. "Especially you two." He turns back to me. "This story spans 20 years, but it'll answer a question that has been bothering you for over a decade."

"What?" I ask.

"Who killed your mother."

"I assumed it was my father–Viktor?" He shakes his head and I glance over at Nithe, who is watching silently, avoiding my gaze.

"Your mother and Amaya, Tobias's mother, were childhood best friends. They met when Sybil was about two or three, well, we were all that age." All? I open my mouth to interject, but he cuts me off. "They were close, closer than siblings. I think on some unconscious level, they loved each other. Amaya's father worked for Sybil's mother. Sybil's mother, your grandmother, she is High Witch of Zivell, she reigns over the land of magic and aether. Amaya's family were not born witches, but they wanted magic, they wanted power, so they took it. It is not common for siphons to be born, much less one who could siphon magic and then transfer it to someone else, but they found one.

"They found someone who could pull from the lands and redistribute that magic. So they did it, and Amaya's parents stole from the very ground our world was built on. Amaya wasn't born yet, but when she was, she was gifted as well. It took a very long time for your grandmother to figure out the blight placed on the lands, why everyone's magic seemed to dampen almost instantaneously, but when she did, she killed Amaya's parents. See, the land always needs balance, everything does. So instead of pure aether, Amaya's parents were cursed. While the blight on the land reversed and everything seemed fine, they passed that curse onto Amaya.

"She was nearly ten the first time her curse appeared. Sybil's magic was silver, bright, so much so that she was called Moonlight. You see, all aether is pulled from something, some *form* of energy. Sybil got hers from the moon, you got yours from the stars, Nora, and your grandmother pulled hers from flames. Firelight." *Firelight*. "Amaya's magic was dark, fueled by hatred, greed, and shadows. In order to keep her safe, she needed the curse siphoned away. She needed me. Your mother and I, we are twins, and one of the small magics I was born with, was siphoning." My mouth falls open and I glance over at Enzo, whose eyes are just as wide. Twins?

Enzo is my *cousin*.

"We fell in love. I siphoned away the curse on a routine basis, so the High Witch, my mother, never found out and Amaya stayed powerless and happy, but she was sold. Our mother needed an alliance in the north, so she sold Amaya to the Rosenthal's, whose family was the richest in Noterra. They were just lords at that time. Sybil met Archie right before Amaya left, and after some convincing, their engagement became a political alliance that was unforeseen but welcomed. They were engaged for nearly a year before Jahara was murdered. They were set to get married right after, but that never happened." He paused and looked over at me.

"My mother was pregnant when he died, wasn't she?" My voice is soft, quiet as the pieces start to fall into place. My grandfather was High King Jahara, and my father was his heir, Argent Nottingham. Which means I am the heir. The heir to *everything*.

"Yes. Pregnant with twins." Twins? I sit up, my legs dropping back to the ground, shock pummeling through me. "She was sold by Evreux to Viktor, and they wed within days of Archie's murder. But she knew whose children were in her. She knew all along."

"I have a sibling out there?" I whisper. I have a brother or a sister somewhere in the world. *Wait*. He hesitates for a moment before he looks at

Enzo. Scarlett's hand flies up to cover her mouth as we all stare at him. "Enzo—he's my brother?" Kass nods and Enzo lets out a trapped breath, silence filling the room. Argent, *King* Argent was my—*our*—father. And Enzo is my *brother*. Nausea spreads through my belly and I fight the urge to be sick.

"My father—you aren't my father?" Enzo's voice is thick, as he fights through the lump growing in his throat. His hand finds Scarlett's and she squeezes it.

"My gods." She whispers as she looks at me.

"So I am the heir? Or we are the heirs? Enzo and I?" I ask.

"Yes, *you* are the heir to the entire continent. King Jahara was more than just Noterra's king, every kingdom answered to him. That only dissolved when he died, but he was High King, and you will be High Queen."

"Why can't Enzo do it?" Scarlett asks and I glance over at her. "No offense." She says softly and offers me a small smile.

"It is not the way of the gods or the witches. It is you, Elaenor. The female descendent who has to carry the lineage."

"I don't understand." I shake my head.

"You are stronger than your brother. The way your grandmother chose to have children is more or less the same way your mother did. Enzo is the heir to Vodia, but you, Elaenor, are the heir to it all. It's always how the witch lineages have been. It is the female who holds the title and power." Vodia. The mythical water people?

"What does this have to do with Amaya? What does this have to do with who killed my mother?"

"When Amaya was sold to Evreux, she lost me. And not just in a romantic way, but she lost the magic I had used to siphon. She needed me, but I couldn't get to her. I was forbidden. Because of that, the curse grew. Amaya knew all along that you were not Viktor's, she knew who your real father was, and she knew where Enzo was. Without the curse, she would have kept that secret to the grave. But the curse was more than just magic, it was a curse of the mind. She fell ill. Not in a physical sense, but she grew paranoid, reckless.

"One day, when you were seven, she went to Chatis. She was convinced that you were going to steal Noterra from Tobias, from her children. She got it in her head that you needed to die. So she set out to do that. Your mother and her fought, long and hard, but she was weak. She had just gone through another miscarriage. Amaya killed her and then went after you.

"I could tell something was wrong, I could feel the surge of aether all the way in Labisa and then my own magic was gone. It took me days to arrive, but when I did, I was blamed for your mother's death and your disappearance. I didn't do it, and I managed to escape fairly quickly. I don't know what happened to you after Amaya attacked you, but I found your blood on the bridge and in the carriage she used. Amaya had burns on her hands, which is how I realized that you fought back, Elaenor.

"She was taking you; I don't know where, but you fought back. You burned her with your starlight and escaped. You ended up in the lake, where you were able to enter stasis and sleep."

"Stasis?"

"Your grandfather is the King of Vodia, and he is a siren. Sirens are a form of shifter that can shift into merfolk. You don't have the ability to fully shift, not like Enzo, but you can shift your lungs. You can breathe underwater just like your grandfather and his people." This is too much. Too much information. But it makes sense. The water breathing makes sense...

"The bath. I used to spend a lot of time under the water in the bath. Tobias thought I was trying to kill myself." I recall, squeezing my legs.

"Were you?" Nithe asks. I look at him briefly before returning back to Kassius, ignoring his question.

"How did they find me?"

"It was me." Enzo speaks up. "I felt it. I felt when you used your aether to attack Amaya. All I could see was water and all I could feel was pain, I was shocking everyone I touched. It was your aether wasn't it?" He stares at me, and

I shrug. What am I supposed to say?

"When I got home, I learned from Enzo where you were. You were found shortly after, healthy and whole. Viktor was convinced that someone was going to attack you again, so he decided to tell the world you died."

"The secret princess." He nodded. "What happened to Amaya?"

"She killed herself. When the madness dissipated, as it often came in waves, she realized what she did. She killed her best friend and she thought she killed a child. She slit her own throat, taking herself and her unborn child with her." We are quiet for a moment, my eyes frozen.

"Why did my mother separate Enzo and I?"

"She was worried that if she gave Viktor a male heir, he would turn him into a monster like him and Evreux. She did it to protect Enzo and to protect you, Elaenor. He would have treated you much worse if you didn't have any value at all."

"The miscarriages?" My voice is emotionless as I try to get out all of the questions I have lingering in my mind before I break down.

"It was us. I would siphon the fetus's life energy, giving them a quick and painless death before they ever even started to exist, much like the herbs that clean out the womb. When she died—she took everything. She took my abilities with her. That can happen. You either absorb the other or you lose everything. Our mother absorbed her twin's aether, and she had two different eyes because of it."

"I don't understand. All of this…"

"A lot?" I nod. "You will adjust."

"So if I died, what would happen to Enzo?" I glance at my brother for a second, his eyes frozen on the wooden floors.

"He would either absorb your aether or lose his own abilities."

"This doesn't make sense. What about Mali?" Enzo asks, anger fueling his voice.

"Mal is my child, and despite the fact that I did not sire you Enzo, you will always be my son." He stands, pushing Scarlett off his lap.

"Not only have you lied to me about Elaenor, but also my parents? You told me my mother died—"

"She did—"

"*And* you told me that Elaenor was my other half, leading me to believe that she was my soulmate!" My eyes widen as I look at him. His face is flushed, and his brows furrowed, and I realize something. We look almost identical. The freckles, the hair, or at least what my hair used to be. The shape of our eyes. We look the same. "You had me pining after my own *sister*." His voice cracks and he shakes his head. "Excuse me." He leaves the room quickly, Scarlett following after him.

"This is why your father wants me to marry you?" I ask as I look up at Nithe. His face is still filled with shock as he tries to process everything.

"Yes, it is." He responds, clearing his throat and straightening his back as he faces me.

"I won't do it." I say as I rise from the settee and walk to my room without giving him another glance.

Chapter Thirty-Four

The Caged

I walk quickly down the hall to the room that will be mine for the foreseeable future. Tears burn the back of my eyes and I feel as if I am seconds from losing it entirely or passing out.

Probably both.

The door across from mine is open and I stop short, peeking in. Emery is lounging on her bed, golden waves a mess behind her as she reads. She's wearing a tunic and trousers similar to my own but trimmed in gold and cut perfectly for her toned body. I can't tell what she's reading, but she seems bothered, upset even. I take a silent deep breath and knock on her door. Her eyes flash to mine in anger, before dissolving into surprise.

"Elaenor." She whispers as she sits up, her perfect hair flowing behind her.

"Emery." I respond and take a hesitant step inside. Her room is a little smaller than mine, with a huge balcony and sitting room. The sky is a bright, cloudless blue and I can see the tips of wisteria trees brushing the balustrades of the stone balcony. It's peaceful in here, comfortable.

"How are you doing?" She asks quietly and I offer her a small smile.

"I'm not entirely sure. I'm just tired and probably due for a meeting with a mender." My hands knot in front of me, and I can feel my limbs shake as I take another step forward. Her eyes track my steps as if I was a deer she is afraid to startle.

"Well, that's to be expected, we can have someone sent to your room." I can almost taste the awkwardness in the room, but I have to know.

"Your father, have you heard anything?" Her eyes widen and she bites her lip before shaking her head and looking down at her lap.

"Not since we received word that he saw you. I am holding out hope that he isn't dead, but we haven't heard from Ren either."

"Ren?" She looks back up at me.

"Father Reynolds. He was sort of our inside man." Shock settles deep in my belly as it all starts to make sense. How they knew things.

"Can I ask you something?" I ask and she meets my gaze.

"Of course, cousin." She smiles.

"Nithe," a soft laugh escapes her throat as she slides off the bed and walks towards me. Her cold fingers wrap around my hands, prying them apart and lacing her fingers through mine.

"Nithe is one of my favorite people in the world. He's kind and caring, protective and strong. I know you may not want it, nor do you even know him, but you would be lucky to marry him. Anyone would." I stare into her golden-brown eyes for a moment before stepping back and out of her grasp. Her mouth falls as she tilts her head again, studying me.

"I am not in the market for marrying anyone, Emery. I am already wed. I won't be forced into another union. Not like this." I spin around and make my way across the hall to my room, shutting the door behind me and flicking the lock.

I cross the room quickly, climbing through the open window and onto the balcony. I drop down onto my knees, my palms pressing into the stone as the sobs start to build.

Brother.

Twin.

Uncle.

Amaya?

It's too much. And now marriage? Again?

I can't do this. I can't. I have no family. I guess technically Enzo and Kassius are my family, but not the one I grew up with. Not the one I miss.

I have nothing. These people are nothing. The only thing I need to do, the only thing I can do, is kill Tobias.

Tobias.

He is the only thing I can think about. Even now. The way his face looked as I fell over the cliff. He looked terrified for me. He looked like he cared.

Does he care?

I can't tell what's real anymore.

I—

Knocking on my door causes me to jump as I look over my shoulder. Tousled black hair and light purple eyes walk through and close the wooden door behind. He's holding a piece of rolled parchment in his hand as he slowly makes his way to the window.

"Little witch." He says by way of greeting.

"Did you break my lock?" He smiles in response, and I clench my fists.

I turn away from him and clamor to my feet. My hands grip the cool stone railing as I look out over the land. Grassy hills littered with all of the colors of the rainbow, but it's the purple trees that draw my focus.

"When I first came here, I hated it. I hated how quiet it was, how many flowers there were. It felt to open." I stay quiet, letting him speak. "My home is much like yours. Trees filling every inch of open space, cool and humid air. But we also have flowers and plants of all kinds, animals you wouldn't even know about. Everything across The Divide is like that. Beautiful." He says softly, and I can hear the smile in his voice.

"The Divide?" What is that? I turn slightly so I can face him.

"Down the center of the sea, there is an invisible border between the human lands and the lands of magic." He gestures out past the hills, the direction I'm assuming the sea is.

"I don't understand." His face recoils as he looks at me. As if he's only just now realizing how little I know. He stares for a second before his face softens and he starts to explain.

"This side of the sea was created for the humans. The other side was created for those who are of magical blood. Like you and I." He points at me before dropping his hand, his pinky barely brushing mine where it rests on the railing.

"I don't know anything about our world, Nithe. Not a single thing. I was sheltered growing up, barely even knowing about Rakushia and Noterra. I've never seen anything, been anywhere." My throat catches and I look back out towards the hills.

"You can now." I shake my head.

"I can't. He'll come for me."

"We are going to keep you safe, Elaenor. You don't have to be afraid here." His hand covers mine and I pull it away, clutching the hem of my tunic, worrying the stitches.

"We arrived just a few short hours ago and all I have been, is afraid. Your father wants to force me to marry you. He wants me to take over all of Viridiana. I not only have a brother, but I have a twin. Enzo is my *twin* brother who I didn't get to grow up with. Everything has changed. Everything. I have this suffocating need to go home, but it's not Chatis I am craving, it's Noterra." I bite my lip as the admission rolls off my tongue.

"To a husband who tortured you? Are you serious?" Disgust coats his words like ash, and I look back up at him.

"With Tobias, I knew what to expect. I knew that at the end of the day, I'd be fine because he wouldn't kill me. Even if he did, I would be better off for it—" His hand finds my shoulder, turning me towards him. His hand is hot, bleeding through my tunic and scorching my skin.

"Don't. Don't say you would be better off dead." He snaps.

"What do you want from me Nithe? Do you want false confidence in my mental state? Do you want me to wear a crown and a wedding dress and promise to be yours forever? What do you *want* from me? I have nothing to give!" I try to shake his hand off, but he tosses the parchment to the ground, his hands gripping onto my face. "Let go of me." I snap, my fingers wrapping around his wrists.

"No. Listen to me. You are more than what you were made to be. You are more than what you can even imagine. Stop letting him control you—"

"He's my husband." My voice is weak, my shoulders shaking.

"He doesn't have to be."

"I want him! Even now, Nithe, I *want* him. He was the only home I had." A tear trails down my cheek and his eyes follow it down. He closes his eyes and takes a deep breath. He leans forward and presses his forehead against mine, bathing me in the scent of mint and bergamot. I shake my head, our foreheads rubbing.

"This is day one of a new life, little witch. Day one. You get to decide how the rest of the days are spent. You. Not Tobias. Not my father, or your brother, or me. *You.*" His hands slip from my face as he bends down to grab the parchment. He holds it out for me, and I hesitantly take it. "When you are ready, I'll help you burn it. We all will."

He climbs through the window and quickly leaves the room, shutting the door behind him. I stare at the white parchment in my hand, not even old enough to be yellowed by age. I unroll it, tears pooling in my eyes.

"King Tobias Rosenthal of Noterra and Queen Elaenor Rosenthal of

Noterra, bound together forever by a marriage approved by the gods." I whisper, reading the words scrawled across the page.

Forever.

Even if I burn it, I'll still be his.

No one bothered me for the rest of the day. I sat on the balcony, watching the sun go down. At some point someone brought a tray of food in, setting it on the table by the fireplace, but I don't move from my spot. The air grows colder and colder as the darkness spreads, but still, I don't move. Even when the ache of my wounds barrel into my mind until that is all I can think of. When all I can feel is pain, still, I don't move. When exhaustion pulls at my mind and my eyelids grow heavy, I stay on the balcony.

I watch the stars fill the sky, moonlight spreading across the plains, setting everything in a silver glow.

Moonlight.

"Mama?" I whisper, hoping that wherever she is, she can hear me. "I don't know what to do. I don't know how to go on this way, with these people." I clear my throat, forcing the growing lump down. "Why did you keep him from me? Why did you never tell me I had a brother? Why!" I raise my voice, screaming into the night. "How could you do that? I don't understand." The tears fall freely and white clouds my vision. "No, no, no." I whisper, shaking my head.

My limbs begin to vibrate as the aether spreads, turning my veins into a bright white, glowing through my skin. I can see the stars forming on my fingers. I force a deep, slow breath, but it doesn't work. I pull myself up onto my feet, shaking my hands. Panic spreads just as quickly as the starlight as I try to get it to go away. But it doesn't listen.

I don't have control.

"Get off of me!" I yell as I shake them again. Sparks fling off my fingers and tears form. "Stop. Stop. *Stop!*" I repeat as I stare at my hands, almost completely white and glittering. My head feels light, my body dropping to an icy temperature. My feet go numb as I fall to my knees. "What is happening?" I whisper as I fall forward, my cheek slamming into the stone.

The last thing I see before my eyes go dark is a purple glow.

Chapter Thirty-Five

Her skin is ice-cold as I lay her on the bed. Her veins glow a brilliant shade of white, nearly making her skin translucent. It takes everything in me to not recoil as the starlight burns through my own flesh. I keep myself in a semi-stage of shifting, protecting my human skin, but it also means I have very little control. I fight against the urge to shift fully, panic fading into a numbing calm. The room is awash in bright light, coming from both of us. As my hands slip out from under her, the purple glow beneath my skin vanishes. I gently brush a pale lock from her forehead as Kassius and Enzo come in.

"What happened?" Kass's voice is thick with anger and panic as he comes to kneel by the bed, his fingers brushing her forehead.

"She was yelling, I don't know at who. I opened her door and saw her collapse, stars flying everywhere." He sighs and looks up at Enzo, who's staring at her in a new way. Not the desperate love-sick way he used to look when he would think of her, but almost angry. Almost *hateful*.

"Get Master Lenus." Kass snaps at his son. Enzo turns and quickly leaves without giving it a single thought.

"What's happening?" I ask as I watch Kass's eyes close for a moment.

"She's been burrowing deeper and deeper into her aether since she erupted the first time. Her emotions are heightened, and she doesn't have control right now. She's too strong, too strong for only having magic in half of her blood. Her body can't handle it, neither can her mind. Exhaustion, pain, confusion, all of it is eating away at her." He stands, his hand briefly touching the crown sewn to her head.

"What do we do?" My voice wavers and I clear my throat. No, you can't care right now. You *can't*. She's nothing. Just a young girl. That's it.

"The deep sleep, until she's well enough. We may not see wounds physically, but we don't know whether or not she's healed internally. We don't know anything about her." He glances up at me, a silent question.

"She's injured. Her leg, we forgot about her leg. We cauterized it, but it was bad." My voice is rushed. How could I forget? She's been sitting in pain, sitting with her injuries for an entire day.

"Why didn't you say anything?" Kass snaps, his hands clenching into fists at his side. He takes a slow deep breath before meeting my gaze again, as if he has to reign in his anger. This protection he has over her, it's like she's Mal. "It doesn't matter. We need to put her in stasis until she can heal."

"How can we force her into stasis? Isn't that something that happens naturally?" The clinking of tools makes me look up as Master Lenus hobbles in, his right leg stiff.

"A few injections should keep her down for a couple days." My eyes widen and I come around the side of the bed, stopping him before he sets his bag down.

"*No.* She just spent a year being drugged by her husband and you want to do it again?" My hand grips his shoulder, forcing him away from the bed.

"Ni, it's for the best." Kass says from behind.

"I said no." I get out through gritted teeth.

"Get him out of here." I glance up as my father leans against the open door, ordering me to leave.

"Father—"

"Out. *Now!*" He snaps and Enzo grabs my arm, pulling me past him.

"Don't touch her!" I yell as I am yanked out of the room. My father's smiling face is the last I see before he closes the door. "Let go of me." I rip my arm out of Enzo's grasp and reach for the door again. He shoulders me out of the way, knocking me into the wall.

"Enough!" He yells. "Just leave it alone." His voice is laced in irritation. I don't even recognize him anymore.

"What the fuck is wrong with you, man?" His green eyes darken as he stares at me.

"What?"

"All of a sudden because she's not available to you, you don't care. You've been nearly crying every day for a year and now that she's here, you don't even care what happens to her." I spit.

"That's not true."

"My father is in there, doing only the gods know what—"

"*My* father is in there, too. He won't let anything happen to her!"

"Enzo?" A soft, child-like voice pops up from the end of the hallway. We both spin around to Mali, a blanket wrapped around her. "What's wrong with that girl?" She asks. He rushes down the hallway, scooping her up into his arms.

"Nothing, Mali. She's just sick, but she'll be okay. Let's go back to bed."

Erik joins me in the hall a few hours after Enzo leaves. It's the middle of the night, but I can see the stress in his eyes. He offers me a tight-lipped smile as he slides down the wall, sitting across from me.

"Have you seen her?" He asks, but I just shake my head, anger brewing deep in my mind. "She'll be alright. She's strong." He attempts to reassure me, not that I even know why I need reassuring.

"Why didn't you do anything?" His eyes widen and his mouth clamps shut. "All those years, you never did anything to protect her." I shake my head and turn away from him.

"You don't know anything. You weren't there." His tone is filled with venom as his face hardens, which only pisses me off.

"Her father beat her, and you just watched." I snap, fighting against what little control I have.

"I didn't watch, I intervened so many times. You may think the scars on her back are bad, but you haven't seen mine." My mouth falls open as ice spreads through my veins.

"Scars?" I ask, my voice soft. "I haven't seen any scars." His eyes soften as his legs fall to the ground. He sighs before he speaks.

"She has scars on her back from a whip her father used. My own father and brother had to hold me back and forced me to watch her be whipped to near-death. She fell unconscious and I could see her spine, see her ribs through the splits in her back. After she was carried away, I was strapped to the same pole she was and whipped. Except he didn't stop when I fell unconscious. My father and brother allowed him to whip me until I was seconds away from death. Even in the infirmary, they didn't keep me asleep. I suffered in pain for weeks, but I could see her. She was asleep, they kept her that way while she healed. So for weeks, I watched her. Scarlett and I watched her and hoped she would wake." Bile rises in my throat as I listen. His voice is strained, almost as broken as hers.

"I didn't know." I admit.

"Don't say I never stepped in. You don't know her; you don't know her life. I was always there for her. Always. And even on the road when she was kidnapped—"

"What?" I cut him off, remembering what she had said to my father. He shakes his head and scoffs.

"This only proves my point. All you know about her is what you think Tobias did. You filled in everything else yourself. She is a stranger to you, a girl you've barely heard about. But to us, to *all* of us, she's family. She's *ours*. I gave my life for her that day, and I didn't expect to wake, but I did. I gave my life so she could get away, but she didn't."

"What happened to her? She mentioned these men, men she accused my father of sending."

"It's not my story to tell." He responds. He doesn't look at me as he rises. "If anything changes, please let me know." He doesn't wait for a response as he walks down the hall, entering Laenie's room.

He's right. I don't know anything about her. All I see is a traumatized girl, but that's not her. She's stronger than I expected.

Hatred pools deep in my belly as I pull myself up and open the door to Elaenor's room. My father is sitting beside her on the bed, where she is naked and exposed as she lies on her stomach. There is only a thin sheet covering her backside waist down, exposing her back.

"What are you doing?" I ask as I stride in, grabbing a blanket off the end of the bed and throwing it over her, my eyes catching on the purple lines across her back before they disappear under the wool. Kass is sitting by the fireplace, talking to Master Lenus.

"We were cleaning the mess of a leg wound you left behind, as well as the many other slices and bruises you failed to mention." My father says lazily.

"No, it looks like you were eyeing a naked, vulnerable girl." I snap, making sure the blanket covers every part of her up to her shoulders.

"For gods sake, Nithe." He mutters and climbs off the bed. "She isn't your property yet; I don't know who you are fooling." He sneers.

"She will never be my property." I snap as he strolls out of the room. "How could you just leave her exposed like that?" I turn towards Kassius and Master Lenus. "You are supposed to take care of her."

"Did you see her scars?" He asks, and I shake my head. I didn't allow my eyes to linger. "She has no physical wounds on the outside, aside from her leg, a deep laceration on her arm, and a few scratches, but there is something in her, something pulling her strength." He looks back at Master Lenus.

"Like an infection?" I ask.

"Possibly. We won't know more for a few days. We gave her some herbs to reduce infection—" The master starts.

"Take the crown off." I demand.

"We should really wait to see what she wants to do when she wakes." He responds carefully.

"You think she wants it on? Take it off!" I yell louder as I step towards them. Master Lenus nods as he hesitantly rises, coming to the bed.

"Can you hold her up, Your Grace?" He asks while pulling materials out of his bag. I nod as I reach for her. I keep the blanket wrapped around her like a tourniquet as I scoop her up in my arms. I sit down on the bed, resting her head on my shoulder so Lenus has access to her scalp.

Her face is peaceful, calm. Her breath fans around me, bathing me in the scent of vanilla and something floral. Sweet and warm. Her pale skin is flawless, aside from a small sprinkling of light freckles on her nose and cheekbones. Her lips are a deep pink, plush and full. Her eyelashes are dark and long, fanning across her cheeks. But her pale skin is gray, and the bruises under her eyes are deep. She's beautiful, but she's suffering. I brush an icy lock off her forehead, and it falls over the crown in a silky wave. Her eyebrows furrow as if she is dreaming, and I take a deep breath.

What are you doing, Nithe?

"Don't cut her hair." I order as he begins to part the colorless strands, exposing thick, black stitches wrapped around the metal and into her scalp. My mouth dries, dinner turning sour in my stomach as I stare at his handiwork. Her husband did this to her. He sewed a crown to her head as if she were a toy to play with.

Kassius leaves the room, giving me a sympathetic glance on the way out. The minutes are long and silent, the only noise being the sound of thread being sliced by a scalpel. I watch the black threads pull out of her skin and fall to the bed. I watch as Lenus's face pales as he tries to concentrate on the task. What had to be thousands of stitches later, the crown slips free from her head. Blood stains the pale locks as the holes left behind are opened. Gauze is pressed to her head, soaking up the blood before it can stain her hair. Lenus puts a thick cream over the wounds and lets her hair fall back over them.

"The bleeding should stop quickly, Your Grace."

"You may go." I order as I watch her nostrils flare with each breath.

"There are syringes in the bag already prepped for her height and weight. Should she wake before I return, she will need them to fall back asleep. I will return in the morning." He explains, but I ignore him. There is no way I was going to be complicit in drugging her.

"*Go.*" I repeat. He bows deeply before leaving the room and closing the door behind him.

I can't help the tears pooling in my eyes as I think about all she endured. As I picture him hurting her. I shake my head and slide off the bed, setting her down. I can't get attached. I can't allow myself to care for her.

Whimpering pulls me out of my sleep, and I crack my eyes. Her thin body is wrapped in a sheet, sweat beading on her forehead. Her hands are clenched into fists, her brows furrowed.

"No." She whispers and then her eyes fly open. "Tobias?" She whispers again before she sits up. A grimace crosses her face, and her hands find her stomach. She looks down and around the room before her eyes land on me.

"How are you feeling?" I ask as I stretch, leaning forward with my forearms on my knees. It's been two days of her being asleep. Two days of me counting her breaths for the fear she'll stop.

"Who are you?" Her voice is sharp, clear, as she stares at me. Her eyes are wide, assessing, as if she's deciding whether to fight or run.

"My name is Nithe." Her mouth parts and I can see her eyes wash over me, confused.

"Where is Tobias?" I sigh.

"Back in Noterra." I respond calmly.

"He's going to kill you. He's going to kill you for touching me." She's shaking her head, a laugh bubbling in her mouth.

"I didn't touch you, little witch." I sigh and she just laughs again.

"He's going to kill you. He's going to find me." She's fully giggling, and I lean back, arching a brow.

"Elaenor, Tobias isn't a good man. He isn't going to protect you." I say slowly.

"He's going to come for me. You can't keep me forever." I rise and her eyes snap to me. "He will come for me." Something flashes in her eyes and for a moment it looks as if the veins under her eyes have turned black, spreading out to her cheeks. But it's gone a second later.

"I hope he does." I respond, clearing my throat.

"Take me home. It's not too late." She pleads, her voice wavering.

"Elaenor, we rescued you. You were going to die there." She shakes her head. "Tobias isn't a good guy, little witch." I reach for her, and she recoils.

"I want to go home!" The door opens and I turn to see Enzo stride in. His clothing is disheveled, as if he just woke.

"Elaenor." He says softly and her lips part.

"You?" He walks up to the bed, sitting on the edge. "Enzo?" He nods.

"Yes, it's me."

"I don't understand." She reaches forward, her fingers lightly brush his cheek as if she's checking if he's real. "This isn't real. You aren't real." She snatches her hand back, her body shaking. "Wake up. Wake up. Wake up." She covers her eyes, repeating the same thing over and over again. I rise and come over to her side, gripping her wrists and she screams.

Her screams echo around the room, sharp and shrill. She screams as if she's fighting for her life. She shakes the blankets free and kicks at Enzo, who has to grab her legs before she hits him in the face.

"Fuck. Calm down!" He yells at her. Someone barrels into the room and I hear digging around in the medical kit. A tan arm reaches between me and Enzo, and I see the syringe as it slams into Elaenor's leg. Her eyes widen, fixed on mine, before she goes limp.

"What the fuck, Scarlett!" Enzo yells and I slowly lower Elaenor back on the bed. Her eyes are still open, but she's out. I close her eyes gently and brush a lock of hair from her face.

"She was losing her mind. She needs sleep, she needs to rest. We *all* do. None of us have slept in days." He pushes past her, stalking out of the room. "*Enzo*." She calls, racing after him out of the room.

I look away from them, and brush more of Elaenor's hair off her face and neck. She's breathing slowly, deep in sleep. But she's not peaceful. She feels the opposite of peace.

Chapter Thirty-Six

The Caged

It's quiet when I wake. The sounds of trees rustling in the wind, birds chirping in the distance. The fresh smell of flowers and wisteria flowing around me, carried by the summer air. Peaceful. This is what I imagine peace feels like.

My eyes open to the bright ceiling, a mixture of stone and pale wood. The canopy hanging off the four-poster bed is a soft gray, reminding me of home. I take inventory of my body, and for once I actually feel good. I feel fine. I lift my hand hesitantly, feeling for the crown, but there is nothing there. I shoot out of bed, the linen falling around me revealing a black, silk nightdress. Both hands tangle in my hair, but the only part that tells me it was ever there at all, are the tiny scabs across my scalp. Tears pool in my eyes and my breath comes in quick pants.

"Nora?" Kassius's voice is warm, like honey, as it flits around the room. I glance up to where he is lounging by the lit fireplace. "How are you feeling?" My hands fall from my head, my fingers tangling in the white strands.

"How long have I been asleep?" I croak.

"A little over a week." He says hesitantly.

"Why?"

"You weren't well. Your body was exhausted, as was your mind. You didn't have control over your aether, and you became a danger to yourself. We had to put you in stasis to allow you to heal."

"Stasis?"

"Just another word for those who are forced to sleep in order to heal both mentally and physically." I nod and drop my hands in my lap. "What are you thinking about?" He asks softly. They drugged me. Just like *him*.

"Everything. Enzo, my mother, Tobias, you." I recite as if I am reading off a list. "It's hard to decipher what is real." I admit. He smiles and stands, walking over to the end of the bed.

"You have a twin brother, and I am your uncle. Your mother died at the hands of Amaya. You have a magical aether called starlight. You are currently in Rakushia, under the watch of the Labisian King, Davenport. Your friends are here, Scarlett and Erik and Laenie." He pauses as he takes in my furrowed brow. "You are safe." I nod, swallowing against the lump in my throat. "I am going to go have some breakfast sent up for you, alright?" I nod again as he slowly leaves the room, leaving the door cracked.

My mind is reeling after Kassius leaves. My legs are crossed as I sit on the bed, my gaze fixed on the pale linen sheets. I have a brother. A *twin* brother. Rakushia. Tobias?

"Rosie?" My gaze snaps up as Nithe walks in, leaving the door open behind him.

"Stop calling me that." I snap as he collapses on the foot of the bed like a dog. "What are you doing?"

"Making sure you don't kill yourself or run."

"Fuck off." I surprise myself as the words leave my mouth, a gasp following. I don't know why I feel so angry, so disturbed by his presence. I bite my lip and look away.

"I thought you'd be meek and quiet, but my gods you are vulgar." He snorts, rolling onto his back.

"Leave me alone, Nithe."

"Or what?" My eyes narrow and I can feel the electricity trickle through my veins before my peripherals turn white. I scare myself, my breath catching as I slam back into the headboard.

"I don't understand." I say, my voice more breath than sound.

"Maybe little witch is a better nickname than Rosie." He snorts.

"I would like to be alone." I clear my throat and look at him, trying to seem as demanding as possible, but I'm sure I look like a mess.

"Trust me, the last thing I want is to be here, but it will keep my father away." He replies and I don't miss the disgust in his voice at the mention of his father. Davenport didn't seem like a kind man, giving me a weird sensation of repeating time. As if this is all something I have done before.

Because it is.

"Why would you need to keep your father away?"

"He isn't kind, Elaenor. And if I stay by your side, he'll leave you be." His eyes glance down at my dress before returning to my face.

"So you are protecting me?" I say while pulling the blanket up higher around me.

"Unfortunately." He sighs.

"I don't need protection." I mutter, crossing my arms. I am fully aware I may look childish, but I'm tired.

"You need more than most." He snorts.

"Nithe–"

"Look, you just learned a fuck ton of information about your life, found out you have a twin, and found out more about how you almost died. You have been asleep for nine days. You have a lot–"

"I don't need a babysitter!"

"I don't care."

"What is your problem?" I snap.

"I am trying to help you, little witch."

"I don't want your help." I spit, bringing my legs up to my chest and wrapping my arms around them.

"Look at me." I don't, keeping my gaze on the bed. "Elaenor." He says sharper this time. When I don't look up, he sighs. "I can't even imagine what is going through your head, but I am trying to be your friend here. I am trying to make sure you aren't alone, or that you don't do anything stupid." He says softly.

"What would I do?"

"You called out for him. In your sleep." My eyes finally meet his and I can almost see sorrow crossing the bright irises.

"What?" I whisper.

"You cried for him, begging him to come. You woke up once. You were confused and said Tobias would come for you."

"He will." I say slowly, admitting it to myself. He will come for me, it's just a matter of time.

"Do you want him to?" My mouth hangs open as I try to think of what to say. "It's alright if you do."

"I miss him." I admit quietly. His eyes darken for a split second, black encompassing the amethyst irises. A blink and it's gone. "I miss when he was kind. Right before the end, everything was back to normal."

"Normal? How normal could any of it have been if he was abusing you?"

"I don't want to talk about it." I shake my head.

"You can talk to me."

"I don't want to, Nithe. I would like to be left alone." He's silent for a second before he slides off the bed and walks to the door.

"Erik is right outside the door. There are guards in the hallway and at every exit. You can walk around, do whatever you want. They are here for your protection, not to trap you. You are not a prisoner here." He says the last part with emphasis, as if he really wants me to believe it. But he's wrong.

"It is still a prison, Nithe. Even if the accommodations are pretty and clean, I am still caged."

"I know you have been caged your whole life, I know you don't trust us, but I promise you, you are safe here. You don't have to be scared or worried. Nothing will happen to you while you are here." He doesn't say another word before he leaves the room, closing the door behind him.

The silence hits me before everything else does. I can't hear voices, or footsteps. I can't even hear the trees rustling in the wind outside the open window. Everything is silent.

My footsteps are light as I slide off the bed and walk to the balcony, climbing through the open window. There is no wind, no animals. Nothing.

It feels stale.

Wrong.

I look across the land, green hills greeting me. But it isn't the hills my attention is focused on, it's the darkness creeping along the edge of the surrounding wall. As if it's a mist slowly making its way across the land, but instead of white, it's black. Swallowing everything whole.

My hands grip the railing as I focus on it. It takes shape, growing taller and taller. My heart skips a beat, my palms instantly sweaty, as the shape turns into Tobias.

His golden hair is short, groomed perfectly against his head. His armor is a deep black aside from the red rose imprinted on the front of his chest plate. His blue eyes are piercing as he stares at me, stares into my soul. He smiles, his white teeth blinding in the sun.

I blink and he's gone. My heart stutters and I step back from the balcony, slamming into someone. I spin around, a scream lodged in my throat as I stare up at Tobias.

"Ela." He whispers as my lips part. My blood hums in his presence, begging to get closer. I am frozen where I stand, unable to move. His hand lifts, the back of his knuckles brushing my cheek. "I promise to come for you." He whispers again before leaning down and pressing his cold lips to mine. I open my mouth to protest, but—

"Wake up!"

Sweat clings to my forehead as I shoot up, my pulse pounding in my ears. My eyes take a second to adjust to my surroundings, the pale wood and roaring fire.

"Elaenor, are you okay?" He says again, his voice close. I slowly turn my head to the left and see Nithe kneeling on the side of the bed, his brows furrowed.

"What?" I ask, my voice hoarse.

"Are you okay?" I lift my hands as a tingling spreads through my fingers. No sparks appear but I can feel them. I nod and look back at him. His amethyst eyes are dark, almost black as he stares at me. "You were screaming in your sleep."

"I had a bad dream." I respond, lifting my hand to wipe the sweaty tendrils of hair out of my face.

"About what?" I shake my head and slide off the mattress, the floor icy under my bare feet. When did I fall back asleep? It was seconds. Only seconds had passed.

"Nothing." I respond.

"Rosie—" He starts, but I cut him off.

"Please, Nithe. Please just go."

Chapter Thirty-Seven

The Caged

A whole day passes, and I watch the sun set from the balcony. My brain is foggy, stuck in a dream. I feel him. I can feel him all around me, pressing into me. Prying into my mind and making me miss him, *crave* him.

I can smell the cedar and ash, the smell of my husband. The smell of my abuser and lover. The person I shouldn't want to be with right now, but something is digging into my mind, making me ache for his touch. Ache for him.

Something feels wrong. I feel as if I am suffocating. As if I am feeling the pain of a thousand cuts and as if the distance between me and him is somehow killing me from the inside out.

A tear slips out of my eyes, trailing down my cheek as I watch the sun go down. This is my life now. Another prison. Another place for me to be stuck. Another place for someone to control me. I could run. I could make a break for it. But where would I go? I can't go ba—

A loud knock sounds from behind and I spin around. To my surprise, and disgust, King Davenport walks in, shutting the door behind him.

"Princess." He says, crossing his arms. Everything about him exudes power, control. He reminds me of Evreux, of my father—of Viktor. Fury pummels through me, disgust as I stare at this sad excuse of a man.

Why are the people who end up with power always the people who shouldn't have it?

"What can I do for you, Your Grace?" I ask, wrapping my arms around myself.

"I have been thinking." He stares into my eyes before stepping forward, running his hands along the bedspread. "You seem to be under the impression that you have choices here, that you are a free woman." I want to scoff, to laugh, but I don't.

"I will never be free." I say slowly. His brows furrow as the edges of his mouth twitch.

"At least you're smart." He snorts, walking around the bed.

"What do you want?" I ask again, sliding back an inch until my back presses against the window.

"I am here to make a proposition." My eyes widen as I stare at him.

"What could you possibly have to offer me?"

"I want you to marry my son. I want you to unite our bloodlines. In return, I will rule in your place. You will not have to lift a finger. War will be had, and you can live comfortably in the palace in Labisa. You won't have to watch as the world burns, you won't have to be a part of it. Your husband will die, and you will be free. You could do whatever you wished in Labisa." My lips part as I stare at him. As I ponder.

I won't have to be involved. I won't have to go to war or worry about what my life will be like. I won't have to do anything. I could live.

But I would be married.

"Why?"

"I want something else from you." He steps around the bed, pausing a foot from me. My fingers tingle, and as if he can sense it, he smiles. He lifts a hand and traces my arm from my shoulder to my elbow. I flinch, my gaze glaring into his. "I can feel it brewing beneath your skin. I don't think you understand how powerful you are." I step to the side, out of his reach and walk to the door.

"What else could you possibly want from me?" I snap.

"Your brother, he's a siphon. Do you know what they can do?" I spin around, facing him again.

"They can take power." I respond.

"They can take it just as easily as they can give it." My heart skips a beat as I understand what he's saying, what he's asking for.

"You want my aether?" I whisper, my hands falling down to my sides.

"Yes."

"Why?"

"Why would anyone want power, child? To be *powerful*." He snorts before walking towards me again. "You don't want it. You made that very clear. You have no control over it, nor do you want to. Think, Elaenor. Think about this. I may be willing to negotiate." He adds.

"What?"

"I won't make you marry Nithe if you do this, if you give me your aether. You could still move to Labisa, where you will live as a queen, but you will still be free."

"If I annul my marriage, I will already be free, or as free as I can get."

"No, child, you are not. I own you." His hand grazes mine and I pull it away, but he snatches it anyway. His fingers press into my skin and my fingers open, spasming. "Every breath you take, every beat of your heart is because of me. I saved you. I am giving you sanctuary. I am giving you life. You have no more choices, except this one. You will give me your aether or you will marry my son. One of which will happen tonight." I rip my hand from his and he grabs my face, pinching my cheeks and pushing me into the door behind me. "This palace is full of your friends, your family. I will rip each one of their hearts out in front of you until you do as I ask, as I *demand*. War is coming, and I will not be on the losing side." Words fail me as he releases my face and pushes me out of the way. I stumble to the side as he exits the room, slamming the door behind him.

I stare at the empty space he was just occupying. He's not going to let me live, let me be free without giving up everything. My aether is all I have. Despite my friends, and the people in this palace, the starlight is *mine*. It is what saved me from Tobias.

And it will be what destroys him.

My mind is made up before I snatch the cloak from the dressing room, fastening it around me and slipping a pair of boots on. I search the room for a weapon but find none.

I take a slow, deep breath before I open the door and peer out in the hallway. It's empty, quiet.

I cross the hall, quickly pushing open Emery's door. Her room is dark, vacant. I run in quickly, pulling open drawers in her nightstand. The moonlight illuminates the room softly, but I can't find what I am looking for.

I abandon the nightstand and move to the dressing room, pulling open dresser drawers. I hit the jackpot and nearly cry out in relief when the bottom drawer opens.

Daggers and short swords fill the bottom drawer to the brim. I grab two daggers, shoving them in my boots, not that I even know what to do with them. I grab a short sword, quickly hooking the holster around me, before closing the drawer and exiting back into the hallway.

I look down the dark expanse, seeing a small light coming from the library. I strain my ears as I listen, and then I hear it. A soft laugh, the clinking of dishes. They are in there.

I creep closer, my back resting against the wall as I peer into the room. They are facing away from the door, towards the fireplace, eating and drinking. I take a deep breath before running across the doorway to the stairs beyond.

My footsteps are silent as I descend, keeping my eye out for guards. The rustling of armor makes me freeze as I peer around the bend in the staircase. The noise dissipates and I continue.

My hands sweat, my fingers tingling as I reach the bottom floor. There are two guards by the door and one by the entryway to the grand room.

"Damnit." I whisper as I think of what to do. I contemplate just walking by, Nithe said I could, but I feel they would stop me, especially if I look like I'm leaving. I need them to move, to abandon their post for just a moment. I rack my brain, searching for anything when I peer back around the corner. A small gasp escapes my mouth as I see that the guards are gone.

Where did they go? I don't hesitate.

I exit the stairwell quickly, running across the entryway and out into the crisp night. The stars are bright, illuminating the grounds as I make my way to the low wall. I grip the top of it and struggle to pull myself up. I release a breath as I drop to the other side.

I spin around and face a wall of wisteria. The trees are thick, the vines filling every inch. I push them aside with my hands as I walk through, letting them fall behind me, covering me from prying eyes.

My footsteps are quick as I dart through the trees and nearly cry in relief as I exit the orchard. The hills are vast, the green grass glowing from the moonlight. I continue running, nearly slipping as the terrain dips down.

I don't know how long I keep going, my boots slipping on the grass as I get closer and closer to another hill. As I reach the top, I see it. The trail.

I quickly clamor down the hill, finding the trail that leads to the lake. Everything is quiet, peaceful, just the sound of me running, and then I hear it. The lapping of the water as I reach the beach, white sand crunching beneath my boots. My pulse thrums in my veins, adrenaline feeding me.

Pushing me forward.

The small boat is tied off to a short pier, oars already placed in the two holders. I waste no time as I step onto the wooden dock, the sound of my boots echoing around me. I step down into the boat and look over. The lights from the palace are visible, brightening the dark sky.

Friends. Found family. That is who is in there. But if I stay, I will be forced to marry Nithe, forced to give my one source of power away. And if I don't, they'll die.

I don't know Davenport, but he seems ruthless, and he seems like the type of man who gets what he wants. He almost did. Back on the road to Noterra when I was tortured and raped. When I was drugged and kidnapped before Theo and Tobias rescued me. And now. He has me in his palace, in his care.

In his control.

If I stay, I won't make it. He won't keep me around if I continue to oppose him. Why would he?

I look away and unravel the rope holding the small boat to the dock. I push off, letting the current pull me farther from the beach. The bench is cold when I finally sit down, grabbing the oars and pulling them towards me, pushing the boat farther and farther into the lake.

The air is colder, thicker, as I paddle. It makes no sense for the weather to feel so frigid in the beginning of August. It should be warm, humid. But the cold air presses down around me, making my skin crawl. I don't know how much time passes, but exhaustion finds me. I try to pull the oars, but the water resists and I drop them. Resignation falls over me as I curl up on the bench, watching the stars. My fingers tingle, as if recognizing the twinkling lights above.

Nineteen years and I never knew I had magic. I never knew, and not once did it appear. But I felt it. I felt electricity through my limbs every time I was scared or angry. Every time I was happy. As if it was there all along and I didn't know how to wield it. I felt it every time I was touched, every time I was kissed, as if it was reacting to my emotions. It was always there, ready for me. A piece of myself I never knew, a pie—

Chapter Thirty-Eight

The Caged

The boat stops moving, something slamming into it, splashing water into the small craft. I sit up, looking around the dark waters, but see nothing. Ripples extend from the boat in all directions.

I hold my breath as I stare, waiting.

Something hits the side and I fall off the bench, my knees slamming into the bottom of the boat. Water soaks through my clothing as it pours in through the side. Something cracks and I feel the boat jerk again. I stumble and grab the oars, pushing against the water, trying to paddle as fast as I can. The oar rips from my hand, splinters slicing through my palm. I cry out as the other oar is ripped from my hand, disappearing under the black waters.

Silence.

Silence follows.

The only sound is the beat of my heart echoing through my ears.

I stand slowly on unsteady feet as water starts to pour through the cracks in the boat. The water stills, as if it's waiting. Expecting. I spin around slowly, water now up to my ankles. My pulse is beating rapidly, my limbs going numb from the cold water and the starlight thrumming in my veins.

Whatever it is slams into the boat again, and I go flying.

I hold my breath as I hit the water, the liquid infiltrating my nose. I kick out, attempting to swim, but it feels like I'm being pulled down, the cloak making it impossible to move. I struggle to rip it off as I go deeper and deeper. I get the sleeves free, and my eyes scan the dark waters.

I see it.

A black creature barrels towards me in the dark water, its mouth opening. My eyes widen as I thrust my hand out. Star filled lightning shoots through the water, illuminating it. The creature is all black, shaped like a worm. Rows and rows of teeth fill its circular mouth, eyes the color of the depths of hell find mine as it turns away from me.

I exhale, bubbles erupting around me.

Shift. I beg myself as my lungs burn. *Shift, damnit!* I kick and kick, trying to get to the quickly disappearing surface as the creature spins around, heading back my way. I fight against the urge to inhale as much as I can, but the burning is too much, it's too—

I inhale and water shoots down into my lungs. I thrash in the water as its icy embrace wraps around every part of me. I kick and try to cough, but I can feel my heart slowing.

This isn't it. It's not my time.

I can hear a soft wailing as the worm speeds through the water in slow motion, as if time is stopping. The burning in my chest explodes and my mouth opens. I inhale, expecting the water to shoot through once more, but it doesn't.

The burning dissipates and I take a deep breath. My limbs ignite and I thrust my hands out, starlight shooting through the water and hitting the creature straight in its mouth. Fissures crack through its black exterior before it explodes.

I inhale again, but my lungs returned to their normal state, filling with water once more. My limbs twitch as I sink, deeper and deeper. The water is near black, blending into itself. Wrapping itself around me as I drown. I try to kick, but my body doesn't move.

I have no energy left.

I had fight. I had a will to live, that's why I left. That's why I had to leave. I had to fight. To end all of this. To save myself.

But it's all gone as my blood freezes and the starlight fizzles out.

My eyes stay open, but I can feel my heart slow to a stop.

Thump.

I no longer feel cold.

Thump.

Warmth spreads through me as my lips part, a bubble slipping through.

Thump.

And then nothing.

Bright purple light explodes in the water, illuminating everything. More of those worms are circling me, their mouths open. There has to be hundreds.

The light dissipates.

Thump.

It flashes again, this time closer. The creatures look up, as if they are expecting something. Again. Amethyst light that reminds me of someone. Reminds me of...

A creature plunges into the water. Black scales and horns. Wings the size of a house spread around the creatures. Claws reach for me, and I scream with the last bit of energy I have, kicking out. Its head is nearly the size of my entire body as its mouth opens. Purple light shoots out as it turns towards one of the worm creatures, burning it through the water. Its claws wrap around my body and then I am flying through the water.

Warm and sharp claws dig into my sides as I am yanked out of the water.

They squeeze tightly and I vomit, water flying from my mouth and through the air. We climb higher and higher, clouds whipping past us, the ground disappearing.

I inhale, coughing the water out of my lungs, only to replace it with screams. My fingers dig at the creature, at the *dragon*.

It's bigger than anything I have ever seen, nearly the size of the Rakushian palace. Its scales are black, the membranes of its wings reflecting back purple as it beats through the air. Scaled claws hold onto me, legs tucked in behind as the wings bring us higher and higher.

My screams ravage through my throat, tears springing from my eyes as it freefalls back towards the ground. Wind rips at my hair and my clothes, nearly drying me instantly. I claw at its fingers, trying to get free as the snow-colored sand comes into view. I can see it—I can see how close we are. My eyes shut as I brace for impact.

Just as we near the beach, its wings snap out, stopping us in the air, my head snapping from the whiplash. I am set softly on the ground and my shut eyes open slowly. The dragon is standing in the water, its body nearly taking up the whole beach, sitting at almost 30 feet tall. I scramble to my feet and back away, my hands out.

Oh my gods.

Oh my gods.

It's a fucking dragon. An actual fucking dragon. That's the beast I saw. It was a *dragon*.

Its head drops until it's level with my eyes. I could curl up in a ball and fit in its mouth, that's how big it is. Dark irises meet mine and its head tilts to the side, watching me, waiting for something. A low trill comes out of his throat, and I can almost feel it vibrating the air. He exhales through his nose, the hot breath hitting me in the face.

Bergamot.

I take a hesitant step forward and lift my hand higher. The dragon leans its long neck forward, pressing its snout into my palm. It's warm, softer than I expected. Its mouth opens slightly, revealing teeth the size of my arm. I drop my hand as a purple glow spreads across its scales.

I think I knew before I saw him; before the glow dissipated. I think I knew who the dragon was before Nithe appeared where it was just standing.

"Little witch," he smiles, his bare chest glistening in the moonlight. My eyes flit across his muscles, broad shoulders, and— my eyes dip down and immediately shoot back up as I realize he is naked.

"You're naked!" I screech and slap my hand over my eyes.

"That's the first thing you say to me?"

"I think seeing you naked is more surprising than finding out you are a fucking dragon." I mutter. A faint glow makes it through my eyelids and fingers.

"You can look now." I hesitantly part my fingers, glancing through and seeing him fully clothed. My hand drops and my eyes focus on his.

"I don't understand." I laugh, surprising myself, and shake my head. "You're a dragon."

"Technically, no. I am a certain type of shifter—we are called wyvos."

"Wy-vos." I repeat slowly, staring at him.

"Where were you going?" My eyes lock onto his, my mind reeling. He's a dragon. A black and purple dragon. He fit that big of a beast under his skin? Is it like a skin suit? Skin suit. That sounds funny. "Hello?" He snaps in front of me, and I flinch.

"What?"

"Where were you going?" He asks again.

"Home." I mutter, turning away from him.

"To Chatis?" I shrug and he sighs. "Why? You are safe here."

"No, I am not." I snap, stomping through the sand as I trek up the beach. I don't hear his footsteps before he grips my arm, spinning me around.

"What happened?" I pull away and his hands wrap around my face, his palms hugging my cheeks, a position he has grown comfortable being in. "Talk to me." His hands are warm, and I feel the urge to cry, to just embrace the warmth. It feels right. It feels normal.

But it's not.

I hesitate before giving him the truth.

"Your father." His eyes narrow and I feel his fingers twitch.

"What did he do to you?" He says through gritted teeth.

"He told me that if I didn't give him my aether, he was going to kill every one of my friends. He was going to kill Enzo. He was going to kill Scarlett. Everyone." His hands tighten around my face, almost too much, and I lift my hands to wrap my fingers around his wrists.

"How?" He spits, his eyes pupils shrinking.

"He said Enzo can siphon it from me and give it to him."

Chapter Thirty-Nine

The Caged

His eyes darken completely, his irises black as he stares off, the purplish glow spreading across his skin. The light ripples and I can feel heat radiating off him like a furnace. Like *fire*.

"Nithe?" I whisper, my voice weak and tired. He exhales long and slow, smoke billowing out of his nose. I take a hesitant step back and his hands drop from my face. My hand hovers over the short sword I don't know how to use, as fear replaces logic in my mind. "Nithe?" I ask again. His arms shake and I take another step back. The glow spreads and I scream as a dragon—*wyvos*—bursts out of the spot his body was.

Black scales and horns emerge, purple reflecting off his large, leathery wings. His black eyes snap to mine, and I stumble backwards, my arm catching my fall as I land in the white sand. I stare at the large body, the spikes covering his back in a long line of short to tall. The tail that is whipping through the water that ends in an even larger spike. A spike that could tear someone's head clean off their shoulders.

"Nithe!" I repeat for a third time. He lowers his head and then a loud roar echoes around us. I shut my eyes, slamming my hands over my ears as I feel the hot wind flying around me. The roar stops and a shadow falls over my eyelids. I hesitantly open them, blackness obscuring my vision.

Not blackness, *Nithe*.

He's standing over me, his large body nearly swallowing me whole as he stares behind. I scramble to my knees and see the crowd that has gathered. Enzo, Kassius, and the king are standing at the edge of the sand. Enzo has a bow in his hand, Kassius palming a dagger. The king just stands, a smirk crossing his face. I can see Scarlett and Erik up at the top of the hill. Scarlett's eyes are wide, her hand covering her mouth. Erik's sword is out, ready.

I glance back down at Kassius as holds his hand out for me.

"Nora, come here." He says slowly, waving me forward. I crawl a few steps but stop when Nithe growls. My hands cover my head, and a squeal escapes my throat as I am frozen with fear. My hands and limbs are shaking, exhausted. My heart is pounding rapidly in my chest as terror runs through my veins. I think I'm going to vomit.

Nithe roars again and I scream. Vomit.

I am definitely going to vomit.

"We aren't going to hurt her." Enzo says softly. I look up as he slowly sheathes his arrow and throws his bow over his shoulder. "I am not going to hurt her." He steps forward, Kassius's eyes glancing between them. "Elaenor," he says waving me forward, and I slowly pull myself to my feet. The top of my head brushes Nithe's underbelly and I crouch down. My steps are quick as I escape Nithe's reach, Enzo pulling me behind him.

I stare into Nithe's eyes, the black reflecting the light from the palace. He looks scared, upset. He looks as if he's terrified something is going to happen. He bares his teeth as he growls, the sound low and guttural.

"I don't understand." I whisper, my nose brushing Enzo's shoulder blade as he presses me into his back.

"He's territorial. Dragons are territorial over the things they love if they fear there is danger." Love? My breath catches and I glance over at Kassius and the king. The king's smirk is still present, a slight shake to his head. Nithe roars and I slam my hands over my ears again before he shoots into the sky, disappearing into the clouds.

"It appears you have captivated my son in the few hours you have been conscious." I spin around as the king's laugh permeates through the air. "You must have a magical fucking pus—"

"Dav, enough." Kassius snaps, cutting him off.

"I don't understand what is going on." I whisper. Enzo turns around, his hand palming my cheek. I jerk away from his touch and step back into Kassius. "I can't be here. I can't do what you are asking me to do." I spin around, directing the last part to the king.

"What are you asking her to do?" Enzo seethes behind me.

"He wants my aether." I respond and the king grits his teeth, his jaw hardening. "He wants you to take it from me."

"I offered you freedom! I offered you a life."

"No, you offered me chains!" I yell back, my fists tightening. "You want to take the one thing that belongs to me and then force me to marry your son. You want my bloodline and my power; you don't care about anything else."

"Dav." Kassius says a hint of warning in his tone. "You can't take it. Don't you understand how Amaya got her gifts? How her parents got theirs? Balance. If you take her aether by force, you will be encouraging the fates to do something much worse."

"I want to win a war. I want to decimate the child sitting on the Noterran throne and I will do so by any means." He snaps.

"No, you won't. Did you think we would all standby while you ripped away her magic? Do you think we would all standby and watch you destroy her?"

"What does she matter. She is a child—"

"She is our *queen*!" Kass responds. Davenport's eyes widen. "She is our queen, not some child or princess. *She* is the reason the armies are gathering. *Not* you." My heart is pounding in my chest, my eyes glazing over.

This is too much. I don't want this. I don't want to be their queen or their reason for fighting.

I don't want any of this.

"I am the reason you are all here. I am the reason this so-called rebellion is still standing. My money, my men, my country. It's all *mine*."

"My country is gone." I whisper, my voice cracking. "My people. My friends. My parents. Everyone I ever knew and loved is gone. I have no desire to start a war with Tobias. Do you understand what he is going to do if he finds out what is really happening over here? Do you know what he is probably doing to my uncle right now? We will not win. Not against him."

Quiet spreads as the three of them stare at me. A snort leaves Davenport's throat as he shakes his head.

"That is the person you are rallying for. She will lead you into ruin." He turns, heading back up the beach.

"Elaenor, we can win."

"No, we can't." I turn and look at Enzo. "Before you got there, before you saved me, I stabbed him. I shoved a scalpel through his throat, and do you know what happened? His skin knit itself back together and reabsorbed the blood as if it was never shed. The blood that was *black*. He told me that I couldn't kill what was already gone. He *cannot* be killed. What do you expect to happen if we destroy his armies? Do you think we will just walk up and end him? No. We won't. He will burn us to the ground, and I won't let you all die in my name."

"Where were you going?" Kassius responds, ignoring everything I just said.

"Home." I whisper before following the king back to the palace.

I don't sleep. I consider the sleeping draft sitting in the medical bag by the door. I consider a lot of things, but my eyes are fixed on the open windows. The sun rises, but I still sit here, watching it grow higher and higher.

My stomach cramps, my hand resting on it. Hunger settles deep in my belly, but I ignore it. I ignore the wave of nausea and the pain that follows. Weak. That's what I am. The king knows it. He's right, and he's correct in saying they are rallying behind the wrong person. Maybe he would be better suited for this, better suited to take over.

I can leave, go to Labisa. A country I never believed I would see. He could handle the war and the armies and Tobias.

I could be free, or as close as I can be.

But what is the cost? Giving him the starlight that burns through my veins? Giving him the only defense I have ever had? That is the cost? Would I even miss it? It may have always been there, but it has only been present for days.

I could go back to normal. I could *be* normal for once.

I take a slow deep breath, putting the pain radiating in my pelvis behind. I lift my hand, staring at my palm. It only takes a second before a spark appears. Then another.

It forms a ball in my hand, and I finally take the chance to inspect it. It sparkles as if it's filled with glitter, but the more I look, the more I see the individual stars. Each streak of lightning, each spark, is just a tight-knit line of stars.

My free hand lifts and I thread my fingers in between the lines of light. It tingles as it brushes my skin, and a smile passes over my lips.

It's beautiful. So damn beautiful.

Can I give this up?

I watch the stars dance around my palm, tears lining my eyes.

I jump when it sputters. The light winks out before coming back. I sit up, my eyes widening. It sputters again and I flinch.

I see it then.

A shadow seeps from my palm, swallowing the light whole.

The shadows are gone within a blink. I focus, begging the starlight to reappear, but it doesn't.

I don't feel it.

But I have my answer.

Chapter Forty

The Caged

My footsteps are near silent as I make my way down the hall. I can hear chatter coming from the library, but just like last night, I pass by. I take my steps one at a time as I descend the stairs. My mind is empty, quiet, and a familiar calmness settles over me.

I round the corner and stop short. The same exact guards who disappeared last night are back, standing side by side in front of the closed door. My eyes pass over their armor, silver and gold reflecting the sun beating down through the windows.

I hit the bottom step and they both turn and look at me. They nod shallowly before looking back down the hall. My brows pinch together in confusion, but I turn from them, heading towards where I think the council room is.

The large double doors are closed, and I push them open, ignoring protocol.

Davenport and Kassius are bent over the map, hands holding what appear to be mugs of coffee. They look up in surprise as I enter and rest my hands on the back of one of the chairs.

"Princess." The king says by way of greeting.

"I made a decision." I say as strongly as I can. Kassius's eyes widen as he glances between the two of us.

"Enlighten me." Davenport's voice is filled with humor, as if he can't wait to hear what I have to say. I take a deep breath, my fingers flexing on the back of the chair.

"I will marry your son. I will help you go to war against Tobias. And when this over, when *I* end his life, you can have it. You can have every drop of the magic in my veins. You can take it all and I will live out my life as a nobody. You can have the kingdoms; you can have Viridiana—"

"Elaenor!" Kassius cuts me off.

"I don't want any of it." I say through gritted teeth. "I don't want *any* of it." I repeat. Davenport smiles, and I can see the resemblance. The resemblance between Tobias, Evreux, and Viktor. It's the look of someone who feels they have won. "I never asked for this. I never wanted this life. But you do. So take it once the war is over. Take everything."

I don't wait for a response. I turn on my heels and head out of the room. My feet guide me back to my room where I find the rolled parchment, the certificate of mine and Tobias's marriage. I unroll it, my eyes catching on his signature.

I can feel him. I can feel him inside me, destroying every ounce of me that is left. His shadows are flowing through my veins, last night was proof of that, and the only way for it to stop is if he's gone.

If he's dead.

The paper crinkles in my hand and I exit the room, making my way down the hall.

Everyone is there. Enzo, Scarlett, Laenie, Erik, Emery, and Nithe, who's eyes look dark and shadowed, as if he hasn't slept. As if he only just returned this morning. I hold his gaze and lift the parchment.

"Burn it." He looks at my outstretched hand and then back to my eyes. He slowly sets his mug down and takes it from my hand. I quickly glance around the room, everyone's eyes on me.

"Are you sure?" It's Emery who asks and I look at her. Her golden hair is braided in one long plait, hanging over her shoulder. Her eyes are bright, clear.

"I'm sure." I respond. Nithe takes a step towards me as if he is going to say something, but he doesn't. He walks past me to the unlit fireplace. He takes a slow deep breath, and everyone stares at his back. When he exhales, a stream of fire the color of his eyes shoots into the fireplace. I flinch, feeling the warmth from across the room.

He looks back at me once, asking again. I nod and he tosses the parchment in. We are all silent as we watch the paper turn black under the purple flames. I stare unblinking as I watch the black turn to white. I watch until the paper is nothing more than ash and the fire winks out.

My stomach cramps and I feel a cold sweat wash over me. I inhale slowly, fighting against the exhaustion, before turning around and heading back to the room.

A knock sounds on my door. I don't look up from where I am sitting on the settee, staring at the orange flames. Sweat drips from my neck, soaking into the tunic I am wearing. The door opens and I can feel his presence, almost as well as I felt Tobias's, which should concern me, but I feel nothing.

"I assume we will be wed this evening." I say into the silence, my eyes still focused on the fire.

"Is that what you want?"

"What I want is of no consequence, Nithe." I say just as monotone.

"I don't think that's true, little witch." He sounds sad, broken. Like me.

"We will soon be at war, and despite how much I loathe your father, how much I don't trust him, he's right. People are coming together to fight; armies are being built. If I walk away, if I allow myself to just be used, there won't be anything of me left."

"Being wed isn't just a ploy, it isn't just a step towards winning a war." His voice sounds almost hurt, but I disregard it. I have to.

"It is a piece of paper. One I will watch burn when this is over." I respond. He sighs, coming to sit in the settee behind me. "What happened last night, Nithe?"

"I told you; I am a wyvos." His deep voice is hesitant, but I can't ignore the feeling of it snaking down my spine, as if it's wrapping itself around me in a warm embrace.

"Not that, although I still can't wrap my head around that. After. You lost control, you were going to hurt them."

"When I am in that...*form*, I am more animal than human. Instincts take over—"

"Enzo said that you were territorial over things you loved."

"Enzo is wrong." He interjects.

"You can't have feelings for me. You can't." I turn in the seat, staring in his eyes.

"I assure you, little witch, I feel nothing but duty bound." My gaze holds his. He has to be telling the truth. I can't do what I need to do if he falls for me.

"My heart will always belong to someone else." I admit.

"Tobias?" I don't say anything for a moment.

"Tobias owns every single part of me, every cell in my body, but not my heart. I love him, I do, but it's not him who I wish were beside me."

"Theo." He says softly, knowingly.

"I don't know how or why, but I saw him. When I was dying. He's the reason I got up, and part of me feels like when this is all over, I will see him again." I admit, remember the feel of his lips on mine.

"The only reason that would happen is if you died, Elaenor."

"That's the second time." I say, my eyes meeting his.

"What?"

"That is only the second time you have used my name."

"It has been way more than that." He gives me his playful, lopsided grin. "Don't get used to it." I smile softly, my eyes returning to the flames. "Will you be alright?"

"I have no choice. If I have any chance of killing him, I need to be stronger, don't I?" He doesn't answer, but I don't need him to.

I can't be meek; I can't be timid. I have to fight.

I have to be able to fight.

Chapter Forty-One

The Caged

I'm silent as I am readied. The same three women from the other day dress me in a gown of white lace and gossamer. My hair is curled, with half tied up. I stay silent throughout the process, letting them do what needs to be done.

Paints and creams are applied to my face, making me look more human, or as human as they can make me look. I sit still, letting them do what needs to be done.

The dress is simple. It's made of different shafts of gossamer, letting my pale skin show through. Lace makes up the soft, off-shoulder sleeves, and covers the parts of my body that would make it indecent. Honestly the entire dress is indecent, but I am past caring.

I slip white, silk slippers on and give myself a once-over in the mirror. My hair is shiny, longer than it's ever been. The icy locks almost look like they are glittering, matching the starlight I haven't been able to conjure since this morning. It should phase me, it should make me nervous or scared, but the ever-present numbness has settled on my mind, along with stones in my belly making every movement painful.

But I ignore it.

I ignore everything.

My lashes are thick, and they applied a little wing of kohl across the upper lid. My cheeks have been reddened and a soft mauve color has been applied to my lips. I look different. I don't look like myself. I turn away and step into the hall. Enzo is there, his black jacket and tunic cut close to his body.

"Are you ready?"

"This isn't my first wedding." I joke, but it falls flat. A ghost of a smile twitches the edges of his lips, but he doesn't respond. He offers his arm and I take it, letting him guide me downstairs to the throne room.

Everyone is dressed up, and people I have never seen before line the hall. Scarlett's eyes are red, as if she's been crying, her hand clutching onto Emery's. I let my eyes pass over her and towards the front.

Nithe is wearing all black, his jacket much like Enzo's, but thicker, nicer. His hair has been groomed, but its unruly waves still make an appearance. It's the crown that catches my eye.

A tiny, silver skull of what appears to be a deer sits front and center, with silver antlers fanning out from it. Black diamonds are pressed into it and the edges of silver blend into deep brown with green leaves. It almost looks as if it was half crafted out of metal and half out of twigs. My eyes track down to his and he offers me a smile.

The walk down the aisle is a blur and then he is taking my hand in his. His calloused fingers are warm as they wrap around my small hand, swallowing it. I look away from him and towards the man standing at the top of the dais.

"We are gathered here today to wed Queen Elaenor Rosenthal of Viridiana—" My breath catches. "And Prince Nithe Dragehna of Labisa." My eyes flick back to Nithe's as he stares at the reverend. A throat clears in the audience, and I glance over to see the king cross his arms, his eyes digging into mine, burying themselves. I force myself to look away.

Words are muffled as they reach my ears and I nearly flinch when Nithe grabs my other hand. I look up at him, but it's not him I see.

It's Tobias.

His hair shining in the light pouring in through the windows, copper sparkling in the sun. His blue eyes are light, piercing, as he stares into mine. His brows furrow as he opens his mouth.

"I, Tobias, pledge my heart and soul to Elaenor and the continent. I will support and cherish her; I will ensure she lives a long happy life. I will be her one and only." My lips part as I stare into his eyes.

No. This isn't real.

"I love you, Elaenor. You will always belong to me." His fingers tighten on mine, and I take a step back. This isn't real.

"Rosie?" A deeper voice penetrates my mind and I blink a few times. Tobias's hair fades to black and then it's soft purple eyes staring into mine. "Are you alright?" He whispers. I glance around and everyone is staring at me. I had taken a step back, my hands no longer in Nithe's. I nod and step back towards him, offering him my hand.

"As I was saying," the reverend continues. "Do you, Prince Nithe of Labisa, take Queen Elaenor of Viridiana as your own?"

"I do." He whispers, before sliding something cold on my finger. I glance down at the ring, one I never had with Tobias. It's made of a deep silver, nearly black, but it's the stone in the center that catches my eyes. The stone itself is black but inside of it there are tiny white dots. My hand moves on its own and as the sun hits it, the stone glitters, reminding me of the night sky.

My eyes meet his again, shock evident on my face. He smiles shyly and looks away.

"Queen Elaenor, do you take Prince Nithe to be your consort?" Consort? I open my mouth, my throat thick.

"I do." I whisper. Nithe's hand flips over, revealing a black ring entirely made of the same stone that is in the center of mine. My fingers hesitantly grab it and slip it on his finger.

"For the first time, I present Queen Elaenor of Viridiana and King Nithe, consort to the queen." My eyes widen as I realize the wedding is over, completely different to the one I had with Tobias.

Nithe's left hand, the one with the ring, slips from mine and gently cups my cheek. He steps forward, his eyes bright as he looks down at me, his right arm encircling my waist, pulling me against him. His breath fans across my face, bathing me in the scent of him. I look up, my eyes locking on his as he bends down.

His lips are warm, gentle, as they press into mine. It's a quick kiss, one that sends weird jolts down my spine. He pulls back, his eyes still focused on mine.

"Your Grace?" I turn, Nithe's hand still on my cheek, and look at the reverend. "If you will kneel." I look back at Nithe before stepping out of his grasp and kneeling.

The reverend is handed a small tiara and my lips part. It looks nearly identical to Nithe's but has small teardrop diamonds dropping down to hang below the skull, and black antlers stick out of the top, partially hidden by black leaves. A black ribbon hangs off the back of the deep brown twigs, tied in a bow. I dip my chin as it is placed on my head, sitting low on my forehead instead of on the crown of my skull.

Cheering ensues and Nithe offers me his hand while I stand and turn to face the crowd. He steps close to me, leaning down to whisper in my ear.

"The tiara is the crown of Labisa, as is the ring. It belonged to my mother. I thought it was only fitting it now belonged to you." I turn and look at him, my nose briefly brushing his chin.

"Temporarily." I correct. "What does this mean for your father?" I whisper.

"I think it would mean he's been demoted." I turn and look at the king, his eyes shadowed, a smirk plastered to his face.

"I don't think he knows that yet." I respond.

"I don't think so either."

Chapter Forty-Two

The Caged

Nithe's hand stays planted firmly on my lower back as we are congratulated and greeted in the ballroom. I don't know how they were able to set up the room for a reception so quickly, or who any of these people are, but it was done. Just another thing reminding me of the weeklong carnival celebrating Tobias and I, but instead it's Nithe next to me.

I kept trying to step out of his grasp, but all it did was win me sidelong glances from our guests. I have a part to play. I have to act like I am happy for this marriage, for this union.

I sip from my glass of white wine. Both tart and bubbly, a drastic difference to the wine I had last year. A wine that ruined sugar for me.

"How long must I stand here?" I whisper as Nithe gives someone walking by a smile. He exhales through his nose.

"The same amount of time I have to." He replies, his tone dry.

"Which is?" I counter. His hand slides to my hip, and he squeezes, digging his fingers into the flesh.

"Too long." I step slightly away from him, his hand returning to my lower back.

"I need something to eat." I say with a smile, walking away from him. Tingling starts in my fingers, but it's not the same. Something is off, something feels wrong. Not that any of this feels particularly okay since it's so new, but it doesn't feel bright like it did at first. It feels as if the light inside of me is slowly being dimmed.

Slowly dying.

A hand grazes my elbow as I reach a table filled with finger foods. My head swivels, but I catch sight of her chestnut hair before I react. The smile plastered to her face doesn't reach her eyes.

"This should feel different than last time, but it feels the same." She admits quietly.

"Unfortunately it seems I will remember this time around." I pointedly glance at the glass is my hand.

"I'm sure they have hemlock here somewhere." She says with a smirk.

"Not funny." I say dryly.

"I thought it was funny." She pouts and picks up a cube of cheese.

"He won't stop touching me."

"He likes you." I snort, wine shooting up my nose causing me to cough. "I'm serious."

"You can't be. I've only known him for a couple of days."

"Emery propositioned him a few weeks ago when she was bored and lonely." Her face falls a little. "He said no and that he was more or less engaged. That he had no desire to sleep with her." She gossips. My pulse skips and my lips freeze where they are resting on the rim of the glass. I pull it away, my mouth slightly ajar, speechless.

"Why?"

"Why did he say he was engaged or why did he say no?" My words fail me, and she smiles softly. "I think he felt like it would be cheating on you, even if you didn't exist yet."

"Scar, I can't do this. This is too much, too soon." Her hand grasps mine and she pulls me in for a hug.

"Don't do anything you don't want to do. Maybe I'm wrong, maybe it has to do with honor and not his heart." She pulls back. "Or maybe I am right and there is someone in this room who likes you and has no desire to control you."

"That we know of." I retort.

"You know he's different. He reminds me of Theo a little." She looks off into the crowd of guests.

"If Theo had a stick up his ass."

"You only knew one side of him. He had a backbone, and he definitely had a mouth on him." She smirks again and I glare at her. She rolls her eyes before plucking another cube of cheese off the tray. "You may have loved him in the end, Elaenor, but he was *my* fiancé." She walks away, her arm brushing mine.

I can't shake the feeling of dread lingering in my stomach. I lift my glass, downing it before grabbing another and doing the same.

I have no desire to remember this day, and if I don't have Tobias's poison, I can still use alcohol to numb everything.

My head is spinning, my limbs numb, as I grab another glass. I lost count somewhere around five, but I stopped caring. I seemed to have lost that ability too.

My feet feel light as I spin around the dance floor, people dancing around me. I feel free in this moment. As if nothing and no one plagued my dreams or my days. As if for once in my life I can be my own person.

Berry red liquid splashes on the ground as my cup tilts. I don't remember switching the type of wine I was drinking. I giggle at the puddle on the floor. The dark color blending into the light wooden floors.

It could almost be blood.

I stop spinning. My head takes a second to catch up as my eyes stay fixed on the puddle.

Nausea fills my belly, making it heavy. My eyes blur and then I can see it. My hand drops the wine, the glass shattering on the floor. I don't see anyone react; I don't see anyone but him.

I can see his head as it rolls away from the puddle. Light eyes open and lifeless, staring at me. No body connected to it. Just the singular part of him. His lips parted, blood trickling out of the corner. A sense of foreboding, a warning echoes in my mind.

My eyes snag on his dark hair, short and tousled. It's not Theo, it's not Donovan, it's—

"You are causing people to stare, little witch." His breath is hot in my ear as he wraps his arm around me from behind. "Come with me." He grabs my hand, pulling me through the crowd. My feet act on their own, following him blindly, as my eyes stay fixed on the wine until it disappears through the crowd of people.

Sounds return, momentarily deafening me as the laughter and cheers erupt around me. Sweat beads on my hairline, dripping down my temple. He keeps pulling me until we reach the hallway, cool air funneling through the open doors.

"What is it?" Nithe asks as he stops and turns, his hand still in mine.

"I saw—" I stop, my throat thick as I stare up at him.

"What did you see?" I shake my head and pull my hand out of his.

"Nothing. I saw nothing." His amethyst eyes are soft, concerned, but they harden as they shift to look behind me. I spin, coming face to face with King Davenport, his eyes bright and unbothered as my nose brushes his chest.

"Oh, the happy couple." He sneers. Nithe's arm wraps around my stomach, pulling me back against him. I fight the urge to step away, even if his touch makes me nauseous. "I hope you weren't retiring for the evening?"

"No, father. Just getting some air." His chest vibrates against my back as I feel his hand tighten.

"Well I hope you have gotten enough; we have one more activity for this evening." He smiles, a grin so wicked it could rival my father's, before he licks his lips and stares down at me.

"An activity?" I ask, my voice quiet and weak.

"No." Nithe snaps behind me. I try to turn and look at him, but he tightens his grip.

"What?" I question.

"The consummation ceremony." Davenport responds and I feel the wine come back up my throat.

Chapter Forty-Three

The Caged

"No." Nithe repeats as we both stare at his father. My legs go weak, and I probably would have fallen if Nithe wasn't holding onto me. Davenport snaps and two guards walk up, a gagged Enzo between them with a dagger pressed to his throat. Gods. I jerk towards him, but Nithe holds me back.

"What are you doing?" I yell. My nails dig into Nithe's arm as I stare at my brother. He's glaring at the king, blood trickling from under the cloth wrapped around his mouth.

"Everyone is already getting ready. This is happening." He turns and walks back into the ballroom. I can hear him clap his hands and the guests go quiet. He says something and cheering ensues. The guards walk down the hall, dragging Enzo with them, before disappearing.

"Enzo!" I yell, but Nithe still won't let go.

"Stop!" He snaps and I relax, letting my head rest onto his chest as I blink away the tears, only then does his arm loosen.

"Nithe." I mumble, stepping out of his grasp. He steps around me, blocking the door to the ballroom. "I can't." His hand reaches up to touch my face and I flinch before stepping back. Hurt crosses his eyes, but he drops his hand.

"I'll fix this." He responds, before following after his father. I stare after him before turning back the way Enzo went. I start down the hallway, following after him. Ladies appear in front of me, stepping out of the darkness, and smile at me.

"Yes?" I say hesitantly as I stop.

"We are here to ready you, Your Grace." One of them says before they guide me back towards the stairs.

"No, you're mistaken. This isn't happening." I respond as one of their hands clamp around my arm, forcing me up the steps. "Let go of me!"

"The order came from the king, Your Grace." Another says as I reach the second floor. Despite my protests, they usher me into my room and start stripping my wedding dress off of me. A white nightdress that is completely sheer and brushes my knees is pulled over my head. A thin dressing gown is tied around me. White slippers are slid on my feet and my new crown is removed. Pins are pulled from my hair, and the icy strands fall around me like a curtain.

I tried to fight, to pull out of their grasp, but everywhere I turned there was another one of them.

I am once again pulled out of the room and guided down the stairs. I protest, asking them to stop, but their cold fingers stay planted on my elbows. I am led down a different hallway to a door that is open.

"Please, I don't want this." I whisper, but they don't look at me. Their faces are flat, lifeless and a little creepy. They shove me into the door, and I stumble, barely catching my footing.

My breath catches and it almost feels as if my heart will stop as I take in the room before me.

A large bed with gauzy white curtains draped around it, partially blocking the view, sits in the middle. Nothing else is in the room besides torches keeping it alight. The wall on the direct opposite side of the bed is covered in shutters. The shutters are open, revealing the crowd of people who all gathered to watch this horrific moment. They sit in partial darkness, smiles plastered to their faces as they get excited for what they are about to witness.

Noise behind me causes me to spin around. Nithe steps in, his eyes wide as he takes in the room. I don't mistake the hand wrapped around his arm connected to his father. I step forward and he smirks at me before closing the door, Enzo and the guards close behind him. I don't miss the sound of the lock as it clicks into place. My heart drops as I realize there isn't a way out of this.

"Nithe." I whisper, my hand resting on my stomach. His hands clench into fists as he stares at me. His eyes slowly pan down, taking in my nightclothes, before returning to my face. Tears prick in my eyes, and I don't fight as they trail down my cheek. "Nithe." I repeat. He steps closer, hunger deep in his eyes.

He's going to make me do this, isn't he? Scarlett was wrong. He's the same as Tobias. The same as everyone. I shake my head and step back. He glances over at the shutters, the hushed whispers making it through the open slats.

"Don't make me do this." I whisper, trying to keep my voice as low as possible. He steps closer to me, his breath fanning over my face, caramel-scented whiskey coating his breath.

"My father is standing outside with Enzo. If we do not do this, he will slit his throat." His voice is rushed as he says it through clenched teeth. My eyes widen and my knees give out. He grabs my elbow, holding me up.

"Why is he doing this?" I whisper back. "Is this really because he wants us to bear a child so soon? Is that all everyone thinks I'm worthy of? Every person in my life has demanded an heir, demanded a child. *I* am still a child, Nithe." His eyes soften and line with silver as his fingers loosen on my elbow.

"I know, I know." He whispers. "I don't know what to do. He is standing out there right now with a sword to his neck. What do you want me to do?" Hurt fills his voice as he stares into my eyes. "He's my best friend."

"He's my *brother*." I counter.

"I don't know what to do." Resolve settles over me as reality sinks in.

"What's one more night I didn't ask for?" I mumble. He scoffs and releases my arm, stepping back.

"Don't. Don't compare me to the men who raped you, Elaenor. I am stuck in this just as much as you are." My breath lodges in my throat as he spins around, walking to the door. He pulls on the handle, but it doesn't open. He slams his hand against it.

"Don't even attempt it, son." The king's muffled voice filters through the door. Someone laughs from the viewing room, and I fight the urge to scream, to throw something. He leans his head against the door, and I can see his shoulders shake as if he's fighting against sobs that are building in his chest.

You can do this, Elaenor. You can do this. I repeat over and over.

I cross the distance between us and slip in the small space between his chest and the door.

"I'm sorry." I whisper, looking up at him. Tears line his eyes, his pupils darker than normal. "I can do this." My voice cracks and he searches my eyes. "We can do this." I say, my hands lifting to rest on his chest. His breath shudders and he closes his eyes momentarily.

"I am so sorry, little witch." He whispers. His eyes open, and the irises have gone black. His hands drop from the door, grabbing my face. His lips slam into mine, forcing them to open. My hands fist on his tunic as I fight the fear building in my chest. His hands slide down, wrapping around my waist as he pulls me against him.

Tears pour down my cheeks, mixing with his as he turns us around and guides us to the bed. My hands are shaking as the mattress hits the back of my thighs. His tongue caresses mine gently, his lips soft against my own. He leans down, grabbing the back of my legs and hoisting me up. My legs wrap around his waist as he climbs on the bed, the curtain falling closed behind us.

The mattress is soft against my back as he lays me down, nestling in between my legs. His lips release mine as he slides them across my jaw and down my neck. Tears pour from my eyes as I turn to look at the viewers.

"Don't." He whispers, his hand coming up to pull my chin towards him. "Don't look at them." His dark eyes hold mine and a choked sob works its way out of my throat. I nod and his lips find mine again.

I kiss him with everything I have. Begging, pleading for my body to react the way it needs to. The way it needs to in order to make this painless. His arm comes up to rest beside my head, my hands holding onto his cheeks. His free hand slides down in between us. He unties my dressing gown, parting it and revealing the thin fabric that hides absolutely nothing.

His hand slides down, gripping my hip before sliding down to my knee, hitching my leg up and against him. He slowly rests his lower body on mine, and I flinch. Hardness meets my soft flesh, the roughness of his trousers scraping my skin through the thin nightdress.

His lips pull away from mine, his eyes finding mine again before he glances down, his eyes trailing over my exposed body. From the tepid peaks of my nipples to the dip beneath my navel, he sees it all before he tilts his head back up.

"Whatever you have to do, whoever you have to think of to get through this. I understand." He whispers.

"Who will you be thinking of?" His lips part as he tries to find an answer, but none comes. His lips slam into mine just as his hand releases my knee and slides over my backside. He lifts the nightdress up, sliding it up to my stomach. His hand leaves my body, as he shifts above me. My legs shake, my hands sliding down to fist his tunic as he settles back down on top of me. His head comes down, nuzzling my neck as my hands slide to his shoulders.

"I'm sorry." He whispers before sliding into me. A gasp escapes my mouth at the fullness, at the stretching. He stills part of the way in before repeating his apology. He flexes his legs and pushes himself in to the hilt. I gasp again, my back arching as he goes past the point anyone has before. My eyes close and my mouth opens as he moves slightly.

The movement sends a spike of both pain and pleasure through me, and I fight against it. I fight against the warmth I feel low in my core. He slides out before thrusting back in. His hand slides back down to my knee, pulling my leg against him. He lifts up, his hand brushing hair off of my face before he cups my cheek.

He moves again and I fight the small moan hitting the back of my throat. His eyes lighten and I know he can feel the wet heat pooling inside me.

I don't want to like it. I can't. But it was always the same with Tobias. No matter how much my mind fought, my body responded. My body accepted it. Took pleasure in it, and this is no different.

Except it is. He doesn't want to do this either. He doesn't want this. He doesn't want me.

We were forced into this.

"Are you alright?" He whispers and I nod. A tear escapes his eye and I catch it with my thumb.

"Are you?" I respond and he nods hesitantly. I lean up, my lips pressing to his before I arch my back. He flinches and his breath catches, but it causes him to move again.

He kisses me with fervor, with pain. With desperation as he moves. He picks up his pace, his free hand tangles itself in my hair as he thrusts into me over and over again.

Shaking hits my limbs as my core starts to burn. I can't fight the growing orgasm, no matter how much I try.

And maybe I don't want to. Maybe I needed this. I needed a cleanse from what occurred before. Maybe I needed to be touched with affection.

His lips pull from mine again and he presses his forehead to mine.

"*Nora.*" He gasps and my eyes shoot open. *Nora.* Release hits me like a bomb and he catches my cries with his lips, just as release hits him. His body shakes above mine and he empties himself inside of me. As he does as his father wishes.

Tears once again fill my eyes as he stills. They pour freely down my cheeks as his lips slip from mine. I hear a loud *thump* and look over to see the shutters have been shut. A click sounds on the door, and Nithe quickly grabs a blanket, throwing it over us, but the door doesn't open.

He leans back over me, slowly sliding himself out before reaching between us to pull my dress down. He sits up, fixing his pants.

My hands come to my face, covering my eyes as I feel sobs building in my chest. My body shakes as I silently let them out. So many emotions coursing through my body, through my head.

"It's just your body reacting. It doesn't mean anything." He whispers, trying to explain away my body's response. At the betrayal I feel.

It's too much. I can feel their icy brush before I open my eyes and see the stars glistening on my fingers. Nithe gets off of me, collapsing next to me on the bed, watching my hands.

"Let it out, little witch. Sometimes it feels better." I take a deep breath and let it be free. Lightning comprised of a million stars shoots out of my hands, hitting every torch and extinguishing them. The room stays alight with bright white light. It feels good, it feels like I have control over something, as if—

Black streaks start to appear, breaking up the white light, before it all goes dark. Silence fills the room as we lay in the darkness. But we don't talk about it.

We don't talk about what we just did or why the starlight darkened.

We don't talk about anything.

Chapter Forty-Four

The Caged

It wasn't hard to lose Nithe as I weave through the maze of hallways with an ache building low in my core. I knew where I was going, but he stopped along the way to find Enzo. I close the door to my room, flicking the lock.

I abandon the pale dress, letting it fall to my feet in billowy waves, and walk over to the dressing room, slipping a different nightdress over fresh undergarments. I glance at the crown that is set on a shelf in the closet. It's beautiful, albeit creepy with the skull, but it's so different to the one I was forced to wear in Noterra. The one I haven't seen since I got here.

I wonder what they did with it.

I exit the dressing room and a slight shiver slides down my spine. The air is cool, despite the heat during the day. I'm curious how summers in Rakushia will compare to Chatis or Noterra. We are quite a bit farther north, but it's flatter here. There isn't the humidity or fogginess I grew up with, and so far it doesn't seem to get as warm.

I climb through the large window, stepping out onto the balcony. Something of which has become a nightly routine. Being outdoors, it allows me to breathe. I don't feel...suffocated.

The stone feels good against my bare feet, staving off the heat that seems to be radiating from me continuously. I feel ill today, as if food is stuck in my throat. I am nauseous, weak, and tired. I need to sleep, but I can't.

I'm afraid I'll see him.

The door to the room opens and I spin around. Nithe walks in, a smirk plastered to his stupidly handsome face.

"Stop breaking my lock!" I yell and climb back through the window.

"It's not *your* lock, it is *our* lock." He remarks before throwing himself on the bed.

"What are you doing?"

"Relaxing?" He says matter-of-factly.

"Go do it in your own room."

"This is my room."

"No, it is *my* room."

"We are wed, husband and wife, married, tied together–" He starts to joke, and I debate throwing something at him.

"I get it. But I don't want you here."

"Well that's too bad because they already cleared out my room. Yours is bigger and has a balcony." He shrugs before closing his eyes and relaxing into the pillows.

"We are not sleeping together."

"I have no desire to have sex again, Rosie. Maybe tomorrow?" Gone is the tear-filled man who is broken like me, and in his place is the stranger who keeps appearing. The one who uses humor to hide his pain. The one who brushes everything off to seem unbothered.

"That's not what I meant, and don't call me that!"

"I am too tired to argue with you. I am sleeping here, get over it." He sighs as he relaxes deeper into the blankets.,

"Nithe, *please*." My voice cracks and his eyes open. He looks at me, taking in my changed nightdress, clenched fists and furrowed brows. He slides off the bed and walks over to me, I step back but he isn't fazed. His hands find mine and force them to relax.

"I have to stay here. If my father finds out we aren't exactly a happy couple, I am not sure what he would do."

"He knows what we are." I retort. "I can't do this, Nithe. I was forced to marry Tobias, forced to be his in all ways. After earlier, I can't–"

"Hey," he drops one of my hands and cups my cheek. "I know. I'll sleep on the couch." His thumb brushes under my eyes, catching a stray tear, before he bends down and kisses my forehead. His hands leave, taking his warmth with him, before he heads into the bathing chamber.

My hand instinctively goes to my stomach as another wave of nausea hits. Too much wine. Too many emotions. I've been feeling sick for days, but it just has to be everything, I just need to get used to it. I take a slow, deep breath until it passes.

I'm sitting up in bed by the time he returns to the room. My hands are knotted, wringing in my lap. He doesn't look at me as he enters, his skin damp. He's only wearing a pair of sleep shorts, his bare back glistening in the candlelight. He grabs the blanket off of the back of the couch before dropping down into it and sighing.

"Are you alright?" I whisper, breaking through the silence.

"Believe it or not, little witch. I am not entirely thrilled to be married either, or forced to do what we did."

"I'm sorry."

"Don't be. You are stuck in this just as much as I am." He mutters.

"I know." I take another slow deep breath as a lump forms in my throat. I'm cold, but sweating. I feel ill. I feel like I'm going to– "Oh gods." I rip the blanket off of my lap and stumble out of bed. I run across the wooden floors and throw the bathroom door open. I almost don't make it as I fall against the tub, vomit exploding out of my mouth.

"Rosie." A warm hand gathers my hair as I throw up. It takes a few minutes before I am left dry heaving. "You're warm."

"I feel cold." I say through my gasping breath.

"Are you ill?"

"I don't know. I just feel nauseous, and I have a weird pain in my stomach." I admit as I gag.

"It could be all the wine." He ponders, but I just shake my head.

"It started before then."

"I am going to ask you a really personal question." He says after a moment of silence.

"What?"

"Do you know when your last monthly bleed was?" I open my mouth to answer, but nothing comes out.

"I don't know." I whisper as panic courses through my veins. "Nithe, I can't. I can't be pregnant with *his* child. What if it's not even his? It can't be yours!" He drops my hair and I turn to look at him.

"We'll figure it out. It could be nothing."

"Nithe—"

"We will figure it out."

"This isn't your problem."

"Yes, it is. We are married, so whether or not that child is biologically mine, that is my child. If there even is a child to begin with." He stares at me with such devotion, I don't even know how to respond. Scarlett says he's duty-bound. He's here because of duty, and I need to remember that.

"You don't owe me anything." I shake my head and look away from him.

"No, I don't. But you don't deserve to be alone in this either." He uncurls his legs, letting them stretch out in front of him as he sits on the floor.

"Nithe, I don't know what to say."

"I still don't like this, little witch, but at least until this war is over, we are married." He says with a shrug.

"Can we do that? Can we divorce after everything is over?" I ask, hope sparking somewhere inside my black hole of a mind.

"If that is what we want, why not?"

"What do you mean, *if*?" I question. He can't expect me to want to stay married to him forever.

"I don't foresee this being over for a while, who knows where we will be years from now."

"I don't have the capacity to love anyone, I told you that." I say a little harsher than I should have.

"Who said anything about love?"

"Name only, Nithe. I am not offering you anything else."

"I don't care what we do or don't do in this room, but to them," he gestures to the rest of the palace, "to *them*, we need to look like we are trying. We have to give the people hope. Hope that we will get out of this war with Tobias and out of this questionable period of time. They need to believe that we are united." I nod before letting another bout of dry heaving wreck my already exhausted body.

It takes a while before I am well enough to stand. I clean my face and brush my teeth before climbing back into bed. I pushed Nithe away, telling him I was fine, and he curled up on the too-small couch. The candles are blown out, the fireplace unlit. The only light funneling in is coming from the stars.

Starlight.

I curl up on my side and open my palm. It only takes a second and a small ball of light forms on my palm, seeping out of my skin. Relief washes over my body at the sight of it. It sparkles as if it was made of a million little stars. I hear movement and close my fist. Nithe is sitting up on the couch, staring at me. He shakes his head and sighs before dropping back onto the cushion.

Darkness. All I see is darkness. I can hear the sound of leather meeting stone, footsteps echoing in the chamber. I'm cold, freezing. The only things on my body are the metal chains around my wrists and ankles, biting into my flesh.

"You never should have run, Ela." His voice is soft, hurt, but I can hear the anger hidden underneath. "Why did you leave me?"

"I had no choice." My voice croaks and I swallow, trying to ease the scratchiness in my throat. I'm so thirsty. When was the last time I ate anything?

"You had a choice, my love, and you made the wrong one." He's closer and I can feel his fingers gliding up my bare thigh, up and over my breast before gripping my chin. "Now you are going to pay for it." His lips slam into mine just as something stabs into my arm. I scream against his lips, his tongue invading–

"Elaenor, wake up!" I gasp as I sit up, my forehead hitting something hard, throwing me back onto the mattress. "What the *fuck*?" My hand brushes my forehead and I wince. "You just headbutt me!"

"Why were you leaning over me like a creep?" I snap as I rub at the bruise that is no doubt going to appear.

"You were crying in your sleep; I was trying to wake you up." He mutters, rubbing his forehead too. His eyes look tired.

"Oh." I say softly, blinking through the pain radiating down to my eyes.

"What were you dreaming about?"

"Nothing." I mutter and drop my hand.

"Well I know that's a lie, but good try." He snorts and falls back against the pillow next to me.

"Go back to the couch."

"No, you are just going to wake me up again."

"Nithe." I complain.

"Tell me what you were dreaming about, and I'll leave." I groan and roll my eyes.

"I was dreaming about the time I ran." I admit after a second of silence.

"You ran?" He seems surprised.

"Yeah, of course I did."

"Tell me about it." I stay quiet again. Letting my thoughts build, organize themselves. How much do I want him to know?

"I don't know how long it had been at that point, but I woke up unchained. I think Tobias was too drunk and forgot to lock me back up." I snort. "He was asleep and the guards were outside the door, so I slid off the balcony and ran." I shrug.

"Really?" His eyebrows raise as if he's impressed.

"I didn't get very far. I was caught by one of the guards patrolling the courtyard and he brought me back to Tobias. He kept me in the dungeon for a bit after that. He would keep all the lights off so I couldn't see, and he would do things..."

"What kind of things?"

"He would draw on my body with a scalpel. He would write his name, or whore, or something along those lines. It would always be gone when I woke up the next day." My voice is quiet, pained, as I remember the feeling of the blade slicing through my skin. I shudder.

"Gods."

"I don't know how long I was down there, but he just kept asking me why I ran. It wasn't until I gave him an answer that he let me leave the dungeon."

"What did you say?" He asks.

"I told him one of the guards tried to touch me, which wasn't a complete lie." I shrug again. I look up at him, he looks disgusted.

"Did they?" I look away from him, fighting the tears. Disgusted. That's what he feels. Why wouldn't he? His wife has been with more men than she can even count.

"Yes." My voice cracks. "I was left alone a lot, naked and on the bed. He left various guards to watch over me, and sometimes they would find pleasure in my *state*." I sigh.

"Does Tobias know?" I shrug again. "Stop that."

"He knew about one of them, and that guard was placed in the dungeon, but he somehow got out. He visited me a lot during the last few days."

"Rosie..."

"There were so many in the last few days. So many. If I am pregnant, Nithe, what if it isn't Tobias's? What if it's one of theirs?" I sit up and run my hands through my hair.

"It doesn't matter."

"It does!" I yell, turning to face him, smacking him in the stomach. He's looking up at me, my body angled over him. He looks down at my chest and to my hand that's resting on his abdomen. His hand lifts up and closes around mine.

"No, it doesn't. We can't exactly terminate it—if there even is an *it*, so we deal with it. Together."

"I'm so tired, Nithe. I am just so tired." His hand leaves mine and brushes a tear off my cheek.

"I wish I could take away your pain, your scars." I shake my head and fall back against the pillows.

"There is only one that I want gone." I admit. Which is the truth. The only one that labels me as *his*.

"Can I see it?" He asks, curiosity lacing his voice.

"See what?"

"The scar you want gone?" He answers, curiosity filling his amethyst eyes.

"Why?"

"I don't know." He turns so he's looking at me, his eyes soft, curious.

I nod and roll onto my back. He adjusts so he's on his knees, leaning over me like I just was to him. I lift the hem of my nightdress, exposing my underwear and my bare stomach. He sucks in a breath before lifting his hand. His fingers are cold as they brush the two lines carved into my flesh. Goosebump spread across my stomach and my breath catches. "I saw it a bit earlier, but I couldn't make out what it was. Enzo said he branded you; I just couldn't believe it."

"Pretty, isn't it?" I snort and his eyes flash to mine.

"Elaenor..." I push his hand away and pull my nightdress back down.

"Goodnight, Nithe." I roll over, putting my back to him, as I feel the tears form. I keep my crying silent, my breathing even, as I soak the pillow under me with salty drops of sorrow.

"What was it like?" He says after a few minutes.

"It was a nightmare I couldn't wake up from, no matter how hard I tried. And even now, I fear that I am still asleep."

Chapter Forty-Five

The Caged

Breakfast the next day is quiet. I can barely eat, nausea pooling in my stomach making every swallow painful. Nithe was gone when I awoke, much to my relief, but Scarlett made sure I wasn't alone. She's been going on about her situation with Enzo and Emery and I find the whole thing irritating. I don't care what she does and who she does it with, but it's the same situation that she was in with Theo and Rhea.

"I can't choose." She whines.

"Well you might have to." I mutter as I pick at the scrambled eggs.

"Who, though?"

"I cannot choose for you, Scar. One of them is my brother and the other is my cousin."

"Well she's not actually your cousin since Viktor isn't your dad." I roll my eyes and set my fork down. "I love them both."

"You love attention." I retort.

"Yeah, I do." She sighs and takes a sip of her coffee. I can't drink it. Anything sweet or syrupy makes me sweat and I know it's from the drugs Tobias forced me to take.

My heart still clenches when I think of him. I know it isn't right, I know I shouldn't feel that way, but I love him. I remember everything he did, I remember the pain, but I also remember the gentleness, the thoughtfulness. It's hard to separate the two.

I can't love him.

"How was your night after everything?" Her voice cuts through my thoughts and I look away from the window.

"Uneventful."

"No secondary consummation?" She jokes, and I narrow my eyes. "Sorry."

"I don't foresee anything but name when it comes to our marriage, Scarlett. I can't. I can't be close to another." The door opens and Nithe comes in, sweat dripping from his bare chest.

"You sure about that?" She smirks before rising and brushing past him.

"What?" He asks as he turns back to me.

"Where did you go this morning?" I ask as I pick up my glass of water.

"The sparring room. Enzo and I train every day."

"I want to train." He snorts and plops down in the chair Scarlett vacated. He picks up her discarded fork and takes a mouthful of eggs.

"Sure." He says around his food.

"I'm serious." I glare at him, but my eyes trail down his bare chest. Thick muscles line the tan skin, flexing with each breath and swallow. The ink swirling around his forearms moves up to his shoulders and down his chest, as if he's covered head to toe in scales and swirls. It's beautiful. I tear my eyes away.

"You think that's wise given your condition?"

"What condition?"

"Your pregnancy?" He says with wide eyes as if he thinks I forgot.

"We don't know if I am pregnant, Nithe." I snap and cross my arms.

"I don't think it's smart." He shakes his head and lifts the mug Scarlett left behind. He sniffs it and shrugs before taking a sip.

"I don't really care what you think." I retort, rising from my chair. I turn my back to him, stepping into the dressing room. I slip on a pair of leggings and a thin camisole. I step out of the dressing room and slip on a pair of boots I had left by the window.

"What are you doing?"

"Changing." I furrow my brows.

"For?" He presses.

"Training." I say with a sigh.

"You can't just go punch things, Rosie." He smiles as if the idea of me learning to protect myself is comical.

"Don't call me that!"

"Okay, little witch." He says with a smile.

"That's not any better."

"Pick one." He challenges.

"How about, Elaenor? My name?" I snap.

"Mm, no I don't like it. I think I'll stick with Rosie or little witch." He laughs and takes another sip of Scarlett's coffee.

"I hate you." I mutter as I open the door and step into the hall. It takes a few moments and a lot of turns before I find the sparring room on the other side of the palace. A part I hadn't yet explored.

The back wall is gone, leaving the room completely open to the outside. Weights line one wall, and a raised platform sits by the other side. The rest of the room is completely empty. Enzo is on the platform, punching the air. He looks over at me as I step up, his brows raised.

"What's up?" He drops his arms and walks over to me. There is a light bruise along his jaw, and I swallow the bile in my throat.

"I'm glad to see you're okay." I smile and he looks away.

"I don't want to talk about it, Elaenor." His voice is rough, and I don't push it. "What can I do for you?"

"I want to train." He smiles as if I am joking. "I'm serious." He's silent for a moment, before he holds his hand out, helping me up onto the platform.

"Do everything I say, alright?" I nod. He puts his hands on my hips, twisting slightly. One of his feet comes around and kicks my left one forward. "Arms up." I raise my arms, my fists clenched, and he arranges them at an angle.

He holds his hands out and gestures for me to punch, so I do. My knuckles pop and I wince at the contact.

"You are weak." He says flatly.

"No shit." I mutter, throwing my fist through the air again.

"You're small, unstable. You won't win in hand-to-hand combat; you should be training your magic." He drops his hands while my hand is flying through the air. I hit his chest, and he doesn't even flinch. A ghost of a smile passes his face. "See?"

"I want to be able to protect myself." I say softly, my brows furrowing. He takes a long deep breath before raising his hands again. I spend the next hour punching his hands, kicking where he instructs, and attempting to free myself from his grip, which I failed at.

I failed at all of it.

By the time we are finished, I am sweating and exhausted. My leg is cramping, as is my neck. No doubt my injuries I seem to keep forgetting I have. I collapse onto the sparring mat and Enzo sits down next to me. I feel nauseous, but not as bad as last night. Instinctively, my hand rests on my stomach.

"You aren't that bad, but you need a lot of practice if you want to be able to defend yourself."

"Don't lie to me." He chuckles. "I want to be able to fight. I want to be useful.”

“You are useful; you are our queen.”

“I want to be more than a figurehead, Enzo.” He’s quiet for a moment, before the clearing of a throat causes me to jump.

“Come on, little witch. We have things to do.” I sit up and see Nithe standing there, looking stupidly perfect. His tunic is tight, showing off his sculpted chest and I force my eyes to stay on his face.

“What?”

“Hurry up.” He snaps and I roll my eyes. I dangle my legs off the raised platform, that can’t be more than three feet high, and prepare to jump down, but Nithe’s hands grip my waist and lift me. I put my hands on his shoulders as he lowers me to the floor, our chests brushing. He wipes a piece of sweaty hair off my forehead and then steps back and holds his arm out for me to pass him.

“Where are we going?”

“You need rest.” I stop as soon as we get out into the hallway and spin around.

“Are you serious?” I spit, as I rise up on my tiptoes.

“You need to bathe and rest; this can’t be good for you.” He reaches forward to brush hair off my face again and I slap his hand away.

“Nithe, let’s get one thing clear. You do not tell me what to do. You do not control a single thing about me. If I want someone who will manage every second of my day, I’ll go back to Tobias.” He grabs my arm and yanks me closer. Citrus and mint invading my senses.

“Don’t even joke about that. He will kill you.” My eyes widen and I can almost swear he hears my heart beating. My eyes flick to his fingers around my wrist and he drops it.

“Don’t ever touch me again.” I spit before spinning away from him.

He hasn't returned to our room by the time dinner is over. Both Laenie and Scarlett joined me today. We ate roast chicken and laughed. I smiled for the first time in a long time. And it felt good.

They left after dinner. Scarlett had to get to Emery, and Laenie couldn't stop blushing at any mention of Erik, who was convinced he had to be permanently stationed outside my door if Nithe wasn't in here. It took some convincing, but he left with Laenie after dinner.

I'm standing before the floor length mirror in the bathing room, my eyes on my bare stomach. I haven't gained much weight since I've been back, but I feel like there is something there. I don't want to believe it, but I feel it. My hand rests on my stomach and tears form in my eyes.

Tobias.

I probably have a piece of him inside me and I don't even know how I feel about it.

"We won't be able to go to Lenus about this yet." My head swivels and I see Nithe leaning against the door frame. "We have to wait a few weeks." I nod and tear my gaze away from him, dropping the hem of my shirt. I can feel his warmth as I push past him. His fingers graze my hand and I yank my arm away from him.

"Don't touch me." I snap as I step away from him.

"I'm sorry about what happened before."

"Don't be." I say dryly.

"I worry. I know why you feel the need to train, but I'm worried."

"About what? That I'll get stronger? Be able to protect myself? Not have a need for you?"

"Rosie—"

"Stop." I spin around and face him. "Stop calling me that. Stop pretending you care when you don't. You don't have to lie. Neither of us do. We are married. I still love my psychotic ex-husband who got off on torturing me, who you have a need to make a nickname out of. That's what Rosie reminds me of. *Him.*" He flinches. "I still think about what could have been if I had left with Theo when he asked. I don't want to be here. You don't want to be here. I have this primal *need* to go home, but I don't even have a home. I have nothing." My voice cracks.

"You have all of us. This is your home." He gestures to the room.

"No, it's not." I shake my head and step back.

"Labisa can be. Wherever it is you want to rule from, we can call that home." He takes a step forward, closing the distance between us.

"I don't want to rule. Are you not listening? I don't want this. I don't want the crown, or the magic, or *you.* I want to be free. I want to be no one of importance. That is why I did this. So when the war is over, I can be free." My voice cracks and the tears start to pool in my already swollen eyes.

"Well that is too damn bad. You have no choice in this. You think any of us want this? You think Enzo wants to be here? Or Laenie and Erik? What about Scarlett? You don't think she wants Rhea back? Nobody wants to be in this situation. Not a single one of us!" He yells, his breath fanning across my face. I can smell the caramel notes of alcohol on his breath and for some reason, that just breaks me.

Does he need the alcohol to be able to live with the fact that I am his wife? I'm so stuck in my own world that I'm not considering that he was forced into that consummation too.

His freedoms were taken away.

I am not the only person caged here.

"I know." My voice cracks. "I know we have all endured the unthinkable. I know I am not the only one who has been through horrible things. I am not the only one suffering. I know that, Nithe. I do."

"Work with us. Stop fighting against us." He pleads, his hands grabbing my arms.

"I don't know how. I don't know how to not be fighting for my life every second of every day." A tear falls down my cheek and I turn away from him. He hesitantly lets go of my arms and I walk to the windows, looking out at the grounds. I hear his footsteps as they approach and then the sound of his soft sigh. A warm hand brushes my lower back and I lean forward, resting my forehead against the glass.

"You'll learn." He says.

"And what if I can't?" I turn and face him, his hand resting on my hip as if he has to be touching me.

"You have to."

Chapter Forty-Six

The Caged

I don't know where anything stands. My new marriage. My mental stability. Everything is strange and foreign, and nothing fails to make me feel broken.

Like an outsider.

After our argument, Nithe left. I heard him in the library with Erik, Enzo, and Emery. The three E's I'm going to call them now, since they seem to all be joined at the hip. I fall asleep quickly for once, a luxury I never knew.

The air is damp, humid, as I stare at the trees. They are packed in tight, but they look different, foreign. Instead of thick pine trees, the ones in front of me are tall with thin trunks that seem to stretch into the sky. A thick canopy of leaves spreads out at the very top of those trunks, blanketing the woods in a dark shadow.

These trees feel...alive.

I spin around, the moss beneath my feet soft. I take a few steps and I don't feel a single thing stabbing into my bare feet. It's as if the woods were made so that you could be close to the ground.

Close to the magic that brewed underneath.

A giggle escapes my lips as I continue to spin, my thin dress twirling around me. My icy hair falls in front of my face, and I brush it back as I stop. Something rustles behind me, and I turn, expecting a person, but that's not what is behind me.

A beautiful feline of some sort with silky tan fur dotted with black rosettes, prowls through the trees. Its eyes are a deep green, almost as dark as the trees. Its body is long and sleek, its paws big—nearly the size of my head. The animal steps in between the tree trunks, its rounded head low as it gets close.

Fear should be consuming my mind, adrenaline pumping through my veins, but it isn't.

I know that the creature in front of me isn't a threat.

"Hello," I say softly and slowly fall to my knees. Its nose gets close enough that I feel its breath on my cheek, and I close my eyes. I smile as whiskers tickle my face, as it smells me, as it figures out who I am.

Silence blankets the woods, and a low growl vibrates through the air. I hesitantly open my eyes to see the feline is no longer there.

In its place is a white wolf, huge and daunting. It's standing over me, drool dripping out of its open mouth as it bares its teeth at me. I fall back on my arms as it leans down, close enough to bite.

"Please don't hurt me." I whisper, staring into its white eyes. They soften for just a second before the beast lunges.

It's quiet when I wake. The moon is still high, keeping the room bright enough with its silver glow.

I sit up, expecting to see Nithe on the couch, asleep, but he's not there.

I sigh as I slip out from under the thin sheet, my feet meeting the warm floor. I pad over to the bathing room and splash water on my face. I glance up into the mirror and groan. My skin is pale, lifeless.

Nothing new.

I step back into the bedroom and slip a dressing gown over my shorts and tunic. The hallway is dark, the torches burned out, but I make my way over to the sitting room on the upper floor, but as I near the small room, I find that it's empty. I frown as I turn back to the hallway. I almost give up, questioning why I am even looking for him while heading back to the room, but I hear a small laugh. A giggle. It's coming from the room across from mine.

The one belonging to Emery.

I tiptoe over to her door and press my ear up against it. I hear the laugh again and then the sound of something falling over. It's quiet for a second before I hear another voice.

"Just this once." A deep, smooth voice echoes throughout my head.

"Shh." She shushes him and then I can hear shoes hitting the floor. "Hurry up." She whispers and then it's quiet. My hand flies to my mouth and I step back.

Nithe.

He's in there with Emery? My heart skips a beat and I step back again, my shoulder blades slam into one of the paintings hanging on the wall, causing a loud noise. I spin around and try to make it back through my door before Emery's opens, but I don't.

"Elaenor?" His voice is soft, silken and I freeze. My nails dig into my palms, and I turn back around. He's shirtless, his hair mussed, his feet bare. All of that was enough to tell me what was happening, but it's his swollen lips my eyes are fixed on. "What are you doing up?" His voice is quiet, but accusatory. As if I was the one doing something wrong.

But it wasn't me.

It was him.

"I couldn't sleep." I whisper, my eyes finally meeting his. They are lowered, his brows pinched.

"Little witch…" He steps forward and I turn around, heading back to the room.

"Good night, Nithe." I say, cursing how hoarse my voice sounds. I close the door behind me, flicking the newly replaced lock back into place.

I don't know why. I don't understand it, but tears pool in my eyes. I hastily wipe them away as they treacherously stream down my cheeks.

"Gods." I whimper as I let the pain invade my senses. Why? Why her? And why do I care? It's been two days since we wed, but it's not like I am offering him anything. He should be able to get it elsewhere.

I cross the room and crouch through the open window, stepping onto the balcony. The night is warm, the air still and thick. I collapse against the glass windowpane and allow the tears to fall freely.

My eyes fix on the stars, and I feel the thrum of electricity before my vision turns white along the edges.

"Just breathe. Let it out." I whisper to myself as I let the excess power, the aether that is reacting to my emotions, funnel out of me, sinking into the stone floor.

"Let me in." His voice is quiet, saddened and muffled by the door. I don't move. I watch as the aether rolls off of me in waves, getting dimmer and dimmer as my heart slows. It only takes seconds before it stops, and the thrum of electricity is gone. "Please."

I don't move from my place on the balcony, and before long, his soft knocking is gone.

I don't know how long I stay out there, how many hours have passed, but I don't enter the room again until the sun has crested the hills.

The second the sun rose; I was out of the room and in the training ring.

I kicked and punched the air, over and over, until I worked up a sweat and tears poured down my cheeks. I continued over and over, repeating what Enzo taught me the day before.

I won't be helpless.

I won't be weak.

I will be somebody *worth* something.

I scream as I punch the air again, before slamming my hands over my face, trying to stop the tears.

The door shuts and I turn to see Emery walking in. Her hair is in one long plait down her back, her face blank and emotionless. I fight the irritation I feel at her presence. But I know it's not her fault. I told Nithe it was just in name. I told him that's all I wanted.

So why do I feel so betrayed?

She is dressed in what looks like training leathers and boots. Sleek black leather coats her skin in tight shafts, a laced corset across her ribs that houses a couple daggers. She has leather cuffs around her forearms laced with leather cord and part of me wonders if it's stained with dragonink like Theo's?

Or would it be wyvosink?

She looks good, her outfit radiating power, and I made a mental note to ask for clothes like that. Not that I even knew who to ask.

"What are you doing?" She asks, an amused smirk on her face.

"Trying to learn how to defend myself." I spit, my arms crossing over my chest.

"I hate to break it to you, cousin, but your tiny fists are ineffectual." She says, her voice just as perky as her perfect face.

"Enzo already said as much." I snap.

"You need to train with weapons." She says after a few moments of silent glaring on my part.

"What if I don't have weapons?" I counter.

"Then you use magic?" She says as if I'm stupid. I grit my teeth and take a deep breath.

"What if I don't have that?"

"Well, then you better hope someone is around to help you." She says with a snort.

"I don't want to *need* help, Emery. I want to be able to defend myself!"

"Then learn how to not get caught!" She replies just as loud and stares at me, her hands on her hips, before she unsheathes a dagger I didn't even see on her thigh and climbs onto the platform. She holds it out to me, and I hesitantly take it, the hilt cold in my palm.

"Try to attack me." I raise an eyebrow and she smiles, all former irritation gone. "Get all of your unjustified anger out on me. You won't hurt me."

"Unjustified?" I snap. "He's my—"

"He's your nothing! You made that clear!" She yells, getting in my face. I scream before taking a step forward and throwing my arm through the air, attempting to slice her arm. She spins out of the way and ends up behind me. She kicks my wrist and I drop the dagger.

"Hey!" I yell, spinning around and grabbing my throbbing wrist.

"Pick it up." I sigh and bend down to grab the dagger, she lunges for me, throwing her arm around my neck and slamming us both to the ground, with her on my back, knocking the breath from my lungs. "Get free." I scratch at her arms, not even reaching her skin through the thick leather. I kick out, but she moves her legs.

"I can't." I snap, relaxing against her.

"Then don't get caught." She lets me go and my head hits the mat.

"It's not that easy." She points at the dagger.

"Pick it up."

"No, you'll just grab me." I mutter, climbing to my feet.

"No, I won't. Pick it up." I stare at her and then quickly snatch the blade. "Again." I lunge at her, and she steps out of the way.

Again and again and again. I am left sweating by the time Enzo walks in.

"What am I interrupting?" He smirks as he jumps onto the platform.

"She needs to learn evasion and weaponry, not combat." She snaps.

"I know that." He says defensively. I glance in between both of them, and I can feel the anger radiating off of them in waves. My eyes widen at realization that they are probably having a Scarlett caused stand-off. I bite my lip to keep from smiling. Seems I'm not the only one annoyed that Emery is sleeping with their...something. I don't know what Nithe is to me.

"I need food." I say, stepping out from between them and ungracefully jumping off the platform.

They are still silently staring at each other when I leave the room and shut the door behind me. I let a small smile sit on my lips as I walk down the long hallway. By time I turn down the hallway that holds the council room, my smile falters.

Voices carry out. Voices filled with irritation and disdain. I step up to the doorway, glancing in. Kassius and Davenport are staring at each other, their eyes hardened.

"What's going on?" I ask as I step into the room. Davenport takes one look at me and scoffs.

"Nothing of your concern, *princess*." I flinch at the insult to my status but catch Kassius glaring at him.

"Does it have to do with Tobias?" Kassius sighs before turning to me.

"He's filled the woods with these *creatures*," his face pinches in disgust. "Worse than the ones you saw in the lake." I almost forgot about that failed attempt to flee. I don't even think I've fully processed that Nithe is a dragon, or a *wyvos* as he called it.

"What can we do about them?" I ask, stepping up to the table. I glance at the map and see rose shaped pieces scattered around the board. A single white rose piece, like the one Tobias had for me, sits at the center of Rakushia. "Is that me?" I point at it.

"Yes." I lean over and pick it up.

"Can we change it?"

"Change it?" Davenport sneers.

"I am no longer a Rosenthal, thanks to you, so yes. Change it."

"To what?" Kassius asks softly.

"Anything but that." I set the piece back down, glancing at the countries on the other side of the sea. Places like Ovobia, and Dorin, Khailes. All countries I have never even heard of.

Countries I now rule over.

"Anything else, *princess*?"

"I would like to know what is going on with the war. Where are our armies, how many men do we have, what are our chances of survival? All of it." I strengthen my voice, trying to sound as regal as possible.

"Why?" He spits.

"I am the queen, am I not?" I tilt my head.

"In title only."

"No, that wasn't our deal." I lean forward, my hands on the table.

"You are merely a figurehead. The armies you ask about? They are *mine.* All of this is mine." He snaps, gesturing to the entire map. I bite my tongue. How am I supposed to assert dominance if I don't even want this?

"You said I could be involved." I say through gritted teeth.

"You can be involved by giving our troops something to look at."

"Dav!" Kassius interrupts, but I swallow the fury down, letting it fade.

"Fine." I mutter before turning out of the room and heading back to my chambers. There is no reason to fight, no reason to complain.

I didn't want this.

I *don't* want this.

Right?

Chapter Forty-Seven

The Caged

Time moves differently when you aren't happy. I thought it moved weird in Noterra, but here, it's been days, and it feels as if I have lived through weeks, months even.

Nithe snores from his place on the settee, another night where I can't sleep, where I can't even breathe deep enough to get adequate oxygen. Nausea has been coming on in waves, sending me to the bathing room multiple times. Each time, he wakes and holds my hair. He ensures I drink water and make it back to bed.

Each night he cares for me, yet all I feel is fear in his presence. Fear after that first night after our wedding. Fear of what we had to do with an audience. Fear for what I felt and for what I enjoyed. Fear for what he did with Emery.

Fear for the person I am becoming.

We don't speak during the day. I eat my meals alone or with Scarlett, I train with Emery on how to use a dagger, which I feel as if I might be getting good at it. I train with Enzo on maneuvers and attempts to escape captivity. Yet no one teaches me about my aether. No one even attempts to help me control it or learn more about it. I try to learn more about our armies, but everyone shuts me out. I feel like everyone is avoiding me, *afraid* of me.

I can barely channel my aether, no matter how many times I will for it to come. It feels like the connection between my mind and the starlight has been severed or is barely holding on.

I slide out from underneath the covers, my bare feet meeting the warm wooden floors. The night is hot and humid, pressing down on me like a blanket of stones. I climb onto the balcony and rest my hands on the railing. The moon is full, bright. Stars sprinkle about the dark sky, reminding me of glitter.

I stare down at my hands, my palms tingling as they feel the stars presence. I will for the starlight to appear. Lightning flashes through my veins turning them white before they fade to a deep black.

I squeeze my hands shut, a tear escaping my eye.

Something is wrong. Something is eating away at my insides, and I feel like it's going to keep feasting until all that is left of me is skin and bone.

I should tell someone, maybe Kassius. He would know what to do. But do I want him to even try? Why would I give up my one chance at disappearing, if that is what is happening?

I used to tell Tobias everything, but that only got me yelled at, or told I was lying. I used to be open, letting everyone in, but not anymore. I can't let anyone in.

I shake my head and rest my hands back on the smooth stone.

I have a purpose, even if its just a visual one. I need to give the people hope, give them something, *someone*, to fight for. But how could I ask them to fight if I am not even fighting for myself.

The nausea pummels through me and I scramble through the window, nearly falling face first onto the ground. I reach the toilet seconds before what little dinner I ate comes spewing out of me.

My body convulses as I crouch over the toilet, tears mixing with the snot running down my face. A warm hand gathers my hair as another rubs my back.

"Breathe, little witch." He whispers, his voice tired and quiet.

"I can't—I can't keep doing this." I stutter in between ragged breaths.

"What do you want to do?" My back spasms as the dry heaving sets in.

"What can we do?"

"Do you remember what Kass said about your mother? What they did with her pregnancies?" I lean back, resting my cheek on my forearm.

"He siphoned their lives." I whisper. His eyes are dark, the pupils nearly black as he looks me over.

"Your skin is pale. Your eyes are hollow and lifeless. This isn't good for you."

"Are you suggesting we have Enzo siphon the child's life away?" His eyes soften and he licks his lips. His hand drops my hair, but his other one stays planted on my back.

"You aren't healthy. I'm worried this will kill you." I close my eyes for a second, relishing in the quiet. He doesn't speak, his warm hand rubbing up and down my spine, easing some of the tension.

"Do I have to decide right now?" I whisper, my eyes still closed.

"No, this is your decision. I won't make it for you." I nod as his hand slides off my back. I crack open my eyes to see him adjusting, stretching his legs out in front of him.

"I'm sorry I keep waking you up." He smiles, exhaling out of his nose.

"Don't apologize. I don't mind it." I close my eyes again, exhaustion setting in. My limbs ache from training with Emery. My veins burn from the aether that fails to show.

"I can't sleep." I whisper.

"What?"

"I haven't slept since the first night you were in here."

"At all?"

"I can't."

"Why?" I crack open my eyes again. He's leaning forward, his brows furrowed.

"I'm scared." My voice cracks as I hold his gaze.

"What are you scared of?"

"That when I wake up, I'll be back on that table." The whites of his eyes go black, and I can feel the heat radiating off of him.

"You will never go back there. I promise." His voice is thick, deep, as he fights against the beast under his skin.

"Don't make promises you can't keep." I lift my head off the toilet and use it to help me stand.

"Do you trust me?" His hand catches my elbow as he helps me rise.

"I don't know you well enough to answer that question." I reply, pulling out of his grip. I walk to the vanity, leaning against it as I grab my toothbrush and paste.

"Give me your hand." He slices a dagger across his palm before setting it down on the vanity.

"What are you doing?" I say breathlessly as I search for a towel to cover his wound.

"Give me your hand." He repeats. I set the brush down and hesitantly place my hand in his, the blood hot against my clammy skin. "I, Nithe Draghena, pledge my life to yours. I will never harm you, nor will I allow another to harm you. I swear this with my life and with the blood of the wyvos running through my veins." My eyes hold his, my lips parted. I feel a sudden rush of electricity in the room, and I gasp. I rip my hand from his as a purple glow spreads across my palm and up my arm.

"What is this?" Swirls and swirls of purple ink stain my skin. I can make out wings, scales, and stars intertwined within the different twists. "Nithe." My voice cracks as I look up at him.

"I've never had that happen before." His voice is just as hoarse as mine, his eyes wide. I glance back down at my hand and watch as the ink fades until it's gone. I can just make out a small shimmering outline of what was there when I turn my arm, but it isn't visible unless you are looking for it, unless the light catches it just right.

"What did you do?"

"It was an oath, a life oath. I have one with Enzo, but this didn't happen." I glance at his hand and see the same shimmering swirls on his, visible on top of the black ink. I reach for it and turn it over, palm up. Stars and wings intertwined with swirls and streaks of lightning reflect on the torch light as if it's made with glitter. My pulse skips a beat and I drop his hand.

"I don't..." My voice trails off.

"I will never let harm come to you, little witch. And now I have physical proof of that oath." He lifts his tattooed hand, brushing hair from my face and tucking it behind my ear. "I promise." He says again before dropping his hand and exiting the bathing chamber.

I turn back to the vanity, my gaze snagging on the mirror hung on the wall. My face is thin and pale. My eyes truly do look hollow and lifeless. I catch sight of a black line by my temple and lean in. A silent gasp escapes my lips as I realize what it is.

The black line is my vein.

I hesitantly reach up, my tattooed hand causing me to flinch as I press it to the vein. It glows softly and then dissipates.

I return to the bedroom with a clean face and mouth. Nithe is up, sitting on the edge of the bed, staring at his palm as he moves it back and forth in the light.

"Have you ever seen a life oath do this before? I know you said you haven't had it happen, but has someone else?" I ask, walking up the edge of the mattress. My fingers play with a loose thread of the throw, avoiding his gaze.

"No." His voice is choked, hesitant. He drops his hand and stands. "Get some sleep, I'll stay up."

"No, you don't need—"

"It's been days, and you haven't slept, Elaenor. I will make sure that nothing happens." He gestures towards the bed again and I climb in. I curl my legs up against me, my arm wrapping around my knees as I rest my head on the pillow.

Exhaustion pulls at me, beckoning for me to join it in its dark abyss. Fear pulls at the edge of my mind, warning me of what could happen, but I push the thought away.

I can hear him walk to the window before sitting in the chair by the small dining table. His breathing is even, but every inhale causes my stomach to turn. I open my eyes again to see him staring at me.

"Sleep." He commands.

"It's your breathing."

"What?"

"Your breathing is what keeps me from falling asleep. It sounds like..."

"I'm not Tobias."

"I know that." He's quiet again.

"Try." I nod and shut my eyes again. Unconsciousness pulls at me and for the first time in forever, I give in willingly.

Chapter Forty-Eight

The Caged

I open my eyes to bright light, sunshine filtering through the windows at an angle too high to make it morning. I sit up abruptly, hair falling over my shoulders. Breakfast lay on the table untouched, and the chair Nithe was in is empty. I swivel my head towards the sitting area, where the settee sits empty. I sigh and fight the yawn hitting my throat. A soft snore behind me causes me to jump and I scramble out of bed.

Nithe lay on the other side, his clothing fresh as if he already bathed and changed. His deep hair is slightly damp and wavy, tucked behind his ears. The scar running through his eye is nearly the same color as his skin, but still visible. My chest pounds and my hand settles against my throat as I try to take a deep breath. My free hand falls to my stomach, and I nearly cry with what I feel.

I rush to the bathroom and lift up my cotton tunic to see the tiniest of swells in my lower stomach. It's so small that I wouldn't know it was there if I was eating properly. But I can see it.

A choked sob escapes my lips and tears pour down my cheeks. I let them consume me for only a moment. I let the ragged breathing and the tremors take control, but after a few seconds, I take a long, deep breath. I force the lump in my throat to dissipate and the tears to dry up.

I can't keep feeling sorry for myself.

I quickly turn to the dressing room and change. I slide on a pair of leather leggings and a camisole, slipping the leather corset overtop. I mentioned to Emery that I wanted some, and she made sure it happened. They are all black, making me feel like I look as powerful as her, even though I know my nonexistent muscles give my weakness away.

I pull my hair back into a plait, letting it fall down my spine as I slip on my boots. Within seconds, I am out the door and headed to the training room.

Enzo and Erik are sparring, swords out and sweat gleaming. Laenie and Scarlett are lounging on a recently added settee, glasses of something bubbly in their hands. They are both wearing loose dresses that barely brush their knees, probably to stave off the heat.

"Elaenor!" Laenie says with a smile, gesturing for me to join them. I smile back but continue my walk up to the raised platform.

"Good *afternoon*, little sister." Enzo teases and I roll my eyes.

"We have no idea who was born first." I sneer as I plant my hands on the platform to hoist myself up. Two warm hands grab my arms, lifting me onto the mat. I brush off their arms and scowl. "I can get up here myself." Their eyes snag on my arms, as if they can see the slight shimmer. They glance at each other once, but don't say anything about it.

"Where's Ni?" Erik asks, sweat gleaming on his upper lip as he breathes heavily.

"He was asleep when I left."

"Rough night?" Scarlett shouts from where she is stretching out, kicking Laenie in the stomach.

"I was ill, and it kept him up." Enzo raises an eyebrow. "I must have eaten something." I shrug and take a few steps towards their rack of blades. "Can I join?"

"You think you can take us?" Enzo laughs, sheathing his sword on his hip.

"Probably not." I admit, snatching a long, slender blade I have become comfortable with.

"No blades, just evasion right now." I nod and reluctantly set the blade down.

"Emery has been teaching you as well, right?" I nod again. "Well, just follow our lead." Erik says with hesitance in his voice.

"I'm not the same girl I was in Chatis." I snap, noting the glances to Enzo he keeps sneaking. "I need to do this. I need to be able to do this." Enzo nods and gestures for me to move.

I start walking in a semi-circle in front of them. I keep my eyes on their feet, anticipating their movements. Erik lunges forward and I spin out of the way, his fingers grazing my corset and slipping off. I quickly turn around, keeping them in front of me. Enzo is smirking, his hands out and ready. He lunges for my left, and I side-step straight into Erik's arms.

One of his arms goes around my neck, the other reaching for my stomach. I jam my elbow into his ribs, causing him to double over. His arm loosens a fraction around my neck. I use it to my advantage and throw my legs out from under me, landing on my knees. He pitches forward and releases me in time to catch himself.

I hear cheering from Laenie and Scar and I let a smile cross my lips. I motion for him to rise, and he sends me a wild look, something like excitement crossing his eyes.

He climbs to his feet and starts to circle. I keep myself in between them, turning every half second to make sure I have eyes on both of them. Erik lunges and I duck out of the way, his arm connects with Enzo's as they both go for me at the same time. I spin around as I stand, but Enzo's foot comes out of nowhere, catching me in the back of the knee.

I land to the floor with a thud and try to stand again. Enzo's arm goes around me before he throws himself onto his back. One of his legs wraps around mine, pinning me to him. His tightens around me, with the other one of them holding the back of my head. Erik lunges towards us, a blade in his hand. He slams it down inches from my face. I yelp as it stabs into the mat.

"What did you do wrong?" He demands.

"I—I wasn't watching your feet." He nods.

"You have to anticipate their next move, always."

"There are two of you." I counter.

"There could be five men up against you at any point, Elaenor." Enzo says from under me, his leg sliding off of me. I take Erik's outstretched hand and stand.

"You two are so worried about hurting her, that you aren't training her properly." A deep male voice pipes up from the side and the three of us all turn to look at Nithe.

"Fine. You do it then." Enzo snaps as he steps aside. Nithe snorts as he jumps onto the platform, shrugging off his leather jacket. Enzo and Erik walk to the edge of the mat as Nithe gestures for me to move.

I look over at Scar and Laenie, their faces stuck between nervousness and amusement. I step further onto the mat and raise my arms. Nithe smiles and sticks his hands in his pockets. I glare at him and run forward, throwing my arm towards his face. He slaps my hand away and spins around, shoving his elbow up and into my face.

My nose instantly burns and my eyes water. I fall to the ground, my hand coming up to touch my nose. It comes away bloody, and I look up at Nithe, anger fueling my glare.

"Hey! Too rough!" Erik snaps, running over. I hold my hand up, gesturing for him to stay back.

"It's not my fault you ran into my elbow." Nithe laughs, tucking his hands back into his pockets. Gone again is the man who pledged his life to me. He promised to make sure no harm came to me, and the man who uses humor as a front returns. I find myself questioning which version of him is the true Nithe?

I rise, wiping my bloody hand off on my leggings.

"More?" He sneers as he takes a few steps to his left. I don't give him a chance. I run for his left and he moves to his right, but I sidestep, sending my fist flying through the air and hitting him in the cheek. My knuckles pop and instant pain radiates to my elbow, but I don't stop.

His eyes darken as he spins around, reaching for my arm. He grabs my wrist and yanks me over to him. I kick out, hitting his knee as he moves to avoid a foot to the crotch. He stumbles a little before kicking out and sweeping my legs out from under me. I fall back just as his hand tangles itself in my braid and he flips me before bringing me to the ground. I slam my eyes shut, expecting the mat to collide with my face, but it doesn't.

I open my eyes to the mat inches from my nose as I dangle above it. Nithe still has a hold of my hair, my hands wrapped around his wrist. I bend my knee, letting it rest on the mat to loosen the strain on my scalp. He releases me with a shove and my hands catch me before I hit the mat.

"You give your moves away. You don't have any way to surprise someone." He stalks around me slowly. Blood drips from my nose onto the mat. "You are weak, and you won't survive out there."

"Ni," Enzo warns.

"No, she needs to hear this. You think you are all high and mighty. You think nothing can touch you." He continues.

"I know fear." I whisper. He knows what I am afraid of. He knows. So why is he saying this?

"What?"

"I know fear!" I yell, rising to my knees.

"Then *use* it!" He yells even louder. I scream, throwing myself to my feet and rushing towards him. His eyes widen as my peripherals turn white. My hand slams into his chest, sending him flying off the platform. He lands hard on his back, a strained gasp escaping his lips.

My eyes widen and my hands cover my mouth as I stare at his still body.

"Oh my gods." I whisper. Nobody moves, and at once, Enzo and Erik turn towards me. Nithe coughs and the panic slowly subsides.

"You good, brother?" Enzo says. Nithe lifts a hand, giving us a vulgar gesture. Tension dissipates as we all collectively take a deep breath.

He coughs as he stands, his shirt singed where my hand hit him.

"I'm sorry." I say softly.

"Don't be." He brushes his hands off on his pants before stretching his neck and standing. "No matter how much you train, you will not be strong enough to fight. We can do everything we can to make you as strong as possible, but your strength lies in your aether. Use it. Don't be afraid of it. Use the fear, the anger, the resentment to your advantage. It will make you stronger. It will keep you *alive*." He reaches the platform and holds his hands out.

I walk to the edge, and he grasps my hips before lifting me and setting me on the ground. My hands rest on his shoulders as I look up at him.

"Are you hurt?" I ask. He shakes his head, lifting one of his hands to wipe my nose.

"You need to channel your anger, little witch. You have a lot of it, and out there, in the real world, you won't have do overs. You have to use everything you have at your disposal."

I should feel anger at my throbbing nose. I should feel irritated and weak, but I don't.

I feel powerful.

He made me feel *powerful*.

Chapter Forty-Nine

The Caged

Master Lenus's infirmary reminds me of Pakin's on a much smaller scale. Bottles line a wooden bookshelf set against one wall. Beds line the opposite wall with goldish-yellow curtains separating them. A single, metallic table lies in the middle of the room, probably the worktable, with a desk up against it on the left side. I walk up to it, my fingers brushing the cold metal.

I hear his cane before I hear him. He limps in, his face set in a grimace as he watches his feet. His eyes find mine and widen, the wrinkled skin around his mouth tightening.

"Your Majesty, my gods, what happened?" Your *Majesty*?

"She walked into my elbow." Nithe says from where he leans against the bookshelf, reusing his joke. I roll my eyes at him, and Master Lenus sends him a scathing look as he walks up to me.

"Sit, sit." He motions towards the table, and I climb onto it, letting my legs hang off the side.

"I am sure it's fine, just a little bloody." I say softly as he opens drawers and pulls out supplies.

"Hush now." He says as he fills a bowl with water. The scent of lemon and mint hits me along with something floral and sweet. My pulse skips as he walks over, vials in hand.

"*Please*," his eyes flash to mine in concern. "No poppy root." I whisper, my voice cracking. He nods slowly and pulls a vial out of his pile, setting it back on the shelf. I can tell he wants to ask, but I just don't have it in me to explain.

He dips a cloth in the water and raises it, asking permission. I nod and he starts to wipe at my face. The lemony scent is strong, and it burns, but I keep my wincing internal. I shut my eyes, tears pricking the back of them at the pain.

"Your nose is not broken, Your Majesty, but it will be bruised." I nod as he sets the cloth down. A tear escapes my eye and I quickly wipe it away. He opens a small pot, the minty scent hitting me. It's some greenish cream. He dips his finger in it before lifting it and rubbing it against my nose. "This will help with the bruising and the healing. There is no poppy root, just mint and white willow bark.

"Alright." I say softly. My eyes fix on his face, at the shape of his eyes and the subtle dip in his chin. His age, his height, everything about him reminds me of— "You're his brother?" He twitches and pulls his hand away from my face.

"I'm sorry?" His eyes flit back and forth between mine as he figures out what I am asking.

"Master Pakin." I say again, my stomach tightening. He sighs and closes the pot. The glass clinks as he sets it down on the metal table, his hand shaking.

"Yes, Apollo is my older brother." He responds softly, his voice sounds sad—resigned.

"Lenus Pakin." I whisper. He nods again. Nausea hits my stomach and I jump off the table, putting distance between us. Nithe is quiet as he watches, his eyes emotionless.

"I assure you, anything he did—"

"He drugged me. He made the concoction that Tobias used to make me forget. He sewed a crown to my head. He patched me up time and time again just to let—" My hand flies to my mouth as I gag.

"Your Majesty?" He steps forward and I shake my head. I take a slow deep breath and swallow back the bile building in my throat. *Hold it together.* "My brother and I were never close; I can promise you that. He took after our mother, cunning and devious. I favored our quiet and careful father. Whatever he did, I apologize for what you endured." My hand slides to my chest.

"Excuse me." I whisper as I push my way out the door. My feet are quick as I make turn after turn until I reach the front door. I don't spare either of the guards a glance before I run to the wall and straight through the open gate.

Endless grass and hills surround me, and I double over. Bile creeps up my throat and I let it out. My plait falls in front of my face, and I quickly flick it over my shoulder to keep it clean. My breathing comes in shallow pants, and then it calms.

Instantly.

My neck prickles and I feel this pressure on my head, on my eyes. I slowly rise and scan the area around me.

Darkness edges my vision and then I can smell him.

Feel him.

His arms go around my waist, his nose nuzzling my neck. I inhale the scent of cedar and smoke, the scent of him.

"Come home to me." He whispers, his breath tickling my skin. My hands rise, wrapping around his wrists as I lay my head back on his shoulder. "I miss you, Ela." He says softly. Tears prick my eyes as I close them, relishing in the feel of him. I could just run, I could—

No.

I rip his arms off of me and spin around. His face has darkened, his eyes nearly black as the blue is absorbed by the shadows. Black veins spread below his eyes to his cheeks, spreading down his jaw and neck.

"You aren't real." I yell, taking a few steps back.

"I am here. I will always be right there with you." I shake my head, fighting against the pressure building in the back of my skull.

"No!" I scream and thrust out my arms. Starlight pours out of me in electric tendrils, slamming into his body. He vanishes in a dark mist, but I'm not alone.

A young man, with silver and gold armor stands where he was. Shaggy brown hair falling into his eyes. Pale skin that is soft and supple. He looks no older than me. His eyes are wide as they stare at me in shock—in confusion. He opens his mouth to speak, and blood pours out. He grunts and gasps before his eyes roll back, and he collapses.

I scream as I run towards him. His skin is on fire, the smell of burnt flesh filling my nose as I press my hands to the hole in his chest.

The hole I caused.

I can see his sternum, blood pouring onto the grass. *No, no, no, no.* Tears obscure my vision as I tap his face, his eyes unseeing.

"Help!" I scream. "I need help!" I tap his cheek again and check his pulse with shaking hands, but I feel no life inside. Tears stream from my eyes, dripping into his open chest. Men surround us and I am shoved out of the way. I fall back and drag myself away. I don't fight the tears as they pour down my cheeks, the deep sobs causing tremors to run through my limbs. I can't see what everyone is doing as they huddle around the young man.

I stand and hear the murmurs.

Monster.

Out of control.

Murderer.

I run.

Chapter Fifty

The Caged

I killed a man today.

It wasn't on purpose, nor was it in self-defense. It just was.

He was young. I heard the guards say he had just passed his twentieth birthday. And he'll never have another one. He had a wife and a child on the way. A child who will never know their father.

My spine aches from where I am crouched. I ran as soon as everyone started to swarm the courtyard. I ran and kept going until I found a room I'd never been in and hid like a child afraid of getting in trouble.

I ran because I'm a coward.

I've always been a coward and I don't think that'll change.

Except I'm not just a coward, I'm a murderer now too.

I squeeze my knees tighter to my chest and blink back the tears filling my eyes. The room is dark, only one small window on the far wall. Sheets draped over old furniture, a creepy portrait of a woman staring down at me on the far wall. Her black eyes are frozen in a glare as if she, too, is judging my inability to be strong.

"Leave me alone." I whisper at the painting, questioning my sanity for the thirtieth time this month. Her eyes don't move, a grimace plastered to her face as if she is telling me to get it together. "What would you have me do? I killed a man!" I yell at the artwork. I clamp my mouth shut, my teeth clicking as I look around. "Gods, I'm insane." I whisper as I set my chin on my knees.

I hear footsteps down the hall, deep voices filtering through the shut door. I scoot farther behind the chair I'm hiding behind, hoping no one can see me if they peek in. The door opens with a creak, and I hold my breath.

"Your Majesty? Are you in here?" The voice that reaches me is young, crisp, reminding me of icy winter air. Footsteps approach and I shamefully glance up at the man standing before me.

He has dirty blonde hair cropped close to his head, as if he usually kept it shaved. His eyes are a bright hazel, seeming to glow in the darkness. He has a playful grin on his face, showing off his sharp chin and sculpted jaw. He is ruggedly handsome—in a village boy kind of way.

"Is this where all the royals hang out?" He jokes, his smirk travelling up to his eyes.

"Excuse me?" I retort, lifting my head. He crouches down in front of me, his silver armor rustling over his yellow clothing. It looks constricting. I wonder if it's uncomfortable.

"You have the entire palace searching for you." He says softly, his smirk fading into a small smile. "Are you alright?" His tone of voice is so familiar, so comforting. I tilt my head as I stare at him. He glances down, searching my body. I can see when he notes the blood on my shirt as his eyes widen. "You're bleeding!" I ignore him.

"Who are you?" I ask instead.

"Nero, Your Majesty, General of the Rakushian Royal Guard." His voice deepens, diplomacy replacing the playful lilt.

"You look a little young to be a general." I say, cursing the disbelief in my voice. He's going to think I'm a bitch.

"You look a little young to be the queen of an entire continent." He snaps back. My lips part and I fight the urge to smile. *Maybe not.*

"That was rude." I say softly, but I can't help but want to laugh. A small giggle bubbles out of my throat and his eyes widen in surprise. The giggle turns into a full-blown laugh as I drop my knees and hug my stomach. He slowly stands and looks down at me with a cocked eyebrow.

"My gods. Are you mad?" He asks, causing me to laugh even harder. I can't fight the tears coursing down my cheeks as my stomach grows tender from the laughter. When it finally stops, I take a deep breath and glance up at him.

"What?" He shrugs and I roll my eyes. He offers his hand, and I take it. His skin is warm against mine as he helps me stand. "Thank you, general." I smile and he returns it.

"You are very welcome, my queen." My cheeks heat and I step around him, heading for the door, but I pause before I open it.

"I don't know if I want to go out there." I whisper. He walks up behind me, the clanking of his armor giving him away.

"You can't move forward unless you go out there. You need to accept what happened." His voice is soft, concerned. I look over my shoulder at him.

"What if I can't handle it?"

"You do it anyway."

"What if I can't bear the thought of being a murderer? What if everyone hates me?" I press.

"You go out there anyway." He repeats. He nods and I turn back towards the door, pushing it open. I walk into the hallway and am greeted with a few other guards. I don't look up at them, afraid of what their faces will say, as I follow the long hall to the entryway. Nithe is there, his hands gripping the tunic of a guard, fury filling his face.

"Hey!" I yell as I run towards them. "What's going on?" Nithe spins around, his eyes scanning my body for any sign of harm before relief finally crests his eyes.

"Where have you *been*?" He snaps, grabbing my face. I push his hands out of the way and step back into someone. I quickly move to the side and watch as Nithe looks behind me.

"General." He says by way of greeting.

"Your Grace." Nero responds with a subtle dip of his chin. "If you are no longer in need of my services, my queen, I have matters to attend to." His hazel eyes meet mine and I smile. He bows deeply before turning and walking back down the hall we came from.

"Services?" Nithe snips as my eyes follow Nero until he disappears. I turn back to Nithe and catch his glare. "*My queen?*"

"He found me hiding, made me laugh, and made sure I returned." I say with a shrug, heading towards the stairway, avoiding the glances of the guards gathered around.

"He made you laugh?" I nod and climb the tall steps. "How?" I turn around to face him on the stairs. He's a few steps below, making our eyes even. He leans forward, his breath cascading across my face. I inhale softly and relish in the relaxation that follows.

"What do you mean how?" I say softly.

"How did he make you laugh? Was he being inappropriate? Speaking to you in a way that is above his station?" Jealousy crosses his eyes and I snort before shaking my head.

"He spoke to me like a person, unlike everyone else." I start to turn again, and he grabs my arm.

"Look at me." I glare at him, and his eyes soften. "Be careful, please." His voice softens as if he's worried.

"Of what?"

"Adultery is punishable by death." My jaw drops and I can see the regret fill his eyes. My pulse skips and an overwhelming sense of disappointment fills my mind.

I was right all along. He's not different. He isn't similar to Theo or that of a decent man. He's the same as *him*.

The same as Tobias.

"For someone who keeps assuring me they are not like Tobias, you two seem to be identical." I rip my arm from his and quickly walk to my room, shutting it behind me.

The day is long and by the time night appears, Nithe still hasn't returned. I climb into bed, my eyes affixed to the stars outside. Exhaustion pulls at me, and I fight it. I can't sleep.

It's not safe.

But it is.

It is safe. Nothing will happen to me here.

When will I finally realize I'm safe? When will I finally trust that I am free?

I close my eyes and relax against the pillow, my heartbeat slowing as I drift off into sleep.

Blood splatters across my chest and I scream. Fire rages on around us and I quickly scan the area for someone to help me.

"Help!" I yell as I press down on the wound. "Somebody help me!" My screams tear through my throat. I look down at his face, the tan fading with the seconds. "Don't go. It'll be okay. Just stay with me." I whisper, tears dripping off my chin and onto his paling skin.

"I'm sorry—" His voice cracks as he coughs, blood hitting my face as I—

My head is pounding, sweat dripping from my hairline as I sit up. I suck in deep, ragged inhales. Blood. Ash. His face. Images flicking through my head. The first time in a while. The first time I have dreamt of something without looking for it since...since Noterra.

But that's not true, is it?

At the wedding, I saw his head rolling on the ground. And just the other day I dreamt of a forest and a wolf.

My hands are shaking, and I glance over to where Nithe is stretched out on the couch. His soft breaths are the only noise in the silent room. I slide off the bed and silently walk over him. Tears form in my eyes as I trace the path from his forehead to the tip of his nose, over his rose-colored lips.

No. This isn't happening. It's just a dream. I tear my eyes away from him and curl up on my side, cradling the tiny swell of my belly.

I'm gone before he awakes in the morning, the sun beating down on my face from the courtyard. I can feel him approach before he speaks. I can feel the bond in the air like static.

"The weather is warming up quite slowly this year. It's normally blazing." Enzo says as he comes to stand next to me. I turn to face him, noting the small sunburn on his nose and cheekbones.

"You seem to have gotten quite a bit of sun." I remark. "I haven't seen you in a few days."

"I was off doing some surveillance at the border. It seems more and more men are arriving every day. Nearly fifteen hundred." My eyes widen.

"Is it safe for you to be so close?"

"I stay in my raven form; they don't even see me." I nod, but I still feel hesitance. "I heard you've had some...difficulties the last few days."

"You heard about the guard?" He nods. "I don't know what happened, it was an accident."

"You don't have a handle on your aether, it makes you dangerous."

"I know. I need help, Enzo." I plead.

"There is a professor in Labisa, Professor Melner. He taught Nithe how to shift, and me how to manage my abilities. He knows everything there is to know about aether and magic. At some point, we will have to arrange our journey home, and when we do, you should spend some time with him." He turns to face me.

"Labisa isn't my home, Enzo."

"It can be." He shrugs.

"Only because I don't have a choice."

"Why are you fighting everything, Elaenor? I know what you've been through, or at least some of it, but you don't let anyone in. You don't even attempt to heal. You sit with your misery and push everyone away. I know you haven't been seeing Laenie, and Scar hasn't mentioned spending time with you either. You spent the entirety of yesterday in your room, what will it take for you to heal?" Anger brews deep in his chest, I can feel it—*hear* it in the way he speaks.

"It's not as easy as you think, Enzo. Do you think I want to be miserable and in pain? Don't you think I want to find love and be happy? How are you so okay with everything? Davenport held a blade to your throat to ensure I slept with his son. Your life was forfeit. You should know how lost I feel. You should know what it feels like to be weak." I bark, anger fueling my words. How can he be so okay? How can he act as if nothing is wrong, and life is perfect?

"Having a weakness does not make me *weak*, Elaenor." He says, his voice even and emotionless.

"It makes you vulnerable." I retort.

"No. It makes you strong. It gives you something to fight for."

"It gives you something to lose!" I scream and turn away from him.

"I will not lose you. Not again, Elaenor." He grabs my shoulders and forces me to face him.

"I am not yours to lose." I say softly.

"You are my sister! You have always been my weakness, even before you knew I existed. I know I may have had feelings for you, but that was natural given what I was told. But now? Now you are my *family*. You are my twin and the other half of my soul. And yes, that gives me a weakness, but that gives me even more to fight for. It gives me a reason to do more than just sit here and wait for Davenport to give commands. Commands that should be coming from you, I might add."

"He's the king—"

"No. He's *a* king. You are *the* queen. This is your country. Your continent. Every person in this palace and in every other kingdom, is *yours*. You need to start acting like it."

"What would you have me do? Boss him around and give orders?" I slap his arms away, but he grabs me again, forcing me to stay still.

"I expect you to use your power and influence to prevent a war."

"They don't listen to me!"

"Make them listen!" He silent for a mere second before he opens his mouth. "Come with me."

"What?" My brows furrow and I glare at him.

"Come. With. Me." He repeats again, this time slowly.

"Where are we going?" I ask as he drags me towards the palace.

"You need to see what it is we are fighting for."

Chapter Fifty-One

The Caged

I wrap a cloak around my shoulders, fastening it below my chin, before stepping out of the dressing room. Nithe is eating breakfast, his eyes looking everywhere but at me.

"Where are you going?" He asks, staring at his eggs.

"Are you asking me or your breakfast?" He sighs and then looks up at me.

"Where are you going?" He asks again.

"Enzo is taking me somewhere, getting me out of the palace for a while." I say dryly.

"Let me come with you." He stands and steps in my way.

"*No*, Nithe. I'll be fine with him." I put my hand up, keeping him from coming closer.

"At least take a guard." I hold his gaze and offer him a nod before walking past him and out the door.

I find Enzo in the entryway, talking to another guard. He looks at me and smiles.

"Nithe said I should bring a guard." I say, failing at hiding my irritation.

"Okay, anyone you'd like?" Hazel eyes and a smirk fill my brain and I fight a smile.

"Nero."

"The general?" I nod and he shrugs before instructing the guard to find Nero. "Why him?" He asks when he turns back to me.

"I met him yesterday and he made me feel almost...normal. I need that right now." He nods again as we walk out to the courtyard where two horses are saddled and waiting. Their saddles are plain, no markings that signify our status. One of the horses is chocolate brown, the other gray with darker spots along its legs.

"Oh, this reminds me! Some girl with red hair took your horse. She told me to tell you thank you." He says with a small chuckle.

"What?" I smile and look at him, my brows raised in confusion.

"When we rescued you, we ran into a woman in the stables. She told us where to go and then she took a big black horse with her." He shrugs.

"Sybil." My smile widens as I remember my sweet mare who seemed to be double the size of a normal horse. I believe someone called her a Percheron, but I don't even know what that is. I smile even more thinking of Nylah, and how she is probably back in Tatus with Cyn. My face falls as I think of the small child I will probably never see again.

"Our mother?" Enzo asks, interrupting my thoughts. I bite my lip and nod, turning back towards the horses.

"That horse was a gift from King Evreux to me. He named her Sybil, and when he died, I kept her." I explain as we approach the horses.

"I think there might be a lot of family history I am unaware of." He mutters.

"I can tell you anything you'd like." I offer. Not that there is much I remember about my childhood, but I do remember enough to give him some insight into our mother.

"Tell me on the journey." I give him a soft smile as I turn to see an approaching man. His armor is gone and in its place is a white tunic and cream pants. Two short swords are strapped to his back, but he looks almost normal. Not like a general of the army.

"You requested me, my queen?" He asks as he bows deeply.

"Yes, my brother and I are going on a day trip, and I figured it would be safer to have a general at our side. Who knows what men are creeping about in the wisteria." I attempt to keep my voice stoic, but something about Nero brings out a smile in me.

"My pleasure." He purrs while righting himself. He nods once at Enzo before gesturing to my horse. "May I?" He holds out his hand and I step into it, throwing my leg over the saddle as he hoists me up. "I will fetch another horse." He says before disappearing around the backside of my chocolate mare.

"*My queen*," Enzo mocks with a snort before climbing into his own saddle. "That man is going to get himself killed."

"How is him calling me 'my queen' going to get him killed?" I snap, surprised at my irritation. He gestures towards the entryway where a figure cloaked in shadow stands.

"Nithe is going to gut him like a fish."

"Nithe can go fuck himself." Enzo coughs out a laugh, the sound echoing through the nearly empty courtyard as he guides our horses towards the road.

"Gods, you have a way with words."

Nero trots in front of us, his golden horse shining in the sun. His head is on a constant swivel as he scans the surrounding area. We are on a hill-lined path, but I can't tell what direction we are going in.

"Where are we going?" I ask after a bit of silence. I'm enjoying the slight breeze, the cool air licking my cheeks. It really is a nice summer. Not scorching like home would have been. Clean and crisp air.

"Wistervale." Enzo responds.

"I don't know what that is." I admit.

"It's Rakushia's largest city. By comparison, that would be Tellavid or Cragport in Noterra." He provides, looking around as if he, too, is expecting someone to jump out of nowhere and attack.

"Oh." Is all I say as I look out at the endless fields. We pass farms and tiny homes that are secluded, hidden from people who pass by. I wonder what it would be like to live out in the open like this. No guards, just land and animals. I feel like it would be a peaceful life. "Why are we going to Wistervale?"

"Because you have been locked in three palaces your entire life and I figured you would want to live a little." He looks over at me, a smirk quirking up half his mouth.

"What are we going to do there?"

"Whatever you want. We can eat pastries and all sorts of foods, we can go dancing in one of the many halls, we can get drunk at a tavern. We can explore or sit in one place. Nothing is off the table. I want you to see what it is we are fighting for. Who we are protecting by preventing a war."

"You want me to see our people." I look at him, his back straight and shoulders back as he watches our surroundings, just as protective as the general leading the way.

"*Your* people." He corrects.

"Is it safe?"

"They won't recognize you. And if they do, neither of us will let anything happen to you." I stare at the back of Nero's tunic. The summer heat is enough to make me sweat with this cloak on, but I keep it fastened. For some reason, it makes me feel safe.

We ride in silence for a few moments, enjoying the fresh air and the scenery. It's quiet. Silent. As if no one is here. It feels almost suffocating. As if the silence is pressing down around me.

"I need to tell you something." I whisper. Nithe said it was my choice—my choice in what we do with our situation. But an outside perspective might be better. Maybe he'll know what to do?

"Is it about the guard?" I shake my head. That's the last thing I want to talk about. "Elaenor, what is it?" I pull back on the reins slightly, slowing my horse. Nero trots up ahead, just out of earshot.

"I'm pregnant." I whisper. His eyes widen and then a smile crosses his lips.

"What! That is incredible. It's early though, how do you—" His voice stops as he takes in my face. "No." He whispers. I nod and look away from him, tears pricking my eyes. "Elaenor, I am so sorry."

"Nithe says it's my choice what we do, but he says he'll claim it as his own."

"That is a very Nithe response." I nod again. "What do you mean 'what you do'?"

"If we keep it." I whisper and look back at him. His face softens knowingly.

"You mean whether or not you ask me to siphon."

"Yes." He sighs and tightens his hands on the reins. "I don't know what I want."

"What is your heart telling you?" We are quiet for a minute.

"That this child inside me is somehow connecting me to Tobias." My voice cracks. "The guard—when I killed him, I thought it was Tobias. I saw him. I *felt* him. He was there."

"Have you told Nithe, or my father?" I shake my head. "It could be in your head."

"That's not all." I bite my lip and take a deep breath. He needs to know everything. Someone does. "Sometimes when I am using my starlight, shadows appear. They snuff out the sparks or turn them black. And more than once my veins have turned black in my face." He pulls his horse to a stop. "Before you ask,

Nithe only knows of it happening one time, but it has happened a lot."

"Elaenor, we need to go back."

"No, Enzo—"

"We need to tell Kassius." He cuts me off.

"No!" I snap, stopping my own horse. I glance forward and see Nero stop as well. "No." I say softer. "I don't know what any of this means."

"When you first got here and you were sick, Lenus said that something inside was eating you alive, making you sick. It's him. It's the child. It's making you sick. It's spreading his curse through your veins." I stare at him, and I know in my heart he's right.

"So what do we do?"

"We tell my father." I brush the hair out of my face.

"When we get back. Please. Just let me have this one day." He sighs reluctantly and kicks his horse forward. "Talk about something. Anything." I say, my hands tightening around the reins as I follow after him.

"When I was younger, I used to beg my father for a sibling. I cried and cried until he introduced me to Nithe. I think we were maybe four or five—I'm not sure—and I threw an even bigger fit. I was a small child, and Nithe wasn't. Mostly due to his wyvos genes, but he just grew faster than I did. So I asked for a sister, and he introduced us to Emery." He smiles.

"I always wanted siblings, too."

"The three of us got along fairly well. Emery called Nithe out for being a bully, but then she'd turn it around and call me a child. But we loved each other as if we were related. I never thought I would have a sibling until my father came home with Mali." He ends his sentence with a smile as he pictures the young girl I rarely see.

"Who is her mother?"

"He said she was some woman he'd known for a long time. They saw each other again after years apart and had a single affair. It resulted in her getting pregnant. She died during childbirth." My throat constricts at the fact that nearly all of our mothers have died. I change the subject.

"How far away is Wistervale?" I ask, my voice cracking.

"Not far at all, maybe an hour at this pace." He responds. We stay quiet for a while, and I relish the silence. I don't know what to do, what to think. What option to choose. He can take the child's life. He can remove the curse that is flowing through my veins.

But is that even what it is? Would that even do anything?

I get lost in my thoughts as we continue on. We pass farms, trees dotting the vast plains and hills, and then we reach the crest of another green hill, where we stop.

Down below in the valley lay a town larger than I have ever seen. Rows and rows of houses, stores and taverns fill the maze of streets. A large building sits in the very center, made of pale stone. Ships of all sizes are docked off land, smaller boats line up against the many piers. Smoke billows out of the different chimneys, the different buildings.

I have never seen anything like it.

"My gods." I whisper, my mouth staying open like a fish.

"I say we stop at the inn, board the horses, and then find something to eat." Enzo says and all I can do is nod.

He pulls his horse towards the path and mine follows. I watch the town, the *city*, as we grow closer and closer. No walls border the outside of it. No fear of invasion. No fear of anything, really. The cobblestones under the horses click as we trot through the town.

People stare as we pass, their shops open. I see roasted meats and bread. Cloth, and small toys. I even see a bookstore.

I can't keep the smile off my face as our horses stop in front of a two-story white building. Enzo dismounts and hands his reigns off to a man who comes out of the building. Nero does the same before walking over and offering his arms. I nod, and he grabs my waist, helping me off my horse.

He lets go of me quickly before turning and scanning the area.

"What do you think?" He asks as he looks around.

"I have no words. I have never seen anything like this." I smile up at him and he places his hand on my lower back, guiding me towards the street where Enzo is waiting.

We walk up and down the cobblestones. Children scream as they play, candles on strings are woven between windows of tight alleyways, probably to keep the area well-lit at night.

Everywhere I turn there are more people. The salty sea air fills the town, and I can't stop breathing it in. I have never been this close to the sea.

We stop in front of a darker wood building with a fish on a hook sign above the door. Nero opens the door and glances in before I follow him.

The tavern is dark, only torches on tables to light the room. Men shouting with laughter, music playing as a man with a stringed instrument strums in the corner.

The smell of fish and something salty permeates the air as Nero leads us to a table in the corner. I sit in between them, my mouth still frozen open as I take everything in.

No one pays us any mind. No one cares.

"You look like a fish."

"I don't care." Nero laughs as I look at every single person in here. Young and old, clean and dirty. Every type of person imaginable. "This is incredible."

"You truly have never been anywhere?" Enzo asks as he flags down a barmaid.

"I haven't." A stout, older woman approaches with three mugs of liquid spilling everywhere. She sets them on the table and slides them over to us. I quickly grab mine before it topples over the edge. Her graying hair is pulled back into a bun, her apron covered in stains.

"What'll it be?" She barks and I just stare at her.

"Whatever the special is." Enzo responds. She just nods and walks away, maneuvering her way through the crowd. I look down at the mug in front of me and sniff. Something kind of sour makes my nose crinkle and Enzo laughs.

"What is this?"

"Ale. Smells disgusting, tastes even worse, but the more you drink, the better the smell and taste become." I glance up at him with my eyebrows raised. He lifts his own mug and takes a swig before exhaling like it was the most delicious thing he has ever tasted. I look over at Nero, who isn't touching his, and then back to my mug.

I grab the handle and bring it up to my lips. The first taste nearly makes me gag as the warm and fizzy liquid slides down my throat. It tastes like old bread mixed with overripe fruit. I set the glass down and smile up at Enzo, who looks at me as if I'm a whole different person.

Chapter Fifty-Two

The Caged

We dined on grilled fish and crusty bread. I had way too many mugs of disgusting ale, but I laughed. We joked and talked about random things. Nero joined us as we enjoyed ourselves.

As we *lived*.

When we were done with our meal, Enzo set gold coins on the table and gestured for us to leave. The sun was getting lower in the sky by time we exited, and I realized we had spent hours just inside the small tavern.

Torches were being lit around the city, lighting up the small streets and alleyways. I followed Enzo down one, Nero close behind, as we descended. We turned a corner and I realized we were at the docks.

The boats I thought were small before, weren't. They could fit twenty or so men, and they lined the piers and docks. Men and women were working on the boats as well as carrying different barrels and boxes back and forth. The salty air was sharp as I inhale, causing me to sneeze.

The ships docked way out in the water had lights on, making them glow against the darkening waters. The sea seemed to stretch forever, and only the smallest sliver of land across from us was visible.

"What country is that?" I ask, pointing at the dark line.

"Ovobia and Khailes are directly across from us." Enzo responds.

"What are they like?" I ask, as we watch the water.

"Ovobia is what people call the land of savages. It's run by a monster of a man named Selkath. His entire country is filled with for-hire mercenaries. Men are bred to be killing machines, women used as cattle. It's not a very nice place, if I'm being honest. The men, they are another breed. They can be nearly double the size of a human man and can replace ten men on a battlefield." I swallow as I stare at the dark sliver across the sea.

"My gods."

"There may come a time when their services are needed." I don't answer.

"What about Khailes?" He laughs.

"Khailes is the exact opposite. It's a country of great beauty. Women there tend to have an ethereal nature to them, almost too perfect to seem real. Grottos and hidden caves fill their country, making it possible for almost the entire population to live underground. Most cloths and silks come from Khailes. However, much like Ovobia, men are used as cattle there. There aren't really families. The women find men to mate with, and then send them back to wherever they came from."

"Really?" I ask, surprise coating my voice.

"Yeah. I've never been, but Nithe said it was one of the most insane places he's ever been." He snorts.

"Of course he's been." I sigh, swallowing my insecurities. "What queen reigns there?"

"No one knows. It's rumored to be run by a goddess, but unless you live there, or are the High Queen," he glances at me. "No one knows."

We stay quiet as the sun dips down below sea level, turning the sky a deep purple.

"I wish we could stay longer, but we should get going. Travelling at night tends to be questionable." Nero interjects.

"You said it was safe." I counter, turning away from the water.

"It normally is, my queen, but with the Noterran men on our border, it's better to be safe." I sigh and nod. Enzo offers me a tight-lipped smile as we turn away from the sea and head back towards the inn.

The slope isn't as forgiving on the way back to the inn and I can feel the ale coming out of my pores as I sweat. I'm panting by time we get to the stables and Enzo pays the stablekeep. Our horses are brought out, and I use one of the nearby stools to mount, instead of asking for help.

We turn away from the bustling city and the sea as we trek back through the hills. The air turns sweet as the salt dissipates and I sigh.

"Can we come back?"

"Of course. Maybe we can make a trip out of it, stay for a few days."

"I would really like that." I turn and smile at him. His eyes are shining in the moonlight, his face relaxed. "What do you think it would have been like to grow up together?" I ask. He laughs.

"I heard you were pretty wild as a child, so I imagine we would cause a lot of trouble."

"I wish we were never separated. I was so alone." I admit, biting my lip.

"I wish for nothing more than to have grown up with you, Elaenor. Truly. But if we had, I wouldn't have Mali. She may or may not have existed, and I love her. She's everything to me." He offers me a sad smile, and I know I could never ask for him to give her up.

"I understand. I can't imagine having to give up a sibling either. It would be like giving up Scarlett or Laenie." *Or Rhea.* I don't finish the thought.

"I wonder if she would even exist, or if her mother would still be alive." He ponders. We stay silent for a moment and then it hits me. Why did I never consider it? Why has no one ever considered it? Especially after what Kassius told us about them. About their history. I pull my horse to a stop and look at him.

"How old is she?" I ask.

"Eleven, why?" He stops his horse and looks over at me.

"Her hair, it's so similar to his..." My voice fades as the wheels turn in my head. There is no way. There can't be. Light blonde with a hint of copper.

"Elaenor?"

"I remember something."

"What does it have to do with Malathea?" A gasp escapes my lips as a pounding pressure erupts in my head. I grip the sides of my scalp, digging my fingers in as images flash through my mind. The pain is all-consuming, and I feel like I might pass out.

A scream escapes my lips and I vaguely feel arms pulling me off the saddle. I can feel the ground on my back as I scream. Someone is talking, but I can't make out what they are saying.

Trees, young boys, my mother's soft smile. Amaya cloaked in black. Tobias pushing me down a hill. Running through the halls and the trees. Teleporting in clouds of silver mist. Theo's beautiful blue eyes as he helped me up time and time again. Theo protecting me from Tobias and getting beat for it. Theo telling me how he was going to marry me some day, only for Tobias to say that I was his and always would be.

I remember Rakushia, and a young Emery. I remember an older boy who seemed disgusted by my presence, sulking in his room while Emery and I tore through her mother's closet. His dark hair and purple eyes.

I remember the wisteria and the hills.

Kassius time and time again chasing me through the trees. My mother's tears as she lost another child. My mother's worried face as she pried Amaya's hands off of me.

Amaya's cold eyes as she stabbed me over and over again in the stomach. I remember the carriage. I remember the water.

The pain.

"Malathea isn't ready to come out yet."

"You're going to be so powerful, little love."

"Malathea isn't ready."

Malathea.

Mal.

"She's his sister." I spit out, the images flashing through my mind, slowing until just one remains.

Amaya standing in the woods, her hand on her swollen belly. Anger brewing deep in her eyes as she stares at me like I will be the cause of her destruction.

And I was.

"What?" My eyes open and the pain in my head disappears. Enzo's brows are furrowed as he stares at me. Nero is standing, his eyes also filled with panic, his hand on a short sword ready to fight an unseen threat.

"Malathea is Tobias's sister." Enzo's mouth falls open as he leans back. I sit up and stare at him. Emotions flick across his face as he processes through each one. Denial. Confusion. Questioning.

Realization.

"No, that's impossible." He shakes his head and stands, leaving me on the ground.

"Malathea was the name of Amaya's child, the one she was carrying when she tried to kill me." I pull myself to my feet, ignoring Nero's outstretched hand.

"You can't know that. You don't remember!" He spits, misguided anger coating his words.

"I remember everything." I say softly. His face falls as he stares at me, silver lining his eyes. It's then that I see acceptance.

We abandon our leisurely ride and race back to the palace, our horses moving faster than I ever thought possible the entire way. Enzo doesn't wait for me to dismount as he runs for the front door. Nero helps me down, his hands on my hips.

"Are you alright, my queen?" He asks, looking down at me.

"Yes, I'll be fine." I respond, my eyes holding his gaze.

"Should you need anything, I am at your service." I offer him a smile and step out of his arms. I don't look back, even though I want to, and follow after Enzo.

"What is going on?" Scarlett scares me and I jump as she rounds the corner. "Enzo is in there, yelling at his father. What happened?" Her eyes search mine frantically and I reach for her hand.

"I remember everything."

"Everything?" Her free hand flies up to cover her mouth.

"Everything, but..." I glance down the hallway towards the council room.

"What?"

"I remember Malathea. When she was still in her mother's womb." I admit, her hand drops, and she furrows her brows.

"How is that possible?" She shakes her head.

"She's Amaya's. Mal is Tobias's sister." Her eyes widen as it sinks in, I release her hand and follow the sound of Enzo's voice as he yells at someone. I let it carry me down the hall, Scarlett's heels clicking behind me.

"Who knew?" He yells. I step through the entryway and see Davenport sitting in his chair at the head of the table. Kassius's eyes are wide, and his mouth is open as his eyes flick back and forth between me and Enzo.

"You remember."

"I remember." His eyes widen as he realizes he'll have to tell the truth. Anger brews deep in my belly as I stare at him. Lie after lie. What else is he hiding?

"Why didn't you tell me?" Enzo interrupts, screaming at his father.

"What would I have said? That your little sister's older brother is torturing your *other* little sister? That would have confused you even more than it did just now. Her mother doesn't matter. *She* does."

"You went to her, to siphon the curse nine months before she died. You tried to help her." I say.

"And I failed. I couldn't stop it; it was too far gone. It had been too long since the last time I helped her." His face falls and I can see the pain.

"Does she know her older brother is a king?"

"No, and she *never* will." Kassius spits.

"She deserves to know!" He snaps.

"No, she doesn't." I say quietly. They both turn to look at me and I step up to the table. "The less people who know, the better. What do you think Tobias will do if he finds out he has a sister? Probably the same thing he's doing to find his son. He will tear the kingdom apart and anyone who stands in his way. She is safe with us; she won't be safe with him."

"That's her brother." Enzo grits out.

"No, *you* are her brother, Enzo. He is just someone who shares her blood." I say sternly, forcing him to listen.

"How can you say that? Would you say that about me?" His voice cracks.

"Gods no, Enzo. But you aren't a monster. He is." I hold his gaze and reach out for his hand.

"Two siblings you have lied about, father. Is there a third somewhere I should know about?" He turns and faces Kassius.

"No, son. I'm sorry."

"No more secrets. We can't do this anymore. We can't have new bombs dropped on us every single day." I say loudly, getting everyone's attention.

"Figuratively speaking." Scarlett interjects.

"Agreed." Kass replies, defeat makes his eyes darken.

"Well isn't this sweet?" Davenport smirks from his place at the table.

"You." I say through gritted teeth. "We are done with whatever game you are playing. I am sick and tired of being controlled and cornered. Everyone wants something from me. Every single person in this damn palace. I am done." My hand slips from Enzo's as I grip the back of the chair. "This is my council room. This is *my* palace. And this is *my* continent. I haven't been given very many choices in my life, but that stops now. Your reign is over."

"I beg your pardon?" He says with a choked laugh. I can feel heat barreling through my veins, begging to ignite.

"Then beg." My eyes narrow and I lift my chin to stare down my nose at his scrawny figure. This poor excuse for a man and a king. His smile fades as he looks behind me. To the place where Kassius and Enzo moved, the place where I can feel Scarlett, and smell Nithe's citrusy scent. My people.

My *court*.

"I don't know who you think you are—"

"My name is Elaenor Dragehna, first of her name. *I* am High Queen of Viridiana. Child of King Argent Nottingham and Queen Sybil Monvoison. I am the granddaughter of the High Witch of Zivell and the King of Vodia. I have been sold *twice*. I have had things done to me that people can't even begin to comprehend by more men than I can count. I am the vessel in which starlight sparks and my heir grows." I can hear someone gasp behind me, and I realize I just revealed my pregnancy to *everyone*. A pregnancy that would only be a couple weeks old if it was Nithe's. I silently curse myself. "I am not *a* queen; I am *the* queen. And if you want to take residence in my home, *my continent*, you will learn your place. Now *beg*." I can feel my fingers spark and I don't have to look down to know that the starlight is there, listening to me for once.

Davenport stares, his eyes icy and filled with rage. He slowly stands, planting his hands on the table.

"You may—" He starts.

"Your queen gave you an order." A voice pipes up behind me and I glance slightly to the side to see Nero, his hand on a sword strapped to his waist.

Nithe steps forward, blocking my view and puts a hand on my lower back.

"*Beg*." He says, his voice filled with years of rage and resentment as he stares at his father. His fingers flex against my back and I lean into it. Into him. Into my people.

I have people. I felt so alone. But I have people and that feels *empowering*.

Davenport slowly lifts his hands from the table, one finger at a time, before stepping out from behind it.

"Your Grace—"

"On your knees." Nithe says. He glares at his son before dropping to the floor. His trousers brushing the dirty wood.

"Your—"

"Hands on the floor." Nithe's hand flexes on my back again as I speak. A silent acknowledgement. I'm not just doing this for me, I'm doing this for him. For the years of abuse he suffered from his father's hands. Davenport complies, his face going red. His palms touch the floor and I feel an overwhelming urge to vomit. Sweat beads along my hairline and I swallow.

"Your Grace. I beg your *forgiveness*." The room stays silent for a minute, until Nithe slides his hand from my lower back to my hip.

"You can say whatever you want, but I'd recommend letting him stand. We may not approve of him, but he controls our armies." His breath is hot as he whispers in my ear.

"You may rise." He stands quickly, his face red from anger and embarrassment. "Don't speak to me like that again. Don't speak to anyone, regardless of their station, as if they are beneath you. You do as you're asked without hesitance. Do you understand?" I command.

"Yes, Your *Majesty*." He responds through gritted teeth. I nod once before stepping out of Nithe's arms and into the hallway. My hand finds my stomach, my free hand resting on the wall. I lean forward, taking deep breaths.

"I guess the question of are you actually pregnant already has an answer." Scarlett's arms wrap around me. "Lean on me." She whispers and I relax my weight into her. I let her guide me to the stairs before another pair of arms go around me.

"She's burning up, she needs to go to the infirmary." Someone says as my eyes close.

"Alright, well I will take her there." An arm goes around my knees and then I am resting my head on someone's shoulder. "Excuse me! Ser!" Scarlett yells as the person starts to walk. My eyes open slightly, and I see dirty blonde hair.

"Theo?" I whisper. Blue eyes meet mine and I nearly gasp. I blink once and they return to hazel.

"You're alright." Nero whispers before I pass out.

Chapter Fifty-Three

The Caged

"She's dehydrated and malnourished. If we'd known she was pregnant we could have given her herbs to ease her sickness." Master Lenus's voice is rushed and panicked.

"We only knew because she missed her monthly bleed." Nithe speaks softly. I can feel him standing close to me, his hand brushing through my hair.

"It hasn't even been that long since the wedding, how can you know for sure?" A female voice this time. Emery.

"She *is* pregnant." His voice is little more than a snarl, his hand freezing in my hair.

"Gods. You can't make her do this. After everything she's been through, you're going to force her to carry a child?" Scarlett yells. I can hear the panic in her voice.

"How is this my fault?" It's Nithe who is yelling now.

"There are so many things you could have done to prevent this." Scarlett snaps.

"Shouldn't we be excited about an heir, not mad at the father?" Emery says, her voice stoic and emotionless.

"I am excited, but I am also worried about her. She can't be a mother, not now!" Scar responds.

"Let her decide that." Enzo. His voice is soft, calming, compared to Scarlett's shrill voice.

"The last thing she needs is all of you standing here staring at her when she wakes up." Emery snaps, the boredom in her voice replaced with irritation.

"I'm just standing here! Ow!" Erik yells as I am assuming Emery hit him.

"Everyone, out."

"I'll keep watch." Nero is here.

"Who the hell even are you?" Nithe yells, his voice louder.

"Nero, Your Grace. We've met. General of the—"

"I don't give a fuck. Get out!"

"Your Grace, respectfully, I don't serve you. I serve the queen." I can feel a wave of heat and smell something akin to smoke.

"Nero, she's fine. She's safe. We got it from here." Enzo says, probably ushering him out of the room.

"Of course." Footsteps dissipate.

"Where the fuck did he come from?"

"He came from the frontlines. Sent to help train the troops here."

"He needs to go back." He snaps, his breath fanning over my face.

"Is that jealousy I hear?"

"I'm not jealous." His voice pitches and I fight the urge to smile, not that my body is really responding to me. Did they drug me again? I try to move my hands, but nothing happens.

"Could have fooled me." A sarcastic female voice chirps from the other side of where I am laying, another one of Emery's many voices.

"Emery! Go away." Her laughter fades as she leaves.

"I knew she wasn't sleeping, but I didn't even realize she hadn't been eating." His voice sounds sad, broken.

"No one expected you to have to notice. All of this was supposed to be in name."

"It was never going to be like that with us, you know that."

"Speaking of things between you guys..." Enzo asks the question without asking.

"It's not mine." Nithe says after a second.

"I know. She told me today."

"We are assuming it's Tobias's, but she said there were a lot of men who visited her while she was in the dungeons." Enzo inhales sharply, and I can picture his face. His green eyes filled with pain. He's had enough pain today.

"Who?"

"She doesn't know. Just that there was a rotation."

"Gods."

"Yeah."

"It has to be Tobias's. She told me about the shadows. That she's been seeing him."

"What?" Nithe's voice deepens and the smoke returns.

"She's been seeing him. She thought she was attacking him when she killed that guard. She thought she was defending herself."

"Why didn't she tell me?"

"She's not well. She's scared." It's silent before Nithe speaks up again.

"Is it horrible if I say that I wish it wasn't his? That I wish it was one of the other men who raped her?"

"No. Because if it is his, I don't know what we will do."

"Exactly."

"When were you going to talk to me about the tattoos?" Silence follows. "I know what a tattoo for a life oath looks like, Nithe. You seem to forget that Fleur and I had them, although ours didn't shimmer. They were just slightly darker than our skin tone." More silence. Who's Fleur?

"It's not the same." His hand untangles from my hair, and I feel his fingers brush my left arm.

"Are you serious? It's exactly the same. Only people who are—"

"Stop. Okay. *Stop*. It's not that." He cuts him off. Who's Fleur? What is he talking about?

"Why can't you just accept that there is a chance she might love you someday?"

"She won't. She stills loves Tobias. She cries for him in her sleep. She even told me she still loved him. But she also said she was in love with Theo. She doesn't have room for me."

"Both of which aren't here. One is a demented asshole, and the other is dead."

"Great, so I'm third place."

"She needs space and time. She's been through so much the last nineteen years of her life. We all have. And we are all so young. She just needs time."

"We don't have a lot of time. I have a weird feeling that our lives are so close to being over." Nithe's voice trails off and I get the feeling that he's right.

"Since when did you become a prophet?" He snorts, and then I feel the brush of a finger on my forehead. I feel exhaustion pulling at my senses and I try to push it away.

"She looks so peaceful. I think being asleep is the only time she looks this way. Like she isn't burdened with everyone's problems." *Wake up, Elaenor!*

"I can't believe she went off on your father like that." I can feel my consciousness slipping away and I fight it.

"I can. She's strong. She just needs to realize it." But it wins.

My eyes open to a darkened room. A few candles are lit, casting a faint glow across the pale wood. Windows are open, letting a nice breeze in. I am laying on something soft and warm. I flex my fingers and feel the fur slip between them. I glance around the bedroom, looking for Nithe, but he isn't there. My hand finds my stomach and the small swell sitting there. I sit up, my hand still holding my belly.

Noise from the bathing room causes me to jump. My heart races and I frantically look for a weapon but come up empty. I clamor off the bed and run to the open dressing room, hiding in the darkness. I hold my breath as I wait, panic overtaking my senses.

After what seems like forever, the door opens, and I run at whoever it is. My arms go around their neck and I try to yank them back, but they are too strong. I'm flipped over their head, my back headed towards the ground, when I catch Nithe's eyes. They widen and he twists midair throwing himself under me. I land on top of him with a thud, my head slamming into his chest. I gasp as the wind is knocked out of me.

"Gods!" He yells as we both catch our breath. Once my breath has finally stabilized, I lift my head slowly. A smirk is plastered to his face, revealing a dimple.

"I prefer all greetings to end like this, little witch." I glance down and see my thighs on either side of his, my nightgown bunched to my hips, exposing my undergarments. I sit back, attempting to climb off of him when he sits up, grasping my backside and flipping us over. My back ends up on the rug, his lower body nestled between my legs.

Hardness meets softness and I fight the urge to arch my back. I glare at him, fighting the arousal pooling in my belly.

"Get off of me." I push on his chest, and he grabs both wrists in one hand, pinning them above my head.

"You attacked me, little witch. I was just defending myself." He leans down, his nose almost touching mine. The minty scent of toothpaste mixes with the citrusy scent of him and I breathe deeply. "What were you going to do if it wasn't me?"

"Kill you."

"I highly doubt that." I roll my eyes and tilt my head, exposing a bit of my neck. His eyes trace the line of my jaw down my neck and to my collarbone. "Your nightdress isn't very queenly." He muses.

"I'm not the one who put me in it." I retort.

"That would be Scarlett."

"Of course it was." He adjusts, settling in deeper against me and I bite my lip. He doesn't miss the movement. What is wrong with me? "How are you feeling?"

"Tired. Like I can't breathe because I have 200 pounds of wyvos on me."

"I can make it 2000 pounds if you want." He quips with a lopsided grin.

"I *don't* want."

"What about—"

"Don't finish that thought." I whisper.

"You want me to get off? Make me." He threatens, leaning close.

"I can't, you're too heavy."

"You can."

"I am ill." I pout.

"No you aren't, you're pregnant." He rolls his eyes and I glare at him.

"Same thing."

"No it isn't, now make me get off of you." I pull at the hand holding onto my wrists and he relents. I push on his chest, but he doesn't budge. His hand slides down from my shoulder and I shudder as his thumb brushes my ribs. I kick my foot at his thigh, and he shifts slightly, pressing further into me. His hand travels from my ribs to my hip. I slap his arm away and he holds it out for a second before starting at my shoulder again.

I squirm under him, sliding my body down, but all that does is rub the apex of my thighs against him. Damnit. His eyes heat as he stares down at me, and I suddenly question why I am fighting him. Fighting this.

This doesn't have to be serious. This could be something fun, something

I control. I think he senses my change of thought as his hand stills. His body freezes as his eyes lock onto mine. A shallow breath escapes my lips, following another shudder.

"Elaenor…" He whispers. My head tilts back so I can look at him fully. His eyes search mine before his hand slips from my hip to my knee, holding my leg against him.

"Nithe." I say breathlessly. I can hear his heart racing in tune with mine as we lay in silence. He presses his hips harder against me and I arch my back as a tingling hits my core.

"Don't fuck with me." My lips part to speak and he takes it as his opportunity. His lips crash into mine, his tongue curling into my mouth. My hands find his chest and fist his tunic. He leans back, taking me with him, so I am sitting on his lap. His hands cup my backside as I wrap my arms around his neck. His kiss is like a drug, one I could get lost in. His hands slide up from my back to my hair, pulling my head back. His lips break from mine as they trail down my jaw and to my neck. I arch my back as he nips at my shoulder. His teeth pull at the thin strap of the nightgown, letting it fall down my shoulder.

His lips press into my collar bone as his hand pulls the other strap down.

"Nithe." I whisper. The strap slides down my arm and the cool air brushes the hardened peak of my nipples. I can feel him hardening underneath me and I arch my back again, pushing myself harder against him. "Nithe." I say a little louder.

"What?" He responds, pulling back to look at me. "What's wrong?" His eyes search mine frantically.

"I can't. I can't do this if strings are attached."

"What?" He freezes.

"No feelings." I repeat.

"Are you telling me, or yourself?" He spits.

"I told you, name only." He sits back slightly, and I bite my lip. "Nithe."

"I'm not going to use you like a whore. If I have sex with you, I'm going to do so as your husband. I'm going to fuck you as a man should fuck his wife and nothing less." My face falls and I slide my hands down his chest. I look down, my forehead brushing his chin. I don't fight the tear that escapes my eye, trailing down my cheek.

"I can't do feelings, Nithe. I can't."

"At all or just with me?" My head snaps up and my nose brushes his.

"What?"

"Nero?"

"You mean the guard I met like two days ago?" I snap.

"The way he looks at you, and you look at him like—"

"Like what?"

"Like he's a breath of fresh air." The similarities between this moment and one I had with Tobias is disheartening—is terrifying. My throat constricts and I scramble out of his lap, pulling my strap back up.

"And I look at you with duty." I whisper.

"Yes."

"I had this same exact conversation with Tobias about Theo."

"And which one of them did you fall in love with, Elaenor?" He snaps as he gets to his feet.

"The one who didn't make me feel like I was an object, like I was more than just the blood that runs through my veins."

"And I do? What do you expect from me?"

"If this marriage wasn't arranged, *forced*, would we have been together?"

"What?" He recoils as if I hit him.

"Answer the question. If you weren't forced into this and I was just some girl who is your best friend's sister. If I was just a queen who you assisted in rescuing. Would we even be interested in one another?"

"I don't know!" I sit back against the mattress and shake my head.

"That's my point. You see me as a duty as well. You see me as a burden."

"No. I do not. Don't tell me what I see." He snaps.

"You go from being a jerk to being sweet. You make me feel powerful and weak at the same time. You make me want to scream and hurt you but simultaneously want to be the one who hurts those who do the same." I admit.

"That is called love, Elaenor."

"I don't love you!" His head snaps back as if I struck him. "You couldn't have expected me to say anything different."

"Because you love Tobias."

"No! Not everything has to do with him!"

"Yes, it does, Elaenor! You base every decision, every interaction off of ones you've had with him. And I can't blame you. You've been through so much and gods I am so sorry for what you've been through, but you need to grow up."

"Excuse me?" I step back, my lips parting in shock.

"You need to grow up and realize that life isn't easy and it's going to suck, but for people like us, it stays that way. We don't get happy endings and the sooner you realize that the sooner you can begin to live."

"Get out."

"This is my room too."

"Get out!" I yell as I step towards him. He steps out of the way of my hands.

"No! You don't want to stay in here with me? Fine. *You* can leave. I'm done catering to you." My hands ball into fists and I push past him, heading towards the door. "Elaenor." He says softly, but I ignore him, slamming the door behind me.

Chapter Fifty-Four

The Caged

The palace is silent as I creep down the halls. All of the doors are closed, only a few torches lit. I must have slept the entire day away.

I wrap my arms around myself, cursing the fact that I am wearing a short nightgown. I descend the stairs quietly. The entry door is shut, a single guard standing in front of it. He nods in acknowledgment and then averts his eyes. I stroll past him down a hall I haven't been before. The smell of fresh bread awakens my senses as I reach an archway.

The archway opens up to a huge kitchen, steaming pots are on the wood burning stove. Loaves and loaves of crusty bread sit on a shelf. Right below it, pastries of every kind sit, dusted with chocolate or powdered sugar.

I step into the room, my feet protesting the warm wood. I glance around but don't see anyone. I walk in further, heading towards the bread. I inhale deeply, the scent of sourdough enveloping my senses. I reach for the loaf when the clearing of a throat makes me squeal. I spin around, my hand on my chest, to see a short woman. Wrinkles line her tan, freckled skin. She looks angry, as if she's constantly frowning. She reminds me of Estelle. Her gray hair is tied in a knot on her head, a bonnet secured around it the same color as her loose dress.

"I am so sorry." I whisper, unsure of what to say.

"Why on earth are you in here wearing bed clothes, girl?" She snaps, her voice thick with an accent I can't place.

"I was hungry, and I smelled bread." I admit quietly.

"Which one of them boys dragged you into the palace without givin' you a proper meal?" She rolls her eyes and I realize she thinks I'm some random girl someone brought to the palace.

"Nero." I whisper in panic, and she shakes her head. If I said Nithe, word would get around that the king consort has a mistress.

"That boy." She shakes her head and walks over to me, plucking a loaf of bread off the shelf. She gestures for a barstool, and I sit. "Jam and butter?" She asks.

"Yes, please." I respond softly, tracking her every movement. She pulls on a rope connected to the wall before she cuts the bread. She sets a plate in front of me with butter and various jams and then another plate with steaming slices of bread. I look up at her and smile. The wrinkles set in her face remind me so much of what a grandmother would look like. Maybe it is what my grandmother looks like.

"Eat." She orders and I dig in, dipping the bread in a pinkish jam. Strawberries and something floral hits my tongue and I groan. I can't remember my last meal. She glances at my arm, at the slight shimmer of a tattoo in the torch light and lifts an eyebrow. "Kids these days." I smile at her, and she returns it, showing a mouth full of yellowing teeth. "Where did he find you?"

"Noterra."

"Gods, what a beautiful country. Shame it's run by the devil." She snorts and I don't attempt to hide the smile this time.

"I can't imagine a worse king than Tobias." I say as I take another bite.

"Ain't that the truth." Nero's voice startles me as I look behind the woman. "You rang, Mama Collette?" He says as he walks over and kisses the top of her head. She shoos him off, but I don't miss the blush crossing her cheeks.

"Rang?" I ask and she points at a wall of bells with numbers.

"Each one connects to a room." I nod, my eyes widening. I wonder if they have that in Noterra? "Your missy here is starving. You could have at least fed her." She hits him with a towel and goes about mixing something on the stove.

"My missy?" He cocks a brow and looks at me. His eyes widen as he takes in what I'm wearing, before they darken. "Oh, right." He holds out his hand. "Come on then." I hesitantly take it.

"Thank you, Miss Collette." I whisper and dip my chin as a sign of respect.

"You can call me Mama." She says back with a smile as she clears my plate. I thank her again and let Nero pull me out of the room.

"Please tell me why the *queen* is in the kitchen in the middle of the night practically naked?" He says sternly, his hand still gripping mine. I pull my fingers out of his grasp and wrap my arms around my stomach.

"I couldn't sleep, and I was hungry." I say quietly.

"You have servants."

"I am more than capable of getting myself food." He leads me back up the stairs, his tunic wrinkled. "Were you asleep?"

"What else would I be doing at two in the morning?" He asks with a snort.

"Sorry." I mutter. I stop in front of the library and step in.

"What are you doing?"

"I want to stay in here." I say softly.

"Well you can't stay by yourself."

"Why?"

"Safety."

"I am capable of defending myself." I roll my eyes and drop down on the sofa.

"At least let me get someone. Your brother or the king?"

"Do *not* get Nithe." I snap as I pull my legs under me. "You can stay if you must, but I can't go back to my room tonight.

"And why is that?" He pushes and I avert my eyes.

"He kicked me out."

"What?" He crosses the room and kneels down in front of me. "Are you alright? Did he hurt you?" His hands grab my shoulders.

"Gods, no." I push him away. "You are getting too comfortable, general. You need to be careful." I warn as I lean back against the couch.

"Being comfortable is what got me promoted in the first place. If I treat you royals like equals, you tend to treat me like one too." He admits, a half-grin on his face.

"I see us as equals."

"But we aren't." I stay quiet as he rises from where he was crouched down and sits in the settee across from me. "What happened?"

"With?"

"The king."

"We fought, as couples do." I shrug and pull a blanket on my lap.

"About?" I lift my gaze and narrow my eyes.

"You can leave now, Nero." I order. His eyes widen slightly before he rises again and walks to the archway.

"Have a lovely evening, my queen." He smiles at me, and I roll my eyes at his back.

I nestle into the cushion and close my eyes.

Dirty blonde hair and blue eyes smile at me. I take his outstretched hand as he pulls me deeper into the woods.

"Mama is going to be mad."

"No she won't. I'll protect you, Nora." I follow after him, a giggle escaping my lips as we run between the trees. "We should stay out here forever."

"But how will we get food?" I ask, looking around.

"I can hunt, and you can gather berries and herbs."

"You can't hunt a pastry, Theo. I can't live without pastries." I laugh and his hand squeezes mine.

"I can learn how to make them. Or we can run away to a village and live there." He stops and looks at me. "We can be free."

"Free?" I whisper and look at our adjoined hands.

"Ela! I'm going to find you!" His voice echoes around the trees and we spin around, searching for the source.

"It's Toby!" Theo whispers and takes off into a run, leaving me standing in the woods alone.

"Nora, wake up." His voice is calming as he pulls me out of sleep. My eyes meet his, bright and yellow. "What are you doing out here?" Kass asks as he brushes hair from my face.

"Nithe and I had a fight." He smiles and exhales before shaking his head.

"Knowing you two it was probably worse than it should have been."

"I think it was my fault." I respond, keeping my voice quiet. He nods and stands, his knees cracking as he does. "Did you hear about the..."

"Pregnancy? Yes." He sighs and sits down. "Why didn't you tell me?" He asks, concern crossing his face.

"I was scared."

"Enzo told me about the shadows." I nod and bite my lip. "If that's truly what's happening, Nora, I worry for your safety. If that child is his, it will carry the curse. It will carry the darkness, and that is transferring to you."

"I've had this magic for weeks and it's already in jeopardy?"

"Enzo also mentioned that you spoke about siphoning." He says softly, tilting his head.

"I feel like it's my only option." I admit, my hands pulling at loose threads on the blanket.

"I'm not going to tell you what to do."

"But?" I counter.

"I think you should. I think you should end this before it gets worse. Before *you* get worse." I nod and look away.

"Is it painful?"

"Yes. It is. And it doesn't heal instantly. You'll be weak for a few days." I nod again. "Come on, you need to get to bed before the whole palace sees you out here." I hesitantly push the blanket off my lap before rising from the couch. He holds his arm out, gesturing towards the door, and I walk towards my room. I turn the handle, surprised it isn't locked and glance back down the hallway to where Kass is tilting his head, gesturing for me to go in.

The room is dark when I enter, but I can see his form on the bed. I walk quietly to the other side and step up to the windows. The moon is low, stars sprinkling about. Peaceful.

If I do this. If I let Enzo end this pregnancy, then what? What will happen to me? Will I still be shadowed, literally? Or will things go back to normal, or at least how they should be?

I turn away and climb into the bed, careful not to jostle him. He's underneath the blankets, his face towards me.

He looks peaceful, calm. His face is relaxed, his lips parted slightly. I can hear his soft breathing as I turn to face him in the bed. I pull my knees up to my chest and close my eyes. I count each breath as they lull me to sleep.

Chapter Fifty-Five

The Caged

Soft fingers brush my face. I relish in the feel as I stretch in the bed, my limbs heavy and tired.

"You came back." He says softly and I open my eyes to Nithe's. He has a surprised smile on his face.

"Kass found me in the library and made me." I respond quietly.

"I'm sorry."

"No, I am. I shouldn't have said those things. I know you are not Tobias and I have been comparing you against him. It's not fair to you." I admit, shame coating my voice.

"Yeah, well I could have been nicer too." We are quiet for a second and then he smiles. "Did you really fall asleep in the library dressed like that?" I nod and bite my lip. "Thank gods no one saw you." My eyes widen as I release my lip and roll onto my back.

"Well, someone did see me. Three people actually." I admit reluctantly.

"Who?" He says, his voice a little rough.

"Mama Collette and Kass."

"You met Mama wearing a nightgown? I bet she thought you were one of the—wait. You said three people."

"Nero." His silence is palpable as he slowly sits up and slides off the bed.

"Of course." He clears his throat.

"Nithe."

"Don't."

"Stop acting like this is a relationship."

"Stop acting like it's not!" He snaps. I sit up and watch him step into the dressing room, his bare back flexing, scales and swirls of dark ink coating the tan skin.

"Name only."

"No. Stop fucking saying that." He steps out of the dressing room pulling a shirt on. "You want to go around and screw every guy here? Fine. But the second you do that; I can't protect you. I can't keep you safe."

"I don't need you to keep me safe!"

"Yes, you do! You think you are safe in here? Safe with Nero? You're not. Nobody knows him, he just appeared. What about with my father? You think your little stunt was enough to keep him checked? It *wasn't*. You are so gods damn strong, Elaenor. But you are untrained in magic and combat *and* court affairs. I am trying to help you, but you are too damn stubborn to see that."

"I know you are trying to help me. I know that, Nithe." I scoot over to his side of the mattress and sit up on my knees, making us level. I reach out for his face, and he slaps my hands away. "I know." I try again and he lets me. His stubble pokes into my hands, but I just hold his face tighter. He reaches up and grabs my wrists. "I don't know how to act or what to do. I don't know how to be anything other than scared."

"Let me help you." He whispers, pleads. I hold his gaze, light purple eyes meeting mine. "Let me be there for you." He releases my wrists and wraps his arms around my waist, pulling me against him. "Let me help you heal." My eyes search his as he hesitates.

"Okay." I whisper, my heart racing. His lips brush mine softly, and I lean back. He pulls me tighter against him and when his lips brush mine again, I let him. He kisses me slowly, softly. No sense of urgency, no carnal need. Just softness, gentleness. His arms stay wrapped around me, his hands brushing underneath my breasts. My fingers slide into his silky hair, getting caught in the small tangles. The kiss doesn't deepen, it doesn't escalate. It just stays pure, and when he pulls away, I'm not left in pain.

I feel almost whole.

"No expectations. A kiss doesn't have to have expectations." Our foreheads touch and I nod. "We can do everything and nothing, whatever you want." I nod again. One of his hands slides off my back to brush my stomach, his fingers skimming over the barely there bump.

"I'm estimating at least 2 or 3 months." I whisper. "Otherwise I wouldn't be showing."

"It doesn't matter." He says.

"It does, because if it's been a few months then I know without a doubt that it's his, and not one of theirs."

"How does that make you feel?"

"Scared. Kassius and I spoke."

"And?"

"He thinks we should have Enzo end this."

"Why didn't you tell me about the shadows? About seeing him?" He presses.

"I didn't know if it was real or not. I thought it was just in my head. No one has even attempted to teach me how to use this aether. Nobody is doing anything. Enzo says when we get to Labisa someone can help, but I need help now. And I can't even properly use it if I have Tobias's shadows flowing through my veins." He opens his mouth to speak but the door opens, and Enzo's voice replaces his.

"Why the hell did I just hear from a kitchenmaid that the queen fucked the general?" Nithe's head whips around, his arm tightening around me.

"I did not!" I yell, my mouth falling open.

"Well apparently Mama Collette saw you two together last night with you dressed, well like that, holding hands." Nithe turns back towards me and drops his arm.

"Enzo, shut up!" I snap. "Nothing happened, Nithe. I swear. I found myself downstairs after our fight and ended up in the kitchen. Mama Collette gave me some food and asked which one of the guys brought me here. I didn't want her to know who I was, so I lied." My words come out rushed and panicked as I try to get him to look at me.

"She knows who you are!" He snaps and I bite my lip. "She was at the wedding, Elaenor. She's brought you food. You have *white* hair, of course she knew who you were."

"I was trying to not get caught."

"Sneaking around with Nero?"

"I was not! He brought me to the library, and I told him he was getting too comfortable, too outspoken so I made him leave. I promise." My voice raises an octave as I beg for him to believe me. Things just got better. Things just started to feel right.

"That's not what I heard." Enzo pipes up.

"Shut it!" Nithe says this time. I reach for his face.

"You have to believe me." I whisper, holding his forehead to mine. Tears well up in my eyes as he stares at me.

"Enzo get out." He snaps and I glance up to see him roll his eyes and shut the door. "You don't speak to him or see him." I push him away.

"No. That's not how it's going to go. You can't order me not to talk to people—"

"I'm not ordering, little witch, I'm asking. You can say no and you can tell me to fuck off, but I am pleading for my sanity, just stay away from him. Something feels off. I don't trust him." I stay silent and hold his gaze. I don't answer, I just reach up and press my lips to his.

He kisses me back, hungrier this time. I can feel his need for me as he pulls me against him, as his hands dig into my hair. His teeth bite my lower lip and I wince. My hands slide down his chest before I grab the hem of his tunic and pull it up. He needs this. *I* need this. His lips break from mine for just a second as he rips his shirt off. They slam back into mine, his hand coming around my back, holding me as pushes me onto the bed. My legs wrap around his hips as he grinds into me. I gasp against his mouth, and he takes that as his chance to explore my mouth with his tongue.

My legs tighten around him as he moves again, my back arching as heat pools deep in my belly. My nails dig into his back, and he flinches. I do it again, this time harder, and he groans into me. He slides his hand in between us, lifting my dress. His lips part from mine as he kisses his way down to my abdomen. He tenses and I lift my head up. His eyes are on the brand, the letter carved into my stomach. He bends down and brushes his lips across the flesh-colored bump.

"Never again." He promises as his tongue flicks out and touches my skin. A sickening feeling rushes through me and I sit up, nearly throwing him off of me. "What's wrong?"

"I can't." I whisper, my voice pained as I try to inhale. I gasp trying to inhale sharply, my hands going numb. I force another inhale and a raspy squeak happens instead.

"Hey, it's alright. You're just having a panic attack." He brushes hair from my face as I start to hyperventilate. "Breathe. It's alright." He breathes with me for a second and I dig my nails into his arm. "In and out. Nice and slow. Whenever you feel this way, just breathe in and out." I copy his breathing and he smiles. "That's it, come on little witch. You got it." I blink away the tears as I hold his gaze. My heart calms and I take my first full deep breath. "That's my girl." He smiles and kisses the tip of my nose.

I have breakfast with everyone in the library. Scar sits between Emery and Enzo, both of them touching her any chance they get. I almost feel sorry for one of them, and then she gives them equally loving glances. I don't pity them in their little relationship, but I don't ever foresee her giving either of them up. Maybe she doesn't have to?

Erik and Laenie are quiet and oddly sitting on opposite sides of the room. Neither of them will look at each other and I catch Scarlett watching them too. She shrugs and goes back to eating. I'm sitting on the floor in front of the table and Nithe is sitting behind me on the settee. His knees cage me in between his legs and every time he leans forward, his free hand touches my face or my hair. Any part of me.

I keep flicking between enjoying it and feeling suffocated. But he doesn't expect anything from me. Only what I am willing to give, and I can live with that. For right now.

I meet Kassius in the training room after breakfast. He stopped by and said we had to start training, and I was quick to accept.

Across the line that separates the stone floor and the grass, targets are set up. Canvas and hay made to look like chests and arms. I stare at their figures, ten of them lined up and ready. Ready for me to aim at? Hit?

I don't know.

"I need to see them." I spin around, my boots squeaking against the floor, to face Kassius.

"See what?"

"The shadows. Call your aether." I sigh and look down at my hands. Pale palms stare back at me and I dig deep, searching for the spark. A tiny tingle starts in my palm, but nothing appears.

"I can't call it."

"Try harder." He snaps and I look up at him.

"It's not for a lack of trying, Kassius." I snap back and he glares.

"Again!" He yells and I stare back at my hands. I dig my nails into my palms and then throw them open. A spark appears and is quickly snuffed out. I groan and try again. Another spark appears and this time I feel it in my arms.

Stars explode out of my hands, shooting straight to the ceiling. I squeal and throw myself back as debris rains down.

"Again." He repeats. I stare up at him with renewed energy and open my palms. The sparks come easily, and I feel my entire body light up. I laugh as I stare up at the sparkling light in front of me.

"It's so beautiful." I whisper. I will for more power, more strength and then I spin, shoving my hand through the air and towards the first dummy. A bolt of star-filled lightning hits the target in the arm, the entire thing going up in flames.

"Again." Kassius repeats it time after time until every target is burnt to a crisp. Men with buckets come and extinguish the flames before righting them back up on their stands. I smile and spin to look back at him. His eyes widen and he takes a step back.

"What?" I whisper.

"Your face." My hand reaches up, but I feel nothing.

"What is it?" I say louder, panic coating my tongue like venom.

"Your veins, your eyes. They are black." He stutters and takes a step forward. His fingers press to my cheek, and he gasps. "Gods, it's true. It *is* the curse." Tears prick my eyes, and he grabs my arm. "Come on."

"Where are we going?"

"You can't keep this thing inside you." He snaps as he drags me into the hallway.

"Kassius, wait!" I snap and pull myself to a stop.

"It will kill you. I can feel it. It feels just like her—Amaya. I don't know what will become of you if we don't deal with it now." His voice is rushed, urgent.

"I'm scared." I whisper and he grabs my arms.

"I won't let anything happen to you."

Chapter Fifty-Six

The Caged

The day is still bright as we round the corner of the hallway and take the stairs. I chase after him as fast as I can, sweat beading on my neck and dripping down my back. Kassius opens the door to Enzo's room without knocking. Scarlett is standing there crying and Enzo is glaring at her.

"What is it?" Enzo snaps, turning towards us.

"We are doing this." Kassius snaps back before turning out of the room.

"Scar, are you alright?" I ask, stepping up to her. She shakes her head and pushes my hand away.

"I'm fine." She mutters as she runs out of the room. The only sound we hear is her door slamming.

"Enzo, what is going on?" I ask. His face is red, his eyes bloodshot as if he, too, has been crying.

"It doesn't matter." He sighs and walks up to me. "Is this what you want?"

"I don't think I have a choice. My eyes, they were black. I think I'm turning into him."

"That isn't going to happen." He grabs my shoulders and forces me to look at him.

"I'm scared. He said it's going to hurt." I whimper, tears pricking my eyes.

"Come on!" Kassius yells from the hallway. I pull myself out of Enzo's grasp and walk to my room. Nithe looks broken, defeated. He walks over to me and brushes hair out of my face.

"Is this what you want?" He asks, the same way Enzo does. I nod and lean forward to press my head against his chest. His hand comes up to tangle in my hair, holding me against him. "Alright. How do we do this?"

I wasn't prepared for what came next. Kassius laid towels out on the bed, and I changed into a nightdress. A medical bag was brought in, and needles were prepared. I watched everyone move silently from my place sitting cross-legged on the bed. Nithe was following Kassius around, concern and anger fighting for their place in his eyes.

Enzo sat silently off to the side, as if he was unsure what to do. I look over at him.

"What's going on with you and Scarlett?" I ask, hoping to distract myself and him. He sighs and rubs his hands on his trousers before looking up at me.

"Emery mentioned to her that I have an old girlfriend back in Labisa. She was worried that when we left and returned, that I would also return to her."

"Fleur?" I ask, and his eyes widen. "I heard you both talking while I was in the infirmary. You had a life oath with her?"

"We were in love. Had been for years. We pledged ourselves to one another, the only thing we could do as we weren't old enough to marry. When we did, we both were inked. Swirls and feathers. It only happens to certain people."

"What people?" I press.

"Soulmates." He responds. I gasp and look over at Nithe. His arm shimmers in the sun, swirls around his already present black ink. Soulmates. That's impossible. That can't be right. There is no way. If I were to have a soulmate, wouldn't it be Theo? It would have had to be Theo.

"What happened to your soulmate, Enzo?" I whisper, my eyes not leaving Nithe.

"She left me." Kassius walks over, a handful of vials in one hand and a pot of something in another.

"Are we ready?" He asks as he sets everything down on the bed. I nod hesitantly. "Okay, lay back. I'm going to give you something to relax you and hopefully reduce pain."

"No poppy root." I say quickly.

"Elaenor, it is the only thing that will help during this."

"Please, I can't." I shake my head and Nithe sits next to me.

"Hey, it'll be alright. Nothing will happen to you. This is just to help you." I whimper and look into his darkening eyes.

"You're scared." I whisper. He smiles softly and brushes a tear from my eye.

"Of course I'm scared." He responds and leans forward, his lips pressing to my forehead. I nod and look back at Kassius.

"Alright." I whisper. He steps forward, a syringe in one hand. I close my eyes and look away and he sticks it in my arm. Sharp pain is replaced by ice spreading through my veins, a feeling I know too well. I inhale slowly and open my eyes. Enzo steps up, his eyes full of concern and hesitance.

"What do I do?" He asks.

"Place your hands on her stomach." Kass instructs and Enzo listens. His hands are shaking as they reach for me. I lean back, nestling in the cushions as I feel the poppy root spreading through my veins. "Close your eyes and feel." I watch my brother's face as his eyes close and his brows furrow.

"I can feel...a flutter." He whispers. I start to feel this cold pressure on my stomach, this desire to take a deep breath. So I do, and I exhale with a rasp.

"Good. What else?" He scrunches his forehead further and then he smiles.

"It's a boy." He whispers and his eyes open. My pulse skips and I push his hands off of me, my limbs humming.

"Stop!" I cry out. "Stop."

"Little witch—"

"I can't do this. I can't." I shake my head.

"It's okay." Nithe shushes me as he pulls my weak body against his chest.

"Nora—" Kassius starts.

"No! She doesn't want to do this. She said stop." Nithe yells back and I hear Kass sigh. He's right. I need to, but I can't. It's a boy. There is a boy in my stomach. A small child who isn't at fault for what his father has done.

I have a *son*.

Nithe stayed with me while the poppy root worked its way out of my system. Every breath, every muscle twitch, made my heart race. It's not the same. I keep reminding myself. This isn't the same.

I lay on the bed, curled in a ball, while Nithe reads something next to me. My eyes stay fixed on the torch lit by the door, growing brighter by the minute as the sun sets.

I chickened out. I stopped what I should have allowed to happen. But I got scared. And then, I felt something else. I felt a sense of relief—of love—as I pictured the little boy I would have.

"Do you think less of me?" I whisper. Nithe drops his hands, the parchment crinkling on his lap.

"Of course not, little witch. I told you it was your choice." He responds, his fingers brushing hair off my cheek. I tilt my head and look up at him.

"What if it kills me?" I say just as quietly. He smiles softly and tangles his fingers in my hair.

"I won't let that happen." He releases me and picks his parchment back up, diving into whatever it is he's reading. I give into the exhaustion and let it lull me into a deep sleep.

Chapter Fifty-Seven

The Caged

Three weeks come and go. Nothing has changed. Nithe and I haven't progressed our relationship, in fact it seems as if we grow apart as irritation comes with the shadows that seem to want to infiltrate my mind. I see Tobias.

Everywhere.

Everywhere I turn and look, I catch sight of his hair, or his hands clenching the doorway.

I'm going mad.

Nithe doesn't understand. Scarlett doesn't understand. The only one who does is Kassius, although he keeps pressuring me to allow Enzo to siphon away my son's life, but it's too late. I'm halfway through this pregnancy. This child is coming, and I will be grateful for his presence.

Maybe then Tobias will stop following me around.

When I have the willpower to get out of bed, I train with Kassius. While my aether seems to come when I reach for it, the colors are changing. Gone are the bright white stars, and in their place are glittery black orbs hellbent on suffocating every spark I conjure.

My aim has improved, the strength in which I can wield is even better, but my starlight isn't pure anymore. And instead, I am learning how to wield both of the magics dueling inside me.

If I learn to manage it, I can control it. And then it won't control me.

My tunic is tight against my swelling belly, my breath coming in pants as I lean against the fighting platform. Kassius hands me a cold glass of water and I down it.

"They come as easily as the stars." He says as he stares at the targets. The shadows don't burn like my starlight does, instead, they disintegrate. Everything they touch turns into black ash immediately.

"I'm getting stronger, then." I reply, setting the glass down.

"Or he is." He responds, turning back to me.

"*He* is a fetus. His strength is non-existent."

"That's not true and you know it." He snaps and takes the glass from the platform, turning back towards the table. The door opens and I turn to see my least favorite person, the man who happens to be my father-in-law, stroll in.

"I see your aether has become even more unpredictable in your...*state*." He sneers, gesturing towards the destroyed targets.

"Excuse me?" I retort, stepping away from the podium and towards him.

"Correct me if I'm wrong, but starlight burns, not destroys. Correct?" I don't respond. "I thought so. Also, correct me if I'm wrong, this change in abilities has something to do with the demon in your womb. Correct?"

"Dav—" My mouth gapes as I stare at him.

"Do you think I am stupid?" He snaps walking quickly towards me. "I know the child in your womb isn't of my blood and I will not allow you to sully this line."

"What are you going to do about it?" I respond just as loud.

"Your child is a bastard, and you are a *whore*." I slap him. *Hard*. His face turns red, and he spits on the floor, blood landing on the gray stone.

"Don't you ever speak to me like that again." I sneer, stepping closer.

"Your child will not be named heir. Your child will be ignored by these courts and by the continent. That child will be nothing!"

"This child will be *king* someday!" I yell, getting in his face. His iron laced breath fans across my face, and I fight the urge to gag. He turns away without a response, slamming the door behind him. "What is he going to do?"

"I don't know, Nora. But whatever it is, can't be good."

The horns sound, pulling me out of my sleep. Sweat clings to my hair, plastering it to my face. My stomach cramps and I look down at the slightly swollen belly underneath the shirt I stole from Nithe's side of the dressing room. The horns echo throughout the room again and I glance towards his side of the bed.

"Nithe?" I whisper, but he doesn't answer. I slide out of the bed and walk to the windows. I can't see anything, the night blocking out the courtyard. "Nithe are you he–" The door flies open, and I spin around. A black cloak runs at me, and I duck out of the way just in time to miss his fist.

He spins around, reaching for me, and I twist out of the way. What the fuck? I run to the bed, my hand sliding under the pillow for Nithe's dagger he always keeps. My fingers graze the hilt before a hand goes around my waist. My arm flies out, slamming the dagger into his shoulder. He drops me and I land on the floor with a thud, my stomach taking the brunt of it.

I shoot up, aiming for the door, but it flies open again, nearly hitting me in the face. I run right into the arms of another person, the stench of ash coating my nose. His arm goes around my neck, and he lifts me off the ground. His other arm snakes around my waist, holding me to him. I kick out, my nails scratching at his forearm.

He lifts me up before slamming me face down onto the wood. My nose burns and tears well up in my eyes. I can feel his thighs digging into mine, but he's too slow. I roll under him and get a leg free. I slam my foot into the apex of his thighs, and he falls to the side. I scramble to my feet just as a fist comes out and slams into my jaw.

My eyes go dark for just a second before white sparkles in my peripherals. I grab the man's wrist and he screams as my aether pours into his body, slipping through his veins to his heart. He goes limp within seconds. The other man rises, and his hand goes around my mouth. Something sweet tickles the back of my throat and I inhale. I can smell the sticky sweet scent of hemlock on his hand, before my eyes roll back.

He drops me to the floor again, grunting as my weight nearly takes him forward. I stay conscious, but my limbs aren't responding.

No.

I dig deep, as deep as possible. Willing the aether to burn away any trace of the drug. Something is tied around my ankles before he yanks my arms behind me and ties something around my wrists.

The door opens again, and I try to look back, but I can't move my head enough to see. I hear a grunt and then pain as something lands on top of me.

"Elaenor! Are you okay?" Bergamot and mint invade my senses as I hear ropes being cut. I try to speak, but nothing comes out. "Hold on." My arms are free, and he rolls me over. I'm frozen, paralyzed as his eyes frantically search my body for harm. "Did they drug you?" I don't answer. "Blink if they drugged you." I blink. "Fuck, okay."

Running footsteps sound behind him and he's yanked away from me. My feet tingle and I get the sense that the drug is wearing off already. It was probably only enough to render me immobile so they could tie me up. I wiggle my toes and work a swallow. My pulse races and I beg for the burning sensation of sparks travelling through my veins.

I hear fighting in the hallway, and I try to lift my arm, surprised when it cooperates. I push myself up into a sitting position, my head swimming. I don't try to stand, but I crawl to the hallway. I groan as my nails dig into the wood, pulling me farther out of the room. At least a dozen cloaked men are in the hallway. Swords are flying, grunts and screams echoing.

I place my hand on the wood of the floor and close my eyes, willing my aether to come. I feel it as it rises in my chest and snakes down my arm. My eyes open and my hand is a sparkling white. I look back into the hallway and picture all of the assailant's necks snapping. And they do.

Men drop to the floor, their bodies making a sickening noise as stars fly off of them. Then everything goes dark. Arms grab my shoulders, pulling me up. Nithe's purple eyes are wide, bloodshot. He wipes under my nose, and it comes away bloody.

"Are you okay?"

"The baby." I whisper. He glances down at my stomach and bends down to hoist me up into his arms. Enzo's face is bloody as he comes into view. His hands reaching for my stomach. His eyes close as he listens.

"Everything is alright, I can feel him." I nod and a sob shudders out of me. "You need to rest." Cold fingers brush my forehead and I narrow my eyes, looking up at Nithe. His arms are under me, holding me tightly to his chest.

"You said I'd be safe."

"What?"

"You promised I would be safe in this palace. You said I didn't have to be scared. You've been telling me that for weeks!" I struggle and he sets me down.

"How was I supposed to know?" He snaps, running his hands through his hair.

"Where were you?" I yell back.

"He was with me." Emery says from behind. I feel the anger boiling inside me as I turn, lifting my hands. Arms wrap around me, keeping me immobile.

"Don't do what I think you are going to do." Enzo says slowly.

"I am so tired of everything. Of all of you!" I scream as I struggle.

"This is what I said would happen." Kassius's voice pipes up. And Enzo whirls around, taking me with him.

"You aren't helping!" He yells at his father.

"Let me go." I spit.

"Elaenor, it isn't what you think. We were in the council room—"

"I don't care!" I scream, feeling the shadows creep along my skin. I can feel them begging to be let out. Begging—wait. What are you doing? This isn't you. This isn't—

Chapter Fifty-Eight

The shadows fade from her skin as I pull them into my own body. I can feel their power—dark and ancient. Calling for me to release them. Calling for me to explode.

This is what she's been feeling. This is why she's volatile.

Her body falls limp in my arms, and I bend down to scoop up her legs, holding her to my chest. Blood is pouring from a wound on Nithe's head, his eyes red and tired.

"Get yourself cleaned up." I say as I push past him, headed for her room. Nobody speaks. Not even Emery who seemed to disappear once she realized she wasn't going to be eviscerated by our deranged queen. I set her body down on her bed, stepping over a body. Her breathing is slow, even. Her skin isn't as pale, her cheeks red and flushed. Even her freckles have deepened.

She looks healthier. Her belly is swollen, stretching the cotton of the shirt she's wearing. I reach forward, my hand resting on the small bump. I push inward until I feel the thumping of his heart. It's even, strong. I push further until I dig into his little mind, until I feel what he feels.

Warmth.

He feels so warm. I can feel his attachment to Elaenor, the love he already holds for his mother. I can even feel a little bit of light in his soul, but all of that is overshadowed by darkness.

I can see the color of his blood, black as night. I can see his veins pulsing beneath his unformed skin, black. I can see his eyes from where they sit half-made in his skull.

Black.

I can also feel what he isn't.

He isn't human.

Chapter Fifty-Nine

The Caged

There is sweat beading on my forehead as the cramping in my abdomen grows in intensity. My eyes open to the darkness of the room. It's hot, sweltering. The windows are open, but the lack of wind is just making me feel stagnant. I groan as I force myself up, my hair plastered to my neck with sweat. I glance over at Nithe passed out next to me. He's sweating just as much as I am. He has kicked the blankets off, leaving him just in his undershorts.

What happened? I remember feeling this pressure, this need to scream. Almost as much as I needed to that very first day. But this was different, this was darkness begging for destruction.

This wasn't light.

I look away from him and push the thin sheet off my legs. My shorts and camisole are doing little to keep me cool. My swollen belly is starting to push against my clothing. I am going to need more soon, so I can stop stealing Nithe's

I thought I would be able to go the whole pregnancy without needing new clothes, but that isn't happening.

I slide off the bed, the floor warm. I groan against another wave of cramping, grabbing the bedpost to steady me. *Gods* this hurts. I never knew pregnancy was supposed to hurt. I feel something wet on my thigh and I look down, as best as I can, over the swollen bump. Something deep is running down my thighs. Something black.

No.

"Nithe." I call out as another wave of cramping erupts through me. "Nithe!" I cry louder this time.

"Little witch, what is it?" He murmurs sleepily. I drop to my knees as I fight to inhale a deep breath. "Elaenor!" I can hear him fighting against the blankets before sliding on his knees over to me.

"Something is wrong with him." I stammer as I feel the sweat dripping down my neck.

"Guards!" He yells out and I whimper against another cramp.

"*Ni.*" I cry.

"Fuck!" He yells before scooping me up and standing. He kicks the door open and starts running down the hall. "Guards!" He yells again and I can hear the clink of armor.

"Your Grace!"

"Wake Master Lenus. Now!" He screams as he continues down the hallway.

"Nithe, what the hell– Elaenor!" Emery's shrill voice cuts through the fogginess in my head.

"Elaenor?" Scarlett says from somewhere. Oh gods, this hurts. Nithe ignores them as he barrels down the hallway. I can feel my body jostling as he runs down the stairs.

"It hurts." I whimper and he tightens his arms around me.

"I know, I know." He says breathlessly. Another door is kicked open and then I am being set on a table.

"How long?"

"Not that long."

"Okay, I don't have time to give her any pain reliever, she needs to push."

"No, it's too soon." I cry, trying to pull out of his grasp.

"Shh, it's okay." I can feel Nithe lift my arms as he settles in behind me, pulling me onto his lap. My legs are lifted and placed in stirrups. "This is going to hurt, but I am here. I am right here."

"No, it's too early!" I cry out. I can feel poking and prodding against my vagina and I flinch.

"She's bleeding a lot, this isn't good." I scream as I feel the scalpel slice into me, spreading me open.

"Why is her blood black?" I hear someone say, but I can't listen. I can't think.

"Push, Your Majesty."

"No. No!" I scream against the pressure. The *pain*. I'm dying. I think I'm dying.

"Come on, push." Nithe's lips press to my temple as he wraps his arms around my chest. I scream as I bare down, pushing with everything in me. The pressure is debilitating, the pain of my skin ripping open.

"Keep going." I can hear Master Lenus speaking, and I keep pushing. "Almost." I dig my nails in Nithe's forearms as I push. "The head is out." I don't hear crying. No.

"Nithe, I don't hear crying."

"Keep pushing." The scream barrels out of me as I feel the release of pressure. The master cuts something and then turns around, taking the baby with him.

"No." It's silent. It's too silent. "No, no, no." I shake my head. "Ni." I whimper, my eyes too weak to open.

"What is happening, Lenus?" He turns around, a tiny bundle of black goo covered infant wrapped in a blanket in his arms.

"I am very sorry, Your Majesty. It appears your son did not survive." He says softly.

"No. Don't." I cry as he walks over with the too small bundle. He bends down, placing him on my chest. His skin is thin, and I can almost see the veins running below it. The black veins. He has a small sprinkle of black hair on his head, his eyes closed. His tiny nose and tiny lips, this can't be true.

He can't be gone.

"I am so sorry, little witch." Nithe says behind me.

"I am so sorry, little one." I parrot with a whimper and press a kiss to his forehead. His skin is hot, bloody. The sobs barrel through me and I can feel Nithe's arms tighten around me. I glance up at him and see the tears lining his eyes. He presses a kiss to my forehead and just holds me as I say goodbye to my child.

The only piece of happiness I had in my life. The only piece of hope.

This baby was supposed to be the thing that brought me back to life.

I don't know how much time passes, but I stay on the table. Nithe stays behind me, holding me as I cry. Lenus left us at some point, but Erik stays posted at the door, keeping anyone from entering. He refuses to look at me, but I don't mind. I just want to be alone. Alone with my son. Alone with the last piece of me that was good.

"We need to take him now, Your Grace." Lenus speaks and I jump.

"Please, I need more time." I beg, meeting his dark eyes.

"We have to, Your Majesty. I am so sorry." I press my lips to his forehead, his tiny, tiny forehead. I pull back and he takes the tiny bundle from my arms. As soon as he is lifted off of me, I cry. I cry so hard I can't breathe through the snot in my nose and my throat.

"Elaenor." Nithe holds me tightly. Holds me as I cry. As I scream. As I lose my mind. "I am so sorry, Elaenor."

"How? How did this even happen?" I cry as I dig my nails into his arms. I can't think. I can't breathe. All I see are his tiny lips. His tiny hands.

His tiny, dead body.

"I don't know. I don't know."

Chapter Sixty

The Caged

Everyone filters into the council room, taking up what little space there is. And by everyone, I mean everyone. Every single one of my friends, close to twenty guards, and even Mama Collette who winks at me. I'm standing next to Scarlett, her limbs buzzing with nervous energy as she watches Emery talk to a guard I haven't seen before. I nudge her arm and she looks over at me, offering me a sheepish grin.

It's been two weeks since we lit the pyre. Two weeks since I said goodbye to my son. Nithe is convinced his father had something to do with it, and I don't blame him. He was the first person I thought of.

But it's also a possibility that he just wasn't healthy. Maybe he wasn't meant for this world. His blood was black. His veins were black. He was darkness made into a person.

But he was also my son. He was my child.

"What's wrong?" I ask her as she stares at me intently. Concern crosses her face. She's been treating me like glass, as has everyone, but I have been adamant about moving forward. About moving on.

"I have this weird feeling that this isn't going to be a pleasant meeting. Why else would everyone be here?" She whispers. I shrug and look around. She's right. Why else would the entire palace be present. Except for one person. "Where is your father?" I lean to my left, my shoulder brushing Nithe's ribs. He lifts his hand and squeezes my arm.

"Probably waiting to make a grand entrance." He snorts, his hand sliding down my arm to thread his fingers through my own. He hasn't left my side. He's been a constant, a crutch for me to lean against. And I will always be grateful for it, but the hole that was in my heart when I left Noterra has reappeared. And the numbness I never wanted to feel again is back, making everything feel as if it isn't important.

Everything except killing Tobias.

"You don't know what this is about?" Enzo asks from Nithe's other side. He shakes his head. "Well it has to be something important."

The doors open and Davenport strolls in, guards following him like he's afraid for his life. He catches my eyes as he walks to the head of the table, the slight narrowing of his gaze tells me he's not exactly thrilled.

"It has been brought to our attention that our border has been breached." Gasps erupt around the room and Nithe pulls me closer to him, but I step out of his grip. "Five hundred men are now camped right past the border wall, readying themselves to strike. A thousand more stationed right against the border on Noterra's side. As of right now, they have not come closer. They have only breached the wall." He looks around, his eyes landing on me. "We have a choice to make." Everyone follows his line of sight, staring at me.

"What choice?" I ask, my voice clear for once.

"We can stay and fight, or we can begin evacuation protocols." Silence spreads along the room as all eyes stay on me.

"How many men do we have in Rakushia ready to fight?" I ask no one in particular. It's Nero that answers.

"We have less than a hundred at the palace. We had close to four hundred at the border, but we lost over one-hundred and fifty during the siege last night. In the neighboring towns, we have a total of a thousand men at our disposal."

"What about our armies? Where are they?" I ask.

"The core of our army is in Labisa, they would not make it here in time." My eyes water as I absorb the information, trying to figure out the right answer.

"How many civilians?"

"Ten thousand." Davenport answers. *Ten thousand.* Oh gods. "What will it be, Your Majesty?" My heart stutters in my chest as I run through all the numbers, run through the very little battle strategy I have. As panic courses through my veins.

There is only one choice. We won't survive an attack.

"Begin evacuation protocols. Get every civilian out of here." Nithe exhales in relief, the only affirmation that I made the right call.

"Get every ship loaded and ready to depart. Everyone needs to be gone by this afternoon!" Davenport yells into the crowd as everyone starts bustling around. "General! Every single civilian needs to get on a ship. Have them depart for Labisa, have them go the long way. We don't want Noterra to see the ships headed right towards them."

"Yes, Your Grace." Nero bows and runs out of the room, giving me a sidelong glance as he passes. The room empties aside from my friends and I. Davenport collapses into the chair before looking at me.

"You need to be on one of those ships." He states dryly.

"I'm not leaving until everyone else has gone."

"You don't have a choice."

"I will not get on that ship until everyone else is gone." I repeat. "I will not be responsible for leaving someone to die."

"We can't fight them, Elaenor. We can't protect anyone, not without our armies." Nithe says.

"I'm not saying we fight; I'm saying we *wait*, or at least I do. I am not leaving anyone behind." I repeat.

"Don't be a martyr." Davenport scoffs as he looks at me with disgust.

"I don't want to die, that's not what I am saying."

"No, but you will if they get to the palace." He adds.

"They won't kill me. He won't let them." I admit. It's the truth. He won't kill me.

"Elaenor, he's right." Enzo speaks up. My head whips in his direction. "You have to go."

"*No.*"

"If they make it to the palace, none of us are surviving."

"He *won't* kill me." I repeat, again.

"You can't know that." Enzo scoffs. But they don't know him. Not like I do.

"I do. Trust me."

"You are out of your depth." Davenport states. I look around the room, doubt filling everyone's eyes. I turn to Nithe.

"You are the one who keeps telling me I'm powerful."

"Yes, but I also keep telling you you're untrained."

"So *train* me."

"We have hours before we need to evacuate. We don't have the time." He shakes his head. I grit my teeth and step away from him.

"Every civilian gets on that ship, and then all of you. Once Rakushia is empty, I will board. And not a second sooner. That is an order." I snap, my tone venomous as I look around the room. Everyone stays silent as they stare at me, until one by one they depart the room. Nithe is last, and all he does is shake his head before walking out.

How did I go from protecting our people to being called a martyr for wanting to ensure they are actually protected?

I exit the room and am immediately thrown into a rush of people. I stumble and barely catch onto the wall to prevent getting run over. Once the coast is clear I cross the hallway and exit the front door. At least twenty horses are saddled outside the wall, waiting for riders. Multiple carriages and wagons behind them, prepped to transport people.

"Your Majesty." I spin and see a couple of guards walking over. "All transports have been prepped. The royal carriage awaits you and the king consort."

"Thank you, but I'm not leaving until every single person has been evacuated."

"Yes, Your Majesty." They head towards the wall, and I follow after them, crossing through the open gate. I can feel his presence, my palms tingling.

"Where are they going?"

"Wistervale, they'll board the ships from there." I nod, staying silent.

"How close are they to being at the palace?"

"If they leave now, they could be here in a few hours at most."

"Is—" My voice cracks. "Is he with them?"

"I don't know, Elaenor." I turn and look up at my brother, his green eyes bright and clear. "You need to go."

"No, don't start this fight again. You heard what I said."

"Yes, and I get why you are staying, but you shouldn't."

"You and Nithe need to stop treating me like I am incapable of doing anything." I snap. I'm tired of feeling like a child—like someone who has to be protected.

"We aren't. We know you are capable of whatever you set your mind to, but you don't have your starlight under control. You are weak—"

"Do not call me weak. Just because I can't fight, doesn't mean I am weak. And if you and everyone else would take a second and stop treating me like I'll break, I might actually learn how to protect myself."

"Elaenor—"

"No. I am so godsdamn tired of this, Enzo. So tired of being told what to do. Tired of being sheltered and lied to. I will be the queen my mother would be proud of. I will find a way to kill Tobias. I will end this. But I can't do it alone and I need you to get your head out of your ass and *help* me." My voice cracks and I swallow the lump growing in my throat. He stays silent for a second before he sighs.

"What do you need me to do?"

Chapter Sixty-One

The Caged

The palace is silent as I watch the last of the horses depart with a wagon full of people. Only five horses remain, waiting for us. Scarlett refused to leave without Enzo but was finally convinced to go with Emery. Laenie and Erik left too, taking Mali and Kass with them, and I pray that they get to the ship in time.

The council room is quiet as we stand around. Enzo, Nithe, Davenport, Nero, and myself. Nero refused to leave without me, stating the general needs to stay with the queen, which just pissed Nithe off. But that's not why he's staying.

"Are we free to leave, Your Grace?" Davenport sneers.

"Every single person has been evacuated?"

"Yes."

"Not a single soul resides in this palace besides us?"

"No." He says with a sigh.

"Then, yes." He sighs and stands, everyone heading for the door.

"If I may, Your Grace, I would like a word." Davenport says.

"I'll be right there." I say to Enzo, who drags Nithe out with him. Nero glances my way once and then follows. "Yes?"

"I've been doing a lot of thinking, about our situation."

"What situation?" I say, stepping back.

"You are going to get him killed. You are going to get us all killed." He spits, and I feel his breath from a few feet away.

"What are you talking about?"

"I know what you have planned." He snorts, stepping away from me and towards the door.

"Stay away from me." I say through gritted teeth.

"I won't need to be your downfall; you'll do it on your own." He reaches back for my arm, and I slam my hand into his chest. Aether sparks at my fingertips and he gasps as they burn his skin.

"Stay. *Away*. From. Me." I repeat. He scoffs and shakes his head before leaving. I stare after him as he walks out the door, a single tear sliding down my cheek.

I wipe it away quickly before following after him. The chocolate brown mare is waiting for me, Nithe standing next to it. He looks between me, and his father and I shake my head. I reach him and he wipes the remnants of the tear off my cheek.

"It's nothing." He exhales loudly as his eyes track his father. I grab the saddle and he hoists me up.

"We will deal with it once we are safe. Once we are on the ship. Then you can tell me what's going on with you." He vows and I touch his cheek. He turns his head, kissing my palm before walking to his own horse.

I look around the palace. The open windows, the warm breeze causing the vines of wisteria to sway. I don't think we'll ever come back here.

I fall to the back of the group as we head towards the sea, towards the ships ready to evacuate us.

But I'm not getting on that ship.

Enzo slows down, his horse's speed matching mine.

"Elaenor." He says softly.

"Is it done?" I whisper.

"Yes. I already spoke with Nero. It'll happen right outside Wistervale." He's quiet. "What happens after you get away?"

"I kill him."

"This is risky, Elaenor." He whispers under his breath.

"I don't care."

"What if you don't come back?"

"Then Nithe will rule without me." I say bluntly. He stops his horse and reaches over to grab my reigns. Nithe glances back and slows his too.

"Don't do this. We can find another way." He whispers as I shake my head.

"Enzo. I am so tired. So damn tired. And if we keep going this way, a war will start. We will lose thousands of civilians and maybe even our own lives. This is between me and him."

"Nero can't protect you once you get there."

"I don't need him to. He will *not* kill me." I say for the thousandth time.

"You don't know that for sure." He says through gritted teeth.

"The second I tell him I am pregnant; he won't touch me." I place my hand over his.

"You aren't even pregnant anymore."

"He doesn't have to know that." I retort, squeezing his hand.

"I just got you back. Don't make me lose my sister."

"I love you, too." I say with a smile. He releases my reigns and trots up to Nithe, forcing him to move. I take a long, deep breath, before squeezing my thighs against my horse. She starts to move, following after them.

Time passes and we crest the hill. Wistervale looks empty, dead. No smoke coming from the chimneys. No people running around the streets. Ships have already taken off, heading up instead of down towards Noterra.

There is a single ship left in the harbor. The one I am supposed to be on.

Nero glances back from where he is trotting behind the king. I nod once and he returns the nod.

My heart skips a beat as I try to lull myself into a sense of calm.

I think I see them before they attack, but I was ready for them. I was ready for all of this. Enzo glances back, a pained expression on his face as he reaches towards Nithe. Nithe opens his mouth in confusion before his eyes widen as he looks at me.

"Elaenor!" He yells as Enzo's hand clamps around Nithe's arm, and I see the purple glow spreading through his veins. Nithe's eyes roll backwards, and he slumps against his horse. Enzo grabs his reigns and pulls.

I see them take off with Davenport following. He glances back at me once and I almost think I see a smile before I'm surrounded.

A hand grabs my ankle and I'm ripped off my horse. Nero is at my side in an instant, pushing people off of me. The hilt of a sword is slammed into his face and my arms are wrenched behind me.

"Nero!" I yell as I grimace in pain, begging the starlight to come. He was supposed to keep them off of me.

Red tunics and silver armor emblazoned with a rose fill my vision as I am grabbed and pulled in all directions.

"Get off of me!" I scream as I kick out. I feel the pinprick in my arm and my legs go numb instantly.

"She's pregnant!" Nero yells as he's shoved forward. I fall to my knees as my arms are released. Silence spreads like the plague and an uneasy feeling skates down my spine. Nobody is shuffling. No one is fighting. Not even Nero. I glance up to see one of the men handing him a handkerchief. My eyes widen as he takes it and wipes his bloody nose.

"Nero?" I ask as he looks back at me. His eyes narrow as he stares down at me. Horses surround us and I know in that moment he betrayed me.

"Cousin." His voice is like ice, cutting through my mind with the swipe of a blade. I fall forward, my hands catching me.

"No, no, no." I repeat as I roll onto my back.

His head blocks the sun, copper hair glinting in the light. "My Ela." He whispers as he reaches for me. His hand touches my stomach, and he smiles. "You came back to me."

Chapter Sixty-Two

I look back as she's ripped off her horse. Men surround her and panic spreads. Nero's face, he's smiling. He's smiling as if he expected this.

I stop my horse, the king racing past me to the harbor. I don't even care. He's there. His blonde hair shining in the sun as he stands over her.

"No." I whisper. It wasn't supposed to go that way. She was supposed to kill him. She said she was going to kill him.

Nithe stirs to my right, and I glance over as he shoots off his horse. I lunge after him, grabbing his arms as we both fall to the ground.

Sparks fly, shooting off in all directions as she attempts to hurt him, as she attempts to do what she had planned.

"Let go of me!" Nithe screams, but I hold on.

"She needs to do this!" I scream back as we watch. Men fly off in all directions, hitting the ground in smoking piles. She's kneeling on the ground in front of him, her skin glowing. I can't hear what she says, but he laughs.

Tobias's laugh is loud, commanding.

She pulls herself to her feet.

"Come on, Nora." I whisper. Nithe stops fighting as we stare, barely seeing over the crest of the hill. Her hands shoot out and star filled tendrils snake towards Tobias. He falls to his back as they slam into his chest. She's shaking, her hands still held outward.

Tobias doesn't move and relief pummels through me. She did it. She actually did it. She drops her arms and turns slightly, looking at us.

That was her mistake.

I drop my arms as Nithe clamors to his feet and takes a step forward, a smile passing across Elaenor's face.

We don't see him until it's too late. He stands quickly, thrusting his arms towards her.

Shadows in the form of a blade cross the distance, slamming into her chest. The blade breaks through her skin, blood shooting off in all directions.

Time moves so slow, I don't think I was able to process what happened after. Nithe's scream filled the air as Nora's head slowly tilted down at the gaping hole in her chest. She looks up as she falls to her knees, her mouth parting.

Disbelief fills the air as a sound so primal and animalistic crashes through my ears, as it barrels into my soul. Nithe starts to run, and I grab him, both of us falling to the ground again. His fingers dig into the hard dirt, and I see blood and skin leaving trails as he tries to get away.

Silence fills the small road, the road between the hills as I stare at my sister.

The sister I have only known for a few months.

The sister who promised she would come back.

She falls forward, her face landing in the dirt as blood spreads around her, soaking into the ground. I could feel it. I felt her last heartbeat as if it was my own. I could feel as she took her last breath.

I gasp as the pain slams into my mind. My hands go numb as I collapse next to Nithe. He is sobbing, screaming as he tries to get to his feet.

"Nithe." I whisper. He glances over at me once, his eyes catching on mine.

"No!" He screams, *cries*, as he grabs my shoulders, shaking me. And I know what he sees when he looks in my eyes. I turn my head slightly and watch as Tobias bends down and picks Elaenor up. "*NO!*" He yells again as he watches her.

Her head hangs over Tobias's arm, her eyes open and unseeing. Blood pours out of her mouth as Tobias starts to walk.

He doesn't look at us. He doesn't even pay attention.

He just carries her body between the trees before disappearing into a cloud of dark mist.

Nithe collapses next to me, grief filling his veins.

Shock fills mine.

Power.

I felt it the second her power filled my veins. The second the starlight became mine. The second every single vein in my body lit up with the light of a million stars.

I felt the entire world shift the second Elaenor died.

ABOUT THE AUTHOR

Celaena Cuico *(sell-ay-NUH coo-WE-co)* was born and raised in Southern California. She was raised with two parents and an older sister, as well as an army of animals. Celaena endured hardships such as an abusive significant other and the unknown that comes with moving across the country twice for a job. She is the author of The Diadem, a series about a young girl thrown into a life of jumping from kingdom to kingdom to survive, and The Soulless, a series about the God of the Underworld's minions and their lives forced to collect souls for him.

NOTE FROM THE AUTHOR

I want to thank each and every person who made this second installment in The Diadem Series a reality.

To my best friends and my sister – Ris, Vee, Jac, and Vilandra – you guys are truly my rocks. I couldn't do any of this without the four of you. You keep me grounded, you keep me sane, and you keep my ego at a very respectful level. I love you guys so much!

To my dear friends – Cyd, Annie, Savannah, Haydn, Sara, Meghan (Fireheart), Madeline, Thea Green, Thea Guanzon, AND SO MANY MORE – I am so grateful to have you in my corner. You all provide so much happiness to my life, and without you, I wouldn't be here.

Maggie – My fiancé, my favorite human. This story only came to fruition because you believed in me. Because you *told* me I could do it. And I did. I did it in spite of the obstacles and pain, in spite of the mental gymnastics you had to deal with while I put this story into words. I love you beyond words. You are my Theo in a world of Tobias's.

My readers – all of this is for you. For without you, I would be nothing.

Forever yours,

XO Cel